Just Making Out

Just Making Out
© 2010 Mark A. Roeder

Cover Photo Credit: on Rui Vale De Sousa on Dreamstime.com

Used under a Standard Royalty-Free License

Cover Design: Ken Clark

All Rights Reserved

ISBN-13: 978-1456331443
ISBN-10: 1456331442

Printed in the United States of America

Acknowledgements

I'd like to thank Ken Clark, Jennifer Tripp, Kathy Staley, and Robbie Ellis-Cantwell for proofing this manuscript. Their job is a difficult and laborious one and I can't thank them enough for the many hours they dedicated to improving this volume. I also want to thank Ken for creating the cover and coming up with the title for this novel.

Dedication

This book is dedicated to Ken Clark. Ken runs my website and my yahoo fan group. He critiques my work, offers his input, and doesn't get upset when I go my own way. He not only created the cover for this novel, but came up with the title.

Thanks, Ken, for all you do!

VHS Cafeteria—Verona, Indiana

Thursday—February 11, 1982

Shawn

"You suck, Brandon."

"Blow me, Jon."

"You wish, Brandon."

"No. *You* wish, Jon! You know you dream about it."

"Sometimes, it's hard to believe you guys are friends," Tristan said.

"They've been going at each other like this for as long as I've known them," Ethan said. "It's their way of expressing love."

"Yeah," Brandon said. "We don't want anyone to get the wrong idea and think we're homos!"

Brandon was immediately pelted by wadded-up paper napkins, straws, and the odd green bean. This came as no surprise, since Brandon was sitting at the "homo table." That's not what those of us sitting there called it, but I'd heard the name. Just about everyone sitting there, except Brandon Hanson and Jon Deerfield, were indeed gay.

Not all of us were out, but Ethan, Nathan, Brendan, Casper, Tim, Dane, Casey, Tristan, and myself were all gay. Both Ethan and Nathan and Brendan and Casper were out couples. Tim, my little brother, and Dane were a couple, too, but not quite out yet. They weren't making a secret of their relationship, however, so I figured word would get out any day now. Casey, my best friend, had a girlfriend, but her girlfriend went to another school. That just left Tristan and me. We weren't a couple—but, oh, how I wanted him to be my boyfriend!

Tristan had come into my life only recently. I could remember it as if it was yesterday...

I sat by myself in Ofarim's. The bell on the door rang. I looked up. That was the first time I ever laid eyes on Tristan Graham Cole.

I sighed at the sight of him. He was perfect, but oddly enough not any perfect I had ever imagined. He was my height, about 6'1" but had a slimmer build. His hair, which he wore shoulder-length and loose, was black, luxuriant, and ever so slightly curly. His eyes were deep and dark, a chocolate brown. He was Calvin-Klein-model good-looking, with full red lips, high cheekbones, and arched eyebrows. He wore small, round glasses, a brown-suede duster over jeans and a dark-green sweater. I had never seen anyone more beautiful in all my life. Even his glasses made him look incredibly sexy.

If someone had described him to me, I wouldn't have been the least interested in Tristan. I was more into studly than studious, but words could not do justice to the boy who walked through the door of Ofarim's...

"Shawn! Hello, Shawn! Earth to Shawn!"

"Huh?" I asked as I looked around the table.

"Who were you daydreaming about, Shawn?" Brandon mischievously asked.

I couldn't help but glance at Tristan for a moment. I turned red.

"Ohhhh," Jon said. "Homo-love blossoms."

"Yeah, you'd know. Wouldn't you, Deerfield?" Brandon asked.

"Screw you, Hanson."

"I seriously think Jon is one of you guys," Brandon said.

"Oh, I don't know if Jon could make the cut," Brendan said.

Jon stuck his tongue out at Brendan, who only laughed.

I was thankful attention was no longer focused on me. The guys knew I was gay, but it wasn't general knowledge—yet. I wasn't too concerned about coming out, but I wasn't accustomed to anyone openly talking about me like that. Neither Brandon nor Jon meant anything by it. They were the best friends a gay guy could have. It was just new territory for me. I was also a little embarrassed that the guys knew I had a crush on Tristan. Casey smiled at me across the table. That small gesture put me at ease.

I stole another look at Tristan, but nothing more than a glance. I was afraid the guys might tease me if they noticed. I wasn't fearful of Tristan himself taking note. He knew I was interested in him. I had brought up the possibility of us dating and had been gently and kindly rebuffed. Still, there was hope. Tristan's response was more of a "perhaps someday" than a "no."

Devon, the resident homo-hater of Verona High School, walked past and scowled. That was standard operating procedure for Devon. I'd never quite figured out why he hated gays so much, but he sure did. Brandon hated Devon every bit as much as Devon hated gays, if not more so, but that's another story. There were a lot of stories at VHS and a lot of drama, too. A soap opera could have been based on my classmates. I could see it now: *Days of Our Teen Lives*.

I didn't like the way Devon eyed Tristan. Word was slowly spreading about my dream boy. Girls were naturally attracted by his good looks. Tristan had deflected the interest of one of his admirers by telling her he was gay. News like that usually spread like wildfire, but I think Tristan's "secret" was whispered in confidence from one girl to the next. The news would no doubt escape soon and engulf the school, but so far its progression had been slow. Devon was the first sign that word had reached the guys. I think it was still in the rumor stage. Devon's gaze was one of curiosity and mild animosity. If he was certain Tristan was gay, he would have stared at him with baleful hatred.

Devon moved on and was soon forgotten. My friends and I joked and laughed our way through lunch. Tim and Dane sat next to each other, of course; they were so close together that their shoulders touched. I hadn't heard any rumors about them yet, but it was only a matter of time. They were so obviously a couple that no one could fail to notice. Then again, perhaps I only thought it was obvious because I knew about them. I was there when they met. I had stepped aside so my little brother could have someone to love. That's another story, too. See? I told you there were lots of them!

Tristan took off with Ethan and Nathan right after lunch without so much as looking back at me. I frowned. Part of me felt like crying, which was weird because I'm not a crying kind of guy. Something about Tristan walking away from me with nothing more than his general "bye" broadcast to the group got to me. I picked up my tray and walked across the cafeteria to dump it.

"Hey, Shawn."

I turned. I hadn't even noticed Casey following me.

"Give him some time," Casey said.

I smiled wanly.

Casey knew about my feelings for Tristan. As my long-time confidant, she knew everything. Until recently, she'd also been my "girlfriend." Okay, I should probably explain that. For most of my life, I didn't dare come out. I feared my father would kill me—literally. I had an older brother who would've beaten me senseless—or worse. The situation had changed dramatically (which is one of those many other stories), and Casey and I no longer pretended to be a couple. We are still extremely close. She'll always be my girl. I love her.

"It's hard," I said.

"I bet it is," Casey said with a smirk.

I gave her a look that said, 'Don't go there.'

"You're almost as bad as Brandon and Jon," I said.

"Sorry. I couldn't resist."

"I finally found someone I really want to be with. After all those losers I met, I finally meet a guy I truly want to get to know, and he holds me at arm's length."

"Just take it slowly, Shawn."

"That's easy for you to say. You have Sandy. I'm dating my hand. I need sex!"

"I thought you were looking for more than sex."

"I am. I could call up Blake if I just wanted sex, and believe me I've thought about it! If it was just about sex, it wouldn't be nearly as difficult, but I really like Tristan. I want him to like me."

"He does like you."

"I mean *like* like."

"At the risk of repeating myself: give it time. Tristan laid down the ground rules. He told you he wanted to take it slowly. He wants to be friends first, so be his friend."

"Some friend. He didn't even say 'goodbye' to me after lunch."

"Shawn, you're too sensitive when it comes to Tristan. Relax. So he didn't say 'goodbye.' That doesn't mean anything. He is coming to your birthday party this evening. Happy Birthday, by the way."

"Thanks. I can't believe I'm seventeen now. Do I look older?"

"I can't really say you look older than yesterday, Shawn, but you're definitely a hottie."

"Oh. Like your opinion counts. *You* like girls."

"I know a good-looking boy when I see one. Why do you think I sit with all the hunks?"

"There are some majorly hot guys in our little group."

"Yes, and you're one of them."

"Thanks, Casey."

"What are ex-girlfriends for?"

Casey kissed my cheek. We parted ways. I felt much better as I walked to my locker. Casey had a way of putting things in perspective. That was one of the many reasons I was glad she was my friend.

***

My birthday party was held at the Selbys. The loft I shared with Tim was large enough to host a party, but was not well-equipped. We were still missing…well, most things. It's not easy setting out on your own when you're my age. Besides, Ardelene was fixing us all supper and baking me a cake. I could barely feed Tim and myself. If the party was at our place, about all I could scrape together would be some peanut-butter-and-jelly sandwiches.

I smiled when I thought of my party. This was going to be my first birthday party since I was a little kid. Someone actually cared enough about me to throw me a party—several someones. I had no right to be down. I had some truly great friends. Things were not as I wanted them to be with Tristan, but how could I complain about that when everything else was going so well? Besides, as I pointed out before, Tristan didn't say "no." There was still hope.

"Are you ready yet, Tim?" I called out from the kitchen.

"Just about."

Tim walked up the hall, naked, drying his hair.

"I hope that's not what you're wearing."

"It does look good, doesn't it?" Tim said, flexing his biceps.

"Yeah, yeah. Go get dressed, or we won't have time to pick up Dane."

Tim shot back down the hall in a flash. I knew that would get him. If he'd stopped to think, he would have known I was bluffing. Sometimes my little brother doesn't stop to think. This time, it worked to my advantage.

I finished unloading the dishwasher and closed the kitchen cabinet. I almost couldn't believe we had a dishwasher—or a loft, for that matter. I looked around the home I shared with my brother and smiled. We lacked a lot of things, but I was very pleased with what we had. The loft came furnished with a gas stove from the 1950s, a refrigerator, and the dishwasher. The kitchen was small, but it didn't look small because it was separated from the living area by an antique counter that looked as though it had come out of an old store. The kitchen and living area took up the front half of the loft. Two big windows in the front looked down onto Main Street. Two smaller windows looked to the south.

A hallway ran on the right side of the loft. There were two large bedrooms and a large bathroom. We didn't have much furniture. There was a couch and an armchair in the living area and beds in the bedrooms, but there were no kitchen table and chairs, no dressers, no TV, and no desks. Tim and I did our homework on the kitchen counter or on our beds.

I didn't think too much about what we didn't have. I enjoyed what we did have, instead. Our loft might be spartan, but it was beautiful. The living area, kitchen, and hallway had polished hardwood floors, while the bedrooms were nicely carpeted. The bathroom was tiled floor to ceiling with large white square tiles about a foot across on the floor and smaller tiles, about 5 inches across, on the walls. The smaller tiles were cream in color, except for three bands of dark green tiles near the floor, ceiling, and about halfway in between. I especially liked the shower. It kind of reminded me of the shower room at school, only this one had just one shower head and was nicer. There was no curtain or any kind of division from the rest of the bathroom. The shower area occupied one corner, and the water ran down a drain. All in all, our loft was much nicer than any place we'd ever lived.

"I'm ready!" Tim said.

"That was fast."

"I haven't seen Dane since school let out!"

"Wow. That's three whole hours. I wonder if he's taller now."

"Shut up."

I laughed. "Just let me get my coat on."

We walked down the stairs and out onto Main Street. My beat-up, old Cutlass Supreme was parked just down the street. I didn't know what I'd do if it conked out. Well, yeah, I did. I'd walk. I guess Tim and I could get by without a car. VHS was a fair walk from our loft, but it wasn't all that far. I could walk to my job at Ofarim's without too much trouble. It was even easier to commute to Café Moffatt, which was located directly below our loft. Still, it would suck to be without wheels. I wasn't going to worry about it until it happened. Life was too short to worry about all the bad stuff that could happen. Besides, it was my birthday!

In practically no time at all, I pulled up in front of Dane's house. Tim hopped out, but I stayed in the car. Dane and his family had only recently moved to Verona. They were renting a small house until the place they had purchased could be made livable. They'd bought the old Verona school and were having some work done on it. Poor Dane. Once they moved in, he'd be at school even when he came home from school. I guess it would be kind of a cool place to live.

I looked across the street. There sat the old Graymoor Mansion. Just looking at the place gave me the creeps. It had been abandoned forever, which showed. Tall grass grew in the yard, and the immense gates were permanently rusted half open. There was nothing but darkness behind the windows. There were so many stories about that place and all of them terrifying. I wondered how many of them were true.

For a fleeting moment, I thought I caught sight of a boy staring down at me from one of the third-story windows. I was almost certain my mind was playing tricks on me. Even guys my age didn't dare enter that old house. A mere boy surely wouldn't. I stared hard at the window, but there was only darkness. There was a lingering image of curly blond hair and purple cloth in my mind. I tried to bring the memory of the boy into clearer focus, but I couldn't. I didn't have time to think about it long before Tim was back with Dane. They climbed in the back seat.

"Hey, Shawn. Mom and Dad say 'hi.'"

"Hey, Dane. Say 'hi' back to them for me."

That was the end of the conversation. Tim and Dane locked lips. They were much too busy sticking their tongues in each other's mouths to speak. I tried to ignore the sounds from the backseat as I headed toward the Selby Farm. The Selbys lived just a couple of miles outside of town, but it seemed as if the farm was deep in the country. There were nothing but trees, fields, and an occasional farmstead out their way.

As I drove down the winding gravel drive that led to the farmhouse, I noticed a few cars already in the small parking area near the house. One was Brendan's. He drove a Cutlass Supreme, too, but his was newer and in much better shape than mine.

Brendan also had a red '79 Corvette convertible. That was one sweet car. He only drove it in the summer, however, so I guess it was stored in the barn.

"We're here," I announced.

"Already?" Tim said.

I shook my head. Tim and Dane lived in their own little world. I envied them sometimes.

"See if you two can pull apart long enough to make it inside."

Tim and Dane both giggled. Yeah, they had it bad for each other. There was no doubt about it.

We walked down the sidewalk, past the screened-in front porch, and around back to the kitchen door. I knocked, then entered.

"Hey, Shawn! Happy Birthday!" Ethan said as he gave me a bear hug. Ethan was a wrestler and built, so his hug just about squeezed the life out of me.

"Thanks."

My next hug was from Ardelene. It was much less life-threatening.

"Happy Birthday, Shawn."

"Thank you, and thank you for going to all this trouble for me."

"You are more than worth it. Besides, I love a party. Now, you make yourself at home. I have to get back to my oven. Supper will be ready shortly."

Brendan, Nathan, and Casper were already there. This was no surprise because this was their home. Brandon and Jon yelled 'hey' from the living room. I lingered in the kitchen because I caught sight of Casey through the window. In moments, she was walking through the back door with Sandy, her girlfriend.

"I thought I said no presents," I said as Casey hugged me. Both she and Casey were holding gifts.

"You're not my boss," Casey said with a grin.

"Heaven help anyone who tries to boss you around. Hey, Sandy."

"Hi, Shawn!"

Sandy gave me a hug, too. I liked Sandy, mainly because she made Casey so happy.

Everyone was present, with the notable exception of Tristan. Unpleasant thoughts of Tristan skipping out on my party began to creep into my head, but then Tristan walked through the back door. He was wearing the brown-suede duster he wore the first time I saw him. He looked both studious and beautiful with his long dark hair and small, round eyeglasses. He grinned when he spotted me.

"Happy Birthday, Shawn."

"I'm glad you could come."

"I wouldn't miss it."

The sound of Tristan's voice just about made me melt—and I thought Tim had it bad for Dane!

Casey gave me a look that said, 'See, I told you that you were being stupid.' She was right. Just because Tristan wanted to be friends first didn't mean he'd never be my boyfriend. Damn, how I wished we could start dating right now! I didn't want to wait. Tristan was the boy I wanted. I knew what my birthday wish would be.

In only a few minutes, Ardelene called us into the kitchen to eat. It was going to be a tight squeeze, even with the extra leaves in the table and an additional table added to one end. Jack came in at the last minute. He'd no doubt been out in the barn doing some chore or another. Dave, Nathan's eleven-year-old brother, came downstairs just after Jack joined us.

Okay, all the names might be confusing if you're not familiar with the Selbys, so let me stop and explain. There's Jack Selby. He's seventy-something, I think. He owns the Selby Farm. Several years back, his nephew Ethan came to live with him because his parents had been killed in an accident. Later on, Nathan and his little brother, Dave, started living on the farm, too, because of troubles at home. Nathan has also been Ethan's boyfriend now for quite a while. With me, so far? Later, Brendan and Casper came to the farm from down in Kentucky. They were runaways. They are also boyfriends. They started working for Jack and have lived with the Selbys ever since. Casper's grandmother, Ardelene, came to check on Casper once she found out where he was. She never left and ended up marrying Jack. Most recently, Jack and Ardelene have taken legal custody of Nathan and Dave. So, Ethan is Jack's nephew, Casper is Ardelene's grandson, and Nathan and Dave are the adopted sons of Jack and Ardelene—close enough, anyway. That almost makes Ethan and Nathan related, but not quite. That would sure be weird, since they are boyfriends. Confusing, huh? The rest of us are just friends of the Selbys, so there's no need to worry about us.

All of us, related and not, sat down to eat. Ardelene fixed lasagna, with cooked apples and garlic toast, which was one of my favorite meals. Her lasagna was even homemade, with an unbelievable amount of gooey cheese! Tim and I were mostly existing on cereal and ramen noodles, so the home-cooked meal tasted extra good!

I'm not ashamed to say I stuffed myself. I wanted to save room for cake and ice cream, but I couldn't make myself quit eating. It was my birthday, after all, the first one to be properly celebrated since Mom left.

Luckily, there was a break between supper and the cake and ice cream. When the supper dishes were cleared away, gifts began to appear on the kitchen table.

"You guys didn't need to get me anything," I said. To be honest, I was feeling overwhelmed.

"What's a birthday without presents?" Jon said, as if that explained everything.

"Well, thanks!" I said.

"Here, open mine first," Tim said.

Tim handed me an envelope. Inside were three certificates for cleaning the bathroom. There were another three certificates for taking out the trash. I looked up at Tim.

"Sorry. I didn't have any money for a real present."

"Are you kidding? There is nothing you could have bought me better than this! And, if you think I'll forget about these and not use them, you are out of your mind."

"Drat!" Tim said. "There goes that plan." He grinned.

"Thanks, Tim."

"Mine next," Casey said as she pushed a big box toward me.

I tore away the blue-and-white-striped paper and opened the box. Inside were a skillet and pots and pans.

"I scoured the resale shops for the best I could find," Casey said.

"Thank you!" I said. "We've been using one saucepan to cook *everything.*"

Ethan and Nathan presented me with a gift next. It was in a rather large box, too. I opened it to find a set of pastel dishes in blue, yellow, green, and pink.

"Casey said you needed dishes. She helped us pick them out," Ethan said.

"Yeah. We hit the resale shops hard," Casey said.

"This is great!" I said. "Tim and I have been using two cracked bowls, three old plates, and a couple of mugs. Our place has a dishwasher, but we have almost nothing to wash."

"Yeah," Tim said. "We're down to sharing a glass. We had a couple, but I broke one."

Casper smiled.

"This is from Brendan and me."

I opened a slightly smaller box to find lots of glasses.

"Hey, look Tim," I said, holding one up. "We don't have to share anymore."

The theme of gifts to use in the loft continued. I received some much needed towels, washcloths, dishtowels, and dishcloths as well as some silverware and some wooden spoons.

Tristan handed me a large rectangular package. I didn't have a clue as to what was inside, although if I had any sense at all, I would have figured it out. I tore away the purple-and-silver wrapping paper to find a beautiful painting of Café Moffatt that showed Tim and me hanging out the upper windows smiling and waving. Everyone oohed and aahed over it.

"Tristan, I don't know what to say. It's incredible!"

"I thought you could use it to decorate your living room. Or, if you don't like it, your bathroom." He grinned.

"Not like it? Are you kidding?"

Everyone had to get a good look at the painting. Tristan was truly talented. There was no doubt it was Tim and me in the windows. He even captured the mischievous look that Tim often gets.

"Our present is upstairs," Jack said. "We had to put it in one of the spare bedrooms."

We all followed Jack up the stairs. He opened the door, and my breath caught in my throat.

"Casey said you didn't have a kitchen table or chairs," Jack said. "Ardelene and I found these at an auction."

"I don't know what to say. This is too much. Thank you!"

The table and chairs looked new. They were all painted white, except the top of the table was natural wood. It was beautiful.

"Time for cake and ice cream, I think," Ardelene said.

Everyone went back downstairs. I really was overwhelmed. I'd been having a really hard time getting the things Tim and I needed for our place. I'd just started working part-time at both Café Moffatt and Ofarim's. So far, all my earnings had gone for food, electricity, and other necessities. There just wasn't money for things like dishes and furniture. Now, we suddenly had most of what we needed. Yes!

Casey covered my eyes while Ardelene brought out the cake. When Casey finally let me look, I gasped. My birthday cake was shaped like an oversized football. I don't mean it was a flat cake with a football drawn on it. It was actually shaped like a football. Seventeen candles burned above the laces.

"Make a wish," Nathan said.

"Yeah, maybe to become quarterback this fall," Brendan said.

That would've been a good wish, but I already knew what I was going to wish for. I glanced at Tristan for a moment before I drew in a big breath and blew out all the candles.

Dane

"Mom, when can we move into the new place? I feel as if I'm living in a shoebox."

"Be patient, dear. Just a few more days."

"How long can it take to turn on the electricity and water?"

"It's a little more complicated than that."

"Can I go over and study at Tim's then?"

"Will Shawn be there?"

"Why does Shawn have to be there? I'm going to study with Tim."

"You need a chaperone."

"Mom, this is the twentieth century. We aren't living back in the olden days."

"If you want to go, call. I want to talk to Shawn to make sure he's there."

"It's a Friday. Shawn doesn't work on Fridays."

"Call."

I gave up and called. Tim answered. He was all for me coming over, of course. It took him only a few moments to put Shawn on.

"Here he is," I said, handing the phone to Mom.

"Hi, Shawn. Are you up for babysitting? Dane is pestering me to study with Tim."

"Mom!"

I could hear a laugh on the other end of the line, but I couldn't tell what Shawn said after that.

"If Dane becomes an annoyance, send him home. I'm sure you've got a lot of work to do."

Annoyance? Me?

Mom finished up her conversation with Shawn.

"You are in luck. Shawn will be there this evening. I want you home no later than ten."

"Mom!"

"Ten is late enough. I'm sure Shawn has things to do. Remember, he has a lot of responsibilities on his shoulders right now."

"How about eleven?"

"Ten, or you can stay home."

"Ten sounds great! See you later."

Mom presented her cheek, and I dutifully kissed it. I put on my coat and toboggan and walked toward Tim's and Shawn's place.

Parents could be such a pain! Mine really weren't that bad, though. My parents had actually moved so I could go to a different school. There was some serious trouble back in Marmont when word got out I was queer. I became a punching bag for former friends and enemies alike.

I don't see why I needed a chaperone. Mom was no doubt worried Tim and I would get it on. She was right to worry, too! We were going to get it on—as often as possible. No one could watch Tim and me all the time. We were going to do it one way or another, so why make things difficult? Did my parents really believe they could keep me under surveillance twenty-four hours a day? I think they knew they couldn't. They just wanted to make themselves feel better and assure themselves they were fulfilling their parental duties.

I'd only been over to Tim's and Shawn's a couple of times so far. Both times, Shawn made us keep Tim's bedroom door open. He'd changed from my once-upon-a-time lover to my "parent." I guess I should explain that. I knew Shawn before I knew his brother. Shawn saved my life once, in fact. We also messed around once when he came to visit me in Marmont. That was what was so bizarre about him being my chaperone. He was now in charge of keeping Tim and me from doing what he once did with me. I thought maybe he'd just look the other way, but noooooooooooo. He wouldn't let us do more than make out. Mom would probably freak if she knew he let us do that. We actually did a little more than that, but we had to sneak it in. The world was against us having fun, but the world was going down!

I still almost couldn't believe I was living in Verona. Maybe wishes do come true sometimes. As bad as things had been at the end back in Marmont, the pain and suffering was worth it, because it brought me here. Tim, Shawn, Ethan, Nathan, Brendan, and Casper were real friends. They weren't at all like the guys back in Marmont whom I thought were my friends. I didn't have to walk the halls of VHS in fear like I did in my old school. Sure, there was danger, but not like in Marmont. I couldn't believe how many out gay boys there were here! Best of all, of course, was Tim! He was so sexy and such a great kisser. I loved the way his sexy body felt in my arms.

I walked up Main Street and entered the door just to the right of Café Moffatt. I climbed the stairs and knocked on the door at the top.

"Come on in," a voice called. I was confused. It sounded like Ethan.

I was right. There was no sign of Tim, but Shawn, Ethan, and Brendan were moving furniture around in the living room.

"Hey, what are you guys doing here?" I asked.

"Delivering the kitchen table and chairs," Ethan said.

"I think over by front windows," Shawn said. "There's a lot of light there and a good view."

The three set the table in place.

"Now all we have to do is organize the rest of the furniture," Shawn said. "Hey, Dane, could you and Tim bring up the chairs?"

"Sure thing."

"He's back in his bedroom."

I walked down the hallway to Tim's bedroom. The door was open. Tim was just pulling on a shirt. I caught a quick glimpse of his sexy abs. Dating a football player had its perks.

"Oh, baby, leave it off," I said.

Tim grinned. He hugged me and kissed me on the lips. I hugged him back tight.

"Shawn wants us to bring up the kitchen chairs," I said.

"He thinks I'm his slave boy," Tim said.

"I thought you were *my* slave boy."

"Mmm. Hold onto that thought."

"Maybe Ethan and Brendan will keep Shawn distracted and we can have a little…quality time," I said.

"Let's hope so. I could use some…quality time."

"I've been needing it all day."

Tim kissed me again, and we walked out into the hall and to the living room. Shawn and Brendan were in the process of moving the couch.

"So where are these chairs you want us to bring up?" Tim asked.

"In the truck," Ethan said. "It's just up the street."

Tim and I walked downstairs. It didn't take us long to spot Ethan's ancient, green Ford pickup. Tim and I both grabbed two chairs and carried them back up to the loft. We had a bit of trouble coming up the stairs because we had to walk sideways. Carrying one chair at a time would've been wiser.

"Thanks, guys," Shawn said as we placed the chairs around the table.

"Looks good," I said.

"Yeah. I'm thrilled with all my birthday presents. You guys are the best. It was such a pain trying to get by with one glass, one pan, and very few dishes."

"Maybe you should have another birthday," I said.

Shawn laughed.

"If you need money, I can help you out," Brendan said.

"Thanks. I appreciate the offer, but we'll get by. I really want to make it on my own. I've got to if Tim and I are going to stay together. A social worker will be checking on us every two weeks, so I have to stay on top of things."

"A social worker?" I asked.

"Yeah. There was some talk about putting Tim and me in foster homes, but I was able to convince the social worker I could make it on my own. She's actually really nice. She was impressed with our loft and that I found two part-time jobs so quickly."

"If things get tight, don't forget we're here for you," Brendan said.

"Thanks. I'll remember that, but I'm determined to make this work."

"Hey, we really need to go," Ethan said.

I glanced at Tim. There went our chance of keeping Shawn distracted.

"Going out, huh?" Shawn asked.

"Yeah, we're all going to catch a movie at the Paramount. You guys want to come?"

"We'd rather stay here," Tim said, grinning.

"I've got a lot to get done," Shawn said. "This is one of my few nights off."

Shawn seemed kind of sad, but I wasn't sure why.

"Well, we'll see you Monday at school at the latest," Ethan said.

"Bye, guys. Thanks for bringing the table and chairs over."

Soon it was just the three of us in the loft.

"I guess we'd better get to studying," I said.

Tim and I headed for his bedroom.

"Leave the door open," Shawn said.

"Shawn…"

"Don't 'Shawn' me."

Tim looked more than a little pissed. He turned back toward Shawn.

"Why do you have to act so different now? You're my brother, not my father. You weren't like this when we were living at home. Back then, you wouldn't have cared what Dane and I did."

"I'm different because things are different. You know that. I'm responsible for you now. I'm trying not to butt in, but I can't just let you run wild. Do you want to end up in a foster home?"

"No. I still don't see why I have to leave my door open. What's wrong with Dane and me having sex?"

I suddenly felt as if I shouldn't be there. This was a family argument.

"Um, should I go?" I asked.

"No. It's okay, Dane," Shawn said. "I think maybe the three of us should sit down and talk about this."

"Or you could just let us do what we want," Tim said.

"Not a chance."

Tim shot Shawn a rather nasty look. The three of us sat down at the newly arrived kitchen table.

"So, why can't you just let Dane and me have sex when we want?" Tim asked. That's one thing I liked about Tim: he wasn't shy.

Instead of answering Tim, Shawn looked at me.

"Would your parents let the two of you have sex at your house?" he asked.

"No way. They'd freak if we even made out."

"What does that have to do with it?" Tim asked. "Those are Dane's parents. Like I said, you're not my dad."

"No. I'm not your dad. I am responsible for you, though. That puts me in about the same position. Tim, I truly don't want to stick my nose in your private life. I really don't. What you've got to understand is that I have responsibilities."

"Dad didn't care."

"Tim, do I have to remind you that Dad didn't give a damn about us, period?"

"No."

"He wasn't a good parent. Yeah, he let us do pretty much what we wanted, but he also let Tom terrorize us. Our lives wouldn't have been so hellish if Dad was a better parent. He damn near lost custody of us. If we had told anyone about what was going on, he would have. We'd both be in a foster home right now. I love you, Tim and I want to keep us together."

"I know that, but...it's just sex."

"Sex isn't just sex, Tim. It's a lot more than that. There are risks involved."

"So? I know you've had sex!" Tim said. "Hell, you had sex with Dane! So what's the difference between that and Dane and me getting it on?"

"The difference is that when Dane and I had sex we did it in my car. His parents didn't know about it."

"So, what are you saying? That Dane and I should fuck in a car?"

"No."

"We're going to have sex, Shawn. One way or another. You're not that much older than I am. You know what it's like!"

"Yeah, I know. Believe me. I know."

"So why cause us problems? We're going to have sex. You can't stop us. Dane's parents can't stop us. If you don't let us do it here, we'll find someplace to do it. We'll get it on in the woods, or a barn, or wherever, but we'll do it. Why not just let us do it here?"

"I bet you two wouldn't put it to Dane's mom and dad like that," Shawn said.

"No way!" I said.

"You're not them," Tim said. "You're not much older than we are. You know how bad guys our age need it. You understand in a way Dane's parents can't. They've forgotten what it's like to be young. You haven't. Which makes it even worse that you won't just let us do it."

"You make some convincing arguments, little brother. If it was just me, I'd let you go at it. The thing is, Dane's mom expects me to keep an eye on you two. She trusts me, and I can't betray that trust. Also, most people freak out when they think about anyone under eighteen having sex. It's as though it's some horrible crime. I don't believe that. It's just plain stupid, but I've got to deal with these people. What if our social worker dropped by while you two were going at it? What if someone else found out?"

"No one is going to find out, Shawn," I said.

"We don't know that for sure. If they did…that would be it. I'd be considered unfit to watch over you. It's stupid, but that's the way it is."

"Shawn. Come on," Tim pleaded. I could actually hear the sexual need in his voice.

"Here's the bottom line, guys. Personally, if you're safe, I think it's fine if you two have sex. But, since I'm responsible for Tim, and Dane's mom expects me to act as a chaperone, I can't let you have sex. I'm trying to allow you as much freedom as I can. I'm sure your make-out sessions get intense. It can't go any further, though. Surely, you can understand that. I'm caught in the middle here, guys. I'm doing the best I can."

"I don't like it, but I understand," Tim said grudgingly.

"Thanks," Shawn said. "This isn't exactly easy for me either, you know."

"Yeah. I know. I'm sorry if my being a horny little bastard is causing you problems," Tim said, then grinned.

"It's okay. I'm used to you being a horny little bastard—and just a little bastard, period."

"Funny!"

"Seriously, I'm letting you do as much as I can."

"Thanks, Shawn," Tim said. "We'll try and make it easy on you. We won't have sex when you're around. Don't you need to go to the grocery store or something?"

"Nice try. I'll be staying right here tonight. I've got some cleaning to do, some bills to pay, and other equally fun stuff to get done."

"Do you want some help?" Tim asked.

"No. Thanks for offering, but I want you to be a kid while you can."

"Just remember that I'm more than a kid. If you need my help, I'm here, Shawn."

I watched as Shawn and Tim hugged. They were lucky to have each other.

"Your brother is really cool," I said to Tim as we walked to his bedroom.

"Shh, he might hear you. He's impressed enough with himself as it is."

"I heard that!" Shawn yelled.

Tim and I laughed, went into his room, and made out quietly so Shawn couldn't hear us. I wanted to do more, but I understood what Shawn had said. He was kind of caught between a rock and a hard place. My opinion might not count for much, but I thought he was doing a damn good job of taking care of Tim.

Tim and I didn't have sex, but we did have an intense make-out session. We were getting in some good feels, too. It was frustrating that we couldn't be naked, but there was something hot about not being able to do everything we wanted. Don't get me wrong. I would much rather have had sex, but we made the best of the situation.

Still, the circumstances were frustrating. If it was warm outside, Tim and I could have had sex any number of places. I couldn't wait for spring! If we got naked outside now…well, something might freeze off! Of course, we didn't have to get completely naked to have sex, but I knew cold would kill the mood. Icy hands and an icy breeze on sensitive private areas aren't exactly ideal for sex.

I was home by ten. Personally, I didn't see why I couldn't stay out later, but moms are funny like that. I would have liked to have stayed over, but I knew there was no chance of that. My parents weren't that stupid.

On Friday, I got some good news. We could move into our new place sometime the next week! It wasn't really a new place. It was the old Verona school, but it was new to me. I wondered what it would be like to go from living in my tiny little room in our rented house to having more room than I could use. I couldn't wait to find out!

Despite my sexual frustration, and believe me I had that to spare, I was still feeling pretty good. Things were way better in Verona than they ever had been in Marmont, especially during my last days there. I had Tim. I had friends. Tim and I even had a Valentine's Day date planned! I hit Dad up for the cash to take Tim out. I knew Tim didn't have any money, and I wanted to take him somewhere nice. He was going to be so excited when he found out I was taking him to The Park's Edge. I was dying to tell him, but I was determined to keep it as a surprise. I couldn't wait for February 14th. It was going to be my first Valentine's Day ever with a boyfriend!

Shawn

"Service! Service!" Brandon said loudly. "What does a guy have to do to get waited on around here?"

I grinned as I walked toward the booth Brandon shared with Jon.

"Keep your shirt on—or on second thought…"

"Yeah, you wish," Brandon said.

"It's not enough you guys harass me at school. Now, you're following me to work?"

"Don't flatter yourself," Jon said. "Brandon and I eat in here a lot. Café Moffatt is our place."

"Hey, Suzie," Brandon said to the owner as she walked by. "Can't you get some *decent* help in here? I mean—hiring Shawn— what were you thinking?"

"Are you kidding? He's my best waiter."

"He's your *only* waiter," Brandon said. "The other servers are all females. Keep that up, by the way. I like it."

Suzie just laughed, shook her head, and moved on.

"Okay, if you two are done annoying my boss and landlord, perhaps you'd like to order."

"Don't you just hate a pushy waiter," Jon said.

I laughed. I was accustomed to Brandon and Jon going at each other. Becoming their new target made me feel accepted.

"Okay, I'll have a western omelet, sausage links, and coffee," Brandon said. "Oh, and give me an order of those cinnamon donuts they make here."

"Pancakes with strawberry topping, bacon, scrambled eggs, toast, and coffee for me," Jon said.

"Yeah, and be quick about it," Brandon said, "or no quarter tip for you."

"A whole quarter?" I said. "That's very generous. I know how hard it is for you to earn a quarter. It must be especially rough for a straight boy."

Jon laughed, but Brandon just looked confused. I was halfway back to the kitchen before I heard him yell, "Hey!"

I grinned and placed their orders.

"Friends of yours, I take it?" Suzie asked.

"Oh, yeah. How could you tell?"

"I'm psychic."

Suzie was a great boss. She was serious about things being done right, but she was easygoing, friendly, and just plain nice.

"You should hear the things they say to each other at school," I said. "You'd swear they hate each other, but they're best friends."

"I see them in here together a lot," Suzie said. She leaned in close to me and whispered, "For quite a while, I thought they were a couple."

I burst out laughing.

"Brandon would think that's hilarious. He's girl-crazy."

I went off to check on another table. I hadn't been working in Café Moffatt long, but Suzie started me waiting tables my very first day. Café Moffatt was a small place. There were usually only two or three servers, the cook, and Suzie. All of us, except the cook, also worked to clear tables and do the hundred-and-one things that needed doing to keep the place going. Something I really liked about Suzie was that she was right in there with us. She owned the place, but she didn't think she was too good to clear tables. That made all of us willing to do anything she asked.

I kept my mind on my work when necessary, but I did a lot of thinking when I was clearing tables, filling salt shakers, and performing other mindless tasks. Mainly, I thought about Tristan. It was February 13th, and I still hadn't asked Tristan out for Valentine's Day. I wanted to in the worst way, but a Valentine's Day date was serious business. It was a day for lovers, and Tristan and I weren't to that stage yet. I didn't know if we'd ever get there.

I'd been to Tristan's house a couple of times right after I met him, but then things got hectic. Tristan was getting settled into Verona and VHS. I was trying to get the loft in order and learn the ropes at not one, but two new jobs. Tim and I were settled into our loft now, but I was still going to school full-time, working Tuesdays, Wednesdays, and Thursdays at Ofarim's and weekends in Café Moffatt. The café did close at two p.m., but I didn't have much free time. Most of my weeknights were taken up by cooking, homework, laundry, and cleaning up the loft. The only time I had any real free time was on Monday and Friday evenings and after work on the weekend. Even a lot of that time was taken up with schoolwork and things that had to be done at home. I never realized that living on my own would create so much work!

Being so busy was probably saving my butt. I would most likely have already blown it with Tristan if I'd had lots of time on my hands. I was head-over-heels crazy about Tristan, but the feeling was not mutual. I'm not saying he had no interest in me, but where I wanted to get down on one knee and ask him to be my boyfriend, he just wanted to hang out, be friends, and see what happened. Every time I saw him I wanted to kiss him. He was just so damn sexy! Tristan hadn't exactly said I couldn't kiss him, but I didn't know when the time was going to be right. Why did everything have to be so difficult! Anyway, my lack of free time was a blessing in disguise, I guess. It kept me from trying to move too fast with Tristan. Move too fast? Ha! I barely saw him outside of school! It was so frustrating.

When Brandon's and Jon's orders were up, I carried them to their table.

"Here you go, guys. I'll get you some more coffee. You need anything else?"

"When do you get off work, big boy?" Brandon asked, as if he was flirting with me.

"Two p.m."

"So, have you asked Tristan out for Valentine's Day yet?" Jon asked.

He laughed when he saw the flabbergasted look on my face.

"Come on, Shawn. Everyone knows you're hot for him. It's not a secret. You haven't asked him out, have you?"

"No. I'm afraid to."

"You pussy," Brandon said. "Just do it."

"I'm going to!"

"When?"

"Right after work. I'm going to go home, clean up, go over to Tristan's, and ask him out."

"Hmm, should we bet on this?" Jon asked Brandon.

"I think he's going to wimp out," Brandon said.

"I don't know. He is pretty desperate. Desperation can stand in for courage."

"Yeah, you'd know all about that, wouldn't you, Jon?"

"Fuck you, Hanson."

"See?" Brandon said, looking at me. "Jon is desperate. He isn't even into guys, and he wants to fuck me."

"Listen, bitch," Jon said to Brandon, "I asked Kim Haley out for Valentine's Day, and she said 'yes.' I'm taking her to The Park's Edge tomorrow!"

"It's not a date if you have to pay her," Brandon said. "There's another name for that."

I had other tables to serve, so I left Brandon and Jon bickering. I kind of hated to miss the show.

I had not actually intended to go to Tristan's house right after work, but time was running out. Brandon was right. I was being a pussy. It wasn't like me. I was aggressive on the football field. I didn't back down from fights. Why was I being such a coward when it came to simply asking Tristan out on a date? Because it was Tristan, and Valentine's Day wasn't an ordinary date—that's why! I had butterflies in my stomach just thinking about it. I was going to do it, however. I was going to force myself to ask him out.

At closing, I made the long, thirty-second commute to the loft and then took a hot shower. I loved the bathroom in the loft. Back home, we had this little tub and this shower curtain that was always wafting in and sticking to my body. It was all cold and clammy. I loved the openness of the shower area in the loft bathroom, and there was no slimy plastic curtain. There wasn't any privacy if someone walked in, but Tim and I weren't shy about showering around each other. Hell, I showered with as many as two-dozen other guys at school after football practices and P.E. classes. Now, that was some nice scenery.

I had to calm myself a bit. I couldn't go over to Tristan's all sexually revved up. I had to play it cool with him. I was dying to rip off his clothes and ravish him, but I had to keep that to myself.

I reluctantly left the luxury of the hot, steamy water. I dried off as I walked to my room. I pulled on a pair of boxers and then stared at the clothes in my closet. What to wear? What to wear?

I almost went for one of my football jerseys, but I wanted to play down my jock side. Tristan was an intellectual. He was an artist, and he liked to read books. I thought about my black, long-sleeve, button-down shirt, but that was too dressy. Nothing seemed right. I growled.

"Problem, bro?" Tim asked, as he stuck his head in my room.

"I can't decide what to wear."

"Oh. Going out with Tristan, huh?"

"I wish. I'm going to Tristan's house to ask him out for Valentine's Day."

"Go for it. Dane asked me out. He's taking me to The Park's Edge."

"Jon said he's taking Kim there."

"You should take Tristan there."

"With luck," I said, still staring at my closet.

Tim stepped into the room.

"Here," he said. He grabbed a blue-and-white-striped, short-sleeved shirt and held it up to my chest. "Yeah, wear this and a pair of jeans. You're going to get a chill standing here in your boxers."

"Okay, I'll take your advice, but it's your fault if I get shot down."

"No way. If he turns you down, it's all your fault. I'm not taking the blame for your lack of personality or good looks."

I made a fist as if I was going to strike Tim, but he just grinned.

"Good luck, Shawn."

"Thanks. I'm going to need it."

I put on my leather jacket. I reached for my toboggan, but then drew my hand back. The toboggan would definitely mess up my hair. I took my scarf instead. I could use it to cover my ears if necessary. It was cold out, but not *that* cold.

As I walked to Tristan's house, I kept wanting to turn around and go back home, but then I pictured myself alone on yet another Valentine's Day. Of course, I might go through the torment of asking Tristan out and still be alone. At least then I'd know I tried. Brandon's voice taunted me in my head, too, chanting: "You pussy." No, I wasn't going to turn around. I was going to go through with this.

I walked up to the white, two-story home Tristan shared with his mother and knocked on the door. No answer. I waited, then knocked again. I stood there for about a minute. Just as I decided no one was home, the door opened.

"Hey," Tristan said.

He looked so very handsome wearing jeans and a black sweater. His loose, black hair tumbled down to his shoulders.

"Hey," I said. "Uh…"

"Come in," he said.

"Thanks."

"Let's go to the kitchen. I'll make us some hot tea."

We walked through the living room on our way to the kitchen.

"You and your mom are really getting this place in shape."

"Yeah. It takes an amazing amount of time to unpack everything, but you know all about that, I'm sure."

"I didn't have nearly as much stuff to move as you did."

"I'm sorry I haven't come over to help you with decorating, but things have been kind of crazy," Tristan said as he filled a tea kettle with water and set it on the stove. I watched as the blue gas flames shot upward and danced under the kettle.

"Yeah. I've been crazy-busy, too. I hope things will settle down soon."

"I hope so, too."

There was a pause. I should have come right out and asked Tristan what I wanted, but I couldn't make myself. Besides, I was distracted by his sexy, dark eyes.

"Brandon and Jon came into the café while I was working today."

"Yeah?"

"Yeah. They were going off on each other—and me."

Tristan laughed.

"They're crazy. Taylor wrote me about them a time or two. They are just as he described them."

Taylor. Tristan looked so much like his cousin it was scary. The only differences were that Tristan had black hair where Taylor had blond and brown eyes instead of blue. Taylor didn't wear glasses, either, but Tristan was his dark twin. Sometimes, it was as if Taylor was alive again…

Tristan and I talked about school for a bit while I tried to work up the courage to ask him out.

The kettle whistled. Tristan took it off the stove and made us cups of Irish Breakfast tea.

"So what's up?" he asked.

This was it. I hesitated, but then Brandon's voice taunted me in my head again, "You pussy."

"I was wondering…will you go out with me tomorrow?"

"Out with you? Like bowling or what?"

"Well, I'd like to take you to The Park's Edge."

"So, you mean like a date?"

"Yeah, well...it doesn't have to be. Just...you know..."

"I don't know, Shawn. Tomorrow is Valentine's Day. I like you, but... I don't really want to be more than friends right now. Maybe somewhere down the road, but I'm just not ready."

I could feel my face blanching. Tristan was being as kind as possible, but he might as well have been kicking me and laughing at me.

"Just as friends?" I asked. "I promise. I won't read anything into it. We haven't had much time together. I want to get to know you. We have to eat anyway, and who wants to be alone on Valentine's Day? Please."

"Oh, you're bringing out the puppy-dog eyes. That is not fair."

"I have puppy-dog eyes?" I asked.

"You do, sometimes—like now."

"Just as friends, then? I promise to keep my hands to myself."

"Okay, just as friends, but we go Dutch."

"I don't mind paying," I said.

"No. We go Dutch."

"Okay."

It wasn't the way I wanted things to be, but I guess it was about as much as I could expect. Tristan and I were going out on Valentine's Day!

"So what have you been up to?" Tristan asked as he took a sip of tea.

"School, work, organizing the loft, cleaning, prying Tim and Dane apart."

"I bet the last is the toughest job."

"Yeah. I had a talk with the two of them. Tim didn't understand why I wouldn't just let them do whatever they wanted. It's tough being his brother and his guardian at the same time. Well, I'm not officially his guardian, but in a way I am. I hope he doesn't start resenting me. I feel like a villain sometimes when I'm telling him he has to be home by a certain time or follow some other rule."

"You're just trying to take care of him."

"I know, but I don't know if he sees it that way. When I came up with the idea of us moving out and getting our own place, I never thought about the consequences. I knew I'd have to get a job and pay bills, but there are all these other responsibilities I didn't consider. I didn't realize I'd basically become Tim's parent. I don't mind. It's just that I don't know how to do it."

"Look at it this way. Even if you really screw up, you can't possibly be a worse parent than your dad."

"Yeah. Tim won't come home and find me drunk in front of the TV. He doesn't have to worry about me beating him."

"Have you talked to your dad since you moved out?"

"No. He did send me a check for the first two months' rent on the loft like he promised. I was kind of surprised he kept his word."

"At least he's helping you out some."

"Yeah. Dad isn't all bad. I know he has his own problems. Basically, he's a bully, a shitty father, and an alcoholic. He does have his moments, though. He wasn't always like that, either. He was never a great dad, but there was a time when he was, at least, a decent father. He has improved some recently. At least, he respects me now."

"You know, word about what happened between you and your dad has gotten around at school. I don't mean everything, just the fight. I think a lot of people respect you for that—or are at least afraid of you."

"I guess I should have kicked his ass long ago," I said with an insincere laugh. "I used to be so scared of him. Then, when I came in and found him beating on Tim, I just snapped. One thing is for sure, I'm not at all sorry I got Tim out of there. Now, if I can just get Tim to keep it in his pants."

Tristan laughed.

"That will probably be a losing battle."

"Pardon me for being crude, but if I'd let them, Tim and Dane would fuck like bunnies."

Tristan laughed again. "No doubt."

"The thing is, I kind of feel like a jerk for not letting them. I feel as if I'm sticking my nose in where it doesn't belong. At the same time, I feel responsible for Tim. Dane's mom lets him come over when I'm there because she trusts me to keep things under control."

"How do you handle it?"

"When Dane is there, I make Tim keep his bedroom door open. They make out a lot, and I'm sure they do quite a bit more, but at least they're not going all the way."

"That's probably the best you can do. I don't envy you."

"Sometimes, I just want to be a kid again. I never really did get to be a kid. Well, I did for a while, then Mom left, and that was that. Everything began to change."

I was thankful Tristan didn't ask why Mom left. I didn't want to get into it.

"My life has been rough at times, but it's been much easier than yours," Tristan said. "I know what you mean about wishing you could be a kid again. I'm seventeen, just like you. A lot of people think of me as a kid still, but I'm really not. I guess compared to being thirty-five, seventeen is being a kid, but it's not like being nine or ten. I don't have your responsibilities, but still there are all these pressures, all these decisions to make. Sometimes, I wish I could go back to having my parents tell me what to do."

"Yeah. I hope life will get easier. Being on my own and becoming responsible for Tim just happened so fast. It's kind of like someone walked up to me and said, "Congratulations, it's a sixteen-year-old boy. I'm a father, and I've never even had sex with a girl!"

Tristan laughed. He did that a lot. It's one of the many things I liked about him.

"Sorry. I didn't come over here to whine."

"You're not whining. I find it all rather interesting. I don't have a little brother, but I can't even imagine trying to raise one if I did."

"My whole life has changed. My plan was to get the hell out of Verona the second I turned eighteen. Now, I plan to stick around at least until Tim graduates from high school. I don't know what I'm going to do about college. My hopes were never too high when it came to that. I may be working at Ofarim's and Café Moffatt my entire life."

"Your family is not very well off, is it?" Tristan asked.

"No. Dad hasn't had a real job for years. I'm not sure where he gets his money for booze. I'm not sure I want to know."

"I bet you can get financial assistance, then. You might be able to get a scholarship as well."

"I'm going to try, but I've got Tim to worry about as well. I'd like to put some money back for his college education, but right now, it's taking everything I'm making just to keep going. Okay, we need to talk about something else. I don't want to think about this stuff anymore, and I don't want you to think of me as someone who comes over and talks about his problems all the time."

"We can change the subject, but you're welcome to talk to me about your problems anytime you want."

"Thanks."

"Hmm, new topic… Oh, this is kind of related, but I heard a rumor about your brother on Friday."

"Uh-oh. What did he do?"

"People are beginning to notice how Tim and Dane stick together every minute. Someone saw them kiss."

"That doesn't surprise me, the little horn dogs."

Tristan grinned.

"Tim was planning on coming out," I said. "I guess it's no big deal. I'll have to keep an eye on him, though. Once Devon and his minions find out, they'll give Tim and Dane a hard time."

"I'm sure the guys can keep Devon and the others under control. I haven't been going to VHS for a long time but Brendan, Ethan, Brandon, and Jon seem to keep things from getting out of hand—as far as preventing the gay boys from being harassed."

"Yeah, you missed some major drama. Some serious shit went down in the last several months. I was just on the fringe of most of it. I was really scared for quite a while—back when Devon and his crowd were all over Taylor and Mark. Then, when they…died…"

"You can say it, Shawn. My cousin killed himself, and then Mark did, too."

"I just don't want to bring up painful memories."

"Those memories are painful whether you bring them up or not. Taylor was more like a brother than a cousin, even though we didn't get to see each other all that much. I think it's best to just go ahead and talk about what happened. It's not good to repress feelings. Emotions have a way of coming out one way or another."

"Maybe you're right. I don't know."

"My point is: don't ever feel bad about talking about Taylor around me. I'm still adjusting to losing him, but I try to focus my memories on his life, not on his death. In a way, it helps me to truly appreciate what I've got. I'm sure Taylor didn't know he was going to die until shortly before he killed himself. He was sixteen. He probably thought he was going to go on living for years and years, but then his life ended. His death has made me understand the importance of appreciating what I've got right now. Thinking about the future is fine, but it's the present that is truly important."

"You're really smart," I said.

"I don't know about that, but I'm glad I have the ability to live in the moment. Maybe all I'm saying is that I'm an optimist. I think it's a lot better going through life seeing the glass as half full, rather than half empty."

I so wanted to kiss Tristan just then. I wanted to hold him in my arms and kiss him. For now, I had to be content with his friendship. As I sat there and thought about it, I realized his friendship was a pretty valuable thing. I wanted to focus on that. I wanted my glass to be half full, too.

Tristan was extremely intelligent. That much was obvious. He was telling me about this book he was reading on Gutenberg. Luckily, I didn't open my mouth and say anything before he explained that Gutenberg invented the printing press and movable type back in the fifteenth century. When he first mentioned Gutenberg, I thought he was talking about those really awesome cars from the 1930s, but that was Duesenberg. I came very close to looking like a total idiot.

Tristan was also reading *The Iliad*. I didn't know anyone who would read a book like that unless it was a class assignment but Tristan read it just because he wanted to. He was explaining it to me, and I have to admit, it did sound pretty cool. We must've sat there for two hours drinking hot tea and talking about stuff like Renaissance artists and Greek mythology. When my teachers discussed such things in class I was bored, but Tristan made them interesting.

***

When I was in grade school, Valentine's Day meant a party. We'd each make a mailbox out of a shoebox and some construction paper. These shoeboxes always reminded me of covered wagons. Then, we'd all go around delivering valentines to the mailboxes. Everyone got one for everyone else, so it wasn't like on that Charlie Brown special where he's looking forlornly into an empty mailbox. Looking back, those grade-school parties weren't all that much— just some cupcakes, punch, a few games, and those valentines—but I really looked forward to them back then. When I got older, there weren't any parties, and I started to feel like an outsider because my friends would have Valentine's Day dates with girls. It was really only the last couple of years that Valentine's Day began to be a major bummer. I wanted a boyfriend, but there was no way I could have one—even if I could find one. This year was different. Despite the fact that my date with Tristan wasn't really a date, it was the closest thing I had experienced yet. I was excited!

Picking out what to wear for my Valentine's Day date with Tristan was surprisingly easy. I selected my white dress shirt because I knew it would look good with my dark, chocolate-brown hair. I wore a pair of deep maroon corduroys to complete my dressy look.

I wanted to buy Tristan some flowers or candy, but then he'd think I was reading more into our date than I should. I wanted it to be a flowers-and-candy kind of date, but it wasn't. I didn't want to come on too strong or Tristan might decide he didn't want to see me anymore. I had to respect his wishes and just hope he'd take a romantic interest in me—or at least a sexual interest. I wanted more than just sex, but I'd take what I could get! Oh, how I yearned to kiss those full, red lips of his.

It was cold out, but there still seemed to be little sense in driving. Besides, my beat-up car didn't exactly create a luxurious atmosphere. I pulled on my leather jacket and scarf, but once again chose not to wear my toboggan. I didn't want to greet Tristan with messy, static-charged hair.

The walk to Tristan's house was bracing. I enjoyed breathing in the cold air. I liked the contrast between the cold breeze hitting my face and the warmth of my body inside my leather jacket. With my hands in my pockets I felt quite snuggly.

Tristan answered the door wearing a deep-purple dress shirt and dark slacks that were almost, but not quite black. I wanted to just stand there and gaze upon his beauty, but I couldn't for the same reason I couldn't buy him any flowers or candy.

"Ready?" I asked.

"I just have to get my coat. Step inside and I'll run up to my room."

I stood just inside the door for less than a minute before Tristan returned wearing his suede duster. It made him look like some New York model. Together, we stepped out into the chill air of Verona.

"How was work today?" Tristan asked.

"Busy. Sunday mornings are always busy. I don't mind, though. The time passes faster, and I get more tips."

"I actually finished putting my bedroom together this morning. Then I finished up a book report. I'm finally on top of things again."

"Does that mean you'll come over and help me decorate? I've done my best, but I'm not good at that sort of thing."

"Are you sure you're gay?" Tristan asked. "We're supposed to be natural-born decorators, you know."

"Oh, I'm sure."

I resisted the urge to tell Tristan I was willing to prove it right then and there.

"It's nice to get out. I can't wait until spring," Tristan said.

"Yeah. I love warm weather. My favorite weather is when I can run around wearing shorts and no shirt."

"I don't go shirtless very often."

"You should. I bet you've got a sexy body."

"More like skinny. My ribs show."

"There's nothing wrong with skinny."

"That's easy for you to say. Those of us who aren't built prefer not to let others see our skinny bodies."

I struggled hard not to say certain things. My instinct was to flirt and make suggestive comments, but with a supreme effort I controlled myself. I wondered if I'd gone too far by saying Tristan had a sexy body.

It wasn't long before we reached The Park's Edge. It was crowded. While we were waiting on a table, I spotted Ethan and Nathan sitting together. Brandon was with his girlfriend. I spotted Jon with a girl, too. I wondered if they were dating. I caught sight of someone waving at me and turned to see Casey. She was having supper with Sandy. It looked as if everyone was there. The only couple I didn't spot was Brendan and Casper. There was no sign of Tim and Dane, either, but Tim was still primping when I'd left.

I feared all the couples would make Tristan nervous, but he didn't show any sign of being ill at ease. I noticed the guys checking Tristan and me out. They probably thought I'd finally convinced him to go out with me. I kind of had, but it wasn't the kind of date I truly desired. Oh, how I wished it was! We'd have supper, take a romantic walk, and then make out under the stars. That wasn't going to happen, but at least I could dream.

"Thanks for coming with me. I didn't want to sit at home alone on Valentine's Day."

"I'm glad not to be alone, either," Tristan said.

"What is it about holidays?" I asked. "They're supposed to be fun, but so often they end up being sad and miserable."

"Holidays make people think about who or what is missing from their lives," Tristan said. "Mom was really sad this morning. I know she misses Dad. I think a lot of people who don't have someone to be with on Valentine's Day look around at all the happy couples, and it makes them feel really lonely."

"Yeah. It makes me feel lonely. I was determined to have a boyfriend this Valentine's Day. I really worked at it. Casey helped me. I went out with four different guys, and all of them were losers. Well, except Blake. He was hot, but he wasn't looking for a boyfriend. It leaves me feeling as if I've tried and failed."

"At least you tried."

"Yeah."

I looked at Tristan. I didn't voice my hope that by the next Valentine's Day he would be my boyfriend.

We were shown to a table that was located right next to a large tropical plant. It provided a sense of privacy. That's one thing I liked about The Park's Edge. The tables weren't crowded together. They were thoughtfully placed so that no matter where one sat, there was a feeling of intimacy. I knew I could carry on a private conversation with Tristan without being overheard.

"Holidays can be rough," Tristan said, continuing our conversation. "My aunt took Mom out shopping today. Hopefully, that will get her mind off things."

"Yeah, and I'm here with you, so I don't have to feel lonely."

"Looking at the glass as half full, huh?" Tristan asked.

"Yeah."

"The toughest holiday was Christmas," Tristan said. "It was really hard on Mom and me last year. Dad died less than two weeks before Christmas. The holidays weren't the same without him. Dad and I used to pick out the tree together. Suddenly, he wasn't there to do that. Mom went with me. I still enjoyed decorating the tree, listening to Christmas music, wrapping gifts, making cookies, and all that, but Dad's absence was…it was something I could *feel*. I really missed him. I kept thinking about how he wasn't there and wasn't going to be there ever again. I think it was worse than losing him in the first place. There it was, Christmas, the family time that was supposed to be so happy, and my dad was gone. I felt as if everyone else was spending the holidays with their families, but mine was broken. You know?"

I nodded.

"Of course. You do understand. Your mom has been gone for a long time, hasn't she?"

"Yes."

"I guess I'm just telling you things you already know, then."

"No. Well, yes, but you're putting them into words in a way I can't. I'm not really all that smart. I'm just a dumb jock."

"Shawn, you're a lot more than that. Just because you're a jock doesn't make you dumb."

"I know, but I am a jock, and I am dumb. I mean, I'm not completely stupid, but I have a lot of trouble understanding things sometimes. Like in literature classes. There are all these meanings that are supposed to be in these books, and I just don't get them. We read *The Lord of the Flies*. I thought the book was about how certain people will be bullies if they get the chance, but our teacher was talking about the breakdown of society and all this stuff that I didn't get. I felt as though I'd read the wrong book."

"Don't be so hard on yourself. Distilled down to its most basic essence, *The Lord of the Flies* is about the potential some have for being brutal and savage—for being bullies. You did understand; you just phrase the idea in simple language."

"That's because I am simple."

Tristan gave me a look that said, "quit putting yourself down."

"I do a lot of reading," Tristan said. "I love books. What I don't like is when an author tries to be too lofty and artistic or unnecessarily complicates a simple idea. The whole idea of language is communication, and making things unnecessarily complicated defeats that. I've had a few teachers who lost sight of what they were supposed to be teaching because they wanted to put everything in these grand terms that half the class couldn't understand. Literature has always been one of my favorite classes, but I had this Lit teacher back in Tulsa that...well, I don't think he really had a clue. He spent all his time talking about grand themes and imagery. It was as though he was trying to add all this meaning that wasn't even there. He wanted to interpret everything. He seemed to think that nothing in the books we read was what it seemed to be. It was as if they were all written in some complicated code that one had to work for years to figure out. I completely disagreed with his interpretation of every book we read. I have the feeling the authors of those books would have disagreed as well."

I smiled.

"I'm sorry. I tend to go off like that. I get interested in something, and I can't shut up about it."

"I think it's wonderful," I said. "You're so intelligent."

"The only thing I've really learned is that I know nothing," Tristan said. "Everything I learn opens up all these things I never even knew existed before. It's as if...it's as if I started out with the goal of reading every book in a bookshelf, but for every book I read a hundred more appear. They were there all along, but until I read a particular book, I couldn't see them."

"I'm not sure I get what you're saying."

"I just mean that the more I learn, the more I realize that there is far more out there to learn than I ever suspected. It's like starting out on a journey that you think is going to take a week and ends up taking a lifetime."

"Oh, okay. See, I told you I'm dumb."

"You're not dumb, Shawn. Everyone knows things that others don't. I'm sure you know lots of things I don't. You just think I'm smart because I wear glasses. I fool a lot of people that way." Tristan smiled.

"The glasses give you an intellectual look, but you're smart with or without them. You know things I'll never know."

"Yes, but you know things I'll never know. That's what I'm saying. We all have our own types of intelligence. We all have different interests. Lately, I've been getting into medieval history. What I'm learning probably has little or no practical application, but it doesn't matter, because I enjoy it. Lately, you've been learning how to pay bills and be a parent to your brother. I don't know those things. What you've been learning is a lot more practical that what I've been learning. You could say I'm wasting my time while you're doing something worthwhile. I could call myself dumb."

Our waiter finally arrived with our ice water and menus, so we halted out conversation.

"I'm sorry for the wait. We're really packed today."

"We're in no hurry," I said.

"What would you like to drink?"

"Coke," Tristan said.

"Same here."

"I'll be right back with your drinks."

"Do you know why Coke is called Coke?" Tristan asked.

"No, why?"

"Because one of the original ingredients was cocaine."

"This is a test to see how gullible I am, isn't it?"

"No. I promise. It's true."

"Really?"

"Really. They didn't quite realize what it was back then. I think they knew some of the effects but definitely not the dangers. Anyway, that's why Coke is called Coke. That's just another example of the interesting but mostly useless information that's running around inside my head."

"It's not useless. It's entertaining."

Tristan and I browsed the menus. When the waiter returned with our drinks, I ordered Mediterranean Chicken, and Tristan ordered a Filet Mignon Salad.

Tim and Dane entered shortly after we ordered. I smiled as I watched my brother and his boyfriend take a seat at a distant table.

"You're really happy for him, aren't you?" Tristan asked.

"Yes. He's so lucky to have found someone. Dane needs someone, too. He's had a rough time."

"I heard what happened to him at his old school."

"Yes, and what made it worse was that the boy who beat him up so bad was a boy that Dane had a huge crush on."

"He must have been damaged even more emotionally than he was physically."

"Yes. It was hard on him. That's why Tim is so good for him. Just being in Verona is good for him. Things are better here for boys like us than they are in most places."

I spotted Brendan and Casper entering. I couldn't think anyone in my little circle of friends who wasn't in the restaurant. The Park's Edge was definitely the place to be on Valentine's Day. I was grateful I'd had the courage to ask Tristan out and even more thankful he'd accepted.

We talked until our orders arrived and then talked while we ate. I'd been sorely tempted to order a Fried Chicken Hoagie, one of my favorites, but I liked it with so much Honey Dijon it was a messy business. I'm not complaining though. My Mediterranean Chicken was delicious—grilled chicken with pine nuts, olives, tomato, basil, onion, hot peppers, capers, mushrooms, cream, and bowtie pasta. Mmm. Tristan's Filet Mignon Salad was huge! It was covered with Filet Mignon, tomatoes, olives, red peppers, and parmesan cheese.

Tristan and I continued talking right through dessert—incredible chocolate cake with thick butter cream icing. Yum. We talked about anything and everything. Tristan told me things about Tulsa. I filled him in on some of the legends and attractions of Verona. It didn't matter what we talked about; I just enjoying being with my hopefully future boyfriend.

I walked Tristan home. The stars were out by then, so I got my walk in the moonlight with the boy I loved. Yes. That's right. I loved Tristan. I knew he didn't love me back, but I hoped that would change. I knew it was far too soon for me to love him, but things like love don't have to make sense. Love happens on its own terms and in its own time. Okay, so I'm not an expert on love, but I knew what I was feeling.

We lingered in front of Tristan's door just long enough that I began to hope he'd kiss me. I wanted ever so much to lean in and press my lips to his, but I knew better than to make the first move. As much as I wanted to rush ahead, I had to be patient. Waiting was probably the hardest thing I'd ever done in my life, but I'd finally found someone, and for now, that was enough.

Dane

Between my parents and Shawn, my sex life with Tim was mostly limited to make-out sessions. They happen to be way more than what most called a make-out session. There was a lot of rubbing up against each other, groping, and hands wandering into pants. It wasn't all-out sex, and we had to remain almost completely clothed, but damn it was hot! I even tried blowing Tim once, but then we heard his brother coming down the hallway, so that was the end of that. Talk about frustrating! Especially for poor Tim. Half a b.j. can leave a guy in dire straits.

It goes without saying that my parents and Shawn ultimately failed in their efforts to keep Tim and me from getting it on, but I'm going to say it anyway. Tim and I got it on! One day, Tim and I finished our lunches in a rush and then slipped into the auditorium. We almost got caught by Coach Jordan who was on cafeteria duty. Had he looked in our direction he would have nabbed us, but we managed to just make it into the off-limits auditorium before he turned around.

Once inside, Tim and I found a dark space between the curtains. We grabbed each other and made out like crazy for a few moments. We could make out at Tim's, however, so I dropped to my knees, ripped down Tim's zipper and gave my boyfriend head right there on the stage. Tim was so excited it took him no time at all to finish. Tim's moan turned me on like mad, so when Tim dropped to his knees and gave me head, I didn't take long to climax, either. We were back in the cafeteria fifteen minutes later. Shawn gave us a suspicious look, but he didn't know anything for sure. Besides, he had no need to worry; we didn't mess around on his watch. Even if we had gotten caught, it wouldn't have been his responsibility.

***

The day I had long been anticipating finally arrived. No, not the day Tim and I finally managed to have all-out sex, although I was eagerly anticipating that, too. I'm talking about the day when we could finally begin to move into our new home.

I had been packing in anticipation of our move, so when I came home from school I was ready to go. There wasn't all that much to move from our rental home to our new place. All of our furniture and most of our belongings were still back in Marmont. The house there was up for sale but hadn't sold yet. Dad even lived there part-time while he transferred his business to Verona. Dad was an architect and planned to work from home in our new place, but until now he'd been moving back and forth between his office in Marmont and Verona. It was only about a forty-five minute trip, but I was sure Dad would be glad when his commute was reduced to walking from his bedroom into his office located right in the house.

Dad wasn't around when I got home, but Mom had the keys to the new place and was already loading stuff in the car. I jumped in and helped, partly because I was eager to check out my new home again, but mostly because I wanted to make sure some of my stuff got in the car. From the looks of the little rental house, I was guessing it would take no more than three trips to empty the place.

I was kind of going to miss our rental house even though it was tiny and right across from the creepy Graymoor Mansion. I swore I sometimes heard screams coming from the place at night. I was kind of going to miss the place (the rental house, not the creepy mansion) because that's where I'd lived since we'd moved to Verona. True, we hadn't lived in Verona very long, but I was so happy about moving here that anything connected to the move was special to me. Still, I was excited to be moving into our new place!

We pulled up in front of our home after a two-minute drive. I looked up at the old school as Mom and I got out of the car. It was going to be kind of weird living in an old school—cool, but weird. I liked the building. It had a lot of character: red brick, worn stone steps, and even an old bell in a cupola at the top. I wondered if I could find the rope that was attached to that bell—if there still was a rope. Dad had looked into the history of the old Verona School. It had been used for first through twelfth grade from 1874, when it was built, until sometime in the 1930s. A separate grade school was built then, but ninth through twelfth grade continued to use the old building until it closed in 1954. It was odd to think that the building had sat unused for nearly thirty years.

"Do you think you can get used to living in a house this big?" Mom asked.

"No problem. I am so glad to get out of that little shoebox that was called my bedroom."

My bedroom in the rental place was really small. I swear it was about eight by eight feet, although I never measured it.

"I know you're eager to get up to your room, but can you help me carry a few things into the kitchen?"

"Sure, Mom."

I grabbed the box she indicated and followed her as she walked up the steps and stopped to unlock the double doors at the front of the building. We walked into a short but wide hallway, past old, glass trophy cases (still filled with photos and trophies) and bulletin boards. On the right was a water fountain. I heard it kick on as we passed.

Just beyond the water fountain, the short hallway joined a larger one, forming a T. Straight ahead was a wooden door with frosted glass. Old-fashioned lettering on the glass spelled out "Principal."

We entered the larger hallway, which extended to the ends of the building in both directions. Just to our left was a wide staircase leading to the second floor. We turned to the right.

There were no doorways on the left side of the hallway, but on the right were doors marked "Boys", "Girls", and then "107" and "Library." All the doors had the same frosted glass that the one marked "Principal" had. We turned left at the end of the hallway. This hall had only two sets of doors: one on the left and another at the end. We entered the set on the left. This was our kitchen, the former school cafeteria.

All the tables were still there, as was the serving line. The cafeteria looked as if it was waiting for the lunch bell to ring. The only things missing were salt and pepper shakers and condiment bottles on the tables. I followed Mom into the actual kitchen. We set our burdens down on one of the long, shiny metal tables. The kitchen was rather large, but then that was to be expected. When it was in use, it was used to prepare lunch for all the students and faculty. The school was a lot smaller than VHS, but it still had eighteen rooms. That was a lot of kids!

"This place is going to take a lot of cleaning," Mom said.

"It doesn't look so bad."

"I'll be cooking in here, so the place has to be spotless."

"The realtor said everything works, right?" I asked.

Mom turned on one of the gas ranges, and blue flames jetted up instantly.

"Now that the water, gas, and electricity are on, yes."

The stoves didn't look as big as I expected. They weren't much larger than normal size. The kitchen looked quite useable to me, but then I didn't do much cooking.

I made two more trips to the car for Mom, and then I was free to haul my stuff up to my room.

All the old classrooms were much the same: large, mostly empty rooms with blackboards, bulletin boards, and wooden floors. The only exception was room 101 on the first floor. It had been left exactly as it was when the school closed. Everything—desks, the American flag standing in the corner, and even old textbooks—was still there. I guess someone thought the place might be turned into a museum someday.

I chose room 206 on the second floor. I liked that particular room because of the view. The room was located near the center of the building on the front side and looked down upon the lawn and the street below.

I set the first box of my belongings down on the wide window ledge. The windows were huge. They took up one entire wall from waist-high almost to the ceiling. There were no drapes or blinds on the windows, but the room was on the second floor, so they were unnecessary. I suppose someone could peer in at night with binoculars from the houses across the street, but if they wanted to spy on me that bad, they could just go for it. The lack of drapes was another reason I had chosen a room toward the front of the building. My windows faced the west, so I'd have a great view of the sunset. I definitely didn't want a room facing east. I wasn't nearly so fond of sunrises, especially when awakened prematurely by bright light.

I turned from the windows and surveyed my room. I almost couldn't believe I had so much space to myself. The room looked even larger because it was empty—with the exception of my bed and the box I'd carried in. Dad and a couple of his friends had brought the beds from our old home in Marmont only the day before. Everything else would have to wait a few days.

My new room had incredible potential. The wall opposite the windows was almost completely covered by blackboards. The other two walls were bare. I'd have tons of room for posters and pictures! My meager furniture was going to be swallowed up by the room. In addition to my bed, I had a desk, chair, dresser, a table that held my stereo, and a set of bookshelves. I definitely needed some kind of easy chair where I could sit and read or listen to music. I might even get a loveseat or couch. I had the room for it! I was already saving up and planned to hit yard sales and auctions when they began in the spring.

I returned to the car and grabbed another box. The disadvantage of living upstairs in such a big place soon became evident. It was quite a trip to the car and back. It was going to be a considerable hike whenever I wanted a shower, too. There was a boys' restroom about fifteen feet from my room, but I'd have to walk all the way to the boys' locker room in the gym to take a shower. Don't get the idea I'm complaining, though. Living in that old school was going to be awesome! I could rule the school!

Mom and I made a couple of trips back to the rental house to get the rest of the boxes. Soon, it was empty. I wondered when we'd get our stuff from the house in Marmont. Most of the packing was already done. Mom and Dad had been busy getting ready for the move, and I'd already been back once to pack up my stuff.

I wanted to get my room all cleaned up before my furniture and belongings arrived. I'd already tracked down a...well, it wasn't a broom; it was a floor sweeper about five-feet wide with a handle. It did a great job picking up the dust off the floor. There was quite a bit of accumulated dust, but not all that much considering the place was probably last cleaned way before I was born.

I dusted off the window and chalkboard ledges, too. I must have cleaned for an hour and a half, but when I finished, the room looked great.

I needed to make a shopping list. I grabbed a piece of chalk and began to write my list on the chalkboard. I paused for a moment. The last person to write on that chalkboard was probably a teacher writing down a homework assignment. Or, perhaps it was some poor kid called up to the front of the class to do a math problem or diagram a sentence. A weird feeling crept up my spine. Kids had come into this room every day for years and years to attend classes. Now, it was my bedroom. One thing was for sure: I bet I'd have more fun in there than any of those kids, especially when Tim was visiting!

I began my wish list by writing down "easy chair" and "loveseat." I soon added "rug" and "dorm-size refrigerator." I liked the solid-wood floor, but a big area rug would look really cool. It would cut down on the echo, too. I wasn't sure I'd like hearing myself walk across the floor all the time. A little refrigerator was going to be great—if I could find one. It was a long way down to the kitchen.

I remembered I had homework to do, so I sat on my bed and did my assignments. It was kind of funny: here I was doing homework for school in an old school. I'd be the only kid at VHS who went to school when he left school at the end of the day.

It was getting kind of late by the time I finished up, so I grabbed my toiletries bag and walked across the hall to the boys' restroom. Inside was what one would expect: toilet stalls, urinals, and sinks. What surprised me was that there were only four of each. VHS had twice as many and several bathrooms. Still, it felt kind of odd brushing my teeth in what had once been a public bathroom. It was kind of eerie in a way. I almost expected the ghost of a past student to walk in. I put that thought out of my mind fast. I did not want to spook myself on my first night in my new home.

I had some trouble getting to sleep. The lights from passing cars flashed on the walls. I kept hearing odd noises, probably pipes knocking or something like that, but I wasn't so sure. Dad told me old buildings make weird noises, so I wasn't too concerned. Still, it was a little freaky.

My alarm awakened me the next morning. I'd set it for half an hour earlier than usual because I knew it would take me longer to get ready in an unfamiliar place. The walk to school might be a bit longer, too. I didn't like getting up early, but I disliked rushing even more.

I got up, pulled on my robe, slipped on my house shoes, grabbed my towel, washcloth, shampoo, and soap and headed for the showers downstairs. I bet I was the first person ever to walk through the hallways of the old school in a robe.

My house shoes shuffled on the wide, wooden stairs. I walked past door after door with frosted-glass windows. I looked up the short entrance hallway, past the display cases, to the front doors and the street outside. At the moment, my new home felt exactly like what it was: a school. I couldn't shake the feeling that scores of kids would be arriving in an hour or so for classes.

I turned and walked down the hallway that led past the old cafeteria. I pushed through the double doors at the end of the hall and into the gym. I crossed to the middle of the floor and paused a moment to look around. The lights were off, but the morning sun came through the high windows up above the bleachers. The gym was small by modern standards. I wasn't sure, but the basketball court didn't look quite full size. Then again, it probably only looked that way because the bleachers were so much closer to the sidelines than they were at VHS.

"This is so cool," I said. "I have my own basketball court."

Sadness enveloped me as I thought of Billy Holmes. He had a passion for basketball. He'd go nuts over a place like this. I'd had a huge crush on Billy, but he'd turned against me when he found out I was gay. He'd even beaten me up. He was one of the main reasons I couldn't live in Marmont anymore.

I pushed Billy out of my mind. I had Tim now, so Billy no longer mattered. Verona was a hundred times better than

Marmont. I was not going to miss my old home—or those I'd once thought of as my friends. I had real friends now, friends who accepted me just as I was, gayness and all.

I returned my attention to the gym. The wooden bleachers, ten rows high, surrounded the basketball court on three sides. At the far end, beyond one of the basketball hoops, was a small stage. Old light-blue-and-white curtains still hung at the sides. On either side of the stage was a doorway. I headed for the one on the left.

The door was just like all the doors throughout the building: wood with frosted glass. This one read "Boys' Locker Room." I opened it and stepped inside. The locker room wasn't as big as the one at VHS, but it resembled it in that it had lockers on three walls and benches in the center. The lockers weren't like those at VHS, either. Instead of a door, each compartment held a wire basket with a number on a metal plate on the front. Some of the baskets were still locked in place. There were several of these on each side of the room.

I hung my robe and towel on one of the hooks on the wall, feeling the weird sense that I was the first person to do so in decades. I shivered a little in the chill air. I slipped off my house shoes and carried my shampoo, soap, and washcloth into the shower room. While smaller, it was almost exactly like the one at VHS. The floor and walls were tiled, with drains near the center. It was a communal shower with eight showerheads.

I turned on one of the showerheads. In just a few moments the water began to run warm. I was relieved. I'd feared the water might take a long time to warm up or perhaps wouldn't get warm at all. I stepped under the shower and let the warm water pound down upon me.

As I shampooed my hair, I thought about all the boys who had showered in that shower room. The showers back at my old school had always been a place of danger, a place where my desires might be revealed. I enjoyed stealing looks at wet, naked boys, but I always feared I'd get caught, or my own body would give me away. The showers were also a setting for my fantasies, but I'm not telling you about them! No one gets to know about those fantasies but me...and maybe Tim.

I soaped up with my washcloth and thought about the things Tim and I might get up to in the locker and shower rooms. I began to breathe a little harder. Tim was a football player. He could make some of my fantasies come true. I wondered if I could get him to bring over his uniform sometime when my parents weren't home... Okay, enough of that. You're learning far too much.

I will tell you what I did while I was in the shower room alone, wet, and soapy. I just couldn't help myself. All those thoughts of wet, naked jocks... Then again, I don't think I will tell you. You'll just have figure it out if you can.

I walked back into the locker room after I'd...showered, dried off, and slipped back into my robe. I trekked back to my room and dressed for school. I couldn't wait to get my meager furniture in my room. It was kind of awkward living out of boxes and bags. My new home was going to take quite a bit of getting used to as well. I wondered if anyone had written a book entitled *How to Live Comfortably in an Abandoned School.* Probably not; it was kind of a specialized area.

I stuffed my books into my backpack, grabbed my coat, toboggan, and scarf and walked downstairs to the cafeteria.

"There you are," Mom said as I entered. It was weird hearing her voice. I'd begun to think I was the last living person on earth.

"Pancakes?" I asked as I sniffed the air. I walked closer. Mom was indeed flipping pancakes in a skillet on one of the stoves.

"I thought I'd break in the new kitchen. I'm glad you're up. I was afraid I'd have to come after you."

"I got up early."

"Set a table. Everything is in boxes by the serving area. I haven't had a chance to unpack yet. I spent last night cleaning in here."

"I spent last night cleaning my room."

"Oh, I hope I hear that phrase a lot."

"Don't get used to it," I teased.

I set a place for each of us at the nearest table. The old cafeteria seemed so empty. The whole place was full of ghosts. I don't mean ghosts as in the spirits of dead people, but ghosts as in the lingering memory of those who were once there.

In minutes, Mom and I sat down to a breakfast of pancakes and bacon. Yum.

"So, when are we moving our stuff from Marmont?" I asked.

"As soon as your father gets everything organized. Probably later this week."

"Awesome. I can't wait to get my room set up. I love it. It's huge!"

"You seem much happier here in Verona."

"Of course I am. I have friends. I have a boyfriend. No one beats on me. What's not to like?"

"I'm glad you're happy. Just take it easy with your boyfriend. You're only sixteen."

"I promise, no one will get pregnant."

"Dane," Mom said in her warning voice.

"Well, you could lighten up a little. Two guys dating isn't the same as a guy and a girl dating."

"That's what I fear. Remember, I dated teenaged boys. It's been several years, but I remember what they're like."

"What's the danger, though, Mom? It's not as if Tim or I can get pregnant."

"There are other dangers, Dane."

"I know there are dangers. There are also precautions to take."

"I just don't feel you're old enough for sex. Give yourself a chance to be a kid, Dane. You'll have decades to be an adult. Believe me, once you become an adult, you'll want to be a kid again."

"Yeah, but Tim and I want to have fun."

"You can have fun, just don't..."

"What?" I asked mischievously. Mom was turning a bit red. To be honest, I was kind of amazed I was so casually discussing sex with my mom. We weren't talking how to do it, but we were dancing on the edge.

"Just don't try to be too adult too quickly."

"I guess I can understand how you feel, but I'm not a kid anymore."

"True, but you're also not an adult. You're going through a very difficult time in your life. You're caught in between—neither a child, nor an adult. It can be confusing, and it's easy to make mistakes."

"Well, don't worry too much. With Shawn watching us like a hawk, we don't have a chance to do anything."

"That's why you're allowed to spend time at Tim's."

"Would you be watching me this close if I was dating a girl?"

"Even closer."

"Closer? Are you kidding me? How could you watch me closer?"

Mom just gave me "the look," which was a cross between "don't go there" and an elongated "please."

"I want to get a couch for my room or maybe a loveseat," I said to change the subject.

"So, you're exciting about fixing up your room?" Mom asked.

"Of course."

"I can't wait to get going with this place myself. There is so much that can be done. I'm going to concentrate on the kitchen and bedroom first. Your dad will no doubt focus his efforts on his office. It's going to be so wonderful to have him working at home."

We finished breakfast. I bundled up, kissed Mom, tossed my backpack over my shoulder, and headed for school—my other school. Well, you know what I mean.

I thought a lot about Tim and me as I walked to school. I *really* wanted to get with him. Making out and feeling up is all well and good, but I wanted more. Giving each other head in the auditorium was intense. I wanted more of that and more than that, too.

I wasn't entirely truthful with Mom during our talk, but I also didn't outright lie. I could sort of understand her point of view. I just didn't agree with it as much as I let on. I knew there were dangers to sex, but Tim and I didn't have to worry about the biggie. I joked about it with Mom, but seriously, it was impossible for one of us to get pregnant. We were both male—natural birth control. I didn't feel I could be completely honest with Mom. For one thing, it would have been kind of disrespectful to tell her I was going to have sex with Tim no matter what she said. For another thing, if she knew I was determined to have sex, she'd watch me all the closer. Finally, I didn't want to get Mom worried. She was no doubt picturing the worst-case scenario. She probably had a book called *Nasty Sexually Transmitted Diseases Carried by Teenaged Boys* that she read every night. She was a mother, so she didn't truly understand. Guys my age had needs, powerful needs. Our bodies were built for regular sex, and when we didn't get it, we were in imminent danger of exploding!

I was thinking that with my move to a larger abode came greater opportunities for sex. I didn't even bother thinking about getting it on with Tim at the rental house if my parents were there. Even if they didn't see us, they could have easily heard us. There were plenty of places to hide in the new house, however. My parents were not stupid, though. They probably knew I was thinking exactly what I was thinking. Tim and I were going to have to be extra clever if we were going to get away with anything. I didn't even want to consider the consequences of getting caught. There was the embarrassment, of course, but even worse was the possibility that my parents would try to keep Tim and me apart. If they caught us having sex, Tim probably wouldn't be allowed to come over anymore, and I wouldn't be allowed to go to his place. I did not agree with my parents' opinions on the appropriateness of teenagers having sex, but that didn't matter. They would come down on me hard if I got caught. Getting it on in one of the abandoned classrooms wouldn't be safe enough. We had to find a better hiding place. I intended to devote a lot of thought to the possibilities.

Shawn

I browsed through the classics in the public library, but I couldn't find anything that appealed to me. My Valentine's Day "date" with Tristan had been wonderful, but he was so intelligent he frightened me. I don't mean he was a genius or anything, but he was obviously a good deal smarter than I was. I wasn't stupid, well not really stupid, just kind of, but I definitely wasn't cultured. I thought that if I read a great classic I'd have something intelligent to say. Maybe that would help get Tristan interested in me.

The trouble was that I didn't know what to read. It all looked so boring or intimidating. *War and Peace?* Are you kidding me? How could anyone read a book that long? *The Catcher in the Rye?* Wasn't rye something like corn or rice? I didn't think I wanted to read about farming. Maybe "catcher" referred to baseball, but I seriously doubted it. I didn't even bother pulling that book off the shelf. I found a book by Chekhov, but that just made me feel stupid, because at first I thought it was written by the helmsman of the Enterprise. I had no idea why that book was in the Classics section, but it was by another Chekhov. *The Song of Roland?* At least that book was short, but it was one really long poem. I didn't think I could get into poetry. I wasn't accustomed to reading unless I was forced to do so—or it was a football magazine or something like that. I ended up leaving the library without checking anything out. I felt discouraged, but I wasn't giving up. I was going to make Tristan my boyfriend.

My next stop filled me with anxiety. The drug store didn't usually frighten me, but then I was usually in there buying a candy bar or a magazine. This time was different. I actually had to force myself to go in.

Once inside, I felt as though everyone was watching me, as if they knew what I was going to buy. I walked down the aisle where they sold tampons and hemorrhoid cream. I pretended to be checking out suppositories while I covertly browsed the condoms. I'm not exactly sure why I did that. If you think about it, looking at something you stick up your butt is more embarrassing than looking at something to put on your penis.

Purchasing condoms was confusing. I didn't know there were so many kinds! There were ribbed condoms and even flavored ones. I finally decided on a box of lubricated Trojans. I'd heard of Trojan condoms, so I figured they must be pretty good.

Once I had the box in hand, I dashed over to the candy aisle. I picked up a Milky Way and a box of Lemon Heads, not so much because I wanted them, but because I didn't want it to look as if I came in just to buy condoms, which was exactly what I had done.

Thankfully, no one else was in line when I walked up to the counter. I was also thankful it was a middle-aged guy at the cash register. I don't know why, but if it had been a woman, I would've been more embarrassed. The guy didn't bat an eye at the box of condoms. I guess he sold them all the time. I think I turned a bit red, however. Boy, was I relieved when I'd made it out of there!

Okay, now before you go thinking I bought those condoms in anticipation of some future illicit activity with Tristan, let me set you straight. As much as I wanted Tristan, I knew there was no way in hell we would be getting around to doing anything that required condoms for a long time. Maybe we never would. Anyway, the condoms weren't for me at all. I wished I had a use for them, but I didn't.

I walked home from the drug store still feeling as if I was being watched. It was as if the plastic bag I carried had "CONDOMS" written on the side. My palms were still sweaty, and my heart raced as I climbed the stairs to the loft.

Tim was in his room lounging around when I entered. I was glad he was there so I could get this over with. A part of me had secretly hoped he'd be out and about, but it was better this way. I called him into the kitchen, and we sat at the table the Selbys had given me for my birthday.

"I want to talk to you about something," I said.

"It was like that when I got here!"

"Funny."

"So what do you want to talk to me about?"

"Sex."

"Okay. What do you want to know?"

"Don't ever try to become a professional comedian, Tim."

"Okay. Okay. So what is this about? I thought we already had the you-can't-have-sex-with-Dane talk."

"This is related. I'm only a year older than you, so I know what you're going through. I know all about being so horny you can't stand it. I know about walking around with a hard-on half the time. I also know what I'd do if our situations were reversed."

"Yeah? What would you do?"

"If I had a boyfriend like Dane and I wanted to have sex with him—and believe me I'd want to—I'd find a way to do it."

"I think we already talked about this, too. Have you changed your mind? Are you going to let us keep the bedroom door closed?"

"No. I explained why I can't do that. What I am saying is that I understand, and I know you'll probably do it with Dane every chance you get."

"You are pretty smart sometimes."

"So…I bought you these."

I took the box of condoms out of the bag and handed them to Tim.

"You're sending me conflicting messages here. Is it okay for us to fuck—or not?"

"Not, but I know you're most likely going to do it anyway. I wouldn't be a very good brother if I didn't do my best to keep you safe. If you guys screw, I want you to wear those."

"Which one of us?" Tim said, grinning.

"If you're trying to embarrass me, it's not going to work. Whoever is on top should wear the condom. It doesn't make much sense for the guy on the bottom to be wearing it. Or, didn't you know that?"

"Ha, ha."

"There are diseases you can get, Tim."

"Yeah, I know. Dane doesn't have any diseases, though, and I don't. Why do we really need these?"

"Because when it comes to sex, you can't be sure of anything. You don't know for sure who Dane has been with. Personally, I trust Dane to tell the truth, but you never know. It's to protect both of you. He has no way of knowing who you've been with, either."

"I haven't been with anyone except Dane."

"Okay, but Dane has been with other guys. When you have sex with someone, it's like having sex with everyone they had sex with, too."

"So we're talking incest here, huh?"

"No."

"Well, you had sex with Dane, and I've had sex with him, and you just said…"

"I mean that if Dane picked up something from someone else, he could pass it on to you."

"He wouldn't do that!"

"He might not know he's doing it. Here's an example. Let's say I have a venereal disease…"

"Gonorrhea!"

"Okay, let's say I have gonorrhea and I have unprotected sex with Dane."

"Have you had unprotected sex with Dane?"

"No. I haven't, but just remember that just because I say that doesn't mean it's true."

"So, you're lying?"

"No, but I could be. When it comes to sex, you should trust no one."

"Okay, I guess."

"So, I have gonorrhea, and I pass it along to Dane. He doesn't even know it. Maybe I don't even know I've got it. Then, you guys have unprotected sex. You end up with gonorrhea, too. It's the gift that keeps on giving."

"How could you not know you have gonorrhea?"

"If the symptoms hadn't shown yet."

"Have you ever had gonorrhea?"

"No, and I hope I never do. It's just an example."

"Okay, I think I get what you're saying."

"That's why I want you to use a condom if you fuck. Those condoms aren't permission to have sex, but I want you to use them if you do. If you need more, I'll buy them for you and won't ask any questions."

"This is still kind of a conflicting message you're sending me."

"I know, but I'm doing the best I can. Okay?"

"Yeah, okay. I'll tell you something to set your mind at ease. Dane and I have never fucked."

"I'm glad."

"But we will!"

I shook my head.

"Have you fucked?"

"That's really none of your business."

"Hey, you're getting into my business. Fair is fair. So answer the question."

"Yes, and before you ask, we used protection."

"Who did you do it with?"

"A football player from Plymouth."

"Really? Which one? Have we played against him?"

"Yes—I'm not telling you—and yes."

"Ah, come on, tell me. I won't tell anyone."

"Okay. Blake York."

"Damn! He's hot! He's gay?"

"Yeah."

"So…did you bottom or top?"

"I bottomed."

"I always knew you were a bottom!"

Tim laughed so hard I thought he'd fall off his chair.

"Hey. I don't know what I am, okay? That was the first time I'd ever done that."

"Have you topped?"

"No, so I don't know which I prefer."

"Did you guys…"

"No more questions. I think I've told you more than enough. I'm really not all that comfortable discussing my sex life with you."

"Okay. No more questions—for now." Tim grinned evilly. Damn. He was a horny little bastard.

"So, are we done, then?"

"Yes, just remember what I told you. I'm just trying to look out for you."

Tim got up walked around the table and pulled me to my feet. He hugged me.

"Thanks, Shawn."

"No problem, little brother."

I sat back down after Tim went to his room. Our conversation wasn't half as bad as I'd anticipated even though I'd told him way more about my sex life than I had planned. I just hoped he listened to my advice. Too many guys our age made the mistake of thinking bad things couldn't happen to them. Too many thought they were invulnerable, and it just wasn't true.

***

"You are so pathetic. Quit checking the time. Just relax, your dream boy will be here soon," Tim said.

"Shut up."

Tim grinned.

"Damn, you're like a lovesick girl."

"We're just friends."

"Yeah, but you want to be more. Even if I didn't already know, it's so obvious."

"It is?"

"If you could only see the way you gaze at him. You get this dreamy, longing look in your eyes. You practically drool, too."

"I do not."

"Yes, you do, and that's not all! I've seen positive proof that you want him bad."

"What proof?"

Tim didn't say a word, but glanced meaningfully at my crotch. I fought to maintain control when Tristan was near, but my body didn't always cooperate.

"When did you notice that?"

"Hmm, let's see—when you got up to leave The Park's Edge on Valentine's Day, at your birthday party when you were talking to Tristan, at school when you were flirting with him by his locker... I could go on."

"What do you do, go around staring at my crotch all the time?"

"Don't try to change the subject. Just admit it. You've got it bad for Tristan."

"Yes. I do. Damn, do you think anyone else noticed?"

"That you're infatuated with your dream boy? Everyone in our little circle of friends knows it."

"No, I mean..."

Tim laughed. "Relax, it's not that big of a deal. You're seventeen. It's expected in guys our age. Hell, I pop one just *thinking* about Dane. Ha! And you were giving me advice about sex!"

"It's just embarrassing."

"You are such a fag."

"Shut up."

Tim grinned.

"You're evil. You know that, don't you?" I asked.

"Of course. I take after you."

There was a knock at the door. I pointed my finger at Tim.

"Behave yourself or else."

Tim gave me an innocent 'who me?' look. I scowled at him and answered the door.

"Hey, come in," I said.

I feared Tim would embarrass me, but apart from giving me some mischievous looks, he didn't do anything I'd want to pound him for later. He took Tristan's coat and draped it over the back of a chair.

"So what do you think?" I asked.

Tristan looked around the room.

"You definitely need some color. White walls, white table and chairs, white appliances in the kitchen, and a beige sofa and chair."

"Yeah, it is kind of bland, isn't it?" I asked.

"White is a great background color. You'll be surprised at how much we'll be able to do with only a few additions."

"That's good. I've scraped up $30 I can spend."

"We'll see what we can get at the resale shop today, and then we'll go from there."

Tristan continued to assess the decorating potential of our loft.

"That antique counter nicely divides the kitchen from the living area. That will allow us to use a couple of different color schemes. How about yellow for the kitchen? I'm thinking a pale yellow. It's a sunny, cheerful color, and if we go with pale yellow, it won't be too great of a contrast with all that white."

"Works for me," I said. "I know nothing about decorating."

"I'm thinking something stronger for the living room. We'll see what we can find. Anything will go with white, so it's a matter of what's available and what you like."

"Sounds good. You ready?"

"Sure. I'm eager to get started. I can't wait to see what we can do with this place."

Tristan grinned, and my heart melted.

"Want to come with us, Tim?" I asked. I didn't want him tagging along, but this was his home, too. He might want to be a part of things.

"No. This is obviously some kind of homo-bonding moment. Three's a crowd."

Tim meaningfully gazed at my crotch when Tristan wasn't looking. I gave him a warning glance, which he answered with a mischievous smirk.

Tristan and I bundled up and walked down to my car. We could have easily walked to the resale shop, but I hoped we'd find enough stuff that we wouldn't want to lug it back on foot. After a two-minute drive, we got out and entered the resale shop. I went there often to look for clothes. I couldn't even remember the last time I'd paid retail. Maybe part of that was some kind of homo-shopping gene, but mostly I just couldn't afford new clothes.

The resale shop was located in a regular home that was given completely over to the shop. Most of the clothing was upstairs, but the downstairs was filled with all sorts of other stuff. Tristan and I browsed around the 'living room' of the shop.

"Hey, what about this rug?" Tristan asked. "It will add a lot of color."

Tristan held up a large braided rug that was dark red and cream. It was about six feet long and four wide.

"That would look nice on the living-room floor."

"Yes. It's $5, too. What do you think?"

"I think let's get it."

"Red," Tristan said. "Hmm."

He walked back toward a closet that held linens and began searching through the stacks of cloth.

"Here we go!" he said, pulling out a red-and-green-plaid tablecloth. "What about this? It's just $2, and it will match the rug. This will add a lot of color."

"I want it," I said.

Tristan handed it to me. He walked back into the kitchen area. Thanks to my birthday presents, Tim and I had enough dishes, glasses, pots, pans, and silverware. I browsed around with Tristan. I spotted a large, attractive vase and picked it up.

"Could we do something with this?" I asked. "It's pale yellow. You said that color would be good for the kitchen."

"Wow, nice! How much is that?"

"Um, $3."

"Don't put it down! That's an art deco vase made in the 1920s. Not only is it perfect for your kitchen, it's worth several times $3."

"Yes! I have good taste!" I said.

Tristan grinned and pushed the hair back from his face. Oh, how I wanted to kiss him!

"Hey, here's a coffee maker," Tristan said. "Do you guys drink coffee?"

"I'm not much into it, but Tim is a coffee fiend. He's been forced to drink instant, and it's about to drive him insane."

"It's just $2."

"We definitely need that, then. Tim has been bugging me to get one, and new ones are expensive. He already went out and bought coffee and filters with his own money just so he'd be ready when we got a machine."

"He *is* a coffee fiend, then."

We wandered around the resale shop some more. Tristan spotted a brass floor lamp for $4. I found a blue-and-white rag rug for $3. It wasn't yellow, but Tristan thought it would look good on the kitchen floor. We looked around more but couldn't find anything else of interest. Our purchases cost a total of $19, so I was well within my budget. We loaded the stuff in the car and drove back to the loft.

Once everything was hauled up to the apartment, Tristan and I set about decorating. Tim was out. He left a note saying he was going to the library. More likely he was meeting Dane somewhere the two of them could make out.

The braided rug looked great on the living-room floor. I set the brass floor lamp between the couch and chair while Tristan draped the red-and-green tablecloth over the kitchen table. I plugged in the coffee maker and then put the rag rug on the kitchen floor. Tristan looked around the kitchen a bit and then placed the vase on the counter that divided the kitchen from the living area.

"There," Tristan said. "What do you think?"

I focused on the kitchen first. We only added a rug and a vase, but it really brightened the place up. I walked into the living room. The large rug and the tablecloth really made a difference.

"I would never have believed that so few things could make such a big change. Now the painting you gave me for my birthday has company. This place looks great. You should be a professional decorator."

Tristan smiled.

"I think you're overestimating my abilities."

"No, I'm not. You've got a great eye for color. Who knows what I would have picked out?"

"Hey, you picked out the vase. That was the best find of the day."

"I only picked it because it was yellow and you said yellow would look good in the kitchen."

"I don't know a lot about collectibles, but that vase is worth at least $50," Tristan said.

"Really?"

"Yeah."

"Wow, now I like it more." I laughed. "Hey, would you like some coffee? Or, I have tea."

"Tea, please."

"I don't have a tea kettle yet, but a pan works. I'll put some water on to boil."

I set about doing just that. I also got out a couple of mugs, tea bags, and the sugar bowl.

"You'd better write tea kettle down on your shopping list."

"Yeah. I have a feeling that list is going to just keep getting longer. I was so happy with all the things for the loft I received on my birthday. Who would have thought I'd ever get excited over dishes and pots and pans? You don't really think about things like spoons and glasses until you don't have them. It was kind of funny in a way. We had a dishwasher, but almost no dishes."

"I'll probably experience that when I get out on my own," Tristan said. "That won't be until college for me."

"Yeah. You have no reason to leave home. Your mom seems really nice."

"She is. She needs me, too. Losing Dad was hard on her. It was hard on me, but I lost a father where she lost her soul mate."

"I don't think I can even imagine losing a soul mate," I said. I carried the sugar bowl and a couple of spoons over to the table and set them down.

"I hope she will be okay when I leave for college," Tristan said. "By then, she'll have more friends, and hopefully time will have dulled the pain some. It was really rough at first. Mom couldn't handle it. It's odd, but in a way her inability to cope helped me. I had to be strong because Mom needed me so badly. I focused so much on her pain that I largely forgot my own. Suddenly, I was the one she depended on. It was as though I became the parent overnight. The worst was over after a couple of weeks, and things became more normal, but she still needed me. She still does."

I poured hot water over the tea bags in the mugs and carried them to the table. Tristan and I sat down.

"It's just plain tea I'm afraid. I don't have anything fancy."

"Plain tea is great."

"I guess you kind of understand what I'm going through with Tim," I said. "The circumstances are different, but I more or less became his parent overnight."

"You have too much responsibility," Tristan said as he stirred sugar into his tea.

"I do have a lot on my shoulders, but things are much better now than when we were home. I like working and earning my own money. I love living here. I feel safe here, and I know Tim is safe. That's worth more than I can say. There are drawbacks. I don't have much time for fun. I'm not even sure I'll be able to play football this fall. I was really looking forward to football. I thought I might even have a chance at quarterback. Now...it probably isn't going to happen."

"Football is important to you, isn't it?" Tristan asked.

"Yes. Maybe it's silly to love a game that much, but I do."

"It's not silly. If you love something, that makes it worthwhile."

"I do love it. It's just...it's hard to explain. I love getting out there and plowing though the linebackers. I love racing down the field with the ball, running flat out, feinting and dodging my way toward the goal. It's a battle. I work out all my frustration and aggression on the field. There's more to it than even that, but I don't know how to put it into words."

"Then it is truly important to you. The most important thoughts and feelings can't be put into words. No words exist to express them. Poetry can sometimes come close to expressing those feelings, but even at its best, poetry is merely a poor imitation of the real thing."

"I...I think I know what you mean."

"Language is very limited when you think about it. I think that's why music is so valued all over the world. Like poetry, music can sometimes touch upon those thoughts and feelings that words can't express."

We sat there in silence for a while. I enjoyed just being near Tristan. He looked so much like his cousin that it was scary. I'd never had a chance with Taylor, but with Tristan...maybe.

"This tea is good."

"Thanks."

I paused. My heart was racing. I felt so awkward just then. There was so much I wanted to say but so much I feared to say.

"I wish I had more time to spend with you," I said at last. My words didn't express what was in my heart, but it was as close as I dared come.

I reached across the table and ran my hand over Tristan's. He paused before pulling his hand away, but I knew I'd crossed a line I should not have. The only reason he didn't jerk his hand away was out of politeness. I could tell he made a conscious effort to pause for a few moments before he reached for a spoonful of sugar he didn't really want. I didn't quite understand. I had grasped his hand once before. It was when I'd first shown him my loft, but I remembered that moment as though it was yesterday. He had smiled at me then. Was he just being kind that time? Had he decided twice was too much?

I pulled my hand back, and we both pretended nothing had happened. I felt faintly humiliated, but Tristan was so kind that the feeling quickly passed. We talked about school. We talked about the way Brandon and Jon went at each other. It was so wonderful just to have someone to sit and talk with. I had my brother, of course, but our relationship had changed. I was more parent now than brother, and that put a distance between us that had not been there before.

"I should get home," Tristan said later on. "I have homework to finish up, and you probably do, too."

"Yeah. I've really enjoyed our time together," I said.

"Sometime we can hit the Goodwill and the resale shop in Plymouth."

"I'd like that, and if you just want to come by to...talk or whatever, that would be good, too."

Tristan smiled at me and put his hand on my shoulder. That's when I did something really stupid. I leaned in and tried to kiss him. He pulled back as if I'd tried to strike him.

"Shawn, no."

Tristan picked up his coat and put it on.

"I'm…I'm sorry."

"I'll see you at school tomorrow," Tristan said, and then he was gone.

Tristan didn't seem angry, but when I apologized, he didn't say it was okay. He clearly didn't like what I'd done. He just as clearly didn't want to kiss me. Why wasn't he as interested in me as I was him? I felt depression setting in.

I sat back down at the kitchen table, staring at the mug Tristan had so recently held in his hands. I felt his absence like a ghost.

When Tim came home a few minutes later, I was sitting at the kitchen table, banging my head on the tabletop.

"Bad evening?" Tim asked.

"I'm so stupid," I said. "Stupid. Stupid. Stupid."

"You're going to have to be more specific, Shawn."

I gave Tim a 'screw you' look.

"I tried to kiss Tristan."

"And?"

"You have to ask? He pulled away."

"Bad breath? Sorry," Tim said, catching on at last to how rotten I felt.

"I don't think he's interested in me at all—not like I want him to be," I said.

"I'm sorry."

"He knows how I feel about him. I told him soon after we first met. He gave me this let's-be-friends-and-see-where-it-goes line. I wonder now if he was just too nice to say he wasn't interested."

"I hate to say this, but he does seem nice enough to do something like that."

"Exactly. That same day, I asked him about holding his hand and kissing him. He said it was okay to try—that if he didn't feel it, he'd pull away. I tried both today, and he pulled away."

"Why don't you look for someone else, Shawn? I know you really like Tristan, but there are other guys out there. You're good looking—you've got a hot body—there's got to be someone out there for you."

"Maybe, but Tristan is the one I want."

"I hate to say this, but you don't always get what you want."

"I know."

"Listen, Tristan obviously doesn't want to be anything more than friends now. Right?"

"It certainly looks that way."

"If you push too hard, you're going to push him away. I know this is easy for me to say, but why don't you just forget about a romantic relationship with Tristan—at least, for a while. Just be friends. Find yourself a boyfriend and just be friends with Tristan. You can't have what you want, so make the best of the situation. You like hanging out with him, don't you?"

"Sure."

"So, take my advice. You may find a guy you like just as well or better. If you have a boyfriend, you won't be pressuring Tristan. You can relax and have fun with him, and that is the best way to get what you want from him. If you play it cool, maybe he'll begin to feel the same way about you that you feel about him. If you get a boyfriend, he might even get jealous."

"Great. My little brother is giving me dating advice."

"I'm not that much younger than you, you know. I'm not a kid. I don't mean to rub it in—much—but I have a boyfriend. You've never had one. Besides, any idiot can see that putting the moves on Tristan isn't working. Continuing to put the moves on him would just be stupid."

"I feel like an idiot."

"You're not an idiot, Shawn. Right now, you're just down and upset. You've been rejected by someone you really care about, and it hurts. You're smart enough to learn from your mistakes. It's time to try something new."

"I hate it when you're right—especially this time."

Tim reached out, took my hand, and pulled me to my feet. He hugged me close.

"You'll find a great boyfriend, Shawn. I know you will. Maybe you'll even end up with Tristan, but even if you don't, you'll find someone who will make you very happy."

I hugged Tim back tightly, then let him go.

"Thanks."

Dane

Mom picked Tim and me up after school. We tossed our backpacks in the front seat, and then we both climbed in the back. Mom pulled away from VHS and headed for Marmont. Moving day at last!

"Your dad called," Mom said. "The movers have already loaded up everything from his office. They will be emptying out the house by the time we arrive."

"I'm glad I already put my name on my boxes," I said.

"How much packing do you have to finish?" Mom asked.

"Not much. With Tim's help, I can finish up in about half an hour."

"Good, then you boys can help carry things to the truck."

I groaned, but my heart wasn't in it. I was too excited.

Tim and I couldn't make out in the backseat. Mom checked her rearview mirror a little too often for us to get away with that. We did manage to hold hands. Every once in a while, Tim teased me by running his hand up and down my leg. It got me excited, if you know what I mean. I needed some alone time with Tim as soon as possible!

The drive to Marmont went by in a flash because I had Tim to keep me company. Before I knew it, Mom pulled into our old driveway.

"So this is where you lived?" Tim asked.

"Yeah."

I had forgotten Tim had never been to Marmont. Even his brother had only visited me once.

There was a large moving van parked near the front door. Movers were carrying furniture from the house. Mom, Tim, and I entered through the back door. Mom went in search of Dad, and I led Tim to my room.

I closed the door and pressed Tim against it the moment we were inside. I pressed my lips against his and shot my tongue into his mouth. I rubbed up against him as we made out.

We had only gone at it about five minutes before Mom knocked on the door. I opened it, trying to look innocent.

"Dane, when you've finished packing and marking the last of your boxes, carry them into the living room; the movers will load them from there. And keep your door open."

Mom left us alone.

"I guess we should get to work," I said. Tim grinned at me.

"Why don't I carry the boxes to the living room that are ready while you finish packing?" Tim asked.

"I knew having a hunk for a boyfriend would come in handy."

There was very little left to pack. Almost everything was already boxed up. I was amazed at how much stuff I had. It didn't seem possible that it took so many boxes to hold my things. In less than ten minutes, I was helping Tim carry boxes into the living room. Before another ten minutes had passed, my room was completely empty. I walked back into my old room for a moment. When I left this time, I wasn't coming back.

"It makes you kind of sad, doesn't it?" Tim asked.

"Yes."

"I felt that way when I left home, too. I was glad to get out, but it was still hard leaving the place I'd lived in for so many years. All these memories I thought I'd forgotten came back to me when I realized I was leaving."

"Yeah. I'm going to miss this place—my room and the house, that is. I'm not going to miss Marmont, especially my old school."

"Dane, someone is here to see you," Mom called from some distant location.

Tim looked at me. I shrugged my shoulders. We walked out into the hall and toward the living room.

"Simon," I said.

"Hey, Dane. Your dad said you were packing up today. I came to say goodbye."

I smiled. Simon was one of a handful of people from my old school that I actually missed. I turned to Tim.

"Tim, this is Simon, one of my friends. Simon, this is Tim, my boyfriend."

Simon's eyes widened, but he shook hands with Tim.

"Just for the record, he's much hotter than Billy," Simon said.

"I know," I said smugly.

I turned to Tim.

"Simon is one of the few cool guys at Marmont High School," I explained.

"I'm not exactly cool," Simon said.

"Sure you are, and you were there for me when it counted."

"I should have been there for you all along, especially after the way you helped me out." Simon looked at Tim. "Dane noticed I was having trouble with weight training in gym, so we started working out together."

"It looks as if you're still keeping it up," I said. "You're looking good."

"Well, I'm looking better. I don't know about good, but thanks!"

"How are things at school?"

"Homophobic. I keep a low profile so I'll survive. I cannot wait to get out of there! You are so lucky you escaped."

"Well, the price I paid was kind of high, but it was worth it. I love Verona. There are several out boys there, and two or three of them are the hottest hunks in school. Well, just look at Tim."

Tim actually blushed. It was so cute.

"I am not one of the hottest hunks in school," Tim said.

"Yes, you are. You just don't realize it," I said.

"You look hot to me. If you weren't Dane's boyfriend…"

My eyes widened. I'd always wondered, but Simon had never even hinted before that he was gay.

"Hands off, Simon. He's mine!"

Simon grinned.

"I promise. I'll just look. I won't touch!"

"Dane, can you boys give me a hand?" Mom called.

"Yeah, Mom."

"Need some help?" Simon asked.

"Sure."

The movers were emptying the place out fast. Tim, Simon, and I helped carry boxes from the kitchen and other rooms as directed by Mom. We piled everything in the living room, where the movers loaded the boxes onto two-wheeled carts and carted them away. In less than two hours the place was empty. The moving van pulled out, and Dad followed it in his car. Tim, Simon, and I stood in the living room and talked while Mom closed up our old home.

I was kind of sad when I walked out the front door for the very last time. I was more excited than sad, however. I couldn't wait to get to Verona and begin unpacking my stuff. I hugged Simon goodbye. Tim hugged him, too. I almost laughed because Simon rolled his eyes with pleasure as Tim squeezed him. I had one sexy boyfriend.

"You have my new address," I said to Simon just before climbing in the car. "Write me sometime. I promise to write back. You should come and visit sometime, too."

"I will! Bye, Dane!"

"Bye!"

Simon stood in the driveway and waved as we drove away from my old home. I hoped things worked out as well for him as they had for me.

Marmont was behind me, Verona ahead. Moving the last of my possessions marked the end of one chapter in my life and the beginning of another. Verona was my home now. It was where I was meant to be.

Mom had stashed some of her most valuable and breakable objects in the car. The trunk, the passenger seat, and part of the back seat were occupied with boxes of carefully packed treasures. Tim and I didn't mind the crowded confines of the back seat one bit. If Mom had realized how we were going to be squeezed together, I think she would have trusted the movers with a few more boxes.

Tim took my hand even before we were out of the driveway. Before we hit the highway my hand began to roam. I don't think I have to tell you my hand's destination. I almost laughed at Tim's efforts to keep a neutral expression on his face. I soon faced the same fight myself, but it was worth it. There was something especially exciting about doing something forbidden right under my mother's nose. The fact that there was no way she could see what we were getting up to made no difference.

I wanted to kiss Tim, but that Mom could see. I contented myself with driving my boyfriend crazy. We stopped before we reached the point of no return. I was so worked up I was ready to breathe fire. Perhaps I hadn't thought my actions out very well, but it was worth the torment.

We were just a few minutes behind the moving van, but the movers were already carrying boxes into the new house when we arrived. I offered to help Mom carry in the boxes from the car, but she declined. I guess she didn't quite trust me with her most precious possessions. It was probably just as well. I could just picture myself tripping and dropping a box of costly breakables. Besides, I was eager to get at my own stuff.

Dad was guiding the movers, so the right boxes and pieces of furniture would make it to the right rooms. Tim and I each grabbed a box marked "Dane" and carried them up to my room on the second floor.

"You must have the biggest house in town," Tim said.

"Yeah, unless someone moves into the old Graymoor Mansion."

"Yeah, right! Like that's ever going to happen! That place has been up for sale my entire life, but no one is brave enough to even look at it, let alone buy it. Someone would have to be out of their freaking mind to buy that haunted house."

"Maybe the Addams family will move to Verona."

"They are the only people who would live there. Well, perhaps the Munsters. Have you seen that old show?"

"Oh, yeah."

"I'd take your house any day. I can't believe you have your own gym!"

"We should have some of the guys over to play basketball."

"That would be awesome."

Tim and I deposited the boxes in my room and returned to the truck for more.

"You should go out for football this fall," Tim said.

"I'm not much of an athlete. I like playing with friends, but I'm not much into playing for a team. Besides, I've heard about football practices. They sound grueling."

"They are, but it's a lot of fun, too. There is the added advantage of all those hot guys in the showers."

"Hmm, maybe I can be the towel boy."

Tim laughed.

"I'm gonna miss Brendan this fall. Have you ever seen him naked?" Tim asked.

"Unfortunately, no."

"Damn, he's hot! It was worth being on the team just to check him out in the locker room and showers. His pecs drove me insane, and that ass!"

"I hope you were careful."

"He wouldn't mind."

"I was thinking more of the other guys."

"Oh, I'm always extremely careful. I was terrified of going into the showers right after I figured out I was gay. I was afraid I'd get caught looking at some guy the wrong way and they'd all beat the crap out of me. I was scared to death I'd pop a boner."

"Did that ever happen?"

"No. Looking at the other boys just about drove me out of my mind, but I was also so scared I was never in danger of getting aroused."

"Not quite like all those 'in the shower' porno stories, huh?"

"No. I'm out now—at least, I think word has gotten around to everyone by now—so I don't have to worry about anyone finding me out. They already know I'm gay. That creates a whole new problem. I don't want to make any of the guys uncomfortable, you know? That wouldn't be cool."

"What about Brendan? He was out all last season, right? How did the guys react to him?"

"Some of them were a little edgy at first, but he was so damned confident and 'normal' acting I think the guys just kind of forgot he was gay. Everyone knew he was dating Casper, too, so I think that made them relax. It's not as if he was looking to get some."

"He could still have been looking."

"Not Brendan. He's a one-man kind of guy. Maybe that set the guys at ease. Of course, Brendan is like a god. All the guys, including me, are in awe of what he can do on the football field. As far as looks are concerned, well, you can't get much hotter than that. I think the guys were too busy admiring Brendan and wanting to be him to be afraid he was checking them out in the showers."

"Then you should be okay, too."

"I am nowhere near as athletic or good-looking as Brendan."

"You come close."

"Liar," Tim said, grinning. "I'll just have to be careful. I don't think the guys will be freaked out. I mean, they're used to Brendan, and I've been showering with a lot of those guys for years.

I haven't groped any of them before, so why would I start now? I never grope without permission."

I grinned.

"You have my permission to grope me all you want."

"Mmm."

All that talk of football players in the showers got us worked up. That particular task wasn't difficult after the grope session in the car. When Tim and I returned to my room once more, we set our boxes down, pulled each other close, and made out like we were starved for each other. I wanted to rip off all his clothes and ravish him, but that had to wait for who knew how long? We kept going at it until we were interrupted by one of the movers carrying a box of my stuff into the room. We had been caught. The mover, a fairly handsome blond guy in his mid-thirties, didn't say a word, but he winked at us as he left.

"We'd better get back to work. There is no telling who else might walk in," I said.

The moving van was huge, but the old school swallowed up our stuff. Most of the boxes and furniture went to just a few rooms: the kitchen, Dad's office, the living room, and the two bedrooms. I had a feeling most of the rooms would forever sit empty.

It was late by the time the last box was carried in. I was too tired to think about unpacking anything. Mom offered to drive Tim home, but I walked him home instead.

"We've got to have some time alone soon," I said. "I swear I'll explode if we don't."

"I wish we could right now," Tim said.

"If it was warmer, we could just go to the woods."

"I'm about ready to go, anyway."

"I know the feeling."

Mom expected me back soon, so Tim and I hugged and kissed at his door. I walked back home, yearning to be with Tim, angry with the ignorant world. What was the big deal about teenagers having sex? Why did everyone freak out about it? No one had a problem with it in past centuries. It just figured I'd live in the Age of Prudes.

***

"Where are we going?" Tim asked.

"Where do you think?" I grinned.

It was our lunch period. Tim and I had rushed through lunch so we'd have a few spare moments before the bell rang. I checked to make sure no one was looking and then quickly pulled him through the rear entrance of the auditorium.

We stepped into the backstage area. I pulled Tim into the darkness behind one of the huge curtains and pressed my lips to his. We held each other tight as we made out.

We French-kissed for a good five minutes. Our hands wandered and groped as we made out. I couldn't wait any more. I dropped to my knees and acted on my pent-up desires. Tim's heavy breathing, moans, and whimpers urged me on. Tim moaned louder than ever and finished just as the bell rang.

We slipped back into the hallway with no one the wiser. Tim grinned at me. I was drunk with the headiness of illicit sex. I'd blown Tim right there in the school—again. We probably weren't the first to have sex in the school, but the forbidden nature of our encounter made it all the hotter.

Shawn spotted us grinning from ear to ear just a couple of minutes later.

"Why are you two so happy?" Shawn asked suspiciously.

"It's just a great day!" Tim said. "I feel so mellow and relaxed."

Both of us started laughing. Shawn looked at us as if we were freaks.

"Maybe we should have just told him the truth to see how he would react," I said when Shawn had passed out of earshot.

"Um, no. He's edgy enough about what we do as it is. What Shawn doesn't know won't hurt us. Time to get to class."

Tim leaned in and gave me a quick kiss on the lips. Devon was the only one who saw us. He sneered at us and muttered 'faggots' as he went on his way.

"Isn't he charming?" Tim asked.

"He's probably just bitter because he isn't getting any."

"What girl would want him? I mean, he's kind of hot, but he's such a jerk."

"He's probably a closet case. He obviously has emotional issues. No normal person is that homophobic," I said.

"Just watch out when he's around. Don't let him get you alone, especially if his buddies are around. It's been a while since there's been any trouble, but Devon is bad news," Tim said.

"I'll be careful, but I can take care of myself. I was once bad news, too. I'll see you after school, okay?"

"Definitely."

As Tim walked away, I wondered why no other couples had thought of meeting in the auditorium. It was always deserted during our lunch period and probably during all of them. There were plenty of places to hide even if someone came in. I kept my mouth shut about our secret rendezvous spot. All we needed was for football players to start taking girls in there. Someone would get caught, and that would ruin everything.

Those other visits to the auditorium were in the future, however. I sighed, wishing there had been time for Tim to blow me, too. I think I like giving more than receiving, but still, a guy has needs, you know. My time with Tim had satisfied his needs for the moment, but they had intensified mine.

I used the rest of the school day as a tranquilizer for my libido. I'm not saying school is boring, but most subjects don't inspire thoughts of sex. Of course, one look at Tim at the end of the day was all it took to get my mind back on his sexy body.

Shawn was working. I was sorely tempted to ask if Tim wanted to go back to his place. To be honest, I would have asked, but I was expected home thirty minutes or less after school let out. Mom didn't used to be like that. I was tired of being on such a short leash. I knew my parents were keeping such a close eye on me because of Tim. They knew how willing teenage boys are, so they assumed we'd get it on every chance we got. What's more, they were right! It really didn't seem fair, however.

I wasn't ready to push the issue with Mom and Dad yet. They were being unfair, but hell, they'd done so much for me. They picked up and moved to Verona—for me. I didn't even want to think of the inconvenience and expense of that. My parents probably thought I didn't appreciate all the other things they did for me, but they were wrong. When I ran away last summer, I learned the value of a lot of what they did for me. I learned fast! When I returned, home seemed a much better place to be. So yeah, my parents were being unfair, but how could I complain? I knew they were just trying to do what was best for me. I also couldn't argue too hard for my right to have sex, because I didn't want my parents to know how intent Tim and I were on having sex. That sure wouldn't encourage them to give me more freedom. If they found out the truth, they might panic and lock me in my room forever!

After school, Tim and I wanted to go to Ofarim's but figured we didn't have enough time. I came up with the brilliant idea of calling home from Ofarim's and getting permission. I even put Shawn on the phone for a sec to prove we were there and that he was watching over us. The result was I got more time with Tim and polished my wholesome image. Sometimes, you have to suck up to get what you want in the end—um, no pun intended.

Playing the part of a good boy came with a special reward that afternoon. Tim and I had a front row seat for a bit of furtive Verona drama. As Tim and I sat in a booth sharing a huge hot-fudge sundae, a hunky boy with black hair and blue eyes entered. It wasn't the sight of such a hottie that was significant, however; it was what Tim told me about him.

"That's Blake York," he whispered as soon as the stud entered. "He plays football for Plymouth."

"I want him," I said quietly and smiled.

"He's gay," Tim said.

"How do you know?"

"Because Shawn has had sex with him."

"*Seriously?*"

"Yes. He told me."

"Damn!"

"Keep it down."

"Okay, okay," I said.

Tim and I spied on Blake as clandestinely as we could manage. He was leaning on the counter, talking to Shawn. We were too far away to hear what they were saying and didn't dare move closer to eavesdrop. Shawn kept looking toward our booth from time to time to see if we were paying any attention.

"I bet they're up to something," Tim said.

"Maybe, but doesn't Shawn have a huge crush on Tristan?"

"Yes, but Tristan only wants to be friends right now. That means Shawn isn't getting any."

"Yeah, but he *really* likes Tristan, doesn't he? It seems almost like an obsession to me."

"Well, I don't think it's Tristan *per se*," Tim said.

"What do you mean?"

"You can't tell anyone this, okay?"

"Of course, I won't."

"Well, after Shawn and I came out to each other, he admitted he had been head over heels in love and lust with Taylor Potter."

"The boy who killed himself, right?"

"Yes. He was Tristan's cousin, and they looked so much alike that Tristan was called Taylor's dark twin."

"Okay. So what are you getting at?"

"I believe the real reason Shawn is so hot for Tristan is because he reminds him of Taylor. Think about it. Taylor is gone. Tristan is Taylor's cousin *and* looks almost exactly like him."

"Shawn can't have Tristan," I said, "and now here's Blake."

"Exactly."

I stole a look at Shawn and Blake and imagined them together. It was a mistake. I had to force my thoughts in another direction to keep from driving myself out of my mind with lust.

We continued to sneak looks at Shawn and Blake. Shawn was playing it cool, no doubt because he either knew or feared we were watching. I wondered how he would have acted if we hadn't been in Ofarim's.

"Shawn and Blake look like conspirators, and since I doubt they're planning to knock over a bank later, I bet they're going to hook up after Shawn gets off work," Tim said.

"I'd give just about anything to lurk outside at closing time and see what happens," I said.

"You like to watch, huh?" Tim teased.

"I'd just like to know if Shawn is going to get it on with Blake."

"Please," Tim said. "Just look at them. It's so obvious they're going to hook up. Why wouldn't they?"

"You think Shawn will bring Blake back to your place?"

"After forbidding me to have sex with you there? No way! That would make him a hypocrite. I'd go fucking ballistic, too, and Shawn knows it."

"Maybe he'll try to send you off to the movies or something."

"If he does, I'm not budging. Hmm, maybe we can work this to our advantage."

"How?"

"Shawn has got to need it bad, and here's Blake. My guess is that big bro is gonna be pretty desperate to get some. Maybe I can cut a deal with him: I ignore what goes on in his bedroom if he ignores what goes on in mine."

"You really think he'd go for that?"

"When he's thinking clearly, not a chance. When he's under the influence of extreme sexual need, perhaps."

"You'd take advantage of a poor, sex-starved boy?"

"To be alone with you in my bedroom—any day."

"You're devious. That's one of the many things I like about you."

I looked at the clock.

"I'd better go. I don't want to spoil my obedient-son image."

"You're kind of devious, too," Tim said.

"You going to stay and spy on Shawn?"

"No. I think I've seen everything there is to see here. Besides, I want to walk you home."

Tim took my hand across the table. I smiled. Having a boyfriend was the best!

Shawn

The bell jingled. I looked up from the counter to see who was entering Ofarim's. My breath caught in my chest. It was Tristan, accompanied by his mother. My dream boy took a seat in a booth. He was facing me. I grabbed a couple of menus and walked toward the table.

"Hey, Shawn."

"Hey, Tristan. Hi, Mrs. Cole."

"Hello, Shawn," Tristan's mom said.

I'd met Tristan's mom on one of my visits. She was very kind to me. I could see where Tristan got his politeness—and his beauty. Mrs. Cole was a real looker. If I wasn't gay, I'd want her.

"We won't need menus," Tristan said. "We just came in for ice cream. I want a caramel sundae."

"I'd like a chocolate-fudge sundae."

"Coming right up," I said.

Damn, he's sexy! I thought as I walked away from their booth. I didn't know exactly what it was about Tristan, but the very sight of him set me on fire with both love and lust. One fueled the other, so that every time I saw him I wanted to either rip his clothes off, tell him I was madly in love with him, or both. How could one person be so powerfully attracted to another? Tristan was attractive, beautiful in fact, but there were plenty of hot boys around. He was charming, sweet, and kind, but didn't I know other boys with those qualities? What was it that made him so irresistible to me?

Perhaps it didn't matter. Feelings didn't have to make sense. Tristan wasn't interested in me as anything more than a friend, anyway. If only I could take all the love I felt for Tristan and the desire he inspired and lock it away in a box somewhere until it was safe to let it out.

Anger welled up in my chest as I prepared sundaes for Tristan and his mom. Why was I made to love him so, when he didn't love me back? I wasn't angry with Tristan. He couldn't help but feel as he did anymore than I could. I was angry with God or the universe or whatever. It shouldn't be possible for one person to love another with such intensity unless those feelings were reciprocated. Why was the world such a cruel place?

Why couldn't I find a boyfriend? God knows I'd tried. My best friend, Casey, had even provided me with a list of some of the gay boys in the nearby town of Plymouth. I went out with each of them, and what disastrous dates they'd turned out to be. Not one of the boys was boyfriend material. There was Cameron (the Flamer) Camden, Blake (I Just Want to Fuck You) York, Riley (Jail Bait) DeCoteau, Preston (Personality-free) Presley, and finally Webb (I'm Shopping Around for a Better Boyfriend) Castleton. Not one of them could compare with Tristan.

I finished the sundaes and took them out to Tristan and his mom. I returned to the counter and busied myself with cleaning while they talked and laughed. Oh, how I wanted to be sitting across from Tristan talking and laughing like that! I was glad he was with his mom and not another boy. No matter how innocent the relationship, I would've been driven out of my mind with jealousy if Tristan was with another guy. Why did being in love have to be so painful? Why did it have to drive me crazy!

Tristan and his mom were gone within twenty minutes, but the memory of Tristan remained. I would practically have sold my soul just to kiss his soft, pink lips. I daydreamed about pressing my lips to his and kissing him as our tongues entwined.

The bell rang again. My little brother entered with Dane. I could have been jealous that Tim had a boyfriend while I didn't, but instead I was happy for him. I was there when Tim and Dane met. It was lust, if not love, at first sight. Tim deserved to be happy. He'd lived through some hard times. So had Dane, for that matter.

I waited on my brother and his boyfriend and then turned my attention to my work behind the counter. Try as I might, I could not get Tristan out of my head. I wondered what he looked like naked. I undressed him in my mind, revealing his smooth, soft skin and slim, firm torso. I yearned to pull his shirt over his head and run my hands all over his sexy chest and abdomen. Then, I'd run my hands lower and...the bell rang. I looked up. My heart raced as Blake York entered Ofarim's.

Blake shot me a knowing grin as he walked toward the counter. The sight of his black hair and intense blue eyes made me breathe a little harder. Blake was wearing his letterman's jacket and looking so very luscious.

Blake was one of the "disastrous dates" I'd been thinking about not long before. I included him in that list because Blake wasn't the dating type, and I'd allowed him to seduce me into a level of physical intimacy that I'd planned to allow only in a serious relationship. We'd hooked up since then, but things had never gone as far again. I liked to think it was because I had more self-control than I did at our first meeting, but the truth was that things didn't go beyond oral due to a lack of time and lack of a place to do more. Blake was dangerous. He was handsome, had an incredible body, and was the most seductive guy I'd ever met in my life. I had a feeling he could seduce a straight boy into giving him head. For all I knew, he had.

I glanced at my brother and Dane to see if they were watching. They were talking quietly together. So far, so good.

"Where have you been?" Blake asked, looking up and down my torso as if he could see right through my clothes.

"Things have been hectic," I said, unsuccessfully fighting to keep my voice from trembling with desire.

Why did Blake have to show up *now,* just when I had myself all worked up thinking about Tristan's sexy body? I wanted to leap over the counter and rip Blake's shirt off. Damn, he had incredible pecs.

"When do you get off?" Blake asked.

"Nine."

"Maybe we can go back to your place."

Blake knew I shared an apartment with Tim now.

"My brother might be around."

"So?"

"So, I can't...mess around if he's there."

"Why not? He knows you're into guys, right? Didn't you tell me he's gay, too?"

"Yeah, but..."

"Maybe he'd like to join us."

"He's my brother."

"That's what would make it so hot."

"Forget it, Blake. Tim and I aren't like that. Besides, he has a boyfriend."

"Yeah?"

"Yeah. They're sitting right over there."

Blake looked back toward my brother and Dane. I would have told him not to look, but Tim and Dane had been checking us out. They were probably trying to figure out what we were saying.

"Mmm. Is your brother a bottom? How about the other one?"

"I don't know, and it doesn't matter. We are NOT having a four-way."

My relationship with my brother was uncertain enough without adding any more complications, and sex would be the ultimate complication. I didn't think of Tim in that way, and I didn't want to. He was my brother. A sexual relationship just seemed...unnatural.

"Maybe they'd be up for a three-way if you're not interested in joining in."

Blake began to turn, but I grabbed his forearm.

"No, Blake."

Blake grinned at me.

"Well, if I had someone else to keep me busy..."

Blake was so damned sexy. I wanted him so bad I couldn't stand it. I also wanted to keep him away from my brother. Blake was concerned with one thing only: getting his rocks off. If I didn't stop him, he'd seduce Tim and Dane into a three-way without a single thought of how it would affect their relationship. I feared Tim and Dane would go for it, only to be sorry later.

"We can mess around in your car after I get off work," I said quietly.

"I want to do more than mess around, Shawn. Remember the first time we got together. Remember how you cried out my name?"

I swallowed hard, and I could feel my face turning red. I did remember, and I was becoming more aroused by the second.

"We can't use the loft, and it's too cold to do it anywhere else."

"What about here?"

"Ofarim's?"

"Yeah."

"Agnes wouldn't..."

"Agnes, whoever she may be, doesn't have to know anything about it."

"She's the owner. I can't..."

"How is she going to find out? We'll turn out the lights. No one will be able to see us. Besides, Shawn, wouldn't it be hot if I bent you right over this counter and took you from behind?"

I hesitated. I could feel my dick taking control of my thought process. I fought it, but my needs were too strong.

"Okay," I said, my voice throaty with desire. "Come back about closing time. You've got protection, right?"

"Why are you worried about protection? You're not going to get pregnant, Shawn. I promise."

"Just make sure you bring some, or nothing is going to happen."

"You're such a girl."

Tim and Dane left. Ofarim's was empty except for Blake and myself.

"Maybe we can just do it right now," Blake said.

"With the lights on? When someone could walk right in any second?"

"The danger would be such a rush."

The truth was that the idea of it turned me on like mad. There was no way I was going to risk it, however.

"After closing time," I said.

"Coward. I'll see you about nine, then."

Blake left. I noticed he didn't order anything. He was obviously hungry for only one thing in Ofarim's—me.

Ofarim's was dead. I had a lot of time to think as I went around filling salt and pepper shakers, napkin holders, and straw dispensers. Was I doing the right thing? Tristan had zero interest in me as a boyfriend, but did that make getting it on with another boy okay? Was I somehow being unfaithful to Tristan?

How can you be unfaithful to him when you aren't dating? I asked myself. I guess I couldn't be. Still, I felt a little uncomfortable. I wanted Blake so bad I was about to burst, which meant I wasn't thinking clearly. Fuck it. I didn't care. Tristan didn't want me. Blake did. I needed sex, and I was going to get some.

My mind was wholly focused on thoughts of Blake and his hard body. I felt untamed and primitive, as if I was driven purely by instinct. I knew that animals, humans included, were biologically driven to reproduce, but did that really apply to me? There was no way Blake and I could reproduce, period. Still, I was driven by my own body. The things I wanted to do with Blake didn't make sense when I stopped to think about them. Sex didn't make sense. Why did two people ever want to do such things? It was crazy. I still wanted it, though, more than just about anything else.

There were no thoughts of backing out. I didn't just want to hook up with Blake. I *needed* to. My only fear was that Blake wouldn't show up, but no, that was stupid. Blake had the same needs as all guys our age. He wanted me. He'd show.

Blake popped up right at closing time. He was wearing his letterman's jacket again, but what I immediately noticed was the he wasn't wearing a shirt underneath. I began to breathe harder even as I locked the door, turned the sign to "Closed," and turned off the lights.

I boldly opened Blake's jacket, revealing his hard, smooth torso. I ran my hands over his chest and abs and almost immediately replaced my fingertips with my tongue. I thought no longer about why I wanted to do the things I was doing. I just followed my instincts and desires.

Blake wasn't wearing any boxers or briefs. I found that out right after I sank to my knees in front of him. Blake's excitement was obvious, if you know what I mean. I got right to it. A feeling of control washed over me as I listened to Blake's breath grow harder and faster and felt his body respond to me. I was giving him such intense pleasure that he moaned and writhed. I was the one on my knees, yet I felt powerful.

Blake pushed me away after a few minutes. I stood and gazed into his eyes.

"I want to top this time," I said.

"Not a chance."

"Come on. I *really* want to…"

"I don't bottom," Blake said firmly. "Besides, we both know what you *really* want."

"How about we switch off?"

"No, Shawn. I don't take it from anyone. I never have, and I never will."

"Then how do you know you don't like it?"

"I just know. Besides, I'm not a girl."

"And I am?"

"No, but you are gay. I'm bi. We're different."

Anger flashed through my mind, but I was overwhelmed by lust. Blake closed in on me. The proximity of his hard, sexy body made my heart race. Blake leaned in until his lips were an inch from my ear.

"You know you want it," he whispered. "You know you want to feel me inside you. Take off your clothes, Shawn."

I couldn't resist him. I stripped naked. Blake kept his letterman's jacket on. That made it even hotter. Blake leaned me over the counter and let his jeans fall down around his ankles. I fought to control my breath, but it came hard and fast as if I'd been running. How could the mere anticipation of something have such an effect on me?

I felt Blake press against me.

"Wait! Wait!"

"What?"

"Put on a condom."

"We don't need one, Shawn,"

"We used one the last time."

"It feels better without one."

"No."

"I don't have any diseases, Dude."

"Just put one on."

"Okay, okay. You're such a pussy."

My face flushed with anger. I stood up and turned halfway around.

"Don't call me a pussy."

"I'm doing what you want, okay?" Blake said.

He grabbed me by the shoulder, and pushed me over the counter. He pressed against me again. I cried out as a blinding flash of pain ripped through my body. Why did I want to do this again?

I tried to get up. Blake pushed me back down.

"Easy. Easy. I'll go slow at first. It won't hurt long."

I knew it was true, but fuck, it hurt. Was the pain worth it? Another cry escaped my lips despite myself.

"Hang in there, Shawn. You're tough. Besides, you know you want it. You know you dream about it."

I felt so naked in front of Blake, emotionally naked. Blake knew my deepest, darkness sexual secrets—some of them anyway. I felt vulnerable and exposed when I was with him. I did want it. I did dream about it. Blake knew it. He knew something intimate about me that I'd shared with no other.

Just when I thought I couldn't stand it, the pain began to ebb. Pleasure began to take over. Soon, the pleasure consumed me, and I let Blake do whatever he wanted. I felt like such a bad boy for doing it right there on the counter in Ofarim's.

Blake kept going, harder and faster, until he groaned and lost control. I lost it at the same moment and our animal cries of passion filled Ofarim's. Blake let me up. We pulled on our clothes.

"Until next time, Shawn," Blake said with a smirk.

I let him out, closed and locked the door again, and then cleaned off the counter with disinfectant. I was no longer thinking through a haze of lust, and I felt somewhat used. Blake did use me, and I knew it, but didn't I use him, too? Didn't we use each other to satisfy our sexual needs? Somehow, being on the bottom made me feel more used. I was the object acted upon. I was the one taking the pain. I was the one bending over and submitting. I did want it, though, so why did I feel used? As they say, you can't rape the willing.

I didn't want to think about it anymore. Now that I'd relieved my sexual stress, I wanted to move on to other things. Sex was just one part of life, after all. There was plenty more out there to experience.

I locked up Ofarim's and headed for home. Unbidden, my thoughts turned to Tristan. I didn't feel as if I'd cheated on him as I feared, but I yearned to be with him. Sex with Blake was hot, but I wanted to be with Tristan. I sighed. It wasn't going to happen, at least not soon.

Tim was sitting at the table doing his homework when I walked into our apartment. He appeared so innocent my suspicions were aroused, but there was no sign of Dane, so I guess he wasn't up to anything.

"Didn't you bring Blake home with you?" Tim asked.

My first instinct was correct. My little brother was up to something. He was waiting to ambush me.

"No."

"You could, you know. I wouldn't mind."

"That would be a little hypocritical of me."

"You could let Dane and me keep my bedroom door closed. You and Blake could do anything you wanted in your bedroom."

The thought of bringing Blake home was more than a little tempting.

"No deals. Sorry."

"You're later than usual. Did you guys get it on somewhere?"

"That's none of your business."

"So you did!" Tim laughed. "I knew you would! I saw you guys looking all conspiratorial. I knew you were going to do it."

"I didn't say we messed around."

"You don't have to say it. I can tell just by looking at you."

"Whatever, Tim. I'm taking a shower, and then I have homework to do."

"Washing off the scent of Blake's cologne?"

I stuck out my tongue at Tim and headed for the bathroom.

Dane

Verona rocked! It was so-o-o much better than Marmont that there was no comparison. It wasn't so much Marmont itself that sucked, but the people who lived there. Billy Holmes was the worst. There was a time when I had a major crush on Billy. Who wouldn't? Feathered blond hair, blue eyes, a hot body, and a great ass—what was not to like? Billy was beautiful on the outside, but when he found out I was gay, I discovered just how ugly he was on the inside. Billy and I were friends before that, but once he found out about me, he turned on me. That crushed all my hope of making Billy my boyfriend. After the nasty things he did to me, I had no such interest in him, but there was a time when I dreamed of Billy Holmes. Tim was a million times better!

Verona did have some cool places Marmont lacked, like Ofarim's, Café Moffat, and the Paramount Theatre. I liked the park better, too. The high school was a vast improvement, and there were cool paths out past the soccer fields. I could picture Tim and me fooling around back there when the weather warmed. Surely the cold would depart soon. We were getting well into March, after all.

I sighed. Oh, how I wished Tim was with me! We usually hung out after school, but I was on my own this afternoon. I didn't have a lot of time before I was expected home, but I wanted to walk outside in the fresh, if rather chill, air. Not five minutes ago I'd bid goodbye to my boyfriend at his locker. We even shared a brief kiss. I could still taste Tim's sweet lips. Now, I was walking across the parking lot toward the soccer fields.

Verona wasn't perfect. I'd had some rough times here on my first visit. I was on the run then and had to do some things for food I didn't like to think about. One of the things I did to survive was work for a grave robber. Yeah, that's right, an actual grave robber—someone who dug up the dead and stole their stuff. Boothe was a shady character if there ever was one. Of course, I guess I couldn't expect someone who dug up corpses and stole from them to be a nice guy. Boothe had turned out to be a good deal worse than I'd imagined. If Shawn hadn't saved me...I shuddered to think about it. I owed my life to Shawn. If he hadn't stepped in, I would have died a nasty death after Boothe was done with me. Then, there was Austin. He wasn't like Boothe, but he wasn't exactly a nice guy, either. I'd fallen for Austin, but in the end he'd crushed me. I wondered where Austin was now. I guess it didn't matter.

Once I hit the soccer fields, I came soon to the huge boulder that sat there. I stopped and read the bronze plaque:

THIS FIELD IS DEDICATED TO THE MEMORY OF MARK BAILEY AND TAYLOR POTTER. THEY DIED HERE ALL TOO EARLY BECAUSE OF HATRED AND INTOLERANCE. MAY THE FUTURE LEARN FROM WHAT HAPPENED AND NOT LET IT HAPPEN AGAIN.

I knew the story of course; everyone in Verona knew. Mark and Taylor had been driven to suicide by the abuse of those around them. I wasn't around when it happened. I first came to Verona after that, but I could well understand. Back in Marmont, I'd been tormented by my peers. I'd been called names and beaten. It got so bad that Mom and Dad pulled me out of school and decided to move. I don't know how long I could have stood against all the abuse if my parents hadn't pulled me out of school. Just knowing how many of those around me hated me hurt like hell. I would probably have ended up like Mark and Taylor if I'd been stuck in that situation much longer. So yeah, I understood.

Tim said Taylor was like a blond version of Tristan, so he must've been hot. Shawn had had a major crush on Taylor, just like I had had on Billy Holmes. Neither of us got what we wanted. It must have been hard on Shawn when Taylor died. Billy beat the crap out of me, but I think Shawn had it worse. I hoped he could get with Tristan someday. I really liked Shawn, and I wanted him to be happy. I could have easily dated Shawn myself, but then I met his brother, and...I fell for him...just like that.

I walked beyond the boulder and onto the soccer fields. It was beautiful there, but kind of eerie, too. This was where Mark and Taylor had killed themselves—Taylor by downing a bunch of pills and Mark by blowing his brains out. I could almost picture them, lying there... I forced my mind to other thoughts before I freaked myself out.

I walked quickly across the soccer fields, slowing only when I came to the edge of the woods. A clear path led off under the trees, and I followed it. The leaves hadn't come out yet, but the forest was still beautiful.

I walked among the grey trunks and beneath the limbs overhead. There was green in the forest already—the dark green of honeysuckle and the lighter greens of grass and other vegetation I could not name. I stopped to watch some squirrels as they jumped from limb to limb, landing effortlessly. I almost wished I was one of them, but lately I've been having too much fun being me.

I smiled when I thought of Tim. I thought about my boyfriend more times a day than I could count, and those thoughts always made me grin. My feelings for him made me feel completely sappy, but I didn't care. I was happier than I'd ever been in my life. I wished we could be together more, but I remembered only too well when we lived forty-five minutes away from each other. I could actually see him every day now. Yes! I wished he was walking with me in the forest, too, but Tim was with me even when he wasn't with me. I can't really explain what I mean other than to say I carried him in my heart.

I strolled along the path, taking in the beauty of the nature I'd too often failed to notice before. Tim made me appreciate the world around me. Everything just seemed more beautiful to me now, although I was sure that beauty had been there all along. I was just looking at the world through new eyes. In the end, it didn't matter. Happiness needs no good reason to exist.

I really had changed. Was it only last summer when I'd run away? Was it only a few months ago when I'd been such a little bastard? I almost couldn't believe what a vile little creep I'd been. I was hurting, yeah, but that was no excuse for the things I'd done. Don't get me wrong, I didn't kill anyone or anything, but I'd been bad enough. I'd even tried to blackmail Shawn into having sex with me. I almost can't believe I really did that, but it's true. I stopped just short of it, though. I had him right where I wanted him, but I couldn't go through with it. I wanted him so bad, but I just couldn't force him like that. I was kind of mad at myself at the time for being weak, but now I'm proud that I had enough decency not to treat another human being like that. Something inside me wouldn't let me do it. That something saved me.

The word ironic is way overused, but it was ironic that Shawn, the very boy who I'd almost blackmailed into sex, rescued me. He stopped Boothe when Boothe was…well I'm only going to say this once because it's humiliating. I guess it shouldn't be, because there wasn't anything I could do about it, but…Shawn stopped Boothe when he was raping me. He'd just got started, but it hurt worse than anything ever in my entire life. I'm sure he would have killed me when he was done with me, too. We'd just robbed a grave, and it was still open right there beside us. He could have tossed my body in, covered it up, and no one would probably ever have known. Shawn saved me, though. He saved me, and then all the boys I'd been trying to prey upon—Ethan, Nathan, Brendan, and Casper—took me in and helped me. I'd been such a total ass, but they helped me when I'd needed it the most. Talk about a humbling experience. They were nothing but kind to me, but their kindness, coming after my horrible behavior, made me feel about two inches tall.

I'm not sorry I was humiliated and humbled. I needed it. I am a much better person now than I was back then. It didn't happen overnight. I slipped up now and then, especially at first. I still slip sometimes, but I'm not the same little bastard who thought only of himself and was out to get laid no matter the cost to anyone else. I wasn't proud of what I had been, but I was proud of who I'd become. Who knows? Maybe what happened with Boothe was a good thing in that it changed me. If it hadn't happened, Shawn wouldn't have rescued me, and I might still be the same little creep I was when I first came to Verona. I wasn't thankful for what Boothe did to me, but I was thankful for how I'd changed.

I was too busy thinking to pay attention to where I was walking. Soon, I found myself back near the soccer fields. They didn't seem quite so eerie now. Perhaps it was because the love I felt for Tim gave me a hint of the love Taylor and Mark had shared. Their lives had ended in tragedy, but they'd had each other. We all die sooner or later. What is important is how we live our lives. I intended to get all I could out of mine.

As I left the soccer fields and crossed the parking lot, I caught sight of a blond boy. Moments later, I recognized him: Devon. It was too late to veer off, and I didn't want him to think I was afraid of him. To be honest, I was kind of afraid of him. He was a year older and somewhat bigger than I was. I was tough, however, and I knew how to put up a good fight. Still, I didn't want to fight him. Chances were I'd get hurt.

Devon sneered at me as he neared.

"Faggot."

I thought he was going to pass by and leave it at that, but at the last moment he grabbed my shoulder and jerked me around so that I was facing him.

"How do you live with yourself, faggot? How do you walk down the halls with everyone knowing what you are?"

"There's nothing wrong with what I am."

"You're fucked in the head. You're a sick pervert. You disgust me."

"Just leave me alone, Devon."

"Why? What are you going to do about it if I don't?"

Devon shoved me.

"Huh? What are you going to do?"

He shoved me again, harder. I was forced to take a step back.

"You fucking faggot. I should fuck you up right now."

I tensed, ready to fight.

"I should fuck *you* up."

Devon and I both turned at the sound of the voice. Brandon Hanson stood not ten feet away.

Brandon closed on Devon and circled around him, eyeing him as if he'd love nothing better than to tear him to pieces. I had no doubt Brandon could do it, too. Brandon was about six foot, one sixty-five, with broad shoulders and lot of muscles. Devon trembled.

"Come on, Devon. Say something else. Talk some more shit to Dane. Give me an excuse to kick your ass."

"We were just talking," Devon said, holding up his hands.

"Bullshit."

"Hey, I don't want to fight you, Brandon."

Brandon stepped up to Devon and poked him in the chest.

"That's because you know I'll kick your ass, or maybe you're afraid I'll finish what I started on the soccer field."

Devon's eyes widened in what I can only describe as abject terror.

"Please. I'm sorry."

"What's wrong, Devon? Are you gonna cry? You're not such a bad ass now, are you?"

Devon did look as if he was about to cry. I almost felt sorry for him—almost.

"Just let me go, man. We might get in trouble if we fight on school property. I don't want to get suspended."

"Yeah, you're real worried about that, aren't you, Devon?"

"Please. I don't want any trouble."

"Then...Stop...Making...Trouble," Brandon said, poking Devon hard in the chest with each word. "If you minded your own fucking business, you wouldn't have any trouble."

"Please..." Devon said in a pleading tone.

"Get out of here before I change my mind. If I start beating on you, I don't think I can stop myself."

Devon was out of there so fast he was little more than a blur. Brandon turned to me.

"I HATE that fucker."

"I'm not too fond of him myself. Thanks for stepping in. I wasn't looking forward to fighting him."

"I'm sure you could do okay against Devon, but I put an end to his shit any time I get the chance. Hey, want a ride home?"

"Sure. I'm running a little late. I kind of lost track of the time, and then there was Devon…"

"Come on."

I followed Brandon to his car and hopped in.

"If it's none of my business, just say so, but what did you mean by finishing what you started on the soccer field?" I asked. "I thought Devon was going to crap his pants when you said that."

"To make a long story short, I came this close to cutting his throat," Brandon said, holding his index finger and thumb a fraction of an inch apart.

"You really…"

"Yes. I had a knife at his throat. I wanted to kill that fucker more than I'd ever wanted anything in my life."

"Why?"

"Because of what he almost did to Ethan and Nathan. Because of what he did to Taylor and Mark."

"What did he almost do to Ethan and Nathan?"

"Devon and his buddies were going to kill them. They were going to hang them right out there on the soccer fields."

I jerked my head toward Brandon. My eyes widened.

"You didn't know that, did you?"

"No."

"Almost no one does."

"Why isn't Devon in jail?"

"He should be, but Ethan and Nathan wanted us to let him and his buddies go."

"Let them go? After *that*?"

Ethan and Nathan had been forgiving when it came to me, but I didn't try to kill them!

"I know. Crazy, right? I went along with it, though. I was out of my head that night. After almost cutting Devon's throat, I thought it best to let Ethan do the thinking. Believe me, I did NOT want to let Devon go."

"Damn. Um…what did Devon do to Mark and Taylor?"

"He killed them."

"*Killed them?* I thought they committed suicide!"

"They did, but he just the same as killed them. That fucking bastard and the others just like him—they drove Mark and Taylor to their deaths. They're just as guilty as if they'd shot them dead."

"Shit. I knew Devon was bad news, but I had no idea."

"Most people around here don't know the full extent of things. Verona harbors a lot of dark secrets."

"You aren't kidding. You were close with Taylor and Mark, weren't you?"

"Yeah. Real close. Mark was my best friend. I knew him…forever. I didn't know Taylor nearly as long, but we became close, even more so after I found out about him and Mark."

"Did you suspect Mark was gay?"

"No. Not really. I guess I just didn't think about it. It didn't matter. I was surprised, but I guess it made sense. After I found out, some things kind of fell into place. You know? Things I didn't pay attention to at the time. I was a little hurt that Mark didn't tell me the truth when he first realized he was gay, but I also understood how difficult that would have been for him. I loved Mark. Losing him was so hard. Losing Taylor wasn't much easier. I…I found Taylor's body…Ethan, Jon, and I found him. He was there on the soccer field, right by one of the goals—dead. The rain was falling down on him. He…"

Brandon's voice trembled, and a tear slid down his cheek.

"Hey, we don't have to talk about it."

"It's okay. It's something that is always with me. I'm sure it always will be. I'm glad I didn't find Mark. I'm glad I didn't see him...like that."

"Yeah, I understand."

"I feel responsible for Mark's death. I knew in my heart he was going to kill himself, but I wouldn't let myself believe it. When I saw him, that last time, it was just after Mark found out about Taylor. I told him about finding Taylor. Mark was torn up. When I dropped him off at his house, I told him that everything was going to be okay. We both knew it was a lie, but what else was I going to say? I begged him to promise me he wouldn't do anything stupid, and he said, 'Whatever I do, it won't be stupid. I promise.' That's exactly what he said. That was the last time I saw him alive. I thought about telling his parents that I was afraid he'd hurt himself, but they didn't care about him. I even thought about calling the cops, but how could I do that? I kept telling myself that Mark wouldn't kill himself. I guess the possibility was just so horrible I couldn't let myself believe he'd really do it. You don't think something like that is really going to happen. You know? God, I wish I could go back and stop it from happening, but I can't, and I have to live with what I didn't do."

"You shouldn't blame yourself, Brandon."

"That's what everyone tells me, but I do. I was Mark's best friend. I was my job to be on top of things like that. I failed, and he's dead."

"Brandon, I don't claim to understand everything, but don't you think Mark would have found a way, no matter what you did? If he wanted to kill himself, as he obviously did, no one could have stopped him."

"You're probably right, but that's not going to bring Mark back."

Brandon pulled up in front of the old schoolhouse that was my home.

"Thanks for the ride, Brandon, and thanks for saving me from Devon. If you ever want to talk about...anything, I'm here, okay?"

"Thank you."

117

I climbed out of the car and headed for the house as Brandon drove away. I was right on time. What an interesting afternoon it had been!

As I entered the "house," I had the feeling I was stepping into school. You'd think I'd grow accustomed to living in an old school building, but it still felt weird entering the wide hallway and climbing the big stairs up to what had once been a classroom. I guess it would have been much weirder if I'd actually attended school in the building, but no one had gone to school there for some fifty years.

I closed the door to my room. My few pieces of furniture were swallowed up by all the space, but I loved my room! My bedroom was bigger than the entire rental house I'd been stuck in when we first moved to Verona. It was quite a change.

I pulled my books out of my backpack to get a start on my homework, but then I realized I was hungry. Studying would just have to wait. I headed back downstairs toward the cafeteria. It didn't seem quite right to call it the kitchen, although I did sometimes. Like everything else in my new home, it was just too big. The journey to the cafeteria was a long one, at least it was a lot longer than it had been in the Marmont house. The trip from my bedroom to the showers was even longer. I actually had to get up early every morning just because it took so long to get around the old school!

Don't get me wrong. I loved the new place! It had lots of character. I still wasn't used to having my own gymnasium. There was even some weight-lifting equipment, but it was so old it was kind of weird, and I wasn't sure how to use it. There was lots to explore, like the spaces under the bleachers in the gym. The bleachers were enclosed, and there was a little door on each of the three sets of them that led underneath them. There was lots of cool old stuff in there, like old basketball uniforms, basketballs, props from plays, and all kinds of other stuff. I hadn't looked at it all yet. I'd been much too busy!

Mom was in the kitchen of the cafeteria fixing supper. I grabbed a cookie, and I munched on it while Mom grilled me about my day. I told her about walking on the paths behind the soccer fields, but I left out the part involving Devon. Things had been rough for me back in Marmont, but I think Mom suffered more than I did. She'd cried when I got beat up, and her tears hurt worse than Billy's fists. I didn't want her to worry about me. Devon was dangerous, but I wasn't in nearly as much danger in Verona as I had been back in my old hometown. I had friends here to protect me, guys like Brandon, who wouldn't just stand back and let a jerk like Devon beat on me. I didn't intend for Mom to get the least hint that everything wasn't perfect. My task wasn't that difficult. My life was so near perfect now I almost couldn't believe it!

"What are you smiling about, Dane?"

"Tim," I said.

"You really like him, don't you?"

"I love him, Mom."

I blushed slightly. I still wasn't quite accustomed to talking to my mom about how I felt about another boy. Mom and Dad had been accepting and supportive, but it was still a difficult topic to discuss with my parents.

"I'm glad he makes you happy."

"He does. I like being with him. It doesn't matter what we're doing; it's fun because I'm with him."

"I remember when I felt that way about a boy."

"Dad?"

"Before your father, although your father made me feel that way, too."

"What happened? How did you end up with Dad if you loved someone else?"

"Things don't always work out, Dane."

"Did you have a fight or something?"

"No. We just grew apart. He went off for football camp one summer, and he wasn't the same when he returned. I think he met someone there. I don't know what happened, really, but he wasn't the same boy he had been when he left. I wasn't the same girl, either."

"Did you meet someone, too?"

"No, but change can come quickly when you're young. I think, perhaps, that both of us just needed something new. We did remain friends. We dated a little after that summer, but it wasn't the same. Within a couple of months, we were both dating other people."

"Tim and I are going to stick together. We're not going to change."

"Both of you will change, Dane. That doesn't have to mean you'll grow apart, but you will change. You may feel differently about Tim in a few months."

"I don't want to feel differently about him."

"I know, but it's likely."

"Are you trying to depress me?"

"No. If your feelings for Tim change, it will be okay because you won't be the same person."

"Well, I may be a different person in the future, but I'm going to feel the same about Tim as I do now."

"Perhaps you will. Perhaps you'll be one of those who meet someone in high school and stay with them your whole life."

"Do you know anyone like that?"

"Yes, I do."

I smiled. "That's going to be Tim and me, then; just you wait and see."

Shawn

I sat across from Tristan at lunch, alternating between guilt and anger: guilt for hooking up with Blake, anger because Tristan refused to date me. I was also jealous. Tristan had been way too friendly with Nate London lately. I didn't fail to notice the way Tristan looked at Nate. He wanted him. I'd had a crush on Nate before I met Tristan. Nate was on my football team. He had curly blond hair, green eyes, and a killer body. Checking him out in the showers made me breathe harder. I didn't like the way Tristan and Nate gazed and smiled at each other. I'd never been able to figure out Nate's sexual orientation, but I was beginning to suspect he was, at the very least, bi and possibly gay. If Tristan started dating Nate when he wouldn't go out with me, I was going to be pissed!

The more I thought about Tristan and Nate, the angrier I became. Why should I feel guilty about getting it on with Blake when Tristan was flirting with another boy? What happened to not wanting to date? What happened to the whole friends-first idea? If he didn't want to date me, why didn't he just say so and be done with it? Did he find me that freaking hideous?

"Are you okay, Shawn?" Casey asked.

"I'm going to be," I said testily, glaring at Tristan.

A quizzical expression crossed Tristan's face, but I didn't give him time to react. I got up and left the lunch table. My lower lip trembled slightly as I walked away, making me angrier still. I hated to cry, and I sure as hell wasn't going to cry over Tristan! He wasn't like Taylor at all. He was his evil twin! I was willing to bet Taylor didn't put Mark through such hell. Taylor wouldn't have played games with me. If only I'd... I stopped myself. I could not change the past, but I could change the present. It was time to forget about Tristan. Let him date Nate if he wanted. Let him date the whole fucking football team! I was through with pining over him. Why should I obsess over Tristan when boys like Blake York wanted me?

I sat in my afternoon classes steaming. I was angrier at myself than I was at Tristan. It wasn't his fault if he didn't find me attractive. Maybe Nate had something I didn't have. Maybe it was his curly blond hair or his green eyes. Who knew? Maybe my brown hair and eyes were just too ordinary for Tristan. It didn't matter. If he wasn't into me as anything more than a friend, I just had to accept it and move on. I was stupid for denying myself other guys when Tristan didn't want me. Stupid! Stupid! Stupid! I was stupid for feeling guilty for hooking up with Blake York. I was stupid for not being on the make. I'd been looking for a boyfriend before Tristan came along. Perhaps it was time to begin the search again. Perhaps not. Did I really want to put myself in the same situation all over again? What if I fell for another boy who wasn't into me? I was only seventeen! Why should I even tie myself down to just one guy at this point in my life? Why settle for one when I could have several—or at least a few?

I thought about Blake and the things we'd done together the night before in Ofarim's. Damn! That was hot! Blake kind of frightened me. He brought out things in me I didn't even know were there. Something felt so right about it all, though. I couldn't imagine myself having sex that intense with Tristan. No, Tristan was too gentle, too sweet. He'd never be able to give it to me the way Blake did.

The bell rang, and I could not get up from my desk—if you know what I mean. Thinking about sex with Blake had me so worked up my excitement would have been obvious had I stood. I lingered for several moments, slowly putting my book and notebook into my backpack. I forced my thoughts away from Blake. My excitement began to ebb and soon I was able to stand, using my backpack to hide the reminder of my arousal.

The only thing that prevented me from calling Blake after school was the fact we'd hooked up only the night before. I didn't want to appear desperate, although desperate is exactly how I felt. My eyes fell on the counter when I walked into Ofarim's. Remembering what had taken place there the night before, I grinned. Damn, I wanted to do it again!

A wave of shame hit me. I was turning into a real slut. Last night, I'd felt guilty about getting it on with Blake, and here I was wanting it again. How could my feelings change so fast? I knew how. My dick had taken control. Desire had a way of forcing out rational thought. Besides, why should I feel guilty for making both myself and Blake feel good?

The counter was put to more ordinary uses for the evening, and I settled in to waiting on customers, helping Agnes make sundaes, banana splits and various other items on the menu, busing tables, and cleaning up.

I checked out the high-school boys as I worked. I didn't find most of them all that attractive. There were a few I would've hooked up with, but how could I tell if they were into guys? I was back to the old problem of not being able to tell who was gay and who wasn't. I wished Casey could come up with a list of gay boys in Verona the way she'd come up with a list of gay boys in Plymouth. Of course, that hadn't worked out very well, except for Blake. It was too bad there weren't more names on the list. It was definitely incomplete. Still, I would have given a lot to know the names of a handful of gay boys at VHS.

You idiot, you know the names of several gay boys at VHS. A lot of good those names did me, though. There was Tim, my brother, Dane (Tim's boyfriend), Tristan (my unrequited love), Brendan & Casper and Ethan & Nathan—both couples—quite likely Nate London, who was probably doing Tristan, and possibly Devon Devlin. Devon? There was a laugh. If he was gay, he was so closeted and so filled with self-hatred he'd probably grow up to be a serial killer or something.

I knew a lot more gay boys at VHS than I did in Plymouth, but what did that get me? Nothing. There had to be others, but who? No gay guys had come out of the woodwork to join our table. Not one had approached me. I was out now. Either the other gay boys in school were too scared to approach me or they didn't find me attractive. A list of names might not even help. That didn't stop me from wishing for one. I wanted to meet some other guys like me, guys I could experiment with, and I wanted to meet them now!

The following day at school was frustrating in the extreme. I had half a mind to hit on a few classmates I found particularly attractive, but how could I do that? It's not that I feared a fist in the face, a distinct possibility if I hit on a straight boy. Suggesting, even in a vague, roundabout way that I wanted to get naked with a guy was just too intimate for casual conversation. Plus, how would I feel if I was a heterosexual boy and a gay boy hit on me? I think the word uncomfortable might describe it best. I didn't want to make anyone feel like that.

I *really* wanted to call up Blake after school, but it was just too soon. What were the rules about that, anyway? When was someone going to write a guide book!

I headed for my after-school job at Ofarim's just like the day before. Jon and Brandon came in and gave me a hard time. I guess they had to take a break from going off on each other now and then. I didn't mind. My crazy friends made my job more enjoyable. There was often someone I knew in Ofarim's. A lot of the kids from school showed up during the hours I worked there.

About 8 p.m., I looked up to see Blake York enter. He wasn't alone, either. I recognized the boy with him. He went to VHS. I didn't know him. I'd just seen him around—and checked him out a time or two. He played soccer, I think. I wondered what he was doing with Blake. How did they know each other?

If there was something going on between Blake and the blond boy, I could see why Blake was interested in him. Blondie was extremely good looking—slim and yet muscular—and almost too pretty to be a boy. I just stared for a few moments, entranced. He had long blond bangs that gave him a skater look. His build was a cross between a skater and a soccer player. It was a damn nice combination.

Blake and Blondie eyed me momentarily before taking a booth. I wanted to talk to Blake, but even if he had been alone, there were too many guys from school in Ofarim's at the moment. It's too bad we didn't have some time alone like last time. It would have been the perfect opportunity to tell him I wanted to hook up again. It was probably still too early to call, but since he was here… Damn, why did he have to bring someone with him? I suppose that alone should have been enough to tell me he wasn't looking for a hookup tonight (unless Blondie was a hookup), but I wanted Blake so bad I could hardly stand it.

I approached Blake's table hesitantly. Memories of our last encounter filled me with desire, but I fought to rein in my sexual needs. Blake grinned at me, and our eyes locked for a few moments. There was a sense of sexual tension in the air.

"Hey, Shawn. What's up?"

"I'm just having a blast here in Ofarim's," I said with the slightest sarcastic tone.

Blake laughed.

"Yeah, I bet. This is Marc."

"Hey, Marc. I'm Shawn. I think I've seen you around school," I said.

"Yeah, I'm on the soccer team. You play football," Marc said.

"He's pretty good, too," Blake said, "for a VHS player."

"Ha! We kick Plymouth's ass regularly," I said grinning.

"We'll see about that this fall," Blake said. "We'll just see how good Verona plays without its star quarterback."

"Yeah, yeah, so what would you guys like to drink?"

I found it difficult not to stare at Marc, especially since he was surreptitiously checking me out. How could I have missed this hot boy who was practically under my nose? Of course, there was no guarantee he was into guys. I thought Marc was checking me out, but maybe that was just wishful thinking. It could be that Marc and Blake were just friends. I wondered how they'd met.

I walked away from the table with their drink orders, fighting the arousal in my pants, but only partly succeeding. Thankfully, the counter hid my lower half from view, and I got myself under control before I returned with their Cokes.

Blake and Marc eyed me and whispered conspiratorially as I worked behind the counter and waited on other customers. I had the distinct impression Blake was telling Marc all about what we'd done on the counter of Ofarim's. Both Blake and Marc looked back at me a couple of times and then laughed together as if sharing some big joke, and I had the feeling the joke was me. Anger welled up in my chest, especially when Blake locked eyes with me and gave me a smirk.

Oddly enough, I was aroused as well as angered by the thought that the blond hottie was hearing all the intimate sexual details of my encounters with Blake. Did he and Blake have something going, too? Or, did Blake just bring the cute soccer player to show him the rival football player he'd seduced? I felt naked under their gaze.

I was uncomfortable to say the least, but I sucked it up and returned to their table to take their orders.

"I'll have an Ofarim Burger with large fries," Blake said.

"I think I'll have chicken fingers and onion rings," Marc said.

Again, Marc furtively checked me out. I was maddeningly turned on by his gaze but felt slightly embarrassed at the same time because Blake had probably told him all about bending me over the counter and making me moan his name. I was still more than half pissed off, too. I'd never specifically told Blake that what we did was a secret, but I assumed he'd keep it to himself. I definitely didn't want anyone from VHS to know the intimate sexual details of my life. I could feel my face growing hot as I left the table, and I heard Blake laugh as I walked away. Was he laughing at me?

I worked behind the counter, trying and failing not to think about what Blake might be saying about me. I don't think I would have minded quite so much if Marc wasn't so damned sexy! Visions of making out with Marc and running my hands over his no-doubt smooth and firm body just about drove me out of my mind. Did older guys have to go through this? I prayed I wouldn't be this horny all my life. I didn't think I could stand it.

Marc laughed really loud for a moment. I looked up and caught Blake staring at me as he laughed, too. I could feel my face growing hot with embarrassment again, so I quickly turned away.

Blake and I were going to have words when we met next. I was as pissed off as I was embarrassed. He had no right to share the intimate details of our sexual encounters with anyone else, and he definitely had no right to embarrass and humiliate me in front of a hottie like Marc. If that was the way he was going to be, Blake and I had hooked up for the last time.

The bell on the door rang and I looked up. Great! Just what I needed. Devon entered, and he wasn't alone. Zac Packard was with him. I didn't see much of Zac, and that was fine by me. I heard all about how he tried to blackmail Ethan into throwing the wrestling championship back in '80. Zac wasn't as overtly hostile to gays as Devon was, but he was no friend to them, either. He was also rather intimidating. Ethan had kicked his ass in the wrestling championship, but Ethan was probably the only guy who could beat him.

I sighed as I walked toward their table. This was obviously my day for being shoved into uncomfortable situations. Devon came into Ofarim's frequently, and he'd grown increasingly hostile as he'd become more and more certain I was gay. Now, Zac was with him. I didn't like the possibilities of the Devon/Zac combination at all.

"What can I get you guys?" I asked, in professional-waiter mode.

"I'll have a Coke," Devon said. He gazed across the booth at Zac and smiled.

"Same here," Zac said.

"So, I hear you broke up with your 'girlfriend,'" Devon said, making quotations in the air with his fingers.

Here it comes. So far, Devon hadn't talked shit to my face. He'd merely been antagonistic in attitude. I knew about Devon, though. The more backup he had, the bolder he became.

"Casey wasn't my girlfriend, and we're still friends."

"Yeah, but you sure let on she was your girlfriend, didn't you?" Devon said. "Why was that, Shawn?"

"Because you didn't want everyone to know you're a fag?" Zac asked. "I hear your brother has a boyfriend. What's wrong, Shawn? Did your little brother get tired of you sucking his cock?"

"Shut up," I said.

"Ohhh, we've struck a nerve," Devon said. "Incest at the Myers. You know Shawn and Tim share an apartment."

"Shut up, Devon!"

"Are you going to make him?" Zac asked, standing up. "Maybe you better make me shut up then, too."

Were these guys for real?

I stood my ground. The only sign of fear that escaped from me was a quick swallow. I was strong, but Zac could rearrange my face with one punch.

"So, which one of you is the pillow biter?" asked Zac. "You? Your brother? Or, do you switch off?"

"I don't have sex with my brother."

There were other guys from school in Ofarim's, and we were beginning to draw attention.

"Sure you don't," Zac said as insincerely as humanly possible.

"Just knock it off," I said.

"You want to make me? Do you, fag?" Zac asked.

He stepped closer. He was in my face now. I could feel his hot breath on me. I held my ground. I couldn't believe it. I was actually going to have to fight Zac right there in Ofarim's. I wondered if Agnes would fire me. I knew for sure Devon would jump in as soon as Zac swung at me. I was going to get my ass kicked for sure.

"You're a really big man, picking on guys smaller than you," Blake said, stepping up beside me. Marc appeared on my other side.

Zac looked at Blake.

"Ha! I'm just having a little fun. Shawn would be too easy to beat up. It's no fun punching out a pussy boy."

I clenched my fists. I wanted to punch Zac in the face so bad!

"I don't think I like your idea of fun," Blake said.

"Yeah, well, we all have our own hobbies, don't we?" Zac said, looking at me with a smirk.

Zac sat back down. It was only with a struggle that I kept from sighing in relief. Suddenly, I wasn't so pissed off with Blake anymore. He gripped my shoulder with his hand for a moment. When I turned to face him, he nodded, and then he and Marc returned to their booth. I turned back to Devon and Zac.

128

"So, what would you guys like?" I asked, as if nothing had happened.

I walked away trembling slightly after taking their orders. Despite his words, I knew Zac would have punched me if Blake and Marc hadn't stepped in. I would have fought back, but I would've got my ass kicked. I was kind of embarrassed that everyone in Ofarim's had been watching, but at least I had stood my ground. I was no coward. I'd rather take a beating than slink off with my tail between my legs.

Blake and Marc looked in my direction now and then, but they'd stopped laughing. Blake looked over at Devon and Zac a few times, too. I think he would've liked to tangle with Zac. Damn, I hoped Zac wasn't going to be on my ass from now on. I had enough problems. Devon, I could handle, but about the only way I could beat Zac was to kick him in the nuts. If it came down to it, I would.

I grinned for a moment as I pictured Zac doubling over, grabbing his nuts. Yeah, I wouldn't hesitate to kick him in the nads if he attacked me. I wouldn't kick a guy in the balls in a fair fight, but if Zac was going to pick on me, I'd make him pay the price.

Despite the recent drama, it felt good to be out. I hadn't made any big announcement, but word gets around about things like that. I felt better about myself now. Letting everyone believe Casey was my girlfriend was no better than lying. I had my reasons for keeping my sexual orientation a secret, but I hated lying. It was such a relief not to have to lie anymore.

Blake and Marc lingered over their supper and then ordered shakes. Devon and Zac departed, and the place slowly cleared out. Finally, there was a lull, and Ofarim's was empty except for Blake, Marc, Agnes, and me. I walked over to their table.

"Thanks for helping me out earlier. Zac would have rearranged my face if you hadn't stepped up."

"I kind of wanted to see how well you'd do against him, but you were obviously outmatched."

"No kidding. I might have got a few good punches in, but there's little doubt the fight would have ended with me lying on the floor, groaning in pain."

"That took balls to stand up to him," said Marc.

I slid in beside Blake. It was time for a break, anyway.

"I have balls."

"I know," Blake said and smiled. "Is your brother going to be around this evening?"

"Yeah."

"Think you could get rid of him? Or maybe we could use this place?"

"I might be able to get rid of him. I don't know. As for Ofarim's, Agnes will be here at closing tonight."

"Damn. Well, Marc and I wondered if you wanted to get together, but we need a place."

This was definitely getting interesting.

"Yeah?" I said, looking at Marc.

"Yeah," he said. "I noticed you at school, and when Blake told me that you guys...get together..."

It seemed far less likely now than Blake and Marc had been laughing at my expense earlier. I was just being paranoid. I needed to learn to stop assuming things. I was too turned on to think much about that now. Marc was steaming hot, and I wanted him! There had to be a way to get rid of Tim for a few hours—if not tonight, then soon. I wanted it to be tonight, but I didn't get off until 9 p.m., and it was a school night. I couldn't send Tim to run around that late, especially when he had to be up early the next morning. My dick fought to do my thinking for me, but I had to be mature about this. I had to be a good parent.

"I'm off on Fridays. We can meet sometime after school. Tim will probably go out. I'll do what I can to make sure he stays out for a few hours. We can use the loft. I'll call you with the details."

Blake nodded.

"This is gonna be hot," he said.

The hungry leers Marc was now shooting at me excited me even more than Blake's words. He wanted me *bad*, almost as badly as I wanted him. It was all I could do to keep from jerking him out of the booth and kissing him. I wondered if he was into making out. I guess I'd find out soon enough, but soon enough definitely wasn't soon enough!

Blake and Marc departed soon after we'd made our plans. This had been some evening: a showdown with Zac and then an opportunity for my first three-way. I almost pitied poor heterosexual boys like Zac. How often did they get to hook up with two girls at once? Probably never!

I momentarily experienced a pang of regret when I thought of Tristan, but I put him out of my mind. I'd settle down with a nice guy someday, but now was my time to explore. I just had to be sure not to let Blake and Marc talk me into anything I wasn't ready for or anything that wasn't safe. At the moment, I couldn't think of much I wasn't prepared to do, but I remembered only too well Blake's disregard for condoms. On that I was going to stand firm. No condom, no sex.

My mind was buzzing with possibilities the rest of the evening. A few customers came in, but I was barely aware of their existence. I was too busy thinking about Blake's hard, muscular body. I wondered what Marc had hidden under his clothes. He was slim, but he looked kind of muscular, too. He probably had one of those compact, defined bodies that were so sexy. He was a soccer player, so that probably meant he had a great ass. I definitely liked the view when I watched him depart with Blake.

Tim and Dane usually went to the Paramount to catch a movie on Friday nights. I wanted to make sure they were sticking to their usual plans, but I didn't want to tip Tim off to the fact that I wanted him out of the loft. It wasn't easy, but I kept myself from asking about his plans.

Finally, on Friday at lunch I overheard him talking to Dane about catching *Arthur*. Dudley Moore starred in it. The film had been out a few months but was just getting to Verona. I kind of wanted to see it myself, but I wasn't about to pass up a three-way with Blake and Marc to watch a movie! I found Marc and told him we were on for tonight.

I was now guaranteed a good two hours with Blake and Marc, but I wanted more time as well as a little insurance. I waited until Tim was getting ready for his date and then poked my head into his room.

"I have something for you," I said.

"What?" Tim asked suspiciously.

I handed him twenty bucks.

"What's this for?"

"I really appreciate that you haven't been giving me any trouble. I know the whole thing with not being able to do what you want with Dane here in the loft is difficult for you, but you've been really reasonable about it. You're doing well in school and..."

"Yes, Dad."

I grinned. Considering our father, that could have been an insult, but I knew it was meant as a mere joke.

"You can stay out an extra hour tonight, too."

Tim looked at me suspiciously.

"What are you up to?"

Uh-oh. I'd made a mistake.

"You haven't come in late once. This is a one-time deal, so don't get used to it."

"So I can stay out until midnight?"

"Yes, but not one second past midnight. Got it?"

"Yeah, I got it. Thanks, Shawn."

I turned and walked toward the kitchen. That was close. I'd almost blown it, but I'd also made a nice save, if I do say so myself.

I wanted to start getting ready for my "date," but that would have tipped Tim off. My Friday nights were usually not too exciting for the most part. I did go out with the guys now and then, but most of the time I used Friday nights to catch up on homework, get some cleaning done, and just rest. Turn on some soaps, put a robe and slippers on me and I could have been a housewife. Damn. How did this happen to me? I knew the answer to that, and things weren't nearly as bad as I was letting on at the moment. Yeah, I had extra responsibilities now, but I was up to the task. Besides, Blake and Marc were coming over this evening!

Tim departed at about six-thirty p.m. The movie didn't start until seven, and then he'd almost certainly take Dane out to eat with the cash I'd given him. We had three and a half hours at least and probably more. I couldn't picture Tim coming in much before midnight. I called Blake the second Tim was out of the loft and gave him the word. He and Marc were on standby. They'd arrive in fifteen minutes or so.

I bolted for the bathroom and took a quick shower, then I ran naked to my room and put on the clothes I'd selected a day ahead: slightly tight jeans and a snug red polo shirt that showed off my build. I sprayed on some cologne and then impatiently waited for Blake and Marc's arrival.

I hadn't long to wait. I trembled with excitement when there was a knock on the door. I forced myself to walk over slowly instead of bolting and ripping open the door.

Blake was wearing jeans and his letterman's jacket. Marc was dressed in baggy pants and an old worn leather jacket. I couldn't see what they were wearing underneath, but I was already about to breathe fire, so it hardly mattered.

"Nice place. Where's your bedroom?" Blake asked.

That was Blake, right to the point.

"This way," I said, leading them down the hall.

We entered the bedroom, and I closed the door for paranoia's sake. The guys slipped off their jackets and tossed them in the corner. Blake was wearing his football jersey, which stayed on his sexy body for about fifteen seconds until he yanked it off. Marc was wearing a tattered tee-shirt with holes in all the right places. Soon, his shirt was on the growing pile of discarded clothing.

I'd seen Blake's body before, but Marc's was all new. He was compact and defined just like I'd imagined, but a bit more muscular. I wanted to lean over and lick on his small brown nipples.

Soon, we were all naked and I don't think I'd ever been more turned on in my life. If I wasn't very careful I was going to lose control and truly embarrass myself. I drank in the sight of their hard, naked bodies. Blake was gorgeous, and Marc...damn he was sexy! I stepped up to Marc, pushed his blond bangs away from his face and pressed my lips to his. He responded. Yes! The sexy boy was into making out! We stood there and made out like crazy.

"Nice," Blake said.

Things only got hotter from there on. I have a thing for a nice chest, and I was all over both Blake and Marc's torsos. Of course, Blake pushed my head toward his crotch, but I didn't mind that in the least. I just opened up and gave into my desires.

After we'd been going at it for a while, Blake pushed Marc face down on my bed.

"You have supplies?" he asked.

I quickly pulled my condoms and lube out of my dresser drawer. Blake ignored the condoms, but grabbed the lube. I bit my lip to keep myself from saying anything. If they wanted to do it bare, that was their business. Marc definitely had no reservations about it.

I'd never watched two guys get it on before. I'd never even seen something like that in a magazine. I was madly turned on. Marc groaned as Blake entered him, but after that he didn't seem to feel any pain. My own experience bottoming for Blake had been quite different. It felt incredible after a while, but at first the pain was so intense I thought I was going to die.

I wasn't quite sure what to do with myself. This was all new territory for me. I ran my hands over Blake's back and his firm ass. I could feel Blake's buttocks tense and flex with each thrust. I didn't know if I could stand this much arousal for long.

I stood back and watched, feeling slightly like some kind of perv voyeur for doing so. It wasn't as if I was peeking through a window and spying on a couple during an intimate moment, however. This was my bedroom, and the three of us were in this together.

Blake rolled off Marc then motioned for me to take a turn. Marc turned over onto his back as I walked toward him. I was so nervous I trembled. I'd never done this before. What if I wasn't any good? The doubts ripped through my mind, but were quickly shoved to the side by pure animal lust. Nothing mattered to me at that moment but taking Marc.

I entered Marc without hesitation. Marc showed no sign of pain, but I don't think it would have mattered to me if he did. Something primitive was at work here. Something had clicked on in my mind, and I was running on instinct.

I let Marc have it, using every muscle in my body. It was as if I was releasing years of pent-up frustration and desperate need. I felt savage and powerful. I stared into Marc's eyes and saw my own animal passion mirrored there. My heart pounded in my chest. My breath came in gasps.

"Yeah, dude!" Blake said.

It was too much. I completely lost control. I tried, but I couldn't hold back. I cried out in sheer ecstasy, and then it was over. Humiliation crept over me.

"Damn, I thought *I* was wild," Blake said.

I looked at him as I stood there beside my bed. I grinned. Perhaps I didn't need to feel so humiliated after all.

Blake, Marc, and I continued going at it. Marc and Blake were completely different types of guys. There was a lot Blake would not do because he felt it took away from his masculinity. Blake was all about demonstrating his virility, and there was more than a touch of domination in his actions. Marc didn't hesitate to make out or show his appreciation for the male form with his lips and tongue. Marc was masculine, and yet he had a submissive side. He had no reservations about bottoming for Blake and me. Blake would never do that. He considered it being the girl. I was somewhere in between the two. I'd bottomed for Blake more than once—not entirely willingly—yet it wasn't forced on me. Part of me resisted being the bottom, perhaps for the same reason Blake wouldn't do it. I had a feeling Marc was the bravest of us all and more in touch with himself. He wasn't self-conscious like me. He didn't feel guilty about his desires and didn't seem to care what Blake and I thought about his desires, either. I wished I could be as together as Marc seemed to be.

The three of us had sex for a good three hours or more. We just kept going at it. I, for one, couldn't get enough. It was as if my lust was finally being satisfied. Something felt entirely natural about the things we were doing. I was not experienced, but so much of what I did was pure instinct. It was as if my actions were hard-wired into my mind and body, passed down through hundreds of generations.

Blake and I both topped Marc again before the evening was over. I'd never felt anything so intense in my entire life. When I cried out in ecstasy, I felt my orgasm throughout my entire body. I could only describe the feeling as bliss.

Blake and Marc departed at eleven. We could have kept going longer, but the danger that Tim would return would increase with every minute that passed. I wanted a wide safety margin. Besides, we were all well-satisfied. I even gave Marc a lingering kiss at the door. He was so sexy. Now, there was a boy I could date!

It didn't occur to me until I was in the shower that I'd done Marc bare—not once, but twice. All the color drained from my face, and I nearly dropped the soap when I realized I hadn't worn a condom. Fuck. Of course, I immediately began to think of all the diseases I could get. A sense of rising panic began to take over my mind. Blake had done Marc bare, too, and Blake thought condoms were just plain stupid. I wondered how many partners Blake had had, and what about Marc? How could I have been so stupid? I knew the answer to that; it was hanging between my legs. I'd been so worked up I'd allowed my dick to do my thinking for me. I just hoped thinking with my cock hadn't just gotten me into a world of trouble.

I finished showering, dried off, dressed, and made myself a cup of tea in the kitchen. I sat down at the kitchen table and tried to calm myself. It wasn't as if Marc could get pregnant. The chances he had any diseases were pretty slim, too. He definitely looked healthy, but I knew that didn't necessarily mean anything. I guessed I'd just have to wait and see. That was going to be fun. I knew I'd be worrying about it in the back of my mind. I had no one to blame but myself. One thing was for sure, I was going to think with my head and not my dick next time. I could just imagine what Tim would have to say if he knew what I'd done. He wasn't going to find out, however.   There was no way I'd admit to being so stupid.

Dane

Devon looked slightly fearful as he passed me in the hallway. He no doubt remembered Brandon's threat. If the expression on Devon's face was any indication, I didn't think he'd be giving me much trouble. If he did, I'd tell Brandon, and Devon knew it. If I was Devon, I wouldn't have dared to step out of line. I almost couldn't believe Brandon had once come close to killing Devon—actually killing him! Then again, I almost couldn't believe some of the things Devon had done. He was a good deal more dangerous than I'd thought. He was also one screwed-up boy. I still thought he was gay and just couldn't handle it. I couldn't imagine anyone hating gays so much without something to power that hatred. I guess I didn't need to dwell on it; I wasn't Devon's shrink.

I passed Tim as I continued down the hallway. We didn't have time to stop, but we grinned at each other. The mere sight of him made me feel as though I could walk on air. I wondered if guys like Brandon felt this way about their girls? I guess I'd never know, but I hoped so. I wouldn't want anyone to miss out on such a wonderful feeling.

I know I'm probably kind of sickeningly gushing over my boyfriend and how happy I am about him. At least Tim and I aren't like one of those heterosexual couples who think everyone is just dying to watch them paw each other and make out. Tim and I do some limited PDA—that's public display of affection for those of you who don't know—but we mainly keep our physical relationship on the down low. It's not so much because we're gay, either, although some people, guys in particular, probably just can't handle seeing two guys kiss. Giving Tim a hug or even a quick kiss is fine, but more would just be too much. That stuff is between Tim and me, and I don't want anyone else watching—unless they're invited. I'm kidding about the "unless they're invited" part—mostly.

My happiness wasn't all about Tim—mostly, maybe, but not all. I couldn't believe how much I enjoyed school now. Isn't that just sick? If I kept it up, I was probably in danger of becoming a bookworm, but I didn't even care. I guess I didn't hate school in Marmont, at least when I wasn't used as a punching bag, but school was a lot more fun now. Homework was more fun, too, but that's because Tim and I sometimes did ours together. We took frequent make-out breaks whenever possible. It's hard to believe how much more enjoyable it is to study for a test when you know you're going to lock lips with your boyfriend at any minute.

The morning flew by. Tim and I met at my locker as usual right before lunch and made it to the cafeteria a little earlier than usual. There wasn't even much of a line. I caught a whiff of corn dogs before we even reached the silverware. This day was just getting better and better! I followed Tim through the line. In addition to corn dogs, there were macaroni and cheese, green beans, Jell-o salad, and apple crisp. I loved apple crisp!

After we paid, Tim and I headed for our usual table. The table would be filled with boisterous guys soon, mostly gay, but not all, and, of course, the odd girl. I almost laughed when I thought of what Casey would have to say about being called an "odd girl." I don't mean it like that, anyway. Casper and Brendan were the only ones seated at our table at the moment. We joined them.

"Hey, we should get a game up after school," I said.

"A game?" Brendan asked.

"Yeah, the new house, if you can call it that, has its own gym. We could play basketball and maybe even invite some of the guys."

"Invite some of the guys to what?" Brandon said, sitting down with his tray. Jon was a mere step behind.

"Playing basketball in the gym at my place, or something like that."

"Maybe dodge ball," Tim said.

"I am the King of Dodge Ball!" Jon said, standing and flexing his arms over his head.

"You're the King of Cocksucking," Brandon said, "but we won't go into that."

"No way. All the guys say you're the best! You should be, after all that practice."

"You guys are crazy," said Tim. "You know, some of us here could be insulted by your remarks."

"Okay, okay," Brandon said. "You're the King of Cocksucking, then. Isn't he, Dane? Happy now?"

I could feel my face go slightly red.

"Yeah, he is," I said.

Now it was Tim's turn to go a bit red.

"What are you guys talking about?" Casey asked as she sat down. Ethan and Nathan were right behind her.

"Don't ask," Tim said.

"We were talking about getting together at my place to play basketball…"

"Dodge ball!" Jon interrupted. "It's got to be dodge ball!"

"You'll have to forgive him," Brandon said. "Jon developed a fixation for dodge ball in grade school, and he's never gotten over it."

Jon stuck out his tongue at Brandon.

"Okay, dodge ball," I said. "We thought we might break in the gym, so to speak."

"You're not invited, though. You're a girl. Girls can't handle dodge ball," Brandon said.

"Brandon, you truly are an idiot," Ethan said.

"See! I'm not the only one who thinks so!" Jon said.

"Oh, that's it!" Casey said. "I'm in! I'm going to kick your ass, Brandon Hanson. You'll be out faster than you lose control when you're doing a girl."

"Hey!" Brandon said.

"Or a guy," Jon said.

"Hey!" Brandon said, louder. "I have incredible control."

"That's right," Jon said. "It comes from thousands of hours of jerking off."

"Oh, you'd know all about whacking it, Jon. It's a wonder your dick doesn't fall off."

Shawn walked up with his tray just as Brandon was finishing going off on Jon.

"So why should Jon's dick fall off?" Shawn asked. "Has he been doing Brandon's girlfriend again?"

"I don't know why I sit with you guys!" Brandon said.

"Because no one else will have you?" Jon suggested.

"Oh, screw you, Deerfield. Your mom has been paying me to be your friend for years."

"Yeah, well, I don't want to say what your mom pays me for, but you should start expecting a baby brother any time now."

"I'm not going to ask," Tristan said as he sat down.

"You're smarter than everyone else here," Casey said.

"He's not smarter," Jon said. "It's just the glasses; the glasses make him look smart."

Tristan gave Shawn a significant look, but Shawn looked away. I wondered what that was about.

"Anyway…," Casey said, "Dane is having a get-together at his place after school. We're going to play…"

"Dodge ball!" Jon interrupted.

"Yes, dodge ball, and Brandon is going down," Casey finished.

"On my…" Jon began, but I cut him off.

"You're invited, of course."

"Unless you're scared," Brandon said.

"Of you?" Tristan asked. "I don't think so, straight boy."

Brandon grinned.

"Okay, is everyone invited but me?" Shawn asked.

"Leave out my hero? No way! Of course, you're invited," I said. "Besides, we need a lot of people for dodge ball. If any of you want to bring a friend or two, go for it."

"Oh, so I'm really just a filler," Shawn said, unsuccessfully pretending to be hurt.

"I always thought so," Brandon said.

Shawn flipped him off. I loved these guys.

"Damn, I've got work, but maybe I can get off early," Shawn said.

"We have our usual stuff to do at the farm," Ethan said. "What time were you thinking?"

"How about like...seven. Can everyone be done with whatever by then?"

"I'll see what I can do," Shawn said.

Everyone else nodded their agreement.

Lunch period ended without Tim and me slipping away to get it on. We'd talked too much. There was more to life than sex, however, although sex was definitely my favorite! We couldn't rush through lunch and disappear too often or Shawn might catch on. He'd probably crap his pants if he knew what Tim and I got up to in the auditorium. If we ever got caught by a teacher... I didn't even want to think about it. The risk was worth it, however.

Tim and I walked home together. Since we were all getting together at seven to play dodge ball, it didn't make much sense for him to go home only to come back. Shawn said it was cool. My parents were home, and besides, when we were at my place Shawn wasn't responsible for us. I still wished he'd let Tim and me get it on in the loft. That would be perfect!

We didn't really plan it, but when Tim and I reached my room we looked at each other, and that's all it took. Our lips were locked together before our backpacks hit the floor. Our tongues were in each other's mouth before our jackets were off. We didn't dare get naked, but our hands were everywhere.

I thought my zipper might burst from the strain. Whenever I was with Tim, it was instant hardness. When Tim's hand rubbed on the front of my jeans...damn.

I slipped my hand into Tim's jeans as we made out, and his hand was down my pants in seconds, driving me crazy. I think we might have both lost control and made a mess in our jeans, but a knock at the door ended things way fast. Tim and I ripped apart. My hand was still caught in his jeans as Mom opened the door. I barely disentangled myself before she entered. As it was, I had to quickly sit down to hide my obvious erection. Tim dropped into a nearby chair to hide his own.

Mom looked at us suspiciously. Our rumpled clothing and the fact we were teenaged boys no doubt gave us away.

"I didn't know you were bringing Tim home after school," she said.

"Yeah. A bunch of the guys are coming over later to play dodge ball in the gym. It's okay, isn't it?"

"Of course."

"Cool. Tim and I are going to study before they get here. Can Tim stay for supper? Everyone is coming over about seven."

"Yes, he can. You're always welcome, Tim."

"Thanks, Mrs. Haakonson."

"Why don't you two get started on your homework. If your friends are coming over at seven, you don't have much time."

What she really meant was: "I want to see you studying instead of molesting each other."

"Sure thing."

Tim and I grabbed our backpacks and moved toward the library table. Mom lingered until we began pulling books out, then she left us in peace.

"Do you think she noticed?"

I gave Tim a look that said "duh," and he laughed.

"We need some time alone, soon," Tim said.

"Don't I know it? Let's hit the books. You know Mom will be up here checking on us in a few. It's as certain as the setting of the sun."

Tim and I sat side by side, so close our arms were touching, but we did study. Yeah, we took frequent breaks for short make-out sessions, but we did our homework. Mom dropped in to check

144

on us a couple of times, but I guess we looked innocent enough not to worry her too much. Our feigned innocence was all part of our evil plan to lure my parents into a false sense of security. Once that was accomplished, Tim and I could go at it, if we were careful. Until then, we'd get by with what we could. I was giving some thought to sneaking a mattress or something in the storage area under the bleachers in the gym. If Tim and I did it there, I wagered we wouldn't be the first. I bet a lot of fooling around went on way back in the '50s and before, just like it does now.

When the appointed time was near, Tim and I walked downstairs and wandered around the entrance hallway. There was no way we'd hear anyone knocking on the front doors from my room.

"These old trophies are really cool," Tim said.

"Yeah, it's hard to believe they were just left here."

"Same for all the team and club photos on the walls."

"Stuff like that is everywhere here. I keep noticing photos, plaques, and trophies all over the place that I missed before."

"You'd think they would have taken all this stuff to the new VHS when it was built."

"Yeah, but there's so much of it. VHS has stuff like this all over the place, too. Can you imagine what it would look like if all these pictures and trophies were there too?"

"I guess stuff kind of builds up over the decades."

A knock on the glass of one of the front doors caught our attention. It was Shawn and Casey.

"Still pretending to be a straight boy?" Tim asked as he opened the door.

"Screw you, little brother."

Tim arched an eyebrow, and I forced perverted thoughts from my mind.

In short order, Brandon and Jon arrived, then Ethan, Nathan, Brendan, Casper, and Dave, Nathan's little brother. Dave was about eleven and looked like a miniature version of Nathan.

"I guess we're just missing Tristan," I said.

"Why don't you take everyone to the gym," Tim said. "I'll wait here for Tristan. You can give them the tour. I've already seen it."

"Are you talking about the gym, Tim, or something else?" Jon asked.

"You perv," Brandon said. "Only you would make something sexual out of that."

"Oh, like you weren't thinking it, too."

"No. I don't fantasize about dick all the time like you do."

"I think you have me confused with Shawn."

"Hey!" Shawn said. "Leave me out of your verbal warfare. I'm just an innocent bystander."

"Innocent, my ass," Brandon said, gazing at Shawn. "You've had some dick recently. I can tell just by looking at you."

"Yeah, you'd know all about the look guys get when they've had some dick, don't you, Brandon?" Jon asked.

"Yeah, from looking at you."

"I'm going to smack your heads together," Casey said. She looked at Dave for a moment, probably thinking he shouldn't hear such things. He lived in a house full of teenage boys, however, so I'm sure he was used to it. He was laughing, so I doubted it embarrassed him.

"Oh, yeah! I love it rough with a babe!" Brandon said.

"Just ignore them," Nathan said. "Maybe they'll go away."

"Good luck with that. I've been trying to for years, and they haven't gone away yet," Ethan said.

"I'm feeling unappreciated," Jon said. "What about you, Brandon?"

"I'm truly hurt," Brandon said, pretending he was about to cry.

"You can forget an acting career," Casper said.

"Let me show you guys the gym," I said quickly. "Thanks, Tim."

Tim and I grinned at each other, and then I led the little group down the hallway.

"Hey, look, if Brandon went to school way back, he'd be sitting there," Jon said, pointing to a chair outside the old principal's office.

"At least I didn't get sent to the office for jerking off in the restroom," Brandon said.

I wondered if that was true, but I wasn't about to ask.

"Don't you guys ever stop?" Casey asked.

"Stop what?" Brandon and Jon asked together.

"I think they're twins who were separated at birth," Ethan said.

"That's a scary thought," Brendan said.

"It must feel odd living here," Casey said, no doubt to cut Brandon and Jon off. "I think it's incredible, though."

"Yeah, it's cool," Jon said, "but a little like getting life-time detention. Just think about it, Dane will never get out of school."

"Look at it another way," I said. "I rule this school."

"Maybe your parents will buy an old school, Jon," Brandon said. "Then you'd have a chance to rule at school, too. It sure isn't going to happen at VHS."

"Bite me, Brandon."

"Don't say it!" Casey ordered as Brandon opened his mouth.

"You like to order people around, don't you?" Brandon asked. "If we were the Peanuts gang, you'd be Lucy."

"You'd be Pigpen," Casey retorted.

"Hey!"

"In all fairness, Brandon spends more time on his personal appearance than most girls, not that it helps much," Jon said.

"I do hope you're on the opposite team," Brandon said meaningfully.

We entered the gym. Since we'd be using it (and I'd finally figured out where the light switches were), I turned on the overhead lights.

"Now, this is seriously cool," Ethan said.

"Brings back fond memories of molesting all those boys, huh?" Brandon said. "I mean wrestling—wrestling all those boys."

"You want to wrestle now, Brandon?" Ethan growled.

"And make Nathan jealous?"

"Okay!" I said. "While we're waiting on Tim and Tristan, what about teams?"

"How about team captains choosing?" Brandon asked.

"Oh, I hate that," Jon said. "That always sucked in gym class. And don't even say it, Hanson."

"I wasn't going to say anything about sucking. You sound kind of bitter, though. Always picked last, Jon?"

"No, but someone is always picked last. It's so cruel."

"Let's just put names in a hat," Casey said. "I'll write down everyone's name and then one of you can draw for teams."

She pulled a piece of paper and a pen out of her pocket, walked to the bleachers, sat down, and began writing. Soon, she stood.

"Can I borrow your cap, Jon?" Casey asked.

Jon handed it to her.

"Okay, so who picks?"

"Not Jon," Brandon said. "He's too sneaky."

Casey glared at Jon to keep him from retorting.

"How about Casper? You trust Casper, don't you?"

"Well, outside the shower room, yeah, but I wouldn't want to drop my…"

"Shut up, Brandon," said several of us at the same time. Brandon laughed.

"Okay, Casper, you pick."

"If we end up with an odd number, Jon can be the extra. He throws like a girl," Brandon said.

"You know I'm going to kick your ass, don't you, Brandon?" Casey said.

Jon laughed.

"Okay, I'll just pick out names, and that will be one team. Whatever names I don't draw out will be the other team," Casper said.

"Sounds good," Ethan said.

"Okay, here goes," Casper said as he began pulling out names. "Ethan. Dane. Brandon. Nathan. Brendan. Me."

"Who's me?" Brandon asked.

"I am," Jon said.

"No, I am," I said.

"You can't be me. I'm me. Besides, that would mean you were picked twice," Jon said.

"I'm me!" Casper said loudly. "Casper. The last name is Casper!"

"You could have just said so," Brandon said.

Casper growled in frustration.

"I'm so glad you're on the other team, Brandon. I'm taking you out," Casey said.

"On a date? Don't you like girls?"

"Even if I did like guys I wouldn't go out with you, Brandon Hanson. You are so going down."

Brandon started to open his mouth.

"Don't say it!" Casey said.

Dave laughed.

"Okay, now we just have to wait for Tim and Tristan," Casey said.

We hadn't long to wait, but Tim and Tristan weren't alone. Nate London was with them. Shawn didn't look too happy about that.

"Who gets Nate?" Brandon asked.

"I bet you want him—bad," Jon said.

"If I want your opinion, Deerfield, I'll…"

"We'll flip a coin. Call it in the air, Jon," Casey said.

"Tails," Jon said as the quarter sailed into the air and came back down.

Casey uncovered the coin.

"Heads. Nate is on the other team."

"No fair," Jon said. "They have all the big guys."

"Yeah," Brandon said, grabbing his crotch.

"Big guys?" Casper asked. "Have you looked at me lately?"

I laughed. I wasn't especially tall or muscular myself.

"Bigger isn't always better," Casey said. "Especially in dodge ball."

"You hear that, Hanson. Bigger isn't always better. There's hope for you yet."

"I've got more than you've got, Deerfield."

"Anyone have a measuring tape?" Casey asked.

"Why?" I asked. I'm a little slow on the uptake sometimes, okay?

"So we can get this over with. Just pull them out, Brandon and Jon, and we'll measure. We can settle this once and for all."

"Oh, you'd like that, wouldn't you, Casey?" Brandon said.

"Lame comeback, Brandon. You do understand the concept of lesbian, right?" Jon asked.

Brandon stuck out his tongue.

150

"The last thing I'm interested in is what you have in your pants," Casey said.

"Let's just play. We'll flip for who gets the ball first," I said.

Brandon grabbed Dave and lifted him off the floor.

"Okay, heads or tails."

Dave giggled.

"Let's use a quarter," Casey said. "Call it in the air, Brandon."

She flipped the quarter up in the air.

"Tails," Brandon said. "Always tails…"

Jon rolled his eyes at Brandon.

"It's tails. Your ball."

Our team took the end of the basketball court in front of the stage. Brandon tossed the ball up in the air with one hand and caught it while selecting his first target. Brandon eyed Casey and then made a lightning-fast throw towards Jon. The ball smacked the wooden floor hard, barely missing Jon. Shawn captured the ball and rifled it at Nate. Another miss. I caught the ball after it bounced off the floor.

"Let's make this more interesting," I said, walking toward the stage. I pulled another ball out of the box I'd set there earlier.

"Yeah!" yelled Brandon.

I tossed the extra ball to Casper, and we stepped toward the line together. I hurled my ball toward Tristan, and Casper went for Casey. Two misses. Tristan was a lot faster than I'd imagined he'd be. He also caught the ball after it bounced and rocketed it straight back at me. If I hadn't ducked, it would've nailed me. The other ball came close to getting Nate.

It was mayhem after that. The balls flew back and forth with lightning speed. I just barely dodged out of the way three times.

"You throw like a girl!" Brandon yelled at Casey across the court.

"If only you threw that well!" she yelled back.

That was the start of some major insults on the part of Brandon. He taunted Casey every time one of her throws missed the mark. Casey tossed back a few witty remarks, but mainly just grinned at Brandon, the way you'd imagine the Cheshire Cat might grin at a mouse.

"Is that all you've got?" Casey asked after Brandon had hurled the ball toward her with every ounce of his strength.

"Oh, I've got a lot more," Brandon said, grabbing his crotch, again.

"Speaking for those of us who've seen what you've got…," Jon said, and then slowly shook his head.

"Yeah, you've seen it. Right after you… Damn!"

Both balls smacked into Brandon at once; one nailed him in the chest and the other in the left shoulder. Casey and Tristan gave each other a high five and then Jon joined their celebration.

"I told you your mouth would get you in trouble someday," Casey said.

Brandon crossed his arms, glared at them, and growled, but then he grinned and laughed.

"My teammates will avenge me," he said, then walked over and took a seat on the bleachers.

The balls sailed back and forth. Nathan was eliminated next. It wasn't looking so good for our team. We'd lost two players, and the other team hadn't lost any. We had the biggest guys, but this was a game of speed.

I nailed Jon on the shoulder as he dodged a ball hurled at him by Ethan. Brandon howled with delight.

"Way to go, Dane! Yeah!"

Jon gave us both the finger with a double flip-off, but he was grinning as he did it.

"You wish, Deerfield! You wish!" Brandon yelled from across the court.

I began to notice that Shawn was taking special aim at Nate. He tried to hit others, but he went after Nate more than anyone else and tried to nail him hard. There was a look of focused concentration on Shawn's face whenever he stalked Nate. There was a certain amount of anger in his eyes, too. I wondered if there was some history between those two. Shawn was obviously not happy when Nate had arrived with Tristan. Could it be as simple as jealousy? Tristan and Nate had been spending quite a bit of time together. Maybe there was something going on between them more than friendship. If so, I could see where it would piss Shawn off.

Smack! A ball nailed me right in the abs—hard! Owwww.

"Sorry," Dave yelled. "I thought you'd try to dodge it."

"It's okay," I said, walking toward the bleachers clutching my stomach. I guess I'd spent a little too much time thinking about Shawn.

"Taken out by an eleven-year-old. How humiliating," Brandon said.

"Blow me, Brandon."

"Yeah, you'd like that."

"Hell, yeah. I hear you're good."

Brandon grinned and flipped me off. I wished Jon could have heard me. He would have been proud.

Ethan, Brendan, Nate, and Casper of our team remained. We'd made a sad showing. When our side had both balls, Ethan called a quick huddle. I couldn't hear what he was saying, but I hoped he had a good plan.

Dave used the opportunity to come close to the line and shake his butt at his opponents. Ethan whipped a ball at him and just barely missed. Dave stuck out his tongue and ran back to his teammates laughing.

The balls sailed back and forth. Ethan nailed my boyfriend. Well, you know what I mean. Casper narrowly missed getting taken out by Tristan. Brendan was tagged by Casey.

Ethan's plan was executed, and Casey was out before she knew what hit her. I don't know how they coordinated their attack without even seeming to look at each other, but Ethan whipped a ball at Casey, and then Casper nailed her as she dodged to the right.

Things were even, and soon Tristan had been taken out by the same maneuver, only this time Casper made the initial throw while Nate nailed Tristan.

Shawn called Dave over when they possessed both balls. He put his arm over Dave's shoulders, spoke to him for a moment, then they walked away from each other. They both turned after four paces and hurled their balls at Nate. Shawn looked as though he aimed directly for Nate's face. Nate dived to the ground, but both balls nailed Ethan, who was just behind him. A second later, Casper had taken out Shawn with a lightning-fast throw that caught Shawn completely off-guard. Now, it was Casper and Nate against Dave.

"We're coming for you, little boy," Nate taunted just after Dave had thrown at him and missed.

Dave giggled, boldly turned and shook his butt at Nate and Casper, and then darted to the side, avoiding both balls. Now, Dave held one ball in each hand and eyed his opponents with glee.

Dave rapidly fired off one ball and then the next at Nate, who dodged them both. Nate tossed one ball to Casper, then fired off the other at Dave, who caught it in the air.

"Noooo!!!!" Nate yelled in anguish.

"Another one taken out by an eleven-year-old," Brandon said. "It's a wonder our football team ever wins."

"I'm gonna get you, kid," Nate said, crossing his arms and staring at Dave.

"Only if you can catch me!"

Nate walked over to the bleachers. He was a hottie. If Tristan and Nate did have something going, I could understand Tristan's interest in him. I loved Nate's curly blond hair and green eyes and his body...damn. If I wasn't in love with Tim...but I was, so Nate was merely eye candy.

Casper and Dave paced each other. They threw fast and hard when they tried to nail each other, but with one-on-one there weren't many surprises.

"Come on, Casper. Take out the little squirt!" Nate yelled.

"Yeah, come on!" Brandon yelled. "We can't lose to a little kid!"

Dave loved it. He giggled and laughed as he dodged Casper's attempts to take him out. My money was on Casper. Dave barely avoided getting nailed time and again. I was surprised Casper wasn't in some sport. He was good for a little guy.

I thought Casper had Dave, but he missed him by a hair. Casper immediately fired off another shot. Dave caught it. Casper looked stunned. Both Brandon and Nate howled in despair. Dave jumped up and down with his arms over his head. Dave's team put him up on their shoulders and carried him around the gym cheering.

When our opponents finally stopped rubbing their win in our faces, Brandon and Nate stepped up to Dave, crossed their arms and stared down at the eleven-year-old.

"We'll be looking for you in the parking lot, kid," Brandon said.

Dave giggled.

"I give up," Brandon said, shaking his head. "We can't even intimidate a kid."

That just made Dave laugh more.

"Okay, let's play again," Brandon said. "We get Dave this time."

"Forget it," Tristan said. "You are not getting our best player."

"Come on. We'll trade you Ethan and Dane for Dave and your worst player. That would be Jon."

"Hey!" Ethan, Jon, and I yelled simultaneously.

Brandon grinned.

"We'll keep the same teams," Nate said. "They just got lucky."

"Luck, my ass," Jon said.

"What about your ass?" Brandon asked. "Did you say huge or easy?"

"Oh, no. Don't you two get started," Casey said. "Let's play."

"If you tag me out, I'm coming for you, kid," Nate said, pointing at Dave, who just giggled again.

"Let's use four balls this time," I said.

With four balls in play, I couldn't begin to keep track of the action. I was too busy trying to survive. Nathan, Ethan, Tim, and Casey were all eliminated in the first two minutes, followed quickly by Tristan, Nate, Brendan, and myself. Casper took out Shawn first, then Jon. That left Dave facing Brandon and Casper.

"Well, well, well. We meet again," Brandon said.

"Do you want to just surrender now, or do you want to humiliate yourself again?" Dave said.

"You're going down, kid," Brandon said.

Brandon whipped a ball at Dave, who dodged it effortlessly. With four balls and only three players, someone was constantly taking a shot at someone else. Those of us who'd already been tagged out sat on the bleachers and urged the combatants on.

Dave fired off a shot at Brandon and nailed him.

"No!" yelled Brandon. "Noooooo!"

That made Dave laugh.

"Come on, Casper!" Ethan yelled. "It's up to you now!"

"Yeah! Take out that little punk!" Brandon said.

Dave thought it was great fun. I had the feeling he was having one of the best days of his life. Casper and Dave fired off balls at each other fast and hard, but none hit their mark. I thought Dave had Casper with a particularly fast shot, but Casper dived out of the way. He would probably have made a good goalie. Casper came up holding two balls. He whipped one at Dave with his right hand and then nailed him with the second ball thrown from his left. Now it was our turn to cheer and carry Casper around the gym.

We just hung out after that. Some of us played basketball, some just talked, and some explored the gym. I took everyone on a tour of the old school, and then we headed for the cafeteria. Mom had made chocolate-chip and oatmeal cookies! We all had a blast.

Shawn had a good time, but he avoided both Nate and Tristan. He looked at Nate now and then, and I could read jealousy in his eyes. He gazed at Tristan some, too, but then his eyes revealed only sadness. I hoped Shawn could get over Tristan quickly. Shawn could surely find himself a boyfriend. He was sexy, funny, kind, and a hottie! I wasn't quite sure what he saw in Tristan, anyway. Tristan was extremely good looking, but he wasn't athletic, he wasn't built, and…well, he just didn't seem right for Shawn at all. I guess Shawn couldn't help it if he was attracted to him, though. Things like that don't have to make sense. Nate would have been a much better match for Shawn.

Tim and I held hands and kissed now and then. A couple of our kisses were lingering, and we had to break it off before either of us got too excited. Momentary thoughts of slipping off somewhere private entered my mind, but there was no way we'd get away with that. We were surrounded by too many people.

"Damn, you homos are worse than us straight guys," Brandon said when he noticed Tim and me kissing again.

"You're just jealous because you don't get to kiss Tim," I said.

Tim blushed slightly, but he smiled.

"Oh, like I couldn't do a whole lot better than Tim if I was a homo."

"If?" Jon said.

"Yes, if, jock-sniffer."

"There is no one better," I said.

"Oh, please, not another one!" Brandon said. "What is with you gay guys? You all just latch onto each other. Haven't you ever heard of playing the field?"

"Maybe they're just not sluts like you, Brandon," Casey said.

"God help me," Brandon said. "I'm beginning to like you, Casey."

"Oh, you know you already like me."

"I'll never tell. Seriously, though, haven't you noticed all the homos are like…connected for life. It's like they're married!"

Nathan leaned his head against Ethan's shoulder.

"Just like that!" Brandon said, pointing at Ethan and Nathan. "I don't think we could pry those two apart. At least, Shawn has the good sense not to tie himself down."

Shawn didn't say anything, but he couldn't keep from glancing quickly at Tristan.

"I bet Shawn gets more sex than any of you," Brandon said.

The expression on Shawn's face made me wonder if he had been getting some lately. He looked like someone with a secret. Tim and I looked at each other, and Tim raised his eyebrows.

"Not everything is about sex," Casey said.

"You're only saying that because you aren't a guy. Guys need sex constantly."

"Yeah, and don't ever sleep over at Brandon's or you'll understand that only too well," Jon said.

"What's that supposed to mean?" Brandon asked.

That began another round of insults and innuendo between Brandon and Jon. They really went at each other.

"Oh, look, dinner theatre," Brendan said, biting into a cookie.

The rest of us laughed, but Brandon and Jon kept going at each other. I could almost picture them arguing and hurling insults at each other for all eternity.

I was wiped out when everyone left. I went straight up to my room and crawled into bed. I think I was asleep before my head even hit the pillow.

Shawn

"That was a blast!" Tim said as we entered the loft. "We've got to play dodge ball again sometime."

"Yeah."

Tim paused and gazed at me.

"What's the matter, big bro?"

"Nothing."

"Bullshit."

"Did you see Nate and Tristan together?"

"Together? No. Nate was hanging more with Brendan and me. He would've talked to you, too, if you didn't keep giving him the cold shoulder."

"So I was kind of obvious?"

"Duh! You've got to get over Tristan. Get yourself laid already."

I didn't respond. Tim peered at me.

"You did it with Blake again, didn't you?"

"That's none of your business."

"So, I'll take that as a 'yes.' "

"You can take it as a 'none of your business.' "

"Shawn, this is so stupid. Let's just make a deal. Just pretend you don't notice whatever Dane and I do while he's here, and you and Blake can fuck like rabbits."

"We've been through this, Tim!"

"Yeah, and it's stupid. You're horny. I'm horny. We've got our own place. I've got a boyfriend, and you should have no trouble getting guys. I saw the way you and Blake were looking at each other in Ofarim's. You were practically having sex right there on the counter."

If my little brother only knew.

"No, Tim."

"You were a lot more fun when we lived with Dad."

"Maybe you'd like to go back!"

Tim's eyes grew watery.

"Tim, I'm sorry. I didn't mean that. You know I want you here. Just lay off, though, will you?"

"Okay. I'm sorry, too. I just…"

"You're just a horny little bastard."

"Yeah, and you're not helping the situation."

I started to open my mouth, but Tim threw up his hands.

"I know! I know! I'm just saying, and seriously, Shawn, you need to get laid or at least whack off. Go visit Blake…again."

I shot Tim a look.

"Just some helpful advice, big bro. I do, um, kind of like you, you know."

"I kind of like you, too. Now, go away."

Tim grinned and departed for his room. I made myself a cup of tea and sat down at the table. I gazed out the window, thinking. Tim was right about one thing: I needed to get laid. I'd recently had a three-way with Blake and Marc, but I still needed it bad. The pressure was relentless. I thought I might actually go insane.

"Screw this," I said out loud.

I grabbed the phone and dialed Blake.

"Hey, what are you doing tonight?" I asked as soon as he answered.

"Being bored out of my mind. My aunt is visiting."

"Can you get away?"

"I wish, but I've been threatened with death if I try to escape."

"Damn."

"Do I detect a little desperation there, Shawn, or maybe a lot?"

"Not desperation, just intense need."

"I hear ya. I wish I could get away."

I paused for a moment.

"Do you have Marc's number?"

"Of course."

"Can I have it?"

"What's it worth to you?"

I could almost hear Blake's smirk. It made me want him even more.

"A lot."

"Mmm. I like that. I'll remember it, too."

Blake gave me Marc's number.

"You owe me," he said and then hung up.

I dialed Marc's number. Not only was he home and up for meeting, but he agreed to meet me in the parking lot of VHS in just a few minutes. At last, something was going right! I told Tim I was heading out, put on my jacket, and stepped out the door.

It was a short drive to school, but it seemed to take forever. Finally, I pulled into the parking lot. There were only three cars there and only one with its lights on. I pulled up beside Marc, and he hopped from his car into mine.

"I know a dark side street," he said.

I followed his directions. I parked the car, and seconds later we were all over each other. There were no street lights nearby, and in the darkness no one could see in the car. I shot my tongue into Marc's mouth and tried to devour him alive.

Getting naked was a little too risky, but we unfastened each other's belts, and soon our pants were open. Marc's hand drove me insane with need. Before I lost control, I leaned over and engulfed him.

Car head is beyond hot. I went at it like a wild boy. I would have kept right on, but Marc pushed me away and then went down on me. I can't even begin to describe the feeling of pure pleasure that engulfed me. I could feel myself coming closer and closer to the edge. I knew I should have pushed Marc off, but I just couldn't. Instead, I moaned and lost control. I swear my eyes rolled back in my head.

I didn't leave Marc hanging. I went right back to work on him the second he leaned back in the seat. In minutes, his moans filled the car, too. I didn't pull off until he was completely finished.

"We've got to do this more often," Marc said as we both zipped up.

"Definitely." I leaned over and gave him a lingering kiss.

I drove Marc back to his car and then drove home. Tim was studying at the kitchen table when I walked in.

"You look way more relaxed."

"I am."

"You got laid, didn't you?"

"Let's just say I took your advice."

"Who was it? Blake?"

"None of your business."

"Come on. I want a name. I want details!"

"You have a boyfriend. You don't need to live vicariously through me."

"Come on. I'll just keep pestering you until you tell me."

"Okay. His name is Marc. We made out and gave each other car head. That's all the detail you're getting."

"Does he go to VHS?"

"You'll never know."

"Yeah, right! I guess that's good enough for now," Tim said. "Feel better?"

"Yes."

Tim laughed.

"I told you so! You know, I've been feeling a little stressed out recently. If I could have Dane over and…"

"Nice try, Tim. Have a good night."

"You're going to bed already?"

"Yes. I'm tired, and I have to get up early tomorrow, as usual."

"Sex can really wear you out. Pace yourself."

I didn't rise to the bait. Instead, I walked over to Tim and kissed him on the forehead. He smiled at me.

"Good night, Shawn."

I closed my bedroom door so I wouldn't hear Tim moving around, then I undressed and climbed into bed. I yawned. I put my arms behind my head and stared at the ceiling as I waited to drift off to sleep. Getting it on with Marc in the car was exciting. I was getting a little stiff just thinking about it, if you know what I mean. Maybe I'd been wrong to obsess over Tristan. Maybe I should have just been having fun with guys like Marc and Blake all along. I had my whole life to settle down with just one guy. Is that really what I wanted, anyway? I was gay. I didn't have to play by the rules. Nothing said I had to attach myself to one guy for life. I'd thought that was what I wanted with Tristan, but now I wasn't so sure. Being with Blake and Marc made me feel soooo good. Sex felt…natural. Sure, there were a lot of people with religious objections to it, but wasn't that really no more than their personal opinion? Even if the Bible stated flat out that "Sex is bad!" that didn't make it true. I didn't really know what the Bible said. I wasn't all that religious. I did know that God, whoever or whatever he or she was, didn't write the Bible. Men wrote it. Ordinary men. Why should their opinion be any more valuable than mine?

Focus, Shawn. I yawned again. Focusing was easier said than done. There was no need to think about it too much, anyway. Blake and Marc were willing, and they were hot, so I was going to have sex with them whenever I had the chance. Why shouldn't I, after all? I was single and free.

I was going to play it safe from now on. I wasn't going to let myself get caught up in the moment and throw caution to the wind. I seriously doubted I'd catch any diseases even if I did it bare with Blake and Marc all the time, but it was pretty damned stupid to take the chance. Bottoming and especially topping did feel better bare, but not *that* much better.

I had to think of Tim, too. I had to be a good example. Not that I planned on him ever seeing me having sex, but how could I go on about safe sex if I was ignoring my own advice? I was smart enough to be aware of my own ignorance, too. Maybe doing it bare was riskier than I thought. Maybe there was something dangerous about it that no one knew about.

I thought back to Marc and me in the car. We'd both swallowed. Wasn't that kind of unsafe, too? I didn't think it was nearly as unsafe as fucking bare, but maybe it was unsafe in ways no one knew about yet. Where did I draw the line? The only way to be perfectly safe was never to have sex. Like that was going happen! Besides, if I never had sex, I could still get hit by a truck or gunned down or something. Life wasn't safe. I just had to limit my risks.

I slowly drifted off to sleep. I began to dream of Marc and what we did in my Cutlass…

***

I spotted Marc in the hallway of VHS almost the first thing the next day. He grinned at me and wiggled his eyebrows in a way that made me laugh. That wasn't the last Marc sighting of the day, either. I saw him three more times before school let out. It seemed a bit odd that I spotted him so often. It wasn't as if I'd never seen him before we'd hooked up, but I'd rarely noticed him in the halls. He was a very good-looking guy, so he should have caught my attention, but then there were a lot of attractive boys wandering the halls of my high school. I guess it's just easier to spot someone once you've slept with him.

The sight of Marc turned me on like mad, but then the sight of a lot of guys got me going. I was seventeen, after all. I thought about hooking up with Marc again—and as soon as possible—but another thought crept into my head, too. What would it be like to date Marc? I wasn't enamored with him as I had been (and perhaps still was) with Tristan. I wasn't in love with him. He was plenty sexy, however, and he possessed a goofy quality I liked. His goofy side hadn't manifested itself during the three-way with Blake, nor during our mutual blowjobs in the car, but every time I saw him in the hallway he gave me a puckish grin, and his expression was goofy and subtly suggestive. I had a feeling Marc could be fun even when we weren't naked.

I began looking around for Marc during the break between the last two periods and again right after school but failed to spot him. It was Monday, one of the two days I didn't work, and I was thinking about asking Marc out. I thought about it more on the drive home, and by the time I arrived I decided I was going to go for it. What did I have to lose? If he didn't want to go out, maybe we could get together for another session in my Cutlass.

As soon as I got home, I dialed Marc's number.

"Who are you calling?" Tim asked, as he poured himself a glass of milk.

"Marc."

"Ohhhh, round two!"

"Something like that," I said.

"My brother, the horn dog!"

"Shut up, Tim."

"Hey."

"Marc? It's Shawn."

"What's up?"

"I saw you at school today."

"Yeah, I know." I could almost hear Marc smiling at my stupidity. It was time to be direct.

"I was wondering if you'd like to catch a bite to eat sometime—this evening, if you're not busy. I don't work tonight."

"Are you asking me out on a date?"

"Well, yeah, kind of...I just...I just thought it would be cool to get to know you."

"I think you know me pretty well already, at least parts of me." Marc laughed.

"Yeah, and I like those parts, but I thought it might be cool to just hang out…and if anything more happens… well, that's good, too."

"Sounds cool. Where you want to go?"

"Um, maybe for pizza? I kind of want to stay away from Ofarim's. I'm in there enough."

"Yeah, I can imagine. Okay, pizza it is."

"I'll pick you up. How's six?"

"Six is good."

Marc gave me his address, then we hung up.

"So, big bro has a date tonight."

"Sort of. I don't know if I'd call it a date. We're just going out."

"So, you like this guy…Marc?"

"Yeah. I don't *like* like him exactly, but I like him. Damn, I wish I had gaydar. He's been right under my nose all this time."

"So he goes to our school?"

"Yes, eavesdropper."

"What's he look like?"

"He's *really* good looking. He's got longish blond hair, blue eyes, and this cool skater look."

"Wait, are you talking about Marc Peralta?"

"Yeah."

"That's who you were with last night? Damn, he's hot, Shawn! I used to beat it thinking about getting it on with him!"

"Too much information, Tim."

"No. Too much information would be telling you I used to beat off thinking about getting it on with you. I used to think about creeping over to your bed while you were sleeping and…"

"Way too much information!"

"Relax, I've got Dane now."

"Maybe I should start locking my bedroom door."

"This was before we moved into the loft and before I met Dane."

"Okay, but seriously, keep that shit to yourself. I really don't want to know about it."

"Are you sure, Shawn? Even about my fantasy where…"

"YES! Especially about any fantasy that involves me!"

"Oh, but Shawn…"

"Shut up, Tim!"

Tim laughed. I couldn't tell how much of what he'd been saying was true and how much of it was said just to freak me out. I was more than glad to get away from Tim for a while and get ready for my date.

I stripped naked and headed for the shower. The hot steamy water was so relaxing. I loved the sensation of hot water pounding down upon my naked body. It was like my own private rain shower, only nice and warm instead of cold. I loved getting all soapy and wet. I loved the scent of my shampoo and hair conditioner—currently strawberry for the shampoo and lavender and lilac for the conditioner. I loved changing things around, too. This might seem weird, but I have half a dozen different kinds of shampoo, and I change from one to another the first of every month. That way, I take greater notice of the color and the scent. Do hetero guys think so much about shampoo? I had no idea, but I kind of doubted it. If not, it was their loss.

Showering always made me horny, too. Maybe it was because of all the times I'd showered with hot, naked guys after football practice, or maybe it was because I just tended to think sexual thoughts when I was naked and wet. I guess it didn't matter. I was alone, so I enjoyed the feeling in a way I couldn't in the showers at school. Popping a boner there definitely wasn't cool. I'd always carefully avoided it. I'd watch it this fall more than ever. For the first time, my teammates would know for sure I was gay. I hoped they were okay with it. The way they treated Brendan gave me hope. Of course, I wasn't the god on the football field that he was.

Guys like Brendan can get away with a lot. Still, my teammates had been generally accepting. I wasn't going to worry about it. I'd handle the situation, whatever it might be. I just hoped I could play football this fall.

I was going to miss Brendan in the showers. What a body! He was taken, of course, but there was no harm in looking. There were some hot guys on the team, but Brendan...wow...he was something else. Casper was one lucky boy.

My thoughts went to Marc. I'd never showered with him, but I had seen him naked. I'd explored his body with my hands, lips, and tongue. I fantasized about him being right there in the shower with me, all soapy and wet, his blond hair plastered to the sides of his face, his smooth skin rubbing against my own. I was so worked up I could hardly endure it. I closed my eyes, continued my fantasy, and...

After relieving the tension, I finished my shower, dried off, and walked to my room, naked. Tim passed me in the hallway.

"Nice outfit. I'm sure Marc will love it."

I just rolled my eyes and continued on. I had better things to do than spar with Tim—namely, pick out something to wear.

I wasn't about to stand in front of the closet agonizing the way I had when I was going over to ask Tristan out for Valentine's Day. I grabbed the first pair of boxers I spotted when I opened the drawer and slipped them on. Next, I pulled on the jeans I'd worn to school. I opened my closet and stood there no more than thirty seconds before I selected a purple t-shirt with a stylized eagle on it. I checked myself out in the mirror to examine the effect. Not bad. I lifted my shirt and sprayed on a little cologne. I was ready.

It was a bit early, so I sat down and did some homework. It was as good a way as any to pass the time, and the more I finished before going out with Marc the less there would be to do later.

Before I knew it, 6:45 rolled around. I grabbed my keys and my leather jacket, bid Tim goodbye, and headed for the car. I'd never been to Marc's house before, but from the address I knew about where it was located. It was a short-enough drive. I arrived just a bit early. I pulled up in front of a small, white Victorian home decorated with gingerbread trim along the eaves and porch. I wondered for a few moments if I should go knock on the door, but came walking up the drive at the side of the house, pulling on a red hooded sweatshirt. Damn, that boy looked sexy in anything!

"Yo!" Marc said as he opened the door and plopped down in the passenger seat.

"Hey. So...pizza?"

"Sounds good."

I didn't say a lot as we drove back to Main Street. Parrot's Pizza was located across the street from Café Moffatt. If Tim happened to look out the window of our loft, he'd be able to see Marc and me getting out of the car and entering the pizza parlor.

"You go for pizza a lot?" Marc asked. "You sure live close enough."

"Not so much. I have to support Tim and myself, so there's not a lot of extra money."

"Yeah, that would suck, man, but it would also be cool to have your own place! I How did you manage that?"

"That's kind of a long story, but I'll tell you sometime."

"I think I know part of the story. I heard about you kicking your old man's ass."

"Yeah, well, that's definitely part of the story."

"I'd never have the nerve."

"You might if your dad was beating on your little brother the way my dad was beating Tim."

"He was beating him?"

"Yeah, I walked in on it, and the rest just sort of happened. I didn't really think about what I was doing. I was just trying to save Tim. We moved out right then and there."

"You ever talk to your dad?"

"Not much. We actually get along better now, but I don't really want to have much to do with him. It's weird, but he respects me more since I stood up to him. It's almost like he's proud I was able to kick his butt."

"Wow. I sort of have my own place, but not really. I live in the barn loft behind my parent's house."

"You live in a barn loft?"

"Yeah, but it's fixed up like an apartment. It's not like I'm living with livestock." Marc laughed. "Mom and dad keep close tabs on when I come and go and they can see when I bring everyone home, so it's not much better than living in the same house with them."

"Ever take Blake to your place?"

"Yeah, but mom interrupted."

"Shit."

"She didn't catch us doing it, but it was close. It's too dangerous to have sex at my place."

We walked into Parrot's and were shown to a booth.

"I like this place," Marc said. "You'd never think parrots and pizza would go together, but it fits."

"The owner's last name is Parrot," I said.

The interior was done up in a parrot motif. There were a few parrot-themed items hung on the walls. It sounds kind of cheesy, but the effect was exotic and fun. The tables and booths were covered with green-and-white-checked tablecloths, and there were green candles burning on all the tables.

"So, what should we order?" I asked as we sat down.

"You cannot go wrong with pepperoni," Marc said. "What about a pepperoni with extra cheese?"

"Excellent."

When the waiter arrived, we placed our order.

"Last night was hot," Marc said.

"Definitely."

"And the three-way with Blake, well, that goes without saying."

"He's incredible, isn't he?" I asked.

"He's kind of stuck on himself, and he has some issues, but he's hot. He'd be hotter if he'd make out and if he was a little less concerned with his masculinity."

"Yeah, I love to make out."

"I noticed."

"It's just too sexy. In some ways, making out is hotter than sex."

"In some ways," Marc said.

"I wish we could right now," I said.

Marc leaned over the table and kissed me on the lips. I looked around, but the few other customers in Parrot's didn't notice.

"You seem uncomfortable," Marc said.

"I'm not used to kissing another guy in public."

"Well, I'm not into hiding what I am."

"I guess I'm not, either, not anymore. It's kind of hard to break old habits."

"I understand. If I had a parent who would beat me for being gay, I wouldn't be so open."

"Why aren't you out at school?" I asked.

"I'm neither out nor in. I'm just me. If I had a guy to kiss, I'd kiss him."

"So you've never had a boyfriend?"

"I've had three. Two of them were summer flings when I was away at camp. I did have a boyfriend last year, but he was so far back in the closet I'm surprised he didn't end up in Narnia. He would have completely freaked out if I'd kissed him in public."

"It's hard to picture you with someone like that."

"Well, we didn't work out in the end. We were just too different."

"So he went to VHS?"

"Yes. Still does. I can't tell you who he is, though."

"I understand."

"So...we're kind of on a date. What are your intentions, Shawn, besides hot, sweaty sex, that is."

"I'm not exactly sure. I'm going to be completely honest with you. I don't know what I want right now. I've also got a...well, my brother and my friends call it an obsession with a boy at school."

"Who?"

"Tristan Cole—long black hair, brown eyes, glasses, really good-looking."

"Oh, I've seen him! He is sexy! Is he gay?"

"Yeah, but he's not all that interested in me."

"So, you've made your attraction to him obvious?"

"Yeah, we're kind of friends, and I told him how I felt about him. He gave me this let's-be-friends-and-see-where-things-go line. I'm pissed off at him right now because he's tight with Nate London."

"A major hottie."

"Yes. Nate's way hotter than I am, and apparently Tristan is willing to be more than friends with Nate."

"So they're dating? Fooling around?"

"I don't know, could be either. They're together a lot, and they seem too friendly, if you know what I mean."

"You're jealous."

"Yes. I *really* like Tristan, but...he just doesn't seem that interested in me. It's frustrating. I thought he just didn't want to get into anything serious, but now he's with Nate and...well, it pisses me off!"

"Very jealous," Marc said.

I looked at Marc. He wasn't being a smartass. He was merely making an accurate observation.

"I appreciate your honesty. I'll be honest, too. I don't want to seriously date someone who is hung up on another guy."

"Yeah, I want a boyfriend, but..."

"But you want your boyfriend to be Tristan."

172

"Stupid, isn't it?"

"You can't help but feel how you feel, Shawn. It's like being attracted to guys; that's just the way you are. Being attracted to Tristan is just the way you are, too. You have good taste, by the way."

"It's weird. Tristan isn't my type. He isn't the type I fantasize about."

"Hmm, let me guess. Your type is the captain of the football team and other jocks."

"Pretty much."

"I'm not really your type then, either. I guess you can call me a jock. I play soccer but I don't spend much time in the gym. I'm more into skating than soccer, actually, although I do love to play."

"Hey, were you on the soccer team with Mark and Taylor?"

"The boys who killed themselves? Nope. I haven't lived in Verona that long. We moved here in January of '81, so this last soccer season was my first here. We moved from Bloomington."

"That's why I didn't notice you. I went to some of the soccer games back when Taylor played."

"Yeah, I was playing for Bloomington South that season. I would have been kind of hard to notice from Verona."

"So, anyway, I don't know what I want. I'm a confused mess."

"You know what you want, Shawn. You want Tristan."

"Wanting isn't getting. Listen, I'm really sorry. I asked you out, and here I am sitting here talking about another guy."

"It's okay, Shawn, really. I don't know if we'd work out as boyfriends, but that's not the way things are going right now, anyway. I have a feeling we can be friends, though, friends with benefits. The hookups with you were hot, but I like that you're interested in just hanging out with me, too. I'm into having all kinds of fun. That's what life is all about."

"You're being really cool about this."

"Why wouldn't I be? You've been honest with me. You haven't promised me anything you can't deliver. You haven't misled me. It's not as though you're saying things just to get into my pants, either. You can get in my pants any time you want."

Marc wiggled his eyebrows, managing to be funny and sexy at the same time. If I had any sense, I would have completely forgotten about Tristan and dated Marc. My feelings weren't a matter of choice, however. At the moment, I wished I'd never met Tristan so I could date Marc, but then again I didn't wish it. I was in love with Tristan.

"Damn it," I said.

"What?"

"You're really cool and sexy and funny. I wish I could just shut off my feelings for Tristan and ask you to be my boyfriend."

"No can do, stud. Feelings do not work that way."

"Tell me about it."

Our pizza and Cokes arrived. We dug in.

"Mmm. Extra cheese was a good call," I said.

"Of course! I would never lead you wrong."

We were too busy eating for a while to talk much. Pizza is pizza, after all.

"You should sit with the guys and me at lunch—that is, if you don't mind sitting at the homo table. Everyone is really cool. Brandon and Jon are hilarious."

"Are they like, a couple?" Marc asked. "I always see them together, and they're always arguing like they're jealous or something. They crack the guys up in the locker room after practice."

I fought back the laugh that assailed me. I had a mouthful of Coke, and I'd spray the table if I didn't get myself under control fast.

Dead pets. Dead pets, I thought to myself.

As it was, I still nearly choked. I felt foolish coughing and going on in front of Marc, but I ended up laughing.

174

"What?"

"That's hilarious," I said. "Unfortunately, you caught me with a mouth full of Coke. You very nearly received a Coke shower."

Marc grinned.

"What's so funny about Brandon and Jon being a couple? They look good together. I've always suspected they had something going."

"I almost forgot you know them. You're all soccer players."

"Yeah, I can't wait for the next soccer season."

"Brandon and Jon are the homo table's token straights," I said. "Neither of them has any interest in guys, or at least so little it doesn't matter. They're always going off on each other, and most of the time they're accusing each other of homosexual acts."

"You know what they say: methinks thou doth protest too much."

"Nah, they aren't down on gays. I mean, they sit with a whole table of us, and they stand up for us whenever anyone gives us trouble."

"Maybe so, but still, don't you think there might be a little latent homosexuality there?"

"You're just hoping there is."

"Well, yeah. They're hot! I love hot guys, but I'm just saying…"

"I really don't think either of them is interested in guys. If they were, they've had plenty of opportunities to experiment. Hell, I'd give either one of them a blowjob if he asked."

Marc laughed.

"You give many guys a blowjob?" he asked.

"Not many."

"Who?"

"You."

"I remember. I was there. It was fucking fine, by the way. And?"

"Blake."

"Tell me something I don't know."

"My brother's boyfriend."

"*What?*"

I laughed. I wouldn't have told Marc about Dane, but I wanted to see his reaction, and I knew Dane wouldn't care.

"It was before he was my brother's boyfriend. Tim and Dane hadn't even met yet. Dane and I messed around a couple of times. Then he met my brother, and it was love at first sight."

"Aww."

"It was like watching a movie. I wouldn't have been surprised if they ran toward each other in slow motion."

"Were you upset?"

"A little. Dane is a hottie, after all, and it's not as though I was getting any elsewhere. I knew there really couldn't be anything more than sex between Dane and me. It was obvious Tim and Dane could have much more. I wanted them to be happy."

"You're almost sickeningly perfect," Marc said.

"Hardly."

"That's still so sweet of you—and selfless."

"It really wasn't much more than bowing to the inevitable. Besides, there is no way I could deny my brother what I so desperately sought."

"Then along came Tristan," Marc said.

"Yeah, and filled my life with unfulfilled longing and torment."

"Now you're being dramatic."

"Only a little."

"Hmm, I think I might just join your table. If your friends are anything like you, it should be a blast. Maybe we can make Tristan jealous."

"How?" I asked. "Tristan already sits at my table."

176

"Hello! We make him jealous by dating. Maybe if he saw you with me, he'd start thinking about what he's missing."

"Yeah, right! He's got Nate London, and Nate is way hotter than I am!"

"He's hot in a different way, but he's not hotter."

"Whatever."

"What have you got to lose?"

"I don't want to be dishonest. I felt like a big liar when I was pretending I wasn't gay. I had a damn good reason, but I still felt guilty."

"Who said anything about being dishonest? You like me, don't you? You want to spend time with me, don't you? You want to have sex with me, right?"

"Yes."

"So where's the dishonesty? We will date. It just won't be exclusive. If either of us wants to hook up with Blake or anyone else, together or separately, we'll do it. The only teensy bit of possible dishonesty will be in not telling anyone we have an open relationship. That's not even dishonesty. It's just holding back information."

"When you put it like that, it doesn't sound bad."

"Doesn't sound bad? I'm hurt. I'm offering to date you. So, you want me or not?"

"I want you."

"I thought so," Marc said, grinning. "We'll have a blast together, and if it makes Tristan jealous, so much the better."

"Okay, let's say it does make him jealous. Let's say he wants me so bad he comes begging to be my boyfriend. What then?"

"Then you say yes!"

"What about you?"

"You tell him we're about to break up, anyway. Then, you and I can still be friends. We just won't be able to have sex unless your new boyfriend is into three-ways. I'd definitely be up for that with you and Tristan, by the way."

"My mother warned me about boys like you."

"Sure she did."

There were still a few slices of pizza left when Marc and I were both full. We had it boxed up.

"Let's go to your place," Marc said.

"My brother is home."

"So?"

"So we can't have sex while he's there."

"What kind of boy do you think I am?" Marc asked. There was that puckish grin again. "Not everything has to be about sex, Shawn."

"I just figured you meant..."

"You are a horny boy, aren't you?"

"Well, yeah, especially around you."

"I'm sure you can control yourself. I just thought we could hang out, talk, and maybe make out a little."

"Now, who's the horny boy?" I asked.

"You know you love it."

"Yes."

"So, let's go."

Marc and I walked across the street, then up the stairs.

"Tim! You want some pizza?" I called out.

My brother appeared in the living room/kitchen.

"Hey," he said.

"Marc, this is Tim."

"I've seen you at school," Tim said. "So, you're Shawn's new fuck buddy?"

"Tim!"

"Just what have you been telling him?" Marc asked. His eyes gleamed with mischief.

"I…uh…kind of told him about last night. I didn't think you'd mind, and he won't tell anyone."

"Ha!" Tim said. "I already called half my friends."

"Tim!"

"I'm kidding, Shawn. Kidding! Damn! Loosen up!"

"Right after I wring your little neck."

"Aww, brotherly love. To answer your question, Shawn and I are thinking about dating."

"Thank God!" Tim said.

I opened the pizza box and shoved a piece in Tim's mouth to shut him up. It worked.

"Um, want some tea or coffee?" I asked.

"Tea would be great. I never cared much for coffee. It's too bitter."

"That's whaff suffer and creamar isf for," Tim said, with his mouth full of pizza.

"Try to forgive him. He was raised in a cave," I said. "He's also a coffee fiend."

Tim shot me an amused sneer.

I put the kettle on and then showed Marc around the apartment. He'd seen it before, of course—well, my bedroom, anyway—but Tim didn't know that.

The kettle was simmering away when we returned to the kitchen. I placed tea bags into two cups and then filled them with steaming water. The clear water immediately began to turn a golden brown. I carried the cups and saucers to the table, and Marc and I sat down. Tim had already returned to his room with a fist full of pizza.

"I like your brother," Marc said as he stirred sugar into his cup.

"You don't have to live with him."

"You know you love him."

"Yes, but I still want to beat him sometimes."

"He looks a lot like you: very sexy."

"Am I about to lose another guy to my brother?"

"No, I like you better. Besides, he has a boyfriend. Of course, if they wouldn't mind a third..."

"Don't tell him that. I have a hard enough time with him as it is."

Marc laughed.

We sat and talked and drank tea. I enjoyed hanging out with Marc. I'm glad he'd become more than a hookup. Hookups were okay, but they were finished too quickly, and then what was left? Steaming memories, yes, but not much more.

After we finished our tea, Marc and I moved to the couch. We made out, of course. Our hands roamed everywhere while our lips and tongues entwined. I was hard as a rock and wanted Marc in the worst way, but there was something intensely sexy about not being able to take our clothes off. Thoughts of bribing Tim to leave crossed my mind, but the boy wasn't stupid. He'd either refuse to go in an attempt to blackmail me into letting him use the loft for sex with Dane or he'd return a few minutes after leaving to catch me in the act. Somehow, not being able to have sex made making out with Marc that much more intense. There was something to be said for not always getting what you want.

I drove Marc home, and we shared a kiss just before he got out of the car. I liked the direction things were headed with Marc. Maybe I didn't even need Tristan anymore. Only time would tell. For the moment, I was still very much infatuated with Tristan Graham Cole.

Dane

"Guys and Casey, this is Marc," Shawn said as he set his tray on the table.

"Hey," Marc said.

"Finally got kicked out of your place at the skater table, huh?" Jon asked.

"Nope, it was just time for a change of scenery."

"And you chose to sit where you can see Jon? Not too bright, are you?" Brandon asked.

"I am so much better looking than you that it's not even funny," Jon said.

"You wish."

"Don't you guys ever stop?" Marc asked.

"You know them?" Casey asked. "I pity you."

"We're soccer teammates."

"Soccer players? Aren't they those guys who can't cut it in a real sport like wrestling or football?" Ethan asked, looking at Brendan.

"Yeah, I've heard of those guys. Isn't their nickname The Pansies or something like that?" Brendan asked.

"You're just jealous because soccer rules at VHS," Jon said. "Yeah!" Jon stood up and flexed his arms over his head. He had some nice biceps.

"Are you sure you want to sit here?" Shawn asked Marc.

"Oh, yeah," Marc said. "I'm used to them."

Did I catch a dreamy gaze as Marc looked at Shawn—or was it merely a horny stare? I looked at Tim across the table from me. He stuck his finger in his mouth and poked it at his cheek—sign language for blowjob. Tim and I cracked up.

"You've already met Tim, so you know he has mental problems," Shawn said. "Just in case you haven't met, the other mental case is Dane."

Marc smiled at Shawn. Yeah, there was definitely something up between those two. Tim might just have been kidding around, but Marc and Shawn had the look of two guys who'd been naked together. I wasn't the only one who picked up on it, either. Tristan looked at the pair curiously. Both Brandon and Jon had a shared, "What do we have here? Butt buddies?", look on their faces. There wasn't anyone who didn't look as if he, or she, thought there was something more than friendship between Shawn and Marc.

Tim and I finished our lunches quickly and slipped off to the auditorium for a lunchtime quickie. As soon as we hit the darkness between the curtains, our lips joined and our hands slipped into each other's pants. We slipped off nearly every single day to hook up in the auditorium. I was getting used to my daily lunchtime blowjob. It was so much easier to concentrate in my afternoon classes after Tim and I had gotten each other off. If the school board was serious about academic performance, they really should arrange an oral-sex period for everyone instead of a study hall.

Tim and I finished up just before the bell rang, ending our lunch period. We sneaked out of the auditorium and back into the hallway once again without being spotted.

"So, spill it. What do you know about Shawn and Marc?" I asked.

"They went out for pizza last night. The night before, they gave each other car head. They may have last night, too, for all I know," Tim said.

"So, Shawn is finally getting some," I said.

"Yeah, maybe he'll chill out now. I'm also hoping he'll want to get it on with Marc bad enough we can cut a deal about sex in the loft. He can do it with Marc if I can do it with you."

"I wish," I said. "Slipping off is exciting, but I'd rather have more time—much more time."

"We will. We'll find a way."

"You know, if I could get away sometime when your brother isn't going to be home…" I suggested.

"Yeah, but can you? Aren't your parents kind of keeping a tight leash on you?"

"A leash—kinky."

"You know what I mean."

"Yeah, but I figure they'll let their guard down soon. If they weren't both around so much at home, we could find a place to do it there. Maybe we can, anyway."

"We need to do something, or I might explode."

"Mmm, I want to be there when you explode."

I wanted to slip off with Tim after school, but I was expected home. My parents weren't stupid. They knew Tim and I were just dying to get into each other's pants. What they didn't know was that we were getting part of what we wanted at school, but what they didn't know wouldn't hurt us.

I was determined to find a way to be alone with Tim at his place or mine. Sooner or later, both my parents would disappear while Shawn was working. When that happened, Tim and I were going to get it on. I'd been watching for my chance already, but no luck. Mom and Dad were often both home, and not once had they both been gone at the same time. They were putting far too much effort into keeping me from getting laid. In a just world I could have had all the sex I wanted.

I wondered if sex would be as exciting if it was easy to get. What if parents just didn't care? What if no one preached against it? What if I could just say, "Hey, Tim and I are going to my room to fuck. We'll be down for supper later?" Would sex be such a big deal then? The forbidden nature of my encounters with Tim definitely made them more exciting, but wouldn't sex feel just as good if it wasn't forbidden? Would I do it so much it would no longer be thrilling? I guess I'd never know the answer to my questions. There was no way my parents would ever be okay with me having sex. If I told my mom I was going to my room to fuck, she'd probably slap my face for being vulgar and lock me up so I couldn't see Tim. Why did life have to be so difficult, and why was the good stuff always so hard to get?

Tim walked me home. We kissed now and then, but the kisses only fueled my passion. I forgot all about passion, however, when a pickup drove by. Was that...? No. It couldn't be.

"What's wrong?" Tim asked. "You look as if you've seen a ghost."

"It's...it's nothing."

"It's not nothing."

"I just...it can't be, but I thought I just saw Boothe."

"Are you sure?"

"No, I'm not sure. Actually, I'm pretty sure it wasn't him. I'm just seeing things is all. Boothe is still wanted for a whole list of stuff. He wouldn't be caught dead within a hundred miles of Verona."

Tim knew the whole story about Boothe, the graverobber and my former employer, so I didn't have to go into it.

"Do you think he'll be after you if he comes back?" Tim asked.

"I don't know. Maybe. It's probably nothing. I'm just seeing things. You know, like when you think you see a monster when you're walking alone in the dark."

"Yeah, you're probably right, but just be careful, okay?"

"You're going to freak me out if you keep talking like that," I said.

"I'm sorry, but just be careful. Okay?"

"For you, anything," I said.

We were at the old Verona school by then. Tim gave me a kiss, and then I walked inside. I was probably just imagining things, but I began to wonder—what if...

I felt out of sorts as I climbed the stairs to my room. It was as if everything, including me, was slightly off. I wasn't happy, but I wasn't sad. I just felt...blah.

I also felt as if I was being drawn back into my old life, my life before Verona. So much had changed in recent months, including me, and the changes had been for the better. I lived in a new place, had new friends, I got on much better with my parents, I was out, and I even had a boyfriend. Back in Marmont...well, things had been bad. Less than a year ago I'd run away. I'd ended up in Verona, but my time in Verona then wasn't like it was now. I was on my own then, and I was scared. I wasn't a very nice person back then, either. I thought only about what I wanted and didn't much care who got hurt. I was ashamed of what I'd been, but I'd changed. I'd really changed. I had no intention of going back.

As I stepped into my room and closed the door, I realized I was breathing so hard and fast that I was on the verge of hyperventilating.

You're being stupid, Dane, just stupid, I told myself. *You can't be drawn back into the past. You live in Verona now. Everything is cool with Mom and Dad. You have Tim. You're safe. You aren't on your own anymore.*

I really was stupid for letting memories of the recent past bother me so. That was my past. This was my present. I'd traveled a dark road, but I'd turned aside or had been pushed aside onto a lighter road. I could have become something horrible, but I'd been saved from that terrible fate. I really had changed. The past couldn't get me, and there was no way I was going to once again become the Dane I had been. I liked the new me too much. The new and improved Dane was staying!

"Yeah, you're just so perfect," I said to myself as I gazed at my reflection in the mirror.

I laughed. I was far from perfect, but I wasn't a big jerk anymore. That's what was important. I cared about others now. I'd never intentionally hurt anyone.

I walked to the large windows that made up nearly the entire west wall of my room. The sky was darkening even though it was long before sunset. Ominous clouds moved in from the southwest. It wasn't nearly warm enough for a truly terrific thunderstorm, but I thought I could see rain under the clouds. I usually loved storms and rain, but the growing darkness gave me a sense of foreboding. I wished Tim was with me just then. I needed a hug.

I knew all too well that my uneasy mood would keep me from enjoying myself for a while, so I sat down to tackle my homework. I didn't hate homework. Depending on the subject and assignment, I sometimes even liked it. The main thing I didn't like about homework was that I had to do it. Have you ever noticed that having to do something makes it less enjoyable? Since moving in, I've been arranging, rearranging, and organizing my room. I pretty much like doing it, but if Mom told me I had to get my room in order, it would turn into a chore. This may sound a little weird, but I kind of like to mow the lawn. I don't always like it. It sucks when it's too hot or dusty. Dad is really pleased when I mow the lawn without being told to do so, but mainly I do it without being told because I don't want to be told. Mowing after Dad has told me to do it isn't nearly as fun as mowing when the mood just hits me. Okay, enough of my weirdness. Homework awaits.

By five p.m. the clouds had so blotted out the sun it seemed like it was eight. Rain began to smack against the windowpanes, and I could even hear it on the roof overhead. I shivered just thinking about the coldness of the rain. We were getting well into March, but the temperatures didn't get much past the forties most of the time. I liked to walk in the rain in the summer and get all soaking wet, but I wouldn't have stepped outside just now for fifty bucks.

There was a little bit of lightning and thunder, but mostly the rain just fell and fell. It was one of those steady, drizzling rains that could go on for hours. I took a break from my homework and gazed out the window. I could see the lights of cars driving up and down the street below as well as the lights of the houses across the street and beyond. My view from the second floor didn't allow me to look out over Verona as if I was high up in some skyscraper, but I was able to see the lights in the houses for a few blocks. I usually enjoyed the view, but tonight I felt off.

Mom called me down for supper at about six. My parents and I ate meat loaf, green beans, and mashed potatoes in our "dining room"—the old cafeteria. I didn't know if I'd ever get used to sitting in such a big room for meals. I was accustomed to a normal-sized kitchen. In the rental house, the kitchen had been downright Lilliputian. Yeah, you guessed it; I'd just been reading *Gulliver's Travels* for a school assignment. Tonight, the old cafeteria seemed especially dark and silent. The rain pelted against the windows here, too.

After supper, I returned to my room and continued with my homework. I even worked ahead because I just didn't feel like doing any of the things I usually did for fun. By ten, I was tired of schoolwork, but I wasn't tired enough to go to bed. I decided to walk about the old school and explore.

I took my flashlight and walked downstairs. The old building seemed bigger in the darkness. Perhaps it was because the shadows made it seem as if the main hallway went on and on forever, perhaps because each doorway opened into inky blackness. Exploring was a mistake. I made it as far as the gym, but then I began to freak out. I think it was the vast, empty, silent space. Such a short time ago the gym had been filled with the laughter and voices of my friends. Now, it was so quiet I could hear my own heart beat. I wondered if the old school was haunted, and that was more than enough to increase my fear tenfold. I slowly walked back to my room. I had to force myself not to run. I knew terror would overtake me if I ran. Fleeing created the terror.

I felt safer back in my own room with the door shut, but on this night the room was just too big. The rain continued to pelt the windows, and the wind threw itself against the panes. I felt as if the elements themselves were trying to get me.

I undressed, climbed into bed, and pulled the covers up to my chin. I felt safer under the sheet and blankets. I don't know why. It's not as though some cloth could protect me. I didn't even know what I feared. I was just afraid, and I didn't like the feeling. It reminded me of too many nights when I was on the run.

I couldn't get to sleep. I lay there staring at the ceiling, straining my ears to pick up every stray sound. I only succeeded in frightening myself more. Finally, I drifted off to sleep…

The cold rain pelted me as I scrambled backwards on hands and feet in the mud. Boothe stalked me. I twisted to turn and run, but he was on top of me before I got off the ground. He forced me onto my back, straddling me. His hands painfully squeezed my wrists.

"You're hurting me!"

"I'm going to hurt you a lot more before we're done tonight, faggot."

Boothe sat on my chest and glared at me for a few moments. Then, to my horror, he unfastened his belt and pulled down his pants while holding me down with one hand pressed against my chest. I tried to scream, but he slugged me and told me to shut up. I did as he said. He'd hit me again if I didn't.

"Boothe, please dude, lemme go, okay? I won't tell anyone, I swear. I'm sorry, all right? You're the boss, like you said. You don't have to pay me tonight, it's okay man; just lemme go."

"You've sure changed your tune, haven't ya? Aren't you the same boy who was being such a fucker just a few minutes ago? You shouldn't play with the big boys, fag; you'll get hurt."

He pawed at me then. His hands were all over me. I feebly resisted, but I was just too plain scared to fight him. He ripped my shirt in his impatience to get at me. He jerked down my jeans and boxers, tearing them in the process. He groped me while he leaned over me. He shoved his lips against mine and kissed me, forcing his tongue into my mouth. I cried in sheer terror.

"I can make you do anything I want," Boothe said to me when he pulled his lips from mine. "I can do anything to you I want."

Boothe grabbed my hand and forced it onto his crotch. "You like this, huh, do you?"

"Please, Boothe, please let me go."

"You're not going anywhere until we're done," he said. I bawled like a baby. I wanted my mom and dad.

Boothe forced me onto my stomach and used his knee to pry my legs apart.

"No, Boothe! Please, for God's sake, NO!"

I knew what he was going to do to me. I pleaded, begged, and cried, but he had no mercy. I screamed as I felt blinding pain that only grew worse. Each moment was an eternity of pain and humiliation.

"Boothe! No!"

I screamed louder than ever.

"Dane! Dane, wake up!"

I screamed again and nearly clawed my way off the bed, but Dad held me in place.

"Dane!"

"Dad?"

"I'm here. You were having a nightmare."

"Dad," I said.

I grabbed him and hugged him. I sobbed into his shoulder. My breath came hard and fast. I couldn't stop crying.

"It was just a dream, Dane. It was just a dream," said Dad.

"You're going to be okay," Mom said. She was standing nearby.

I couldn't stop shaking. I couldn't stop crying. I couldn't stop breathing so hard.

"Dane, you're okay. No one is going to hurt you," Dad said.

It didn't help. I couldn't stop. I knew it was just a dream, but I couldn't stop. It hadn't even happened like that. It wasn't raining the night Boothe raped me. The rain outside had entered my dreams. It didn't matter. It felt so real.

"Here, Dane, breathe into this," my mom said.

She handed me a paper bag that had been lying on the library table. I put it against my face and breathed into it. I breathed so hard and fast the bag nearly exploded. My breath began to slow, but I couldn't stop shaking or crying.

"Do you think we should take him to the emergency room?" I heard Mom ask Dad.

"He'll be okay soon. It's okay, Dane. We're here with you. We won't leave you."

Dad hugged me harder. Slowly, very slowly, I began to calm. I'd had nightmares before, nightmares that should have been more frightening, but my God…

"Do you want to go downstairs for some hot chocolate or hot tea or something?" Mom asked.

I shook my head violently. I did not want to leave my bed. I felt as if monsters would grab me and jerk me under the bed if my feet touched the floor.

"How about I bring you something up? Hot cocoa?"

I nodded my head. Mom departed. Dad just kept holding me and telling me I was going to be okay.

I took the mug of hot cocoa from Mom when she returned and held it tightly. The warmth of the mug and the scent of the cocoa was comforting. I still trembled, but I no longer shook so violently. My tears had ebbed, too. I took a sip and felt warmed from the inside.

"Nightmare?" Dad asked.

I nodded.

"The worst ever."

"What was it about?"

"Boothe."

Mom and Dad exchanged a significant look.

"Was it about the night he…"

Dad trailed off. He knew I didn't want him to say it out loud. It was bad enough my parents knew what he'd done to me. Having them say it was just too much.

"Yes. It was so scary—so real. I've had nightmares before, even nightmares about Boothe, but this...it was like being there again. I...I know it was just a dream, but even now it feels like it *just* happened."

I'm glad Dad didn't ask why I thought I'd had the nightmare. I didn't want to tell him I'd thought I'd seen Boothe. It probably hadn't even been him. I was eighty percent sure it wasn't him I'd glimpsed, but I just didn't want to get into it. I was too tired and too upset. Boothe was miles and miles away. My own mind had done this to me.

Mom and Dad stayed with me until I fell asleep again. I don't think I could have fallen asleep without them. Damn. Here I was, sixteen-years old, and I needed my parents to hold my hand so I could go to sleep. At the moment I didn't care. The nightmare I'd experienced would have terrified a full-grown man.

Thankfully, the nightmare didn't return. When I next opened my eyes, it was morning. I shut off the alarm that had awakened me. The rain had gone, and so had the clouds. It was almost as if they'd been part of my nightmare.

I felt uneasy as I headed for the showers in the boys' locker room, but the darkness had fled with the morning sun. The old school was still big, but it didn't possess the scary vastness it had the night before.

An edge of fear haunted me as I stripped and stepped under one of the shower heads. The hot water relaxed and warmed me. My thoughts kept going back to the nightmare. It hadn't felt like a dream. It felt as if I'd traveled back in time and experienced those events all over again. Everything was the same, except for the rain.

Enough thinking about my nightmare. Dwelling on it would just give it more power. It was a dream, nothing more. I soaped up my body and then rinsed off. I dried with a towel, wrapped it around my waist, and then walked back upstairs to my room.

I thought about all that was good in my life while I dressed. I loved my new home, school, friends, and hometown. I loved my boyfriend! I had a kick-ass room. My grades were good. Basically, everything was good. A few guys, mainly Devon, were on my ass because I was gay, but I could handle it. It's not as if I was getting a daily beat-down. Devon and his buddies would no doubt kick my ass if they could, but Devon was so afraid of Brandon I seriously doubted he'd have the balls to try. My life wasn't perfect, but I had no reason to complain.

I was in a good mood by the time I headed downstairs for breakfast. Mom and Dad looked relieved. We talked about what happened the night before. All three of us hoped it was just an isolated dream. I told Mom and Dad I just wanted to put it out of my mind, and they thought that was best.

After breakfast, I brushed my teeth in the boys' restroom that was located near my bedroom. I'd already grown accustomed to using a bathroom that had once been public. Fifty years and more ago, dozens of boys had been in there every day. Now, it was just me. I wondered if someone would be living in the current Verona High School someday. I doubted it. It was far too large for a private residence. This old school was really too big, and it wasn't nearly as large as the current VHS.

The sun was shining as I stepped down the worn front steps of the old school with my backpack slung over my shoulder. March was getting on, and the warm breeze carried with it a scent that hinted of spring.

The bright sunlight banished the remnants of my nightmare to the edges of my mind. I intended to lose myself in a good book just before bed tonight. I'd fill my mind with images from the story so it would have something to think about besides Boothe as I slept.

I thought about Tim as I walked along, specifically about slipping away with him at lunch for some action in the dark. I guess all darkness wasn't a bad thing after all. I grinned.

My smile faded when I spotted the truck I'd seen on the way home from school the day before. At least I was pretty sure it was the same truck. I was both frightened and curious. I didn't want to go anywhere near that truck, yet I wanted a good look at the driver. If I could prove to myself I hadn't seen Boothe, I might sleep better in the coming nights.

The pickup drew up to the intersection and stopped. I couldn't quite see inside because the sun was glaring off the windshield, and the truck was on the other side of the intersection. I thought about waiting and letting the truck cut across my path, but I got scared at the last second and hurried across the street. The truck made a left behind me. I closed my eyes for a moment and took in a deep breath. It would be even with me in seconds. I looked to my left just as it drew up to me. I gasped. Boothe was driving! It was him! Oh my God! It was him!

Boothe made eye contact with me. He wasn't surprised to see me. That was for sure. He had a knowing expression on his face. My heart pounded in my chest. He'd been stalking me! I walked more quickly. Boothe sped up. He drove up the street and then turned right into someone's drive, blocking my path.

I bolted. I cut across a lawn and ran through the backyard. I didn't pay any attention to where I was going. All I knew was that I had to put as much distance between that truck and myself as I could. I had to lose Boothe and do it fast!

Tires squealed as Boothe ripped around a corner. I changed course and darted through more yards, hurtling over shrubs and even fences. If I'd been smart, I would have pounded on a door and asked someone to call the cops, but I was in such a panic I thought of nothing but getting away. Bad memories assailed me. I wasn't going to let Boothe get his hands on me again.

I ran until I thought my heart would explode. My breath came in gasps. My side ached, but I didn't stop. I just kept on running. The engine of a truck gunned, then tires squealed as Boothe's truck screeched to a halt in front of me. I darted to the side, but Boothe was out of the truck and pursuing me in seconds. He tackled my legs, and I went down. I turned on my back and came up kicking and screaming, only to have Boothe slam me down and clamp his hand over my mouth.

"It's been a long time, boy. We need to talk."

I looked around as best as I could. Surely someone had called the cops! I didn't recognize the part of town I was in, but it was mostly old abandoned buildings. Boothe jerked me to my feet and twisted my arm behind my back.

"Cry out and I'll break it," he said. "Now get in the truck."

Boothe took me around to the driver's side and shoved me in. Before I could even think of escaping out the passenger side he sped off. Where were the cops when you needed them? Couldn't someone stop him for speeding? All too soon, we were on a country road, and Boothe was driving even faster.

"Jump out if you want. You might survive."

The old fear had returned. Tears rolled down my cheeks.

"Please don't hurt me," I said.

"Has he come after you yet?" Boothe asked.

I looked through the glass at the back of the cab, then at Boothe, confused.

"Has *he* come after you yet?" he repeated.

"He?"

"That answers my question."

"Huh?"

"You and I need to talk. We've got a problem."

"I...I don't understand."

"You will."

Boothe pulled into an abandoned drive. He parked the truck where it couldn't be seen from the road. I was in deep shit. Way out here there was no one to hear me scream.

"Get out," he said.

I had no trouble following that order. I jerked open the door and bolted the second my feet hit the ground. Boothe tackled me before I made it fifteen feet. He pushed me onto my back and slugged me in the stomach.

"Please, no," I said. "Please, don't."

"I'm not going to do anything to you, Dane, if you stop trying to get away."

"You're not?"

"No. You pissed me off that night, Dane. You shouldn't have done that. I was also extremely horny. I get crazy when I'm

194

horny. You brought it all on yourself, boy. If you hadn't been such a little prick, that wouldn't have happened."

I didn't agree at all, but I wisely kept my mouth shut. At the very least he'd slug me again. At the worst... Still, there's something I had to know.

"That night...if no one had come to save me...would you...would you have killed me after you'd finished with me?"

"Yes," Boothe said, staring into my eyes. "You think I'd be stupid enough to leave you alive so you could tell the cops? You are a stupid little fuck."

"Are you going to kill me now?" I asked. Tears flowed from my eyes. I trembled in utter terror.

"No. I have nothing to gain from killing you now. Besides, I already told you I'm not going to do anything to you—if you don't try to escape. I should hurt you. I should pay you back for going to the cops, but I'm such a nice guy I'm going to let it slide. As for killing you, you're more useful to me alive."

I didn't like the sound of that last bit.

"Have you experienced anything...unusual since last summer?" Boothe asked.

"Unusual? Like how?"

"Like...ghosts...spirits of the dead...zombies."

I raised an eyebrow.

"Um, no."

"You will."

"Um, okay."

Boothe smacked me in the face—hard.

"Stop acting like you think I'm crazy!"

"Well, you're the one talking about ghosts!"

"You'd be talking about ghosts, too, if one was after you, and he will be."

"Why would a ghost be after me?"

"Because you helped me rob his grave."

"Hey, I didn't take anything from those graves. You did."

"*He* won't care about that. You helped me. That makes you guilty."

"Well, *he* hasn't been bothering me—only you have."

Boothe raised his hand as if he was going to strike me but then lowered it.

"Your smart mouth is going to get you in big trouble—again."

I swallowed hard. I didn't like the implication.

"What exactly do you want from me? Did you just kidnap me to tell me about this ghost?"

"I want you to help me figure this thing out."

"Why should I?"

"Because, mark my words, he will come after you, too, and when he does... And because, if you don't help me, I'll come after you, and our next trip into the country will not be so pleasant. I'll finish what I started last summer."

I willed myself not to tremble, but I failed.

"I can call the cops," I said.

"You think that will help you? You think I can't get you if I want you? I don't care how well you're guarded. Do you really want to spend your life looking over your shoulder wondering when your buddy Boothe is going to grab you?"

"No."

"I'm not being unreasonable. I just want some help in getting this thing off my back."

"Maybe you should return the stuff you stole."

Boothe punched me in the gut again, only not quite as hard as before.

"You think I have that stuff, you dipshit? I sold that crap as fast as I could. There's nothing left to return, and I couldn't lay my hands on it if I wanted. Who knows where all that stuff is now?"

"Well, I don't have a clue about how to help you."

Boothe picked me up and slammed me up against the truck. I felt as if he'd broken my back.

"You'd better get a clue, boy, and you'd better do it fast. You'll have more incentive to help when he comes for you, and he will."

Boothe put his hands on me then. He ran them down my sides, onto my hips, and around to my ass. I thought he was going to grope my crotch, too, but he only stared into my eyes.

"Your boyfriend is quite a little hottie, Dane. It would be a shame if something bad happened to him, but then, that's up to you."

My face paled.

"I don't understand what you want from me!"

Boothe grinned a horrible grin. He grabbed the sides of my head and kissed me before I could even try to stop him. He pulled away from me, slid into his truck, and backed out of the old drive. He drove away, leaving me standing there frightened and confused. I wiped my mouth off and began the walk back into town.

I was late for school, but compared to what I thought Boothe was going to do to me when he forced me into his trunk, a tardy was nothing. I was in a bit of a daze all morning. I was frightened but even more bewildered. Boothe seemed like the same old Boothe, except he was talking crazy. When he grabbed me, I figured I was done for, but then he started talking about the ghost...

I ran to Tim and hugged him the very first time I saw him between periods. It was all I could do to keep myself from crying. Thankfully, I didn't have any bruises where Boothe had smacked me.

"Where were you this morning?" Tim asked. "Are you okay? What's wrong?"

"I'm okay, I think. I had a horrible nightmare last night— about Boothe. Then, something happened this morning, but it's too long of a story. I'll tell you after school."

"Dane? You don't look okay. You don't look okay at all."

"I'll explain everything later. I promise."

I hugged Tim again. I felt so safe when he held me.

"Faggots," muttered Devon as he passed.

Tim flipped him off, then walked me to class.

At lunch, Tim sat beside me. He was my world. I don't even remember who else was sitting there, although I'm sure it was the usual crew. I spent most of my time gazing into Tim's eyes. I loved him *so* much.

I wasn't looking forward to our after-school talk, and yet it would be a relief to talk about what had happened. Tim knew all about my past with Boothe. It was his own brother who had saved me from him. I now knew for certain that Shawn had saved my life. Boothe himself had told me he would've killed me after he was done with me that night if Shawn hadn't rescued me.

We'd barely stepped out of the school when Tim turned to me.

"So, what's up?"

I told him first about the nightmare. Then, I dropped the bomb.

"Boothe? Boothe kidnapped you this morning? Are you okay? What did he do to you? He didn't...he didn't rape you, did he? You went to the cops, right? You should have told me first thing!"

Tim asked so many questions so fast I couldn't keep up with him. His eyes filled with tears, and his lower lip trembled. I stopped and looked into his eyes.

"He didn't rape me, Tim. He didn't hurt me much. I'm okay. Really, I'm okay. I was scared. I thought he was going to hurt me, but he didn't. Relax, Tim. I'm okay."

I told Tim exactly what happened and what Boothe told me.

"A ghost? He thinks a ghost is after him?"

"Yes. I think he really believes it."

"Do you think he's gone crazy?"

"I don't know what's up with him. He seemed very sincere about it. I'm convinced he really believes that a ghost is pursuing him. I don't know. Maybe his guilt is finally getting to him. I didn't even think he had a conscience, but maybe he's realized what a horrible thing he did—we did."

"Dane, you just helped him. You didn't rob those graves."

"That doesn't make what I did right. I didn't steal anything from those graves, but I still helped. I'm just as guilty as he is. I felt bad about it then and worse since. I should have found some other way to survive."

"Dane, you had to do something. You told me yourself your choices were robbing graves or selling yourself on the streets like Austin. Out of the two, I'd say grave-robbing was the better choice. Hell, if I was dead and buried, I'd rather some kid dig me up and steal my stuff instead of selling his body."

I actually laughed a little at that.

"Well, I would! Grave-robbing is wrong, yeah, but it's not like anyone really needs the stuff they're buried with. If there is a life after death, it's not as though that stuff goes with them. If death is just an end, then that stuff is just as useless. Hell, archaeologists rob graves all the time. It's called science, and they put a lot of that stuff in museums, but it's still grave-robbing just the same. The only difference is there aren't any relatives around to complain about it."

"There's a big difference, Tim. How would you feel if Shawn was dead and someone dug him up?"

"Listen, Dane. I'm not saying what you did wasn't wrong. I'm just saying you did what you had to do. That's all in the past. Don't beat yourself up for it."

Tim and I talked about Boothe all the way home. He even came in for a while. We had some cookies and milk and then played basketball in the gym. I wanted to get in some lip action, but Mom was hovering around, and Tim and I thought it best to work on our "good boy" images. If Mom only knew…

Shawn

"Hey, sexy," Marc said.

Marc gave me a peck on the lips, which was fairly bold considering we were standing in front of my locker just before school. Even hetero couples weren't allowed to kiss on school property, and I could just imagine how the powers that be would react to even the briefest of kisses between two males. There was also the reaction of our classmates to consider, but I wasn't too worried about that. Still, I was uncomfortable. Being out was new to me, and kissing another guy in public was almost more than I could handle. As it was, only two people noticed. One was a girl standing near who wiggled her eyebrows in a "you go, boy" gesture, and the other was a guy who wrinkled his nose and shook his head as if to say "queers." The boy didn't seem overly hostile, which was a sign of how good things were for gays in VHS.

Marc brushed his long bangs back, and I went weak in the knees. I remember reading about people going "weak in the knees" and wondering what the heck that meant. I knew now, but I can't explain the feeling except to say...well, you know. Why is it that feelings are so hard to put into words?

Marc and I talked for the few moments it took me to sort out my books, then we both went our separate ways. That little bit of contact with him made me feel comfortable and happy. Marc smiled at me whenever our paths crossed during the day, which wasn't often, but still his smile gave me a pleasant feeling in my chest. He sat with me at lunch again, and he fit right in.

Marc quickly began to feel like a boyfriend. At lunch, we sat so close our arms touched most of the time. It was actually Marc who scooted in so close to me, but I didn't pull away. I enjoyed the closeness. I liked him being so near I could smell his cologne. I was getting to know Marc a little better, too. It was odd. I knew a lot of guys really well, like Ethan, Brendan, Casper, and all the others who sat at our table. I knew a bunch of guys from football and others from classes. I'd seen Ethan without a shirt before (wow!). I'd seen Brendan and all my other teammates naked (yum!), but I hadn't been intimate with any of them the way I had Marc. I'd thoroughly explored Marc's smooth, sexy body. I knew just where to touch him to make him moan. I knew exactly how big his hard penis was. I knew how his balls drew up just before he came. I knew just what he sounded like when he moaned with passion. What I didn't know was all the little things I knew about scores of other guys. Little by little, I was now discovering those things. It felt like working backwards in a way—not that the ultimate goal of all my friendships was sex, not at all! It's just that I knew a ton of guys well and would have liked to have had sex with quite a few of them. With Marc, it had started with sex. I'd barely noticed him before Blake brought him into Ofarim's. I found I liked getting to know him. The more I found out about him, the more I liked him.

I didn't *like* like Marc. I didn't have romantic thoughts towards him. I thought about sex with him, yeah, but I wasn't in love with him. I enjoyed his friendship, however, and I very much enjoyed the closeness. There were a lot of things that weren't sex but were kind of related that I'd never experienced before: like Marc and me sitting so close at lunch; like the way he touched my arm when we talked, keeping his hand on my arm much longer than anyone else would; like the way he leaned his head against mine, or the way he gazed at me with desire. None of these things were sex, but they were linked, and I liked them, if not better than sex, then almost as much.

Tristan noticed my new relationship with Marc but didn't comment. He was still friendly with me and still spoke to me as if nothing had changed. I could tell in the way he looked at me and at Marc and me that he wondered what was going on between us. Did he also wonder if I'd lost interest in him? It served him right. I'd done plenty of wondering about him and Nate. I wondered if they were seriously dating or just messing around. I wondered if they made out and groped each other and if they'd seen each other naked. I wondered if they took walks in the moonlight and if they'd gone all the way. I burned with jealousy, and I hated Nate. I guess Nate wasn't really a bad guy, but he had what I wanted, so how could I help but hate him?

I felt guilty about my jealousy, but there was this tiny part of me that was happy for Tristan if he was happy. I was pissed off with him at the moment because of the whole thing with Nate. Sometimes, I even hated him a little, but I still loved him, and I wanted him to be happy. I know I'm a mass of contradictions, but I can't help feeling as I feel. Damn, things were so much easier when I was a kid! If I'd known life was going to be this difficult, I would've refused to grow up!

"I think I'm going to be sick," Jon said. "That is just too lovey-dovey."

I looked up. I'd been totally lost in my own thoughts. My brother and Dane were rubbing their noses together and grinning at each other with big, goofy smiles that could only mean they were in love.

"And all this time I thought you weren't prejudiced," Casey said.

"This has nothing to do with prejudice. It has to do with sickening sweetness. I could become a diabetic just watching those two."

"Come on, Jon," Brandon said. "I've seen you kiss girls in public, right before they screamed 'rape', of course."

"Fuck you, Hanson. That's just kissing. I don't care if Tim and Dane fuck right on the table, but this Valentine Day card stuff makes me wanna hurl."

"Well, I care if they fuck on the table," Brandon said. "Who could eat with all that moaning?"

"Look at them! They're not even paying attention!" Jon said.

It was true. Tim and Dane only had eyes for each other. They leaned in to kiss.

"Gentlemen, how are you getting along?" said Mr. Kerr, who was the teacher on cafeteria duty.

That got Tim's and Dane's attention.

"Um, fine, Mr. Kerr," Tim said.

"Good. Good."

Brandon and Jon laughed after Mr. Kerr walked away from the table.

"He could have busted you guys if he wanted," Jon said.

My brother and his boyfriend merely smiled and went back to gazing at each other.

"We've lost them again," Brendan said.

"Yeah, like you and Casper aren't almost as bad," Jon said.

Brendan crossed his arms and mock-glared at Jon.

"Hey, just because you have to beg for your girlfriend to touch you..." Brendan said.

"Hey, she begs me!"

"And then you wake up," Brandon said.

"Get a room, you two," Jon said to Tim and Dane.

"You know where there's one we can use?" Tim asked, hopefully.

"If I knew of such a place, I'd be there now," Jon said.

"Yeah, whacking it to some porn," Brandon said.

"So, they're like this at soccer practice, too?" I asked Marc, indicating Jon and Brandon.

"Practice, the locker room, the showers; of course, they're busy checking out all the other guys in the showers," Marc said.

"Uh, you have us confused with you!" Brandon said.

"If you didn't look so good naked, I wouldn't be looking," Marc said. "You have only yourself to blame."

Thank God, I wasn't taking a drink just then or I would've sprayed the table. Marc had balls.

"Yeah, I guess I can't blame you," Brandon said. "Who wouldn't want to see me naked?"

Jon raised his hand, then Brendan, Ethan, Nathan, and well...everyone, except Marc. He could hardly raise his hand after what he'd said.

"Oh, screw all you guys!"

Everyone laughed.

"So, you are a homo, then," Brandon said to Marc.

204

"You could have asked. It's not a secret. Surely, you had it figured out."

"Yeah. I'm not surprised. Damn, I think the whole world is gay except for you and me, Jon."

"That should solve the overpopulation problem then," Ethan said. "Actually, if it's up to Brandon and Jon to reproduce, we'll probably go extinct as a species."

"Yeah," Brendan said, "we'll probably have to pinch hit for them. I mean, what girl would want that?" Brendan nodded his head toward Brandon and Jon.

"Hey! Insults are our turf! Back off!" Brandon said.

"Yeah, you're working our side of the street!" Jon said.

Ethan and Brendan just looked at each other and mouthed, "Too easy."

"Don't you just hate it when homos try to be witty," Brandon said to Jon.

"I sure do. They should stick to what they know—like decorating, hairdressing, and giving blowjobs. Let's go where *we're* appreciated, Brandon."

"If there is such a place," I said.

Brandon flipped me off but couldn't help but grin. He and Jon walked away, pretending to be incensed.

"Well, there goes the entertainment," Ethan said.

"We can always watch Tim and Dane," Nathan said.

"Nah, I'm tired of that show."

Tim and Dane departed before the end of the lunch period as they had a habit of doing. They probably went to a quiet corner somewhere to steal a few kisses, although I couldn't imagine where they could find a quiet corner in or near the cafeteria. With everyone talking, silverware clinking, chairs scooting on the floor, and people coming and going, it was sometimes hard to carry on a conversation.

Marc closed his hand over mine. I looked at him and grinned. Damn, I wanted him! I wanted him right then and there. I wanted to throw him onto the table and climb right on top of him. That would sure cause a stir! I could just imagine what Brandon and Jon would have to say about that! Marc made me feel aggressive. He liked it kind of rough. Marc and I had only hooked up twice: once in my car and once with Blake. Marc had proven to be very sexual. I think you could describe the three-way as dom/sub, although sub didn't properly describe Marc. He had the submissive role in that he was the bottom and both Blake and I were rough with him, yet there wasn't really anything submissive about him. Someone smarter than I could explain it better, but I'm a jock, so what do you expect?

Near the end of lunch, Marc and I took our trays up together. Marc was telling me about skateboarding and trying to get me to join him sometime. I kind of wanted to, but I'd never skated. I just knew I'd spend more time on my ass than I would on the board.

I spotted Tristan and Nate speaking quietly together a short distance away. I had the strongest urge to go over and shove Nate away from Tristan. I guess I didn't have my jealousy very well under control.

"Ignore them," Marc said. "Come on."

Marc pulled me up the hallway, talking and laughing as we passed Tristan and Nate. It was all for their benefit. I didn't look to see if Tristan noticed us. I didn't want him to know I cared.

"What do you think about my performance," Marc said as we head on up the hall.

"Just now, or the other night in car?"

"Both."

"Incredible," I said, devouring him with my eyes.

"You look like you want to rape me," Marc said.

"Well, not rape you, but...I was having a little fantasy earlier about taking you right on the table in the cafeteria."

"Mmm, that would be hot, but then Mr. Kerr would come over and say, "Gentlemen, I'm sorry, but P.D.A. is not allowed.""

"Yeah, I'm sure that's what he'd say," I said, laughing. "Damn, I want you."

"Maybe after school?"

"I have work."

"Well, I could come over after work. We could at least make out on your couch."

"That might drive me insane, but yes, I get off at nine."

"Interesting choice of words."

I grinned.

"You are so bad."

"Yeah, and you love it."

"Yes, I do."

***

Work went well. I was lucky to have a job, or rather two jobs, that I liked. I didn't want to keep working at Ofarim's and Café Moffatt for my entire life, but both had pleasant atmospheres, easygoing bosses, and generally friendly customers. I felt a little odd serving guys on my football team, but then most of them worked similar jobs, too. They sometimes gave me a hard time, but it was all in fun, and it made the time pass faster.

Brendan and Casper came in at about eight for ice cream. They shared a banana split. I gazed at them longingly as they talked and laughed together. That's what I wanted with Tristan. Brendan and Casper had been together quite awhile now. They weren't all over each other like my brother and his boyfriend, but it was obvious they loved each other. They seemed an unlikely pair. Brendan was a muscular jock, and Casper was so small he looked younger than his sixteen years—make that seventeen—Casper had celebrated a birthday less than a week ago. Brendan was almost two years older than Casper, but he looked four or five years older. The actual difference in their ages wasn't all that much, but I wondered what they'd do after Brendan graduated in a few weeks. Casper was a sophomore and had two more years of school left.

Ofarim's usually cleared out near closing time. When only Brendan and Casper were left, I walked over to their booth.

"How's the loft coming along?" Brendan asked.

"Not bad. We're still missing quite a few things, but nothing we can't live without. Tristan helped me pick out some stuff…"

I trailed off. Talking about Tristan made me sad. Why did I have it so bad for him?

"Our social worker dropped in to check on us. She liked what we'd done with the place."

"So what's up with you and Marc?" Casper asked. "Is he your new friend, boyfriend, or boy toy?" Casper grinned.

"A little of each," I said. "We're kind of dating. We haven't known each other long, and we're just seeing where things go."

"I like his openness," Brendan said. "He's funny, too."

"Yeah, and sexy."

"I never notice things like that," Brendan said.

"Liar," Casper teased.

"Okay, I noticed. So what about you and Tristan?"

"I don't know. He seems much more interested in Nate than me. I guess we're still friends. Well, we're definitely not enemies. I just…I don't know. Marc knows how I feel about Tristan."

"You don't have to explain it to us," Brendan said.

"I know. I just…life's really complicated."

"Doesn't mean it can't be fun."

"Yeah, and Marc is definitely fun."

"I guess your sex life is no longer a problem," Brendan said. "The tone of your voice just then spoke volumes."

I grinned.

"Yeah. *That* part of my life has sure improved. I thought for sure I'd die a virgin."

"I think everyone does," Brendan said. "I know I did."

"You? I figured you always had guys crawling all over you."

"Nope. Most everyone assumed I was heterosexual. That kept any guy who might have been interested at bay. It was frustrating at the time, but it worked out for the best."

Brendan took Casper's hand and held it. They smiled at each other.

"Now I've got him, and I'm not letting him get away," Casper said.

"I wouldn't if I was you. I doubt Brendan will let you get away, either."

"Not a chance."

"If Jon was here, he'd accuse you guys of being sickeningly sweet."

"Yeah, maybe Ofarim's should hire Jon and Brandon to perform. Just give them a booth and let them go at each other. You could advertise it as dinner theatre."

"No kidding. I thought it was hilarious that Marc suspected they were a couple."

"Well, if I didn't know better, I might think that myself. I'm afraid they both have terminal heterosexuality, though."

"Yeah, too bad there isn't a cure for that. Such a pity," I said.

"I just hope neither of them gets himself into trouble," Brendan said.

"Surely they're smart enough to use protection."

"Yeah, but even that isn't a hundred-percent safe. Could you imagine either of them as a father, especially now?"

"Scary," I said.

"No one has it easy. Just think about Stephanie."

"Yeah, her baby is what, like eight-months old now? Can you imagine having a kid to take care of while you're still in high school?"

"He's so cute," Brendan said. "He has the most beautiful eyes and the most beautiful blond hair. Of course, I'm partial to blonds." Brendan looked at Casper, who grinned.

"Has she told anyone who the father is?" I asked.

"Who knows? I've heard it's the soccer coach, and someone said it was Devon. Stephanie isn't saying, so I doubt we'll ever know for sure."

"Yeah. I'm glad I don't have to worry about becoming a father."

"Have you and Marc been trying?" Brendan asked mischievously.

"Just once, but we intend to try a *lot* harder." I laughed. "Do *not* tell Tim I said that."

"Yeah, Dane and Tim were practically having sex at lunch today," Casper said.

"Maybe we should keep a bucket of cold water at the table to throw on them," I suggested.

"Do you think they'd notice?" Casper asked.

"Probably not."

Brendan and Casper departed about ten minutes before closing, and I continued cleaning up. I almost always worked ahead with cleaning and shutting things down so I didn't have to stay too long after we closed. No one else came in, so it didn't take me long at all to get things in order. I locked up and hurried home.

Marc was sitting on the couch talking to Tim when I arrived. I smiled when I spotted him.

"Ten more minutes and I would have put the moves on your boy toy," Tim said.

"I thought Shawn was *my* boy toy," Marc said.

"I could believe that, Tim, if you weren't head over heels in love with Dane."

"We did think about pretending to make out when you walked in," Marc said. "I was afraid you might not realize it was a joke, though, and I wasn't sure how I'd convince you."

"Probably a wise choice," I said.

"Hey, is Dane okay?" I asked Tim. "He seemed a little messed up today, well, except at lunch when you two were fawning over each other."

"I have some big news for you concerning Dane, and it's not good news," Tim said. "This cannot leave this room, however."

"Okay."

"Boothe is back in town—or at least he was."

"*What?* Did Dane call the cops?"

"No."

"Why not?"

"Shut up, and I'll tell you. Dane thought he saw Boothe yesterday afternoon when I was walking him home from school, but he wasn't sure. Anyway, this morning on the way to school Boothe ambushed him, made him get in his truck, and took him out into the country."

"Shit. Is Dane okay? Did Boothe hurt him? Did he…"

"Shut up, will you? He didn't hurt him, except for punching him a couple times and slapping him around."

"Why didn't Dane call the cops? I'm calling the cops."

"Shawn! Chill!"

Marc looked as though he didn't know quite what to think. I was on the verge of freaking out, and I didn't understand why Tim was being so calm nor why the authorities hadn't been notified.

"Boothe just wanted to talk. Well, he wanted Dane's help."

"His help? Why the hell would Dane do anything for that bastard?"

"I'm trying to tell you."

"Okay. Okay."

"This is where it gets interesting and weird. Boothe asked Dane if a ghost had come after him."

"A ghost?"

"Yeah, a ghost, from when they robbed graves."

"They robbed graves?" Marc asked. "Are you shitting me?"

"Yeah," I said. "I mean no. Boothe was a grave robber, and Dane worked for him for a while the summer he ran away from home and ended up in Verona."

"Wow."

"Boothe was serious about this? Was he drunk or high?"

"He was deadly serious, and he was not drunk or high. He said he wanted Dane to help him figure out how to get rid of this ghost or something like that. He'd said the ghost would be after Dane, too, and soon."

"Boothe is messed up."

"That's my guess," Tim said, "but Dane said he didn't seem messed up, other than talking about the ghost."

"Okay, so why didn't Dane call the cops? Boothe is dangerous."

"That's what I said, but Dane said that if Boothe wanted to hurt him, he could have done so when he had him out in the middle of nowhere. He figures he's safe. Boothe split anyway. He's not stupid enough to stay around."

"He's coming back, though? You said he wanted Dane's help?"

"Boothe wasn't very clear on that, but Dane figures he'll be back. How else could Dane help him with his ghost problem?"

"Boothe has finally just fucking lost it. Seriously, I'm calling the cops. Boothe is obviously nuts, and he is wanted."

"I don't know if Dane will like that."

"Tough. Boothe could come back and kill him or something."

"Well, I'm glad you're calling the cops. I wanted to, but Dane made me promise not to. I was hoping you would, but remember it was not my idea."

"Your wish is granted. Marc, this shouldn't take long. I hope you don't mind."

"Not at all. This Boothe sounds like bad news."

"Of the worst sort."

I made the call while Tim and Marc talked. There wasn't much the cops could do, of course, but I was told they'd be on the lookout for Boothe. I didn't give them any details other than that Dane had seen Boothe and he was sure it was him. I didn't want to cause Dane any problems, but I sure as hell wasn't going to just sit and do nothing.

"You look stressed," Marc said when I returned to the couch.

"I have homework," Tim said, winking.

Marc moved in on me and pressed his lips to mine. We started making out, and my worries over Dane left me. I concentrated solely on Marc—the taste and texture of his lips and tongue, the feel of his body as it pressed against mine, his erection as it fought to escape from his pants. All the kissing, hugging, and groping drove me insane with lust, but it relaxed me in other ways. Besides, arousal isn't an unpleasant feeling. It was rather exquisite, actually. I just thought of making out with Marc as a way to sexually torment myself until we could really go at it.

Still, I was sorely tempted to tell Tim he could have Dane in his room with the door closed for an hour if I could do the same with Marc. I had to be strong, however. I had responsibilities. I had to think with my mind and not my penis. At the moment, my penis was screaming for attention, but I willed myself to do what I thought was right.

"We could drive somewhere," I said after we'd been making out for an hour. "We could park somewhere dark again and…"

"I have to be home soon. Sorry."

"Damn. I think you just like tormenting me."

"Oh, I do, and I want you all worked up for the next time we can get naked together."

"If I'm this worked up, I'll explode before I can get it in."

"I'm sure you'll be good for another round," Marc said and kissed me again.

We made out a little while longer, then Marc got up.

"I'll drive you home," I said.

"Walk me home."

"Are you afraid I'll molest you in the car?"

"No. I'm afraid I'll like it too much, we'll be late, and Mom will think I've been kidnapped. Besides, I want to walk with you under the stars."

"It's started raining, Marc. We won't be able to see the stars."

"They're still there, silly, whether we can see them or not."

Marc and I put on our jackets. I grabbed an umbrella for us to share. I called out to Tim that I'd be back in a few, and then Marc and I set out.

It was chilly, but warmer than it had been recently, despite the cold rain. We were just barely into the second half of March. I couldn't wait for spring and warmer weather, but it was quite a pleasant night. I took Marc's hand, and he leaned his head against my shoulder. The rain fell down all around us, but we were safe and dry under the umbrella.

"I could really grow to like you," I said.

"Grow to like me. You don't already?"

I could hear the smile in Marc's voice.

"Of course, I like you already. I just mean I could grow to like you even more."

"Maybe Tristan has more competition than he thought."

"Yeah, I still can't get him out of my mind, though. I want you to know that."

"I know. You already told me."

"I just want to make sure."

"It's okay, Shawn. I know how you feel about him. I don't expect us to get serious. I don't even want to get serious with anyone right now."

"I just want to be honest."

"You always have been...honest and sexy."

"Damn, I wish we could be alone."

214

"Honest, sexy, and horny."

"Especially the last."

"Me, too."

"Waiting only makes it better."

"Maybe, but I'd rather do it all the time."

"I bet you would."

We reached Marc's home all too quickly. I pulled him to me and gave him a lingering kiss. I stood there in the darkness and watched him until he walked inside. I turned and headed for home. Why couldn't I have this with Tristan? Why did he want Nate instead of me? Why couldn't I just forget about Tristan and date Marc? Marc wasn't looking for anything serious right now, but that could change. I liked him better every time we met. If Tristan waited too long to notice me, he might just find he'd waited until it was too late.

216

Dane

I sat in my room doing my homework as the sun set. I took a short break and walked to the windows to watch the orange-golden sky. There were a few clouds on the horizon, and they turned a brilliant rosy-purple. The beauty of the sunset was such a contrast to the cold rain of the night before.

I stood there until the colors faded into the blue, black, and gray of night and then returned to my homework. I had an especially large amount to get done. I was thankful I'd worked ahead the night before. Otherwise, I don't think I could have finished. You'd think teachers could get together and make sure they weren't all making long assignments on the very same day, but nooooo.

Rain began to pelt the window panes as I worked. I stiffened for a moment when I noticed it. I didn't like any reminder of my dream. I shook my head and told myself I was being silly. It was just rain. I liked rain.

I wasn't sure how eager I was to go to bed. I knew my nightmare might be waiting on me. Perhaps I'd never dream it again. I think the nightmare was probably caused by thinking I'd seen Boothe. That brought up old memories and fears. Now, I'd seen him for sure and therefore faced the fear. Maybe the nightmare was some kind of premonition, too, but I didn't want to think like that. What if I dreamed something really bad again tonight?

"D-a-n-e."

I froze. I think my heart might even have stopped. I clearly heard someone calling my name in a whispering, raspy sort of tone. It wasn't Mom and it wasn't Dad. That left...who?

"D-a-n-e."

Shit.

I sat there glued to my seat. My room began to grow chilly. I looked toward the windows. They began to frost over on the inside. I shivered with cold and trembled with fear. Wasn't a room supposed to go cold right before...

"D-a-n-e."

The voice was closer now, much closer—far too close. I closed my eyes. I could feel it. I could feel it standing near me, just behind me and to my left. I slowly opened my eyes. My breath came harder and faster, creating puffs of steam in the frigid air.

"D-a-n-e."

Trembling, I forced myself to turn and look. I didn't want to look, but not looking was worse than looking.

"Shit!" I yelled and jumped to my feet. My chair hit the floor.

I backed into the table that was my desk, causing it to scoot several inches across the floor. There, not five feet away, stood a boy about my own age wearing an old VHS letterman's jacket. Only he wasn't a boy—at least, not anymore. His face was slightly bluish-purple, and he wasn't quite solid. Holy shit! It was a ghost!

"This isn't real," I said to myself. "Not real. Not real."

I closed my eyes hard and then reopened them. It was still there. It reached out toward me. I jerked backward and fell over the chair. I landed on my ass. I stared up. It stepped toward me, and then it was gone.

"Dane. Dane are you okay?"

It was my mom standing at the door.

"Um, yeah. I just...I guess I dozed off and fell out of my chair."

"Maybe it's time for bed, then. I can stay with you for a while if you like."

"Um, no, that's okay. I think I will go to bed, though."

"If you need us, Dad and I aren't far away."

"Thanks," I said.

Mom was no doubt worried I'd have another nightmare. I was now far more concerned with the nightmare that had just entered my waking life. Maybe it hadn't, though. Maybe I had fallen asleep. I didn't think so, but...a ghost? Maybe I'd drifted off while doing my homework and dreamed about a ghost because Boothe had been talking about ghosts. The dream seemed so real, but then my nightmare of the previous night had seemed real, too, and it was nothing but a bad dream.

I set my chair back up, undressed, and crawled under the covers. The cotton sheets felt soft and comfortable against my naked body. I pulled them up close around me and tried not to think about what I'd dreamed. It had to be a dream, after all. It couldn't possibly have been real. I mean…a ghost? Really?

"D-a-n-e."

"Shit!"

I dashed right out of my bed and stood near the windows, naked. It was back, and I was not asleep. I hadn't been in bed long enough to fall asleep.

"What do you want from me?" I asked, my voice barely above a whisper.

The cold felt more intense this time, but that was likely because I was naked. It stepped toward me. I trembled with cold and fear but stood my ground. The ghost would have been handsome if his face wasn't purplish-blue. He looked as though he had a nice build. My thoughts ground to a halt. I couldn't believe it. I was checking out a dead boy! I had some serious issues.

The ghost turned toward my dresser and reached out toward my jeans. I was terrified, but I was also fascinated. A real ghost!

He looked toward me, his face stern. I got the distinct impression he wanted something, but what? I looked at the ghost and then at my jeans. Slowly, I walked forward. It took every ounce of courage I possessed, but I walked toward my dresser. I had to pass way too close to the dead boy, close enough to clearly see the varsity letter for football. I tried not to look at him, but I couldn't stop looking.

I grabbed my jeans and emptied the pockets. I pulled out my wallet, my keys, some change… I stopped, something was there that shouldn't be. I picked up the odd-looking coin and gazed at in the moonlight. It was a half dollar, but it wasn't a normal half dollar. It was silver. Real silver. There was a small hole punched in it as if it had been worn on a necklace. The Liberty Bell was pictured on one side. I turned the coin over. There was a profile of

Ben Franklin and the date 1948. Boothe! That son of a bitch must have slipped it in my pocket this morning! But why?

I looked quickly toward the ghost. I held the coin out to him. He extended his right hand, palm up. It was purplish-blue like his face. He stepped toward me. It took every ounce of courage I had not to back away. I trembled violently as he drew so close I could have felt his breath if he'd been breathing. I dropped the coin into his open palm. I was too afraid to touch him. His fingers closed around the coin, and he was gone.

I darted back to my bed and pulled the covers up to my neck. The sheets and blankets felt so warm against my chilled skin. I was still shaking with cold and fear, but my mind was spinning. I'd seen an actual ghost!

I couldn't sleep, but not from fears of a nightmare. I was too excited. It wasn't a dream. I'd really seen a ghost. It was incredible! It was unbelievable, but it was real!

Damn that Boothe! That bastard had slipped that coin in my pocket! I knew he had! I'd found a couple of silver quarters and dimes in my change over the years but never a half dollar. That coin obviously belonged to the ghost!

Why the hell did Boothe plant the coin on me? Was he too chickenshit to face Mr. Football of 1948? Likely. Still, what was all that about needing my help to find a way to get rid of a ghost?

I thought for a moment. Had I seen the coin before? Had I seen the dead football player before? I concentrated hard, trying to remember a time in my life I'd worked to forget. The image struck me. I did remember! I remembered watching as Boothe opened the lid of a silver coffin. Inside was a teenaged boy wearing a VHS letterman's jacket. Yes! I remembered the coin! I remembered Boothe reaching in the boy's shirt, pulling it out, and ripping it off the chain that held it around his neck. I'd been especially disgusted by the way Boothe had no respect for the dead. That coin had probably meant something special to that boy. Maybe it had been given to him by a friend, a girlfriend, or even a boyfriend. Boothe thought nothing of taking it. I remembered the boy, too, and his handsome face. It hadn't looked quite as purplish-blue that night, but then maybe my memory was off. I remembered his dark blond hair. I remembered he reminded me of Brendan, who I was then trying to blackmail.

I'd long feared my past would come back to haunt me. Now, it had—with more than a little help from Boothe. What was Boothe's game? Had he hunted me down just to plant that coin on me? Was that the end of it? I doubted it. I'd heard ghosts only stuck around if they had some kind of unfinished business. The ghost had his coin back, but surely it wasn't that simple. Maybe Boothe was a big enough coward to want me to face the ghost instead of him, but surely he would have given the coin back himself instead of going to all the trouble and risk of returning to Verona to kidnap me. The cops could've nabbed him. There had to be more to it. I didn't trust Boothe to tell the truth, but I had a feeling this whole thing with Boothe was not at an end. Suddenly, a nightmare didn't seem so bad.

My curiosity helped me deal with my fear. I wondered about the dead boy who had visited my room. I'd been mildly and morbidly curious when I'd viewed him in his coffin, long years after his death. Now, I began to wonder who he was, what he'd been like in life, and how he'd died. I wanted to find out.

***

"Any dreams last night?" Tim asked when he met me at my locker before school. "Any sign of Boothe?"

"No and no. I do have a story to tell you, though."

"So tell me!"

"It has to wait."

"Grrrr," Tim growled. "Another long story I have to wait all day to hear?"

"The story isn't so long, but I'm sure there will be a lot of discussion after. We can talk about it while we explore the graveyard."

"Graveyard? Kinky, but just a bit chilly, don't you think?"

"We're not going to the graveyard to do *that*."

"Then, why...I know, you'll tell me after school."

"You're handsome and smart," I said.

"Yeah. Yeah. Let's eat a quick lunch today."

"Why?" I asked, mischievously.

"You know why. I want you so bad I'm gonna pop."

"Well, don't pop until lunch."

Tim leaned in and gave me a quick peck on the lips.

"Come on," he said. "I'll walk you to class."

Later, Tim and I wolfed down our lunches and slipped into the auditorium. We were all over each other in seconds. I groped the front of Tim's jeans. It was a wonder his zipper hadn't busted from the strain. Our jeans and boxers were down around our ankles moments later. I kneeled down, and soon Tim whimpered with pleasure.

When you're incredibly worked up and short on time, you'd be amazed at what you can do in fifteen minutes. Tim and I were all over each other in an orgy of frantic sex. I yearned for long, slow lovemaking with Tim, but there was something to be said for getting down and dirty right there on the stage.

Tim and I slipped back out of the auditorium relaxed and well-satisfied. Sex truly did calm me. I felt so mellow after relieving the pressure in my groin. How did I survive before Tim?

***

"So, tell me your story," Tim said as we walked away from school. "I've been going crazy wondering about it all day."

"Well, I've been apprehensive about it all day. I'm afraid you won't believe me, or you'll think I've lost my mind."

"Set you mind at ease, sexy. You're as far from crazy as I am, and you know I'll believe anything you say. You've never lied to me, and I know you never will."

"Here goes then. A ghost came to visit me last night."

"*What?*"

"You said you'd believe me."

"I do believe you! That tone in my voice wasn't disbelief; it was shock!"

I smiled.

"Think about how shocked I was."

I told my boyfriend all about my encounter with the ghost and about my thoughts on Boothe and what he was up to this time. We'd reached the cemetery on the edge of town by the time I'd finished.

"So, what are we doing here?" Tim asked.

"Looking for the boy from last night."

"I guess I'm not enough for you," Tim said with pretend hurt.

"You're more than enough, big boy. The boy we're looking for happens to be dead."

"Then, I guess we've come to the right place."

"Are you sure this is the right cemetery?" He asked a moment later.

"Yes, Boothe and I hit some smaller cemeteries, some I didn't even know existed, but this is where we dug him up. I'm sure of it."

"Wow, you really were desperate for a date last summer."

"Funny."

"I'm just trying to lighten the mood."

"What am I going to do with you?"

"I have several good ideas."

Tim pulled me to him and kissed me long and hard. I kissed him back as long as I dared then pulled away.

"No more of that for now or we'll never find him."

"Who cares? Okay, okay. Let's find the dead boy."

The cemetery had a slightly overgrown look. It likely hadn't been mowed since the fall. The grass was just beginning to become green, and it was growing in some places, but not in others. The cemetery was usually well-kept. No doubt someone would be along to mow it in the next few days.

The grave markers varied in age from the early 1800s right up to the present. I knew the grave we were looking for wasn't in the oldest section. No one had been buried in that part for a hundred years. I remembered that well enough from the time I spent here with Boothe. The dead football player had died long ago, but not before 1948. That was the date of the coin, and I was certain it had been buried with him.

"You don't happen to know his name, do you?" Tim asked.

"Sorry, I didn't think to ask. I was too busy being terrified. Besides, I don't think he was in a talking mood."

"I just thought I could be more help if you did."

"I'm trying to remember what was near it, but all I can come up with is ordinary tombstones. I don't think there was anything that stood out. It was dark, too, so that makes it harder."

"Maybe we can look for graves where the grass isn't growing in on top yet."

"Won't help. Boothe was very careful about removing the grass and setting it aside so it could be replaced at the end. When we were finished, it was very hard to tell a grave had been disturbed."

"I guess that makes sense. If people caught on that someone was messing with the graves, they'd keep a closer watch."

"Exactly. Boothe was a bastard, but he wasn't stupid."

"Mark's and Taylor's graves," Tim said, nodding toward two new-looking tombstones sitting close together.

"Taylor Potter," I read. "Born August 21, 1964. Died November 3, 1980."

I looked at the grave next to it.

"Mark Bailey. Born August 21, 1964. Died November 3, 1980. That's really weird. I know why they died on the same day, but to be born on the same day, too?"

"Yeah, I noticed that the first time I saw the markers," Tim said. "Look, someone has been here recently."

It was true. There was a small bouquet of purple carnations in front of each of the markers.

"I wonder who?" I asked. "Their parents?"

"I don't know how likely that is," Tim said. "Mark's dad is buried over there. He killed himself not long after Mark."

"Yeah?"

"With the same gun Mark used."

"Damn."

"It could have been one of the other parents, but I think it's more likely that Brandon put them here. Maybe Jon or Ethan, but I bet it was Brandon."

"Yeah," I said, remembering our talk about the loss of Taylor and Mark. "He's still not over it."

"I don't think he ever will be. Shawn said the guys were worried that Brandon would kill himself after Mark and Taylor took their own lives. They watched him pretty close for several weeks after that."

"It's so sad," I said.

"Yeah."

We walked on, cutting back and forth across the cemetery, but nothing looked familiar. After an hour, we gave it up. Mom would expect me home soon. I'd had to talk her into giving me this much time. She was still convinced Tim and I were going to have sex at the first opportunity. Mom was pretty smart sometimes.

Tim walked me home. Boy, it was great having a boyfriend to walk me home! My life had gone kinda topsy-turvy, but I didn't lose sight of how good my life was at present. I was in love with Tim!

Homework again. That's what my life would be if it wasn't for my boyfriend and the ghost: pure homework. Okay, I'm exaggerating, but I was convinced there was too much homework in the world. There really should be a law against it. Schoolwork should be kept in school and not allowed to creep out and mess up a perfectly good evening. Yeah, I enjoyed my homework sometimes, but there was always the annoying fact that I *had* to do it. That took away too much of the fun.

A thought occurred to me as I sat there in my bedroom. The ghost of the night before was from a time when my home was VHS. The ghost could have attended history or math or some other class right in my very bedroom. If the ghost lived in Verona up until he died, he could have attended school in this building for years. Chances were he'd sat right in this room when he was alive.

That's not all, either. He was on the football team—in this school! This building was used through the 1954 school year. If I was lucky, he might be on one of the team photos on the walls or in the trophy cases! Yes!

I started my search in the upstairs hallway near my room. There were lots of photos in the old school. Some of them were just 8x10s. Some of them were huge—more than six feet across and four feet tall. There were class photos, basketball photos, club photos, and more, but I was looking for football-team photos. I found one quickly, but it was from 1952—too late in time. I found others, from the 1930s, 1920s, and even the 1890s! There were none from the 1940s, however. I spotted the first one of those on the first floor. It was from 1942. I figured it was too early for my ghost, but I carefully scanned each face. Nothing.

I searched the walls and cases top to bottom. I found a couple more football-team photos from the '40s, but no one looked familiar. In the gym, I found a team photo from 1948—the very year on the ghost's coin. It was a huge photo located between the stage and the boys' locker room. I peered at the faces one by one. There he was! Wow. He had been handsome. If I lived back then...but anyway.

There was a list of the team members below the photo. It didn't take me long to find his name: Jacob Brubaker. Seeing his picture and putting a name to his face made him much more real. I knew the ghost in my bedroom had once been a real-live boy. All ghosts had been alive at one time or another. There was definitely an unreal quality about a ghost, however. I didn't think anyone would argue with me about that.

I felt less frightened of Jacob now. I don't mean that I was hoping he'd pop up in my bedroom again tonight, but thinking of him as Jacob made him seem more human than thinking of him as "the ghost," him, or it.

There were old yearbooks in what had once been the school library, so I went there next. It was at the opposite end of the hallway from the gym that led past the cafeteria doors.

It just figured that I couldn't find the yearbook for 1948. It was a blessing in disguise, however, for when I opened the 1949 yearbook, there was a memorial page near the front. It read, "In Memoriam—Jacob Brubaker—1933-1949—Athlete—Friend—Classmate."

I counted on my fingers. Jacob was sixteen when he died, *if* he died after his birthday in 1949. I had no way of knowing that, so he was either fifteen or sixteen. I didn't know how he died, either, but I thought it likely I could find out. If there were newspapers from 1949, they would surely have mentioned the cause of death. I looked carefully through the yearbook. I found another picture of Jacob in the sophomore section. There was a copy of the team photo just like the one in the gym, too, although it was much smaller, of course. There was also a photo of Jacob holding his football helmet under this arm, standing beside another player, an attractive blond guy with intense eyes. There was another photo of Jacob at the prom, escorting a pretty girl with dark hair. He looked so handsome in all his photos. I began to think it was a pity he'd died so young.

I put the yearbook back where I found it. I spotted the one from 1948 then. I yawned. It was getting late. I took the book back to my room with me. I'd look at it when I got the chance.

I drifted off to sleep thinking about Jacob, but I didn't dream about him. I didn't dream about Boothe either. Jacob didn't come to haunt me. I had a peaceful night's sleep.

The next morning, I paused by Jacob's team photo on my way to the shower. There he was with all his teammates, without a clue that he'd be dead in just a few months. You just don't think about dying when you're sixteen. At least I didn't. Maybe I should. Jacob had died at sixteen. So had Taylor and Mark. I bet none of them saw it coming. I bet neither Taylor nor Mark had any idea they'd be committing suicide until shortly before they did it. It made me think. By this time next week I could be dead myself, dead and buried in the very same cemetery as Taylor, Mark, and Jacob. I'd already come close to joining them all on that horrible night with Boothe all those months ago.

After school, I dragged Tim to the Verona library with me. He didn't resist much. I'd told him about Jacob during school, although I'd been careful to do it while no one could overhear. All I needed was for Brandon or Jon to find out I'd seen a ghost. I'd never hear the end of it. I think Tim was just as interested as I was in discovering more about Jacob Brubaker. After all, Tim was the same age as Jacob was when he died. He lived in the same town. He also played football. If Tim had been born a few decades earlier, they would've been teammates and perhaps more.

We hit the microfilm for the Verona Citizen for 1949. We found what we were seeking very quickly. That was good news for us, but not for Jacob. He'd died at the very beginning of 1949—on January 17.

There was a photo of Jacob in his uniform on the front page of the paper. Tim and I read it together.

The Verona *Citizen*—Wednesday,
January 19, 1949

LOCAL FOOTBALL STAR
VICTIM OF HIT AND RUN

Jacob Brubaker was the quarterback of the football team. He was well-liked by students and teachers alike. Now, he is gone, and no one knows why. The cause of his death is not in question. Brubaker's life came to an abrupt end Monday night when he was stuck by a hit-and-run driver on Rogers Road just outside of Verona. What is in question is who killed him and why? Was this an accidental hit-and-run or something more sinister?

Brubaker's body was discovered near midnight on the night of his death by Jack Selby, 26, who was returning from a late-night hospital visit with a relative.

"There was no sign of the vehicle that hit him," Selby said. "He was just lying slightly off the side of the road. At first, I thought someone had just fallen asleep. I stopped to check because I was worried about him being so close to the road. I was also afraid he might freeze to death. Monday night was a nasty night for anyone to be out, and snow was already beginning to cover him. In a few more minutes, I might not even have noticed him. When I got out of the truck and walked closer, I recognized Jacob. I shook him, but he didn't wake up. I held my hand near his mouth, but could feel no breath. Then, I checked his pulse. He was dead."

Selby quickly drove to the nearest home, his own, and called the authorities. They were on the scene in minutes, but it was far too late to help Brubaker.

"We found two faint sets of tire tracks in the vicinity of the body, mostly filled in with snow," said Sheriff Howell. "One set was Mr. Selby's. The other set of tire tracks was closer to the body. It looked as if someone swerved off the road and then back some ten or fifteen feet up the road from where the body was found. We believe Brubaker was walking on the road when he was hit. The driver must have swerved to miss him, but failed. The alternative is that Brubaker was walking alongside the road and the driver swerved and hit him."

Sheriff Howell is asking anyone with information pertaining to the incident to step forward but admits he doubts there were any eyewitnesses. There is slight hope that the driver of the vehicle that struck Brubaker will step forward, according to Howell.

"The driver likely panicked after striking Brubaker," Sheriff Howell said. "The alternate possibility is that the driver was inebriated. There are no skid marks and no evidence that the driver tried to stop. He may have swerved off the road and hit Brubaker without even knowing it due to his inebriated state."

Hit-and-run? Drunk driver? It matters little to Brubaker who is now lying in the county morgue, but friends and no doubt his family (who could not be reached for comment at this time) want to know what happened on the snowy night of January 17.

"He shouldn't have died," said classmate and teammate Will Bailey. "It doesn't even seem real. He was at school on Monday, talking and laughing, and then on Tuesday afternoon we found out he was dead. We were all just stunned."

No further details were available at press time. Funeral arrangements are pending.

"So now you know how he died," Tim said. "Hit by a truck or a car."

"Seems kind of weird, doesn't it?" I asked.

"What do you mean by weird?"

"If you saw someone standing in the road, wouldn't you hit the brakes without even thinking about it?"

"Yeah, probably, but the paper said the driver might have been drunk. Maybe he didn't even see Jacob. Maybe he didn't even know he hit him. He could have hit him, been startled by the bump, and then swerved off the road—all without realizing he'd just killed someone."

"Or maybe someone ran him down on purpose," I said.

Tim just looked at me.

"What?" I asked.

"That seems a little far-fetched. According to the article, everyone liked Jacob. Why would someone run him down on purpose?"

"I don't know, but I bet not everyone liked him. I don't think there is anyone that everyone likes. There could be all kinds of reasons someone wanted him dead. There are people who want me dead."

"Name one."

"Devon."

"Devon is a psycho. He wants a lot of people dead."

"Yeah, and maybe one of Jacob's classmates was a psycho, too. We don't know what went on way back then."

"We probably never will. All this was a long time ago. None of it even matters anymore."

"I guess not. I'm just curious."

"Well, maybe the *Citizen* has more to say about it," Tim said. "You know, you might be able to turn this into a school project. We do have a report due in English by the end of the semester. It doesn't have to be more than five pages. Maybe you can write about Jacob like you would a historical character."

"That's a good idea. I don't know if there's enough material for a paper, but I'd like to find out more about Jacob."

"*Really?*" Tim asked.

"Yes, smartass."

Tim laughed.

"I'm getting a little jealous of you and Jacob," Tim said. "I'm beginning to think you like him better than me—and he was in your bedroom."

"Well, he is kind of hot—if you can get past his bluish-purple face and the fact that he's dead."

"That's kind of a lot to get past."

It was my turn to laugh.

"Okay, let's see what else the paper has to say about your other boyfriend," Tim teased.

We turned our attention back to the *Citizen*. The next week's edition carried the obituary and details on the burial, which had occurred the previous Friday. I wrote down all the names mentioned in the obituary and the short article, but I was already beginning to wonder if there was enough material for a paper. It didn't matter. I wanted to know about Jacob, anyway, but it would've been nice to get a paper out of my efforts, too!

As Tim and I worked our way through issue after issue of the *Citizen*, it became apparent that the driver who ran him down was never found. Jacob was mentioned in every issue for a month, but then he more or less disappeared from the pages of the *Citizen*. We did find one more mention of him about two months after he was killed, but it merely recapped the details of his death and reported that the driver had still not been found. Tim and I kept looking, but all mention of Jacob Brubaker disappeared after that.

"It's sad," I said as Tim walked me home. "He was just forgotten."

"He wasn't forgotten, Dane. Just because he wasn't mentioned in the paper doesn't mean no one was thinking about him. It doesn't mean nobody cared. His friends and family didn't forget about him. You've never been mentioned in the paper, and I care about you a lot."

I grinned.

"Thanks, Tim. I guess you're right. It's still sad that he died like that. He was our age, Tim. It makes you think, doesn't it?"

"Yeah, but I'd rather not think about it."

Tim pulled me to him and kissed me. It was his way of shutting me up, and it worked perfectly. When our lips parted, we walked hand in hand to the old school that was my home. There, we kissed goodbye before I walked inside.

Shawn

"I want you so bad I'm going to explode," I told Marc just after school.

"The feeling is mutual."

"I'm off tonight, and Tim is going to be with Dane."

"Yeah?"

"You want to come over?"

"Trick question?"

"Let's go."

The only thing that kept Marc and me from ripping each other's clothes to shreds was the fact that Tim was coming home to change before going out with Dane. I wanted to pounce on Marc so badly I could barely restrain myself, but I knew that once we started, there would be no stopping. Even if we could limit ourselves to just making out, Tim might think he'd interrupted something. It would be just like him to hang around to torment me.

I made Marc and me some hot tea. When Tim and Dane came into the loft a few minutes later, Marc and I were holding hands across the table. We looked innocent, but not too innocent, as that would make my little brother suspicious.

"I just need to change and grab a couple of things, and we can head out," Tim said to Dane. "Be right back."

"So, anything more on Boothe?" I asked Dane.

"Thankfully, no."

"Don't go anywhere with him alone, Dane. If he does come back and you really feel you've got to talk to him, promise me you'll call me or Brandon or Ethan. One of us will go with you."

"What about Tim?"

"Well, that would be better than going alone, but I don't like the thought of Boothe being around my little brother."

"Me, either," Dane said.

"Call one of us. Don't meet him alone like last time."

"That wasn't by choice, but I'll call."

"Good."

I had the impression Dane wanted to tell me something, but he held back. It surely couldn't be because Marc was present. Marc knew all about Dane's meeting with his old grave-robbing employer and Boothe's warning about the ghost.

"Is there anything else you want to tell me?" I asked, trying to draw him out.

"Um, no. I will tell you if I spot Boothe again, though, or if he wants to meet."

"Okay."

Tim hurried back into the room.

"I rushed as much as I could. I know how boring Shawn can be."

"Funny," I said.

"See you later, big bro." With that Tim and Dane were gone.

"Want to call Blake?" Marc said with a wicked sparkle in his eyes. "I can handle two of you."

I grinned and picked up the phone.

"He's on his way," I said after I hung up. "I told him I'd leave the door unlocked. I don't want to wait for his arrival."

"We're lucky he was free, although I'm sure we'd do fine by ourselves," Marc said.

"He wasn't free. He had plans with his football buds, but he's dumping them."

"I wonder why," Marc said with a smirk.

Marc pulled me, not into my bedroom, but into the bathroom. There we stripped each other. Marc turned on the hot water and pulled me under the showerhead. Our lips met, and we made out like crazy for several moments. Next, we soaped each other up. Once we were all soapy and wet, we went back to making out. We began feeling and fondling and stroking. When we nearly reached the point of no return, we slowed down and made out passionately as the hot water coursed over our hard bodies. After ten or fifteen minutes we rinsed off, dried and headed for my bedroom.

Our make-out, feeling, and fondling session immediately continued. Soon, I was on my back, watching as Marc licked his way down my torso. Those blond bangs of his kept falling into his eyes, making him sexier than ever. Marc licked his way lower, and I nearly went over the edge.

I focused on maintaining control. I was sure I was up for more than one round, but I wanted to play it safe just in case. Besides, holding off was a delicious torment.

Blake entered my bedroom and closed the door behind him. I gazed at him with lust-filled eyes. He stripped off his shirt, revealing his smooth, muscled torso. His shoes, socks, jeans, and boxers followed. He walked toward us, as stiff as he could be...

From then on it was an intense three-way with far too much going on to describe. Sometimes I couldn't tell whose hands or tongue were where. We were all over each other, a writhing, moaning mass of pleasure. I slipped on a condom and took Marc first. It felt so natural to be with him like that. I operated on pure instinct. My focus narrowed to mating with Marc. Nothing else mattered to me then. Nothing could have stopped me. The sensations were way too intense, and I lost control. I rolled off Marc gasping for breath, slightly embarrassed that I hadn't lasted long. I was definitely up for more than one round, however.

We continued going at it. Blake did Marc next. Marc made Blake wear a condom. Blake wasn't happy about that, but he was in too big of a frenzy to argue for long. I watched Blake and Marc together before leaning over and slipping my tongue into Marc's mouth. Marc kissed me with intense passion. Blake lasted a lot longer than I had, but it wasn't a contest. He was a lot more experienced, too. Compared to Blake, I was a virgin. When Blake finally lost control, we all continued. If I described all we did in detail, I bet it would take fifty pages!

Marc was willing, and I was ready to go again, so I slipped on another condom and went at it. Blake put on another condom, too, and walked around behind me. I don't think I have to spell out what he did. Pain flashed in my mind for a moment, but it was soon replaced with exquisite pleasure. I'd never experienced anything like that in my entire life! I didn't know whether to focus on Marc, Blake, or my own body. The sensations passing through my body were too intense. I fought to stave off the inevitable, but I felt myself edging closer and closer. My heart pounded, I moaned louder than ever, and I exploded inside Marc. He moaned at the same moment, and I knew he was sharing my intense pleasure.

"OH, SHIT! I'M SORRY!"

Still in the midst of my orgasm, I whipped my head around just in time to see my little brother whipping out of the room and slamming the door shut.

"Oh, fuck!" I said.

I pulled away from Marc, but Blake wasn't finished with me. He held me down and went at me harder and harder. I was caught between passion and fear. I needed to get to Tim, but...

Blake moaned, his body jerked, and he fell on top of me. I wiggled free and slipped off the bed.

"Guys, I've...I've got to deal with this."

Marc nodded.

"We'll let ourselves out," Blake said as he reached for his boxers. "It was intense." Blake grinned. I only wished I could share his enthusiasm.

I looked around for my clothes and then realized they were still in the bathroom with Marc's. Shit!

I slowly opened the door and peeked out, although I don't know why I bothered. Tim had already caught me in the act with not only Marc but Blake, too! What must he be thinking? I motioned to Marc that the coast was clear, and we slipped down the hall to the bathroom.

Marc and I dressed in silence, but he stopped me before I opened the door.

"It will be okay, Shawn."

Marc leaned in, hugged me tight, and then kissed me.

We stepped out into the hall just as Blake left my bedroom, now fully dressed. Marc kissed me again, and then he and Blake departed.

I took a deep breath, walked down the hallway, and knocked on Tim's door.

"Come in."

He was lying on his bed, reading a comic book, which he put down as soon as I stepped in. His gaze was piercing and accusatory. I knew what was coming.

"So, Dane and I aren't allowed to make love in the loft, but it's okay for you to have a three-way with Marc and Blake? Is that how it is?"

"Shit," I said.

"Yeah, shit," Tim said. "Bullshit!"

My little brother stood up and glared at me.

I opened my mouth to speak a few times but shut it again to keep myself from saying something stupid. I thought about saying that it was different for me because I was older, but I wasn't much older. I thought about getting onto Tim for not knocking, but that wasn't going to fly. Every excuse that entered my mind was useless. I was screwed.

"I fucked up, Tim."

"Yeah, you fucked, and you were getting fucked, right here in the loft when I'm not allowed to make love with my boyfriend!"

"I know, Tim, I..."

"You know, Dane and I love each other! I don't think you love Marc, and I know you don't love Blake! Dane and I together means something, but what you were doing was just sex. How can you tell me I can't make love with my boyfriend when you're fucking everything that moves!"

"That's not fair, Tim. I'm not like that. I just get with Marc and sometimes with Blake."

"Yeah, whatever. How often does this go on? How many times have you done this behind my back? Dane and I have never made love in the loft! Never! We wanted to sooo bad. We both think it's stupid that we can't, but we didn't do it because we understood the position you were in. Now, I come in and catch you going at it with not one, but two guys! Do you want to explain to me how this is okay? Do you?"

"It's not okay, Tim. I fucked up. I'm sorry. I wasn't thinking with my head."

"Yeah, I know what you were thinking with. My dick tries to do my thinking for me, too, but I exercise self-control."

Ouch.

"Tim, I'm sorry. I..."

"Bullshit! This is fucking bullshit! I can't believe I apologized for walking in on you! I am so fucking mad right now I could punch you in the face! Fuck you, Shawn! Fuck you!"

Tim shouldered past me. I heard the door to the loft slam seconds later. I wished he had slugged me. It would have made me feel a little better. I sat down on the edge of Tim's bed and put my head between my hands. I'd screwed up royally this time, and I had only myself to blame.

I just sat there for several minutes feeling like a complete failure. I didn't know what to do. Tim was pissed off, and he had every right to be. Having sex with Marc in my bedroom had seemed like a great idea at the time. I'd wanted him so bad...and then when Marc suggested calling Blake, I didn't even think. I was totally consumed with lust. I didn't stop to think for a moment how things would look to Tim if he caught us in the act. I was a two-faced bastard and a hypocrite. Tim was right about something else, too. Tim and Dane loved each other. I was very fond of Marc, and I knew I could grow to love him, but I didn't love him. I definitely didn't love Blake. Pardon my French, but Blake was nothing more than a fuck.

Tim was right, and I was completely wrong. I was thankful I hadn't tried to rationalize my actions. I was thankful I hadn't said any of the stupid things that entered my mind when I was talking to Tim. That would only have made the situation much worse.

What was I going to do? How could I continue to tell Tim he couldn't make love with Dane in the loft after he'd caught me bare-assed. Worse than that, he'd caught me...I didn't even want to think about it. How humiliating. I had to be the world's worst parent.

I needed to talk to someone, but who? My dad? Yeah, right! Tristan? Yeah, like I really wanted to explain to him that my little brother caught me in the middle of a naked-boy sandwich. I couldn't imagine Tristan ever having a three-way. I couldn't imagine him having sex with anyone he didn't love. I thought of Nate, and suddenly I felt a whole lot worse. If Tristan had something going with Nate, then that meant...no, I couldn't think about it. Tristan would think I was a complete and total slut if I told him what had happened. Who else was there?

Dane's mom? I thought about it for a minute. She let Dane come over because she knew I'd act as a chaperone. I knew I was expected to keep things from going too far. I guess the situation could be worse. I could have caught Dane and Tim going at it. That would have meant I wasn't capable of acting as a chaperone. Still, the chaperone wasn't supposed to get caught having a three-way.

I stood up, walked to the phone, and called Dane's mom before I lost my nerve. I told her I'd made a big mistake and I needed to talk to her. She told me to come right over.

I walked because I wasn't in a hurry to face her. How was I going to say what I had to say? I wasn't going to give her details, but the general picture was embarrassing enough. Worse, she was going to be disappointed in me. I knew she expected more from me. I needed her help, though. I was in over my head, and I knew it. I didn't want anyone to know how I'd failed, but for Tim's sake—and mine, too—I had to face the music.

Mrs. Haakonson was waiting on me at the front door.

"Hi, Shawn. Come on in. I've made us some hot tea. I've set up a cozy little corner where I like to read. I thought we could talk there."

I nodded. I tried to smile, but I felt like crying instead. Abigail put her arm around my shoulder and led me into the building and to a door that had "Principal's Office" painted on the frosted-glass panel in the top half of the door. How appropriate.

Inside, the small room was not at all what I was expecting. I guess I should've known the old principal's desk, the file cabinets, and all the other office paraphernalia would have been removed long ago. Dane's mom had made the old office into a sitting room. Two comfortable sitting chairs upholstered with a light-blue fabric covered with roses were placed near each other with a low, square walnut table between them. Bookshelves were filled with a collection of hardbacks. A large, oval, hooked rug covered most of the wooden floor, and antique botanical prints decorated the walls. It was a very comfortable room.

A teapot and two cups as well as a lavender candle in a jar sat on the table between the chairs. I sat down and watched the flame as Dane's mom poured us cups of tea. She handed me a cup and saucer, and I took a sip before speaking.

"Mrs. Haakonson..."

"Call me Abigail, Shawn. Please."

"Abigail, I need your help. I'm in a spot, and I just don't know what to do. I made a big mistake this evening—a huge mistake—and I...I'm afraid I've messed up everything with Tim. I've tried to be a good parent, but...I'm not a good parent at all. I'm a complete and total failure."

My eyes grew watery. Great, just what I needed: to cry in front of Dane's mom. That would complete the picture of pathetic loser quite nicely.

"Why don't you tell me what happened, Shawn," Abigail said calmly.

"I don't know how to say it, so I'll just say it. Tim walked in on me having sex with...two other guys."

I know I must have turned completely red.

"I've been trying so hard to do what's right for Tim. I've done my best to chaperone Tim and Dane when they're at the loft. I make Tim keep the door to his room open when Dane is there. I've been seeing this boy, Marc. I really like him, and...I just wanted to be with him. And, the other guy, Blake. You must just think I'm horrible."

I couldn't even look at Abigail.

"Shawn, I think you're a courageous and intelligent young man. You're doing the best you can in a very difficult situation. You were thrust into this situation without warning. Overnight, you became, in essence, Tim's dad. Being a parent isn't easy at any age, and it's got to be much more difficult for someone so young. I've felt very comfortable with Dane visiting Tim because I knew you'd make sure things didn't get out of hand."

"But now I've ruined it," I said. "How can I tell Tim he can't have Dane alone in his room with the door closed when he just caught me doing exactly what I'm trying to keep him from doing? I'm a hypocrite. I've completely lost my credibility with Tim. He was screaming at me when he stormed out of the loft."

"He'll calm down," Abigail said. "I think you're being too hard on yourself. This is as much my fault as yours. I didn't mean to put you in such a difficult position. I didn't stop to think I was piling more problems on your shoulders. I was just happy that I knew Dane would be safe when he was near you."

"I've messed everything up!"

"Shawn, you're seventeen. Most boys your age aren't asked to place such constraints on themselves. You've not only become Tim's parent, you've become your own. It's put you in an extremely difficult and trying position. I'm sorry. You should be free to do what you want in your own home, and that includes sex. As a mother, I don't think you're old enough to be having sex, but then mothers aren't objective about such things. I won't be comfortable with Dane having sex when he's thirty. He'll always be my baby. Being objective, however, I know that you are an intelligent, mature, young man who is quite capable of making intelligent decisions about sex."

"I wasn't very intelligent this evening. I let my...body do my thinking for me."

"You shouldn't fault yourself too much for that, Shawn. You are at an age when your body is quite demanding about such things.

Instinct is ordering you to have sex. Fighting against that is a little like trying not to breathe."

I grinned. I was amazed Abigail understood so well.

"That's how it feels. Sometimes, I feel as though I'm going to die if I can't have sex. That just makes me more of a hypocrite, however. I took care of my needs while I denied Tim the opportunity to take care of his."

"Welcome to parenthood. All parents are hypocrites at times, but we mean well."

"I don't really want to say this, but I don't even feel as if I'm doing the right thing when I'm telling Tim he shouldn't have sex. I don't really see anything wrong with it. I did talk to him about the dangers of VD. I even bought him condoms."

"I'm very impressed, Shawn. Most parents don't do such a good job when it comes to sexual matters. Most don't even talk to their kids about sex."

"Yeah, but most parents don't get caught having sex by their kids."

"They don't?"

"Well, I, uh, I figured they didn't."

I took another sip of tea.

"On the contrary, I think it likely that most kids do catch their parents having sex. Think about it. Parents and children live in close, intimate proximity. It's almost bound to happen. Even if it doesn't, the existence of a child is proof that his or her parents do have sex, at least once per child."

Abigail grinned.

"You're making this a lot easier to talk about than I expected. I was not looking forward to this discussion, especially to admitting what Tim caught me doing," I said.

"I'm not surprised that you're sexually active. I'd be more surprised if you weren't. You're a healthy young man. It's almost a given. I would not be surprised to discover that Dane is sexually active as well. I don't like thinking about it, but I do because I want to keep him safe. I talked with Dane about safe sex just like you did with Tim. That wasn't an easy conversation for either of us. It was likely a good deal easier on Tim, because he was talking to his brother and not his mother."

"Yeah."

"The point is that I talked about a difficult topic for Dane's sake. I know this conversation isn't easy for you. I admire you because you have the courage to talk to me about it."

"Well, I'd handle it myself if I could, but I'm in over my head."

"Yes, and you're doing the mature and intelligent thing by asking for help."

"So, any idea of what I can do? If I continue to tell Tim he can't have Dane in his room with the door closed, he's just going to throw this evening back in my face. I can't blame him. I did exactly what I told him not to do. As Tim pointed out, what I did was even worse, because I don't love Marc or Blake. Tim loves Dane very much."

"You have been compromised. I think the best course is to remove the rule."

"You mean allow Tim to have Dane in his room with the door closed? You know what they'll be doing."

"Yes, that's what I mean, and I know what they'll be doing. I'm sure I've gone too far in looking out for Dane's best interests, but I'm his mother so I can't help it. I can't watch over him all the time, and as much as I'd like to, I shouldn't. The truth is that Dane and Tim will have sex if they want to. I don't like to think about it, and I don't know how far they've gone, but I'm sure they've gone as far as opportunity allows. Once the weather gets warmer…well, there is no controlling teenage boys. I dated a few in my past. I know what they're like."

"Tim said as much to me. He said no one can stop them from making love. He used that as a rationale for why I should allow him to make love with Dane in his room."

"That makes a lot of sense, but don't tell the boys I said that."

"Yes, and to be honest, I've felt pretty unreasonable all along. If I was Tim, I'd find a way, no question about it."

"I'm afraid you are right."

"So, how do we handle this? I don't think telling Tim it's fine to make love with Dane is a good idea. Those two do not need encouragement."

"We just tell them that we trust them to make the right decisions regarding sex, and we trust them to be safe. I'll make it clear to Dane I think he's too young, but that I'm also realistic. You may want to stress being safe again. I know you aren't as opposed to the two of them being sexually active as I am."

"This is going to make my life much easier."

"I'm sorry I put you in such a position, Shawn. I really am. Of course, at the same time, I can't help but wish we could continue as before, but that's no longer possible."

"Thanks to me."

"Shawn, I appreciate everything you've done. I also haven't forgotten you saved my son's life. If it wasn't for you..." Abigail stopped. Her eyes grew watery, and for a moment, I thought she was going to cry.

I nodded. I always felt a bit awkward whenever anyone brought that up.

"Thank you so much for your help," I said. "I didn't know what I was going to do. Thank you for being understanding about my, uh, sexual activities, too."

"I'm glad to help. As for being understanding, I've always believed everyone's sex life is their private business. You're a young man, not a boy, and you're mature enough to make your own decisions. You've proved your maturity over and over again. Just remember, doors do have locks."

I smiled.

Abigail and I sat in her cozy little retreat and drank hot tea while chatting about this and that. I was glad to leave the more embarrassing and complicated topics behind. I felt a good deal better when I departed than I had when I'd arrived. Now all I had to do was face Tim.

***

Tim hadn't returned by the time I made it back to the loft. I was tired, but there was no way I could sleep until I'd talked to him. I made myself some hot tea and sat down at the table to do some homework.

It was difficult to keep my mind off what was to come. I could just envision a shouting match, with Tim doing most of the shouting. The minutes crawled by. I did my best and completed a lot of homework, although not as much as I could have if I'd been able to focus properly. Tim came in a little after midnight—later than he was supposed to—but I didn't say a word about that.

"We need to talk," I said.

"Fuck you. Oh, wait, Marc and Blake already have—whore."

"If you're done insulting me, I have some things to tell you."

"I repeat, fuck you. I don't want to talk to you."

"Just listen to what I have to say."

"No!"

"Tim..."

"Just fuck off!"

I stood up and walked toward him. I was getting angry but trying to fight it.

"Tim, just listen to me," I said, putting my hand on his shoulder. He shoved it off.

"What part of 'fuck off' don't you understand? Oh wait, I know you understand fuck, you do it all the time. I guess it's off that has you confused."

"Just listen," I said, grabbing him by the shoulders.

That's when he punched me in face. I tackled him, and we fell to the floor. Tim punched me in the stomach before I managed to wrestle him onto his stomach and get his arm twisted behind his back. That truly set him off, but I was in control now.

"Get the fuck off me!"

"Not until you listen!"

"Fuck off! I'm not listening to you! Whore!"

"You are going to listen," I said, twisting his arm enough for it to hurt, but not hurt too much.

"Fuck you!"

I twisted his arm a bit harder, and I heard Tim sob.

"I'm trying to tell you that you're right about what you said before you stormed out. I'm trying to apologize and tell you about how things are going to change. Will you just talk to me, or do I have to hold you here while we talk?"

"I'll talk to you. Now let me up, fucker!"

"You promise?"

"I promise."

I let Tim up off the floor.

"So talk!" Tim said as he walked to the table and dropped down in the chair.

"You were right. I should not have had sex here in the loft with Marc and Blake when I wouldn't let you do it with Dane."

"Damn right, I'm right!"

"I shouldn't have done it, but I just lost control. You know how it is, Tim," I said as I rubbed my jaw where he'd slugged me.

"Yeah, I know how it is, but I haven't been doing it here with Dane!"

"I know. I'm sorry I did it."

"Are you sorry you did it or just sorry you got caught?"

"A little of both. You were also right when you pointed out that you and Dane love each other, while it's just sex with Marc, Blake, and me."

"Exactly, which makes what you did worse!"

"Okay! Okay! I said I was wrong, and I'm sorry."

"Sorry isn't good enough! You expect me to do what you say when you don't even follow the stupid rules yourself? Dane and I have been as cooperative as possible up until now, but you can forget that! I'm not following rules you won't follow. Fuck that!"

"I know. I know. You're right."

"I know I'm right, but you agree?"

"Yes."

Tim grew a good deal less angry.

"So what do you plan to do about it?"

"I went and had a talk with Abigail. I told her what happened."

"You told her you were fucking Marc while Blake was fucking you?"

"Uh, no. I didn't get that graphic. I did tell her you caught me having a three-way in my bedroom." I held up my hand to forestall more questions. "We agreed that I can no longer expect you to keep your door open when Dane is here."

"So Dane and I can make love in my room?"

"I didn't say that."

"What are you saying?"

"I'm saying you can keep your door closed when he's here and that I will respect your privacy."

"So we can have sex!"

"I'm not putting it into those words, but from now on, what you do in your bedroom is your business, and what I do in mine is my business."

"Yes!"

"This isn't permission for you to have sex. This isn't to encourage you. I know you need no encouragement."

"You've got that right!"

"So, do you think this is fair?"

"I think it's the way things should have been from the beginning!"

"I understand, and maybe you're right, but you've got to understand the feelings of Dane's mom and her expectations of me. I was in a difficult spot. She even apologized for putting me there."

"Really?"

"Yes. Listen, Tim. She just wants what's best for Dane. She's just trying to protect him. I'm just trying to look out for you. I'm sorry I've done such a lousy job, but I'm new to this, okay?"

"Actually, you've done a pretty good job."

"Does this mean you don't hate me?"

"I didn't mean that. I'm sorry. I was just so pissed off. You might call it sexual frustration."

"I know how that is."

"Yeah, right. You just had a three-way, whore."

Tim's tone of voice indicated he was teasing me.

"For your information Tim, a whore is someone who charges for sex. I wasn't charging."

"Okay. So you're a slut, then. You charge? Ha! You couldn't give that shit away for free."

"You know you're contradicting yourself."

"Whatever."

"Listen, I really am sorry."

"Okay, okay. I forgive you. You can stop kissing my ass now."

"Blow me, Tim."

"Sorry, I have a boyfriend. Besides, you have at least two boy toys for that."

We stood up. I hugged Tim, and he hugged me back.

"I love you," I said.

"I love you, too, big bro. Now, I'm gonna call Dane so he can come over and we can have sex!"

"Tim," I said in a warning tone.

"Kidding! I'm kidding."

"Listen, if you guys do…"

"If? You're funny, Shawn."

"*If* you guys have sex, be safe, okay? I'll buy you more condoms anytime you need them. No questions asked."

"Buy a case!"

"You're horrible, but I just want to keep you safe."

"You can't do that, Shawn. No one can keep anyone safe, but thanks for trying. I'm going to try to keep you safe, too. You have your own condoms, right?"

"Of course."

"Yeah, I guess a slut would have plenty."

"Tim!"

"Chill out. I'm kidding, but tell me, how many times did you guys have a three-way here?"

"Um, just two."

"How many times have you had sex with Dane here?" I asked.

"None, like I said, but it's only from lack of opportunity. You're like a freaking watchdog."

I laughed.

"I'm exhausted," I said.

"Yeah, wild sex takes it out of you."

I rolled my eyes.

"Shawn, I'm sorry I hit you. I was just so mad…"

"I understand. I had it coming. Besides, I barely felt it. You hit like a girl."

"Yeah, right!"

"Goodnight, Tim."

I kissed his forehead.

"Goodnight, Shawn."

Tim kissed me on the lips, but it was a nonsexual, brotherly kiss. I smiled and headed for my bed.

Dane

I shivered and pulled the blankets up over my bare shoulders. I was dreaming about Jacob, but I knew it was a dream. I was in that twilight state, somewhere between asleep and awake—in both and neither. In the dream, I became Jacob. I was walking along a dark country road in a snowstorm. A truck was headed toward me. It accelerated. It swerved off the road and plowed right into me, sending me flying. I screamed.

I sat bolt upright in my bed, my heart pounding in my chest. I shivered again. Cold air hit my bare chest. I gasped. Jacob!

He was standing beside my bed, slowly shaking his head from side to side. I fought to control my trembling.

"What do you want?" I asked, my voice quavering. "I gave back your coin. I didn't even know I had it. Boothe stuffed it in my pocket."

Jacob took a step forward, and I scrambled backwards in my bed, which only served to put my back against the icy headboard.

"I'm sorry we disturbed your grave! I didn't want to, but I was desperate! Please."

Jacob's brow furrowed, and he shook his head more violently.

"I don't know what you want!"

Jacob faded until he was no longer there. The air grew warmer. I slipped back down into my bed and pulled up the covers. He was trying to tell me something. I knew he was. But, what?

Jacob had shaken his head when I mentioned his coin. I supposed that meant he wanted more than the coin. That much was obvious, anyway. He had his coin back, but...

I sat up quickly. My hand flew to my chest. I gasped. I ran to the light switch, flipped on the lights, and then ran to the mirror. Jacob's coin hung on a chain around my neck. I just stared at it lying on my chest. How...?

I quickly pulled the necklace over my head and placed it on the dresser. I stood there staring at it. How? I was confused and frightened. I shivered and returned to my bed. I needed the comfort and security of my blankets. This new turn of events disturbed me even more than Jacob returning to haunt me. I was going to let Boothe have it when I saw him again.

***

Tim met me at my locker before school.

"So, anything new with Shawn?" I asked.

Tim had come over the evening before, mad enough to chew on nails. I was somewhat ticked off at Shawn, too, but not nearly as much as Tim was. Sure, Shawn was doing it with guys at his place when Tim and I weren't allowed to mess around there, but come on, I would probably have done the same if I was he. Tim and I would have made love in the loft if we'd had the chance. Tim was really steamed, though. I think part of that was probably because we hadn't been together recently. I don't know about Tim, but I tended to get aggressive and hostile when I was needing it.

"I have big news. Did you talk to your mom this morning?"

"Yeah, I talk to her just about every morning."

"Did she say anything...especially interesting?"

"No. She said she wanted to talk to me about something after school, but that was about it."

"That's it, then."

"What's it?"

"Shawn was at your place last night while we were out. He had a talk with your mom."

"About what happened? He actually told her?"

"Yeah, but that's not the best part."

Tim and I began walking toward class. We kept our voices low, so it wasn't likely anyone could hear us with all the other conversations, locker doors slamming shut, and guys calling out to one another.

"This must be good news. You're smiling."

"Oh, it's beyond good. We don't have to keep the door open when you're in my bedroom."

"Seriously?"

"Would I kid you about something like that?"

"Wow."

"Yeah. How could Shawn keep insisting that I can't keep my door shut after what he was doing in his room?"

"I guess that makes sense."

"It's probably a good thing I got so pissed and left. Otherwise, I would have tried to talk Shawn out of talking to your mom."

"Why?"

"Because she might not have let you come over at all."

"Yeah, now that you mention it, I'm a little surprised that wasn't her reaction, but I guess we don't need to worry."

"No. It's all cool. If you think about it, everything has worked out perfectly. I was royally pissed off, but now I'm glad Shawn lost control."

"So, you're not mad at him anymore?"

"No. I probably shouldn't have gotten so angry at him, but…well, that's the past. We're cool now."

"I'm glad. I'd hate for you guys to be on the outs."

"We fight sometimes, but we're brothers. Even when I say I hate him, I don't."

We wanted to talk more, but we were out of time. I'd reached my class. We would have kissed, but the hall monitor was watching. Instead, we just grinned and said goodbye.

I didn't see Tim again until lunch. We silently agreed to take our time eating and not slip off to the auditorium. We could make love at Tim's place now, so there was no need for a quickie at school. I'd miss the rush I got from the dangerous edge of our auditorium encounters, but recent events had proven the risk was too great. Only the day before, a couple got caught messing around in the balcony. It was a guy and a girl. Word was they were making out and had their hands in each others pants. Both of them were suspended for three days. That could easily have been Tim and me. It might well have been if we'd been in the auditorium, too, although we might have been hidden well enough in the curtains.

"Jacob paid me another visit," I told Tim as he sat beside me at lunch.

"Yeah?"

"I actually had a dream about him, and then, when I woke up, he was standing beside my bed."

So far, I hadn't mentioned the ghost around any of the guys. That's the kind of thing you usually keep to yourself. I figured I was among friends, however, and lots of people believed in ghosts. If I was brave enough to come out...

Nathan gave me an odd look.

"A boy just showed up in your bedroom last night?" he asked.

"Slut," Brandon pretend coughed.

"Well, he's, uh, not a boy, exactly."

"Hermaphrodite," Jon said. "A chick with a..."

"Jon," Casey growled in warning.

"...with a male reproductive organ. You should've just let me said 'dick.' It's so much easier."

Casey rolled her eyes.

"No," I said.

"Is 'not a boy, exactly', like being a little bit pregnant?" Brandon asked.

"Well, he is a boy. He just..."

"So you checked?" Jon asked.

"Noooo," I said.

"Then how do you know for sure," Brandon asked. "I sometimes wonder about Jon. I think he might be a girl."

"Dude, you've seen mine more than my girlfriend has," Jon said. "Ouch. That didn't come out right."

"What he means is he's a virgin," Brandon said, "and he thinks I've seen his in the showers."

"I'm not a virgin, and you *have* seen it!"

"I don't recalling seeing anything like that," Brandon said.

"I can't believe you guys are having this discussion," Casey said.

"I can," Ethan said.

"Anyway," Brandon said. "Just how is this Jacob not exactly a boy?"

"He's dead."

"Dead?" Casper asked.

"Oh, man, Dane offed some boy last night in his bedroom!" Jon said.

"I did not. He was dead when he got there."

"Why don't you just tell us what you're talking about?" Tristan asked.

"Jacob is a ghost."

"A ghost?" Ethan asked, raising an eyebrow.

Now, everyone was looking at me—Marc, Shawn, Tristan, Ethan, Nathan, Casper, Casey, Brandon, Brendan, Jon, and Nate. Tim already knew about Jacob, of course.

"Yeah, a ghost, so he's not exactly a boy."

"I guess that's right," Brandon said. "I think a dead boy is still a boy, but when he's gone all the way to ghost, he's not quite a boy anymore."

"You actually saw a ghost?" Marc asked.

Jon made a circular motion with his finger at the side of his head.

"I'm not crazy!"

"That's what all the crazies say," Jon said. "Honest, officer. I'm not crazy. Satan really did tell me to kill all those people and eat their livers."

"Hey! Lay off my boyfriend!" Tim said.

There was an angry tone to Tim's voice. He meant business.

"Dude, chill!" Jon said. "You're so protective. You know we're just jerking his chain. "

"Yeah," Brandon said, "like you jerk my…"

"Are you serious?" Tristan said, cutting off Brandon. "Or are you just jerking *us* around?"

"No, I'm serious. I've seen him twice now. It all started after Boothe came back."

"*What?*" Ethan asked.

"I guess I should start at the beginning."

I did just that. I told them about being kidnapped by Boothe, what he said about a ghost pursuing him, and finally about Jacob and the stuff Tim and I had looked up on him.

"Then, there's this," I said, pulling the coin out of my shirt.

"That's the coin you told me about," Tim said. "The one Boothe slipped in your pocket and that you gave back to the ghost."

"Yes. Last night, after he left, I found it hanging around my neck."

"Dane's got a new boyfriend," Jon chanted.

"Shut up," I said.

"You found it hanging around your neck?" Tristan asked. "He didn't put it on you?"

"No. It was just there when he'd gone. It doesn't make a lot of sense to me. I thought he came for the coin the first time. Boothe stole it from his grave."

"Fascinating," Tristan said.

"You believe him?" Jon asked.

"Yes," Tristan said. "I don't think he would have carried a joke this far."

"Dane wouldn't joke around about Boothe," Ethan said.

I nodded. Ethan was there the night Shawn rescued me. Really, he'd rescued me, too, although it was Shawn who pulled Boothe off me and punched him out.

"I swear I'm not making this up," I said. "It's okay if you don't believe me. I'm not sure I'd believe any of you if you were telling me the same story. It is true, though, and I've got a ghost who has showed up in my bedroom twice already. I have a feeling he'll be back."

"Yeah, after he gave you his necklace and all," Brandon said. "He's bound to be back. You guys are like...dating now."

"Kinky," Jon said. "Dane is dating a dead boy. I'd be jealous if I was you, Tim."

"Is he cute, at least?" Nathan teased.

"Well, yeah. I'll bring in the yearbook tomorrow and show you. He was cute, although he doesn't look so good now. He's kind of purplish-blue."

"Yeah, I hear being dead does nasty things to your complexion," Jon said.

Jon looked across the table at Brandon, who didn't look as if he felt so well. He almost looked as if he might cry.

"Excuse me," he said.

Brandon stood, picked up his tray, and quickly walked toward the garbage cans to dump it.

"Shit," Jon said. "I'm so stupid sometimes."

Jon got up too and hurried after Brandon.

"It's about Taylor and Mark, isn't it?" I asked no one in particular.

"Yeah," Ethan said. "Brandon has taken it harder than any of us, and it's not easy for anyone. You'd think it would get easier, but..."

"I'm sorry," I said. "I wouldn't have told you about Jacob if I thought it was going to upset anyone."

"No, it's okay," Ethan said. "It's not you or talking about your ghost. It's not your fault."

Ethan got up too and followed Brandon and Jon.

"I still feel horrible," I said.

"Don't," Tristan said. "It's okay. Taylor was my cousin. Ethan meant what he said. It's not you or what you said. It just happens sometimes."

I nodded.

I noticed Shawn watching Tristan with a concerned and compassionate look on his face. He was still in love with him.

"Was it really scary?" Casper asked.

"The first time I about crapped my pants, which would've been especially bad considering I sleep naked."

"Too much information," Casey teased.

"Last night wasn't so bad. I was scared, but I guess the second time is easier."

"I hear it's like that with zombies, too," Marc said.

I flipped him off, and he laughed.

"I'm really curious about him," I said. "I think that helps me be less afraid."

"What concerns me is Boothe," Ethan said.

"Well, Shawn called the cops and told them he was in town. He didn't give them all the details, but he told them I'd spotted him."

"You need to be very careful, Dane."

"Oh, I'm being careful. I really don't think he's a danger right now. I sure as hell won't go off with him somewhere willingly. That would be insane. I figure I'm pretty safe, though. If he'd wanted to hurt me, he could have when he kidnapped me. We were out in the country where there was no one to hear me scream. Believe me, I take Boothe seriously."

Lunch was near the end by then. Tim and I took our trays and dumped them.

"I guess you just came out again," Tim said.

"Yeah, now everyone knows I'm gay and I see ghosts."

"And get presents from them."

"I don't know if I'd call this a present," I said, pulling out the coin.

"I guess I've got some competition," Tim said.

"No way. Jacob is older than my dad!"

Tim laughed.

"I dunno, older guys can be hot."

"Not if they're dead," I pointed out.

"Yeah, dead isn't a turn-on for me either."

"Speaking of turning on…maybe I should come over after school."

"I'd like that, but maybe we should wait a while. Shawn is going to expect us to go at it as soon as possible. It would probably be best to wait a few days. I can't really picture him pounding on the door if he thinks we're doing it, but it would be best if we played it cool for a while. I think it will make Shawn feel better about things. He knows we're going to have sex, but this way it's less obvious. Besides, you mom wants to talk to you after school, right? She probably expects you to rush over and do it with me as soon as possible, too."

"I'd forgotten! You're right, anyway. I guess we should make it easy on them. Besides, now that we can do it we don't have to be in a hurry. Just so we get to do it a lot!"

"Oh, we will. We will," Tim said.

***

I took a walk after supper. I needed to get out by myself and think. I wandered over by the old Graymoor Mansion, across the street from the little rental house where I'd lived not so long ago. I'd once lived even closer, with Austin, in the old summer kitchen of the mansion itself.

I stood and gazed at the mansion. If there were ghosts in Verona, they'd surely be in there, but I had one in my very own home. How did one get rid of a ghost? Exorcism? I wondered why Boothe was so desperate to find a way to keep the ghost away. Jacob freaked me out, but he wasn't that bad. He didn't try to hurt me or possess me. He was basically just a boy. Sure, he was a dead boy, but other than that…

The old mansion intrigued me but not nearly enough to go inside. When I lived in the little rental house, it looked as though there were lights in some of the windows. It was as if someone was inside, walking around with a lamp. When I'd lived in the summer kitchen, I'd thought I heard screams.

The hair on the back of my neck stood on end as I began to hear organ music coming from inside the old house. At first, I didn't even realize I was hearing it. The melody was more like a memory than a sound. I'd heard the melody before, when I lived near the old mansion with Austin. I drew right up to the iron fence and listened. The music called me as if beckoning me closer.

"Going in?"

I jumped.

"Sorry, I didn't mean to startle you," Tim said.

"Do you hear that?" I asked.

"What?"

"Listen."

"It's an organ."

"Uh-huh, and it's coming from in there," I said, pointing to the mansion.

"Cool," Tim said.

"I used to hear that music sometimes. I told you I used to live in the old summer kitchen by the mansion, right over there. Remember?"

"Yeah."

"Austin said it was the safest place to hide out in Verona, because no one would dare get too near the old Graymoor Mansion."

"Let's go inside," Tim said. "I want to check out that music."

"No, thank you. I heard too many strange noises coming from inside—screams and moans. I've heard way too many stories about people going into Graymoor and never coming back out again.

"Ah, come on. Those are just stories."

"Are they?"

"Well, mostly."

"Mostly, huh?"

"Come on," Tim said. "Taylor and Mark used to meet in there. It was their hideout where no one would bother them. Nothing ever grabbed them. We'll just take a peek in the door."

The shadows were lengthening, making Graymoor more foreboding than ever.

"Well, if we're going to do it, let's do it now. I don't want to be in there when it gets dark."

Tim smiled.

"Let's go."

Tim led me to the iron gate, and we entered the overgrown yard. Despite once living only feet from the mansion, I was apprehensive about approaching. The eerie organ music continued. If I was alone, there was no way I'd go inside. With Tim at my side, I felt braver. Even so, I didn't want to go in. I also didn't want my boyfriend to think I was a coward.

Every step forward was a struggle, but I didn't allow myself to stop. The music grew louder as we neared. I could hear it quite clearly as we stepped up onto the porch. We approached the immense front door. Tim reached out and turned the knob. With a push, the door slowly opened.

Tim and I stood on the threshold for a moment. The music was much louder now. The interior was dim, but our eyes slowly adjusted to the darkness. Tim took my hand and stepped forward. He led me across an immense parlor filled with ancient dusty furniture and old paintings. Tim pointed toward an old pump organ. It was the source of the music. We drew nearer. As we did so, the music became more intense as if whoever was playing it had noticed us and was going all out to give a grand performance.

We stood and watched in astonishment as the organ played itself. The keys moved up and down, but there was no one there to see. Then, the music abruptly stopped. I could have sworn I heard a giggle just after the last note.

"You know, if I hadn't believed you about Jacob before, I would now," Tim said.

"Did you hear the giggle?"

"Yeah, it sounded like a boy laughing for a moment there."

"I'm glad you heard it. I almost thought I'd imagined it."

"I don't think we both imagined the same thing."

"This place is so creepy. Mark and Taylor really used to meet here?"

"Yeah, that's what Ethan told me. They started meeting here after things got bad for them. I think it was less scary in here for them than it was out there. I guess ghosts aren't as frightening as bullies."

"It's getting dark fast. I don't know about you, but I've seen enough," I said, hoping Tim didn't detect the edge of fear in my voice.

"Yeah, I don't want to start wandering around in here. There were those boys who got lost in here sometime in the 1940s or 50s. They never could find them. I remember reading it in an old issue of the *Citizen*."

"You knew that and you still wanted to come inside? You said those were just stories!"

"I said they were mostly just stories. Remember, Mark and Taylor came in here several times. Nothing ever hurt them."

"Let's just get out of here."

"Not quite yet."

My heart nearly stopped. It wasn't Tim who spoke. It was Boothe. Where had he come from? Had he followed us in, or had he been here all along?

"Brought the little boyfriend for a tour, did we?" Boothe asked.

Tim stepped up close beside me.

"Don't come any closer," Tim said.

"Relax, I'm not after your boyfriend." Boothe looked me up and down. "Besides, I've already had him."

Tim moved forward, but I grabbed his shoulder to hold him back.

"You're a real asshole, you know that, Boothe," I said.

Boothe frightened me like few others could, but at the moment I was more angry than afraid.

"So I've been told."

"You planted that coin on me, didn't you? It had to be you!"

"Of course, I did. That was the whole point of getting you alone. Well, mostly. I was tempted to...but never mind. I accomplished what I set out to do. He came to see you, didn't he?"

"Yes."

Booth smiled.

"Excellent. He's your problem now."

"What do you mean?"

"He came after me. I thought he wanted that damn coin back. I gave it to him so he'd go away, but he still came back, and when he did, I found the coin hanging around my neck."

"What did he want?"

"You."

"Me?"

"What did I just say, faggot?"

"Why would he want me? How would he even know about me?"

"You helped me rob his grave, remember," Boothe said. He looked at Tim, probably hoping to shock him or mess things up between us, but Tim knew all about my past.

"Why would he want me?" I asked.

"I don't know, and I don't care. I tried to ignore him, but he wouldn't let me rest. He made my life a living hell."

"How?"

"I'm sure you'll find out soon enough. Like I said, he's your problem now. I did what he wanted. I passed the coin on to you. Now you can deal with him."

"You son of a bitch!" Tim shouted. He moved forward again, but I grabbed his shoulder once more.

"Don't," I said.

"Go ahead," Boothe said, looking Tim up and down. "Try it. I'll warn you, though. Winner takes all, and if I win...well, Dane can tell you what I'll do to you."

That infuriated Tim. I used both hands to hold him back.

"No, Tim! Don't! Please!"

Tim stood still. Boothe stepped closer. He mussed Tim's hair.

"Smart boy. Now, gentlemen, our business is concluded. I just wanted to make sure the owner of the coin had paid Dane a visit. I was going to hunt you down tomorrow morning, Dane. Thanks for saving me the trouble. Now, I can get the hell out of Verona tonight and I won't have to hang around this place. It gives me the creeps. The ghost your problem now, boy. Good luck. You're gonna need it."

With that, Boothe turned and left. Tim stood there, trembling with rage. I pulled him to me and hugged him.

"I'm glad you were here. Thank you for not attacking him."

"He needs his ass kicked."

"Yes, but I don't want you trying to do it. Boothe is a nasty piece of work. Likely as not he would've pulled a knife on you. He's capable of anything. Thank you for listening to me."

I kissed Tim on the lips.

"Now, if you don't mind, I really want to get out of here," I said.

"Let's go," Tim said. He took my hand, led me out of Graymoor, and towards home.

"I hope that's the last I see of Boothe," I said.

"I have a feeling it will be. He seems to be finished with you."

"Yeah, but he's stuck me with a ghost! I wonder what he meant when he wished me good luck and said I was going to need it."

"Maybe he was just trying to scare you, make you think Jacob is worse than he is."

"That would be just like Boothe, but I don't think so. It was quite a risk for him to come back to Verona. He could have been nabbed by the cops. He must've been desperate to ditch the ghost or he wouldn't have taken the risk."

"Maybe he was scared enough by Jacob haunting him that he was willing to take that risk. I don't mean to scare you, but I'd be totally freaked out if a dead boy appeared in my room."

"I was."

"So there you go. I think Boothe is a big pussy when you get down to it. He probably just can't take what you've already experienced. I'm sure you're none too pleased about Jacob haunting you, but maybe that's all there is to it."

"Yeah, and maybe he's gonna drag me down to hell for the bad things I've done in life."

"Now you're being dramatic. Don't get yourself worked up over this. You'll be scared of your own shadow if you aren't careful. Hey, maybe that's it! Maybe Boothe hinted that worse is yet to come so you'll worry about it and be tormented by your own fears."

"Isn't that the same as saying he made it up just to scare me?"

"Yeah, but it explains how he means to scare you. He's trying to use your own mind against you."

"If you're right, that is."

"Yeah. All I'm saying is: don't let it get to you. Don't make the problem bigger."

"Easy for you to say. I don't think Boothe was lying or making up stuff to scare me. I don't think Boothe came here of his own free will. I think Jacob made him do it. I'm scared, Tim."

Tim squeezed my hand and held it tighter.

"I'd guard you all night if I could, Dane."

"I know you would, Tim. I'm not going to make this worse than it is. I'm just going to tackle what comes up. I've very likely already been through worse."

"Call me and I'll come running to help," Tim said.

"Thanks."

Tim gave me a hug when we reached my house. We shared a kiss, and then Tim watched as I walked inside. I felt more secure knowing he was watching over me.

Shawn

Tristan walked past just as I leaned over and kissed Marc on the lips. I pulled away quickly and watched Tristan walking up the hallway.

"Shit," I said.

"What?" Marc asked.

"Tristan saw me kiss you."

"So? Isn't that kind of the point?"

"Yeah, but he looked...hurt."

"Isn't that good news? Doesn't that mean he feels something for you?"

"Yeah, but...I don't want to hurt him."

"You're forgetting he has something going with Nate London. He shouldn't be too hurt by you kissing me."

"He still looked hurt."

Marc smiled.

"I like the way you really care about people. I know you've got a major thing for Tristan, but most guys wouldn't care if he was hurt. Like I just said, he does have something going with another guy. It's not as if you're cheating on him."

"Then why do I feel like I am?"

"Because you're in love with him."

"I don't know if I'd go quite that far."

"Puh-lease. You are so obviously in love with him it's not even funny. I see you hide it from him, but when he's around and you think he's not looking...you might as well be holding a sign declaring your undying love," Marc said. "Listen, I don't want to lose what we've got, but if you want to back off and just be friends, I'll understand."

"No," I said. "I'm being stupid. That's all. Maybe I should talk to Tristan, but…well, there's no reason we can't continue seeing each other and having sex. I *really* like the sex."

Marc made a sound of astonishment. "You like it? *Really?* I'm shocked!"

"Yes, smart ass. I love it! It's incredible."

Marc made a move as if he was going to grab the front of my jeans, then laughed.

"I know you love it. I do, too, but I will understand if you want to back off. I can be content with just your friendship. We can still hang out. We can still sit together at lunch. The goal from the very beginning has been for you to get with Tristan and for you and me to just be friends."

"I don't want to hurt you."

"You're not going to hurt me, Shawn. I already know how this is going to end. I've known from the beginning. I'll admit, I have feelings for you. I could see myself falling for you. I know how you feel about Tristan, however. You can't ignore feelings like those. They're too strong. Even if I was set on having you as a boyfriend, it would be in my best interest for you to get with Tristan. Until you do or until something drastic happens, you'll never get over him. Maybe you two are meant to be together. Maybe not. I don't know. Either way, you've got to see where things go with Tristan. If you told me right now you just wanted to forget about him and become my boyfriend, I'd turn you down."

"You would?"

"Yes, because until you get over Tristan—if you get over him—you can't belong to anyone else. Do you get what I'm saying?"

"Yeah. I understand. You're right. I'll tell you something. If Tristan doesn't want me, I'm going to feel a lot better about it because of you. I really like you, Marc. I'm not in love with you. I have feelings for you, sure, but they aren't strong romantic feelings. I can see those feelings developing, though. If I'd met you before Tristan…"

"Oh, so I'm the consolation prize, then? Your backup boyfriend?"

"No! No!"

Marc laughed.

"I had you going there, didn't I?"

"You're evil. I'm so afraid I'll hurt you."

"Well, get over that fear. I went into this with my eyes open. I don't expect you to become my boyfriend. I expect you to date Tristan. If it works out for you I'll be very happy for you. If it doesn't work out...well, then I'll think about making you *my* boyfriend."

"I don't deserve you."

"No. No one does, so you might as well have me."

"You've been hanging around Brandon and Jon too long."

"Perhaps they've been hanging around me too long."

"Come on, I'll walk you to class."

***

Marc was incredible. I was so glad everything was on the up and up with us. If I'd started dating Marc to make Tristan jealous without telling Marc what I was up to, I could have hurt him badly. I would have also felt like a complete and total asshole. I would have been right, too. Things were already more complicated than I'd thought they'd be, and if I'd been dishonest about my intentions, things could've gotten ugly, and people could've gotten hurt.

I needed to talk to Tristan—and soon. I'd seen the look in his eyes. He was hurt. I wanted to make him jealous. I wanted him to start thinking about what it would be like if I dated someone else. But, I never wanted to hurt him. True, he'd hurt me by starting things up with Nate London, but I was sure he had his reasons. Maybe it's something that just happened without any sort of plan. Hell, maybe they looked at each other and it was love at first sight the way it had been with Tim and Dane. Maybe Tristan wanted to experiment with Nate before he got into dating me. I didn't know what was up, but I did know that Tristan would never hurt anyone if he could help it.

I caught up with Tristan after lunch. Luckily, Nate was nowhere in sight.

"We need to talk," I said.

"Uh-oh," Tristan said. "It's never good when someone says that."

"Well, I just…we just need to talk. I'm off this evening. Can we go to my place after school?"

"Sure. We haven't seen much of each other outside of school lately. I'm sorry I've been so busy, but then you've been pretty busy, too."

I wondered if his words had a hidden meaning. Was he referring to my jobs or Marc?

"Yeah, we haven't seen enough of each other. That's for sure. Meet me at my locker after school." I didn't say more just then. I didn't want to get into it. What I had to discuss with Tristan was private.

I tracked down Marc and told him I was meeting Tristan. Otherwise, there might have been an awkward situation if both of them showed up at my locker at the same time. Marc was cool about it. I knew he would be. He'd make someone a great boyfriend. In the short time I'd known him, he'd already became a good friend—and more.

Tristan met me at my locker shortly after school. He smiled at me, and I fell in love with him all over again. Marc was right. As much as I tried to deny it, I was in love with Tristan. I was beginning to feel really guilty about a lot of things: my anger, my sexual promiscuity, my jealousy, my self-centeredness.

Tristan and I talked about Dane's ghost as we walked out to my old Cutlass and I drove him downtown to the loft. Tristan believed him. I did, too.

I wasn't looking forward to our conversation. I was very much afraid Tristan was going to tell me that he and Nate had fallen in love at first sight. I didn't know what I was going to do then. Well, yes, I did. I was going to go and cry on Marc's shoulder. How likely was my greatest fear, however? Why would Tristan look hurt when he saw me kissing Marc if he was in love with Nate? Wouldn't he be relieved instead? It was time to stop thinking and start talking. I'd had enough of jealousy, anger, and wondering.

When we reached my place, I led Tristan upstairs and into the loft. Thankfully, Tim wasn't around. I hoped he remained absent, but I'd convince him to stay in his room if he showed up.

"Make yourself at home. Want something to drink?"

"How about some ice water?"

"Okay, or we have iced tea if you'd prefer."

"Yeah, that sounds great."

I poured us both a glass of iced tea, and then we sat down at the table.

"So…" I said.

"Yeah, so…"

"Okay, I'm just going to get straight to the point," I said. "You looked hurt this morning when you saw me kissing Marc. Were you?"

Tristan paused before answering.

"Who you date is your business, Shawn."

"True, but you didn't answer my question. Did I hurt you?"

"I was…yeah. You've been spending a lot of time with Marc. I figured you probably got tired of waiting around for me. It's okay. I don't blame you. I've thought about asking if you wanted to get together to do something, but you seemed busy with Marc. I wouldn't have said anything about it, but you did ask."

"Yes, I did ask. Listen, I have something I want to ask you. It's none of my business, so you don't have to answer, but…are you dating Nate London?"

"What?" Tristan asked. The look of confusion on his face was a ray of hope.

"Are you guys...messing around?"

Tristan laughed.

"Nate London and me? Are you *serious*?"

I was on the verge of tears. It seemed less likely by the moment, but I was so afraid Tristan already had someone else.

"You *are* serious. No. There's nothing like that between Nate and me. I've been tutoring him so he doesn't flunk and have to repeat this year. We get along pretty well. We even hang out sometimes. There's nothing between us like you mean, though. I'm pretty sure Nate likes girls."

"You guys seem really close. You even brought him when we played dodge ball over at Dane's."

"You guys said you wanted as many people as possible. I was tutoring Nate that afternoon, so I invited him. He thought it sounded like fun. So you really thought we were messing around or even dating?"

"Yeah. I was sure of it, in fact."

"So that's why you're so mean to Nate! I thought you guys had fallen out over something. That's why you were going for blood when we played dodge ball. You were trying to hurt him. Weren't you?"

"Yeah," I admitted. I couldn't help but lower my head. I suddenly felt ashamed.

"That's why you haven't been so nice to me at times. You've been running hot and cold lately."

"I was upset because you said you weren't ready to date, but you were apparently dating Nate or messing around with him. I don't know which would have been worse. You said you weren't looking for just sex."

"I meant it. Listen, Shawn. If I had been dating Nate, I would have told you. I know you're interested in me. At least, you were before you started seeing Marc. I wouldn't hurt you like that. Well, if I had started dating him, it would have hurt you, but I would have been honest about it."

"I'm not dating Marc, not really."

"What do you mean 'not really'?"

"Well, Marc and I are friends—good friends. We hang out, and we, uh, have sex, but he's not my boyfriend. He knows how I feel about you. We, uh, kind of put on a show around you to make you jealous, but we were already friends then, and we've become closer. If the situation was different, we might become boyfriends. Shit. You probably don't even want to talk with me now."

"Why not?"

"I know how you feel about casual sex. You probably think I'm a slut. You're probably mad at me because I used Marc to make you jealous. I didn't really use him, though. He knows exactly how I feel about you. Making you jealous was kind of his idea."

"How do you feel about me, Shawn?"

My eyes grew watery, and my lower lip trembled.

"I'm in love with you."

A tear ran down my cheek. Tristan stood, walked around the table, pulled me to my feet and hugged me. Then he pulled back, gazed into my eyes, and kissed me.

"I'm sorry," he said. "I've made things difficult, haven't I? I really like you, Shawn, but I've let fear get in the way. I didn't want to get hurt again."

"I know you've been hurt before, Tristan, but I'm me. I'm not the boy who hurt you back in Tulsa. I'm not like him. I don't want to change you. I want you to stay just as you are. You said you jumped right into dating him and found out fast you didn't have anything in common. We've been friends for a while now. We have a lot in common. Yes, we have a lot of differences, too, but I like those differences. Don't judge me by what happened back in Tulsa. It's okay to love me, Tristan. I won't hurt you. I'd never hurt you. Please, just give me a chance."

Tristan's eyes grew a little watery, too, and he hugged me close.

"Maybe it's time I showed a little of your courage," Tristan said. "We have been friends for a while now. We haven't spent as much time together as I would have liked, but that's largely my fault. Maybe it is time we started dating, but we've got to take things *slow*."

"I'd like that," I said, smiling.

I leaned in and kissed him.

"What about Marc?" Tristan asked.

"He *really* likes me, and I like him, too. I'm almost positive Marc would be up for dating me if you weren't in the picture. He knows how I feel about you, though. I've been completely honest with him from the beginning. He even said that if I asked to date him, he'd refuse, because he knows I can't belong to anyone else because of my feelings for you. I think Marc and I will be very good friends. I think you and he might make good friends, too."

"I'm glad you were honest with him."

"I had to be. I couldn't get into anything with him without telling him about you. I couldn't take the risk of hurting him."

Tristan smiled.

"Maybe you can stop being mean to Nate now."

"I owe him an apology. I hate to admit this, but I was so jealous when I thought he was dating you. Just the thought of him kissing you drove me out of my mind."

"Are you going to be jealous while we're dating?"

"No, because you're going to be my boyfriend. I trust you. I won't think you have something going with another guy."

"Good. We have learned a lot about each other, and I like what I've seen so far. I'm ready to give this a try. Let's just take it one step at a time."

"That sounds good."

I kissed Tristan again. Tim chose that moment to come home.

"Geesh! Get a room, you two!"

"I can kiss my boyfriend if I want," I said.

Tim didn't miss the key word—boyfriend.

"I can get lost if you two want to be alone."

"It's okay. We're just talking."

"And kissing," Tim said.

"Yes, and kissing."

"I'm glad you're finally dating him, Tristan. Maybe now he can stop pining over you."

"Shut up, Tim."

"It was so pathetic," Tim said.

I grabbed for Tim, but he dodged me.

"He was like some lovesick girl."

I managed to nab Tim and get him in a headlock.

"And the way he gazed at you with longing whenever you weren't looking…"

I clamped my hand down on Tim's mouth. I was embarrassed, but Tristan was laughing.

"Tim has to go to his room now and do his homework," I said. "Don't you, Tim?"

I moved his head up and down, then released him.

"The sighs just about drove me out of my mind," Tim said.

I charged toward my little brother, but he bolted down the hallway, giggling.

"You're so lucky to be an only child," I said.

"I'm sorry I laughed, but you two are so funny together."

"Yeah, Tim's a regular riot."

"Come here," Tristan said.

I walked to him. He pulled me close and gazed into my eyes.

"Were you really pining over me?"

"Yes," I admitted. I could feel my face turning red.

"I definitely shouldn't have waited so long."

Tristan kissed me again. I hugged him tight. I never wanted to let him go.

***

Tristan met me at my locker the next morning before school. I grinned at him. He was my boyfriend at last! I leaned in and gave him a peck on the lips. Marc appeared out of nowhere and draped his arm over my shoulders.

"Well, I guess I don't have to ask how the talk went," he said, pushing his blond bangs away from his face.

"It went well," I said.

"I'm happy for you—both."

"I meant what I said, Marc. I want us to be friends."

"As if you could get rid of me even if you wanted," Marc said. "Chill out, Shawn, you worry too much! I told you it's cool. Now, how about you two invite me over for a three-way tonight?"

"Uh…" I began.

"I'm kidding! I'm just kidding. Damn, you are so easy, Shawn." Marc turned to Tristan. "Hi, I'm Shawn's former boy toy. Nice to meet you."

Marc shook Tristan's hand as if he'd never met him before.

"I'm glad I've been honest about everything, or that boy-toy remark might have caused trouble," I said to Marc.

"You're always honest, Shawn, that's why I knew it was safe. Listen, I've got to run. Now that Shawn and I are just friends, I need to start patrolling for a new guy."

"There's always Blake," I said.

"Yeah, but you know how he is: fun in bed but not much good for anything else."

278

Tristan raised an eyebrow.

"Oh," Marc said. "Haven't told him about Blake yet, huh?"

"Well, not everything...yet. I couldn't get to everything!"

"Just how many guys have you been dating, Shawn?" Tristan said.

"I uh, Blake and I weren't...we were just..."

"You're right," Tristan said. "He is easy."

"Stop ganging up on me!"

"Ah, my work here is done," Marc said with an evil grin. "See you guys at lunch!"

"Bye, Marc."

"I think I'm going to like getting to know him better. So...tell me about Blake," Tristan said as we walked away from my locker.

"Well, there's not much to tell there. To be blunt, he's a fuck buddy."

"You'd better make that a 'was,' since we're dating."

"Oh, certainly. Listen, does it bother you that I was with Marc and Blake? I know you're not into the whole casual-sex thing."

I held my breath while I waited for an answer. Two seconds can be an eternity sometimes.

"You were a free agent, Shawn. You asked me to date you, and I declined. Therefore, you were free to do whatever you wanted."

"Yes, but do you think less of me?"

"No. Casual sex isn't my thing, but that doesn't mean I'm against it. You'll find my ideas about sex very progressive."

"Oh?"

"I think it's an entirely natural act. As long as it's consensual, I see nothing wrong with it—period. Sex has been mystified and demonized, and I think that has caused a lot of problems. If people wouldn't make it such a big deal, there would be far fewer unwanted pregnancies and far fewer problems with VD. It's not sex that causes problems, but ignorance."

"How else are you sexually progressive?"

"You'll find out about that later, but if you think you're getting any right away, you can forget it."

"I've waited a long time already."

"You'll just have to wait a little longer."

"I think you like tormenting me."

"Yes, but I won't torment you too long. I said a *little* longer after all."

"Mmm."

"You are such a horn dog."

"I think you kind of like that."

"Yes, I do. I'll see you at lunch, Shawn."

"Bye, Tristan."

I reached out and brushed a stray hair out of Tristan's face. He grinned at me and walked away. I felt like my heart could burst with happiness. Devon walked past me just then. I grabbed him, hugged him, and then made my way to class, leaving a speechless Devon in my wake.

Tristan and Marc sat on either side of me at lunch. We talked and laughed as always. I even told everyone the story of hugging Devon.

"That was probably the thrill of his life," Marc said. "I have two words to say about Devon: closet case."

"I have two words to say about him, too," Brandon said. "Ass hole, or is that one word?"

"I was thinking four words," Tim said. "Poster child for contraception."

The whole table laughed at that.

Tristan and Marc talked more than they had in the past. The three of us kept smiling at each other as we talked with everyone else at the table.

"Threesome," Jon mock-coughed. "Threesome."

"Nope," Tristan said. "When it comes to boyfriends, I don't share."

Boyfriends. I sure liked the sound of that. My friends didn't fail to catch the significance of the word. They all knew how I'd fallen for Tristan.

"Well, it's about time," Jon said.

"Yeah," Brandon agreed. "So when did you and Marc start dating?"

"Brandon," I growled.

"Oh! Tristan is dating you? Sorry. My mistake. I guess there's no accounting for taste."

"As if you'd know anything about taste," Jon said.

"At least, I don't have to pay for it…"

I tuned Brandon and Jon out. I smiled at Tristan and lost myself in his sexy brown eyes.

Marc went on his way after lunch, and Tristan and I walked back to our lockers together.

"Tristan, I'd like to see you after school, but I have work, and if you don't mind, I'd like to talk to Marc. I just want to make sure he's really okay with all this."

"Sure. Why don't we get together for supper your next night off?"

"That sounds wonderful!"

I gave Tristan a hug. Even better, he hugged me back.

***

I caught Marc at his locker just after school.

"Hey, can we talk?"

"What about your boyfriend? Shouldn't you be spending time with him?"

"Yeah, but I have time for my friends, too, especially such a good friend."

"Oh, please, you sound like a greeting card. I'll talk with you on one condition: that you don't say anymore crap like that."

"I promise."

"Good, I don't want to have to kill you."

Marc slammed his locker shut. We walked out of the school together and sat on the hood of my car.

"You look happy," Marc observed.

"I am."

"I'm glad."

"Are you okay? I mean, with us not being able to be intimate anymore?"

"Wow, what an ego. You must think you're really something in the sack."

"I know I am, but that's not the point."

"I'm okay with it. I already told you that."

"Are you *really* okay with it?"

"Yes. I have feelings for you, Shawn, probably more than you do for me. Of course, I wasn't head over heels in love with someone else when we met. I liked being your almost-boyfriend for a while, but I'm happy things have worked out for you. We can still be close. I'll miss the sex—and the hugging and kissing—but I get to keep the most important parts of our relationship, so I have no complaints. Besides, there has got to be a boyfriend out there for a sexy guy like me."

"Yeah, there must be. As far as hugging is concerned, I don't think Tristan will mind the occasional hug."

"Just watch where you put your hands," Marc said, grinning.

I knew then everything was going to be okay with Marc. I was sure he experienced some sadness over this, but he was right, we still had the best part of our relationship.

Strong arms wrapped around my chest from behind. I flinched momentarily but then felt a kiss upon my cheek.

"Knock it off. You want my boyfriend to catch us?" I said.

I turned around, pretending surprise. Tim grinned at me.

"I think you should forget a career in theatre," Tim said.

"Well, I do kind of have another boyfriend."

"Dead boys don't count. Did he show up last night?"

"I don't think so. I felt really cold at one point and thought someone was in the room with me, but I'm not sure if it happened or if I just dreamed it did."

"I wish he'd just go away," said Tim. "I don't like it."

"I'm not too thrilled about a dead boy in my bedroom, either."

"Who would be?"

"Maybe Devon?" I suggested.

Tim laughed.

"Devon gave me the nastiest look this morning," Tim said. "He shouldered me and called me a pillow-biter, but then he spotted Brandon. Devon disappeared so fast I wondered if he beamed out."

"That boy is going to get his ass kicked if he keeps it up."

"No one deserves it more."

"Come on, let's go eat. I'm starving!" Tim said.

The usual crew sat at our table, but my thoughts went forward to next year. Don't ask me why. I have no idea why I think the things I think. Next year, Brendan and Ethan would be gone. Every year, more of us would disappear, and then there would be no one left. It was sad. I guessed new people would be added every year. Tristan and I were recent additions. By the time the current crew left, a whole new group would probably be phased in. I liked the idea of our table continuing on through the years.

"You look thoughtful, Dane," Tristan said. I noticed Shawn was sitting close by Tristan's side. He looked happy. Both of them did.

"I was just thinking…"

"Ohh, everyone quiet! Dane's thinking!" Jon said.

"Ha-ha. Shut up!" I said.

"I was just thinking about next year and how Brendan and Ethan won't be here. It doesn't seem right."

"Oh, don't worry about that," Brandon said. "There is no way either of them will pass. They probably won't graduate until they're like…forty."

Brendan and Ethan both flipped Brandon off.

"I'm one of the newest guys here, but…I don't know…it just seems like this is how things should be."

"Things change," Brendan said. "You get used to it. Casper and I understand that better than most. We used to live in an entirely different place and attended a different school. I thought my life would just go on and on the same as always, but it changed. Not all of that change was pleasant, but now I'm here, and I like this life. Next fall, if I go off to college, that will be a different life, too, but that's okay. Change is a part of life, and even though most things change, not everything has to do so. I know that Casper will always be a part of my life no matter what happens or where I end up."

"Do you write greeting cards for Hallmark?" Jon asked.

Brendan shot him a look but didn't retort.

"Change can be good. This year is way better than last year!" Tim said.

"In more ways than one," Shawn said as he gazed at Tristan.

"You should go out for football next year, Dane," Tim said.

"Uh, no!" Brandon said. "If he's going to play a sport, soccer is the way to go. Soccer rules here, and everyone knows it!"

Jon didn't argue with Brandon for once, but then he was a soccer player, too.

"Maybe so, but his boyfriend doesn't play soccer. He plays football!" Tim said.

"Are you sure?" Brandon asked. "We all know he cheats on you with Jacob, so he might have another boy or two stashed away somewhere."

"Never," Tim said. "Besides, Dane has way more taste than to go for a soccer player."

"That's true," I said.

"You stay out of this," Jon said.

I stuck my tongue out at him.

"Brandon has a boyfriend on the soccer team, at least that's what I heard," Jon said.

"You wish. You wish it was you! You're the team blowjob boy! You take care of everyone!"

"Only when you're not around to bend over."

"And they're off," Shawn said.

Our table sat back and listened as Brandon and Jon went off on each other. I was so glad they weren't graduating in May. What would I do without The Brandon & Jon Show?

When the bell rang, Tim and I dumped our trays and then walked back towards our lockers.

"Remember how we used to sneak off during lunch?" I asked.

"How could I forget? I miss the noon-time quickies, but now...mmm."

"True, and there's the added bonus of not having to worry about getting expelled if we get caught."

"Yeah, I wouldn't want to face your parents if we got caught doing it at school. Oww."

"They aren't stupid. They know we mess around."

"Yeah, but they're in denial."

"True that," I said. "You think Shawn and Tristan have done it yet?"

"Not a chance! They haven't even gone out on a real date yet. It's as though they're some old-fashioned couple from the 1950s."

"Come on, guys our age were just as horny in the '50s as we are now. I bet they had plenty of sex back then. It just wasn't as out in the open," I said.

"You may be right, but how can they stand it?" Tim asked.

"I bet Shawn wants it bad, but I don't know about Tristan."

"Come on, I know he's like all intellectual, but he's still a guy. Guys *need* it."

"True. I need it right now," Tim said.

"Hold onto that thought."

"You know…we haven't gone all the way yet…" Tim said suggestively.

I began to breathe a little harder, and something else was harder, too. I'd given some thought to what it would be like when Tim and I finally went all the way.

"Maybe we should."

Tim and I gazed at each other. The possibility excited me beyond belief, but frightened me a little, too. Tim and I hadn't discussed going all the way much before, only to say it was something we were saving for later. We had been going together for quite a while now, so I guess now qualified as later. I wondered if Tim was a top, a bottom, or versatile. For that matter, I wasn't so sure about my own preferences. I'd never topped, and I'd only bottomed once. That hurt like hell, but then being forced by Boothe made the experience useless for figuring out if I liked it or not. With Boothe it wasn't sex, it was violence. Tim and I needed to discuss our preferences before we did the deed. That was going to have to wait, though. I could just imagine some of our classmates overhearing that conversation!

Tim and I went our separate ways. My afternoon classes were pretty cool. I had P.E. last period so it was kind of like getting out of school early. Calisthenics sucked, but I mostly liked P.E. at VHS. I wasn't exactly athletic, yet I was in pretty good shape and well-coordinated, so nothing gave me too much trouble.

There was some fine scenery in the showers, but I didn't look around too much. For one thing I was out, and I didn't want to make the guys uncomfortable by checking them out. For another thing, I had a boyfriend, and too much sightseeing in the showers would have felt like cheating. Besides, I had Tim, so I didn't need anyone else. He was hotter than any of the guys in the showers, at least to me.

Tim walked me home after school. It was my favorite part of the day. I not only loved being with Tim, but I loved anticipating that time with him. Tim walked me home most every afternoon. Throughout my day, I went to my classes knowing that, after school, I'd be walking along with Tim at my side. That knowledge made me feel comfortable and warm inside. Our walk home wasn't just a walk; it was more. I don't think I can even put what I mean into words. Walking home together was an expression of our love and our commitment to each other. Our walk was about companionship, friendship, and the intimate connection we shared. To anyone watching, we just looked like two boys walking together, but we were much more.

More often than not, Tim took me home by a roundabout route. I think our after-school walks were as special to him as they were to me. We walked past lawns just now getting to the point they needed to be mowed, freshly hoed flowerbeds with green sprouts that hinted at the daisies, marigolds, other flowers that would soon reach for the sun, and other flowerbeds with tulips and daffodils in full bloom. We walked in the sun and in the shade of the giant oaks and maples. Spring was upon us in full force. I could smell it in the very air.

I wasn't sure how long Verona had been here, but a lot of the trees looked as if they must've been around for at least a hundred years and maybe twice that long. Most of the houses were old, too. I bet most of them were in use when the old Verona School was open. Some of them were obviously a good deal older. I knew the Graymoor Mansion murders occurred in the 1870s, and I doubted it was new then, so it was well over a century old. It was very hard to find a house that looked as if it had been around for less than fifty years. I don't mean they were all rundown. Most were well kept, except for the Graymoor Mansion, of course. I just didn't notice any houses that looked very new.

I was reluctant for our walk to end, but eventually Tim led me to my very own door. We kissed briefly, keenly aware that my parents might be watching. I could feel all the love Tim had for me in that brief kiss. Even the memory of it made me smile. Those end-of-walk kisses might be the best kisses of all.

I watched as Tim walked down the sidewalk and disappeared into the distance. I sighed. He'd barely left, and already I yearned to be with him again. Yeah, I had it bad. I grinned.

The cooler air inside the old school was refreshing after my walk. I'd somehow managed to get a little sweaty even though it wasn't what I'd call hot outside. I didn't really need a shower, but I wanted to take one. I climbed the stairs to my room, stripped, wrapped a towel around my waist, and headed back downstairs toward the gym. I still felt faintly strange walking around the old school practically naked. At one time the hallways had been filled with kids of all ages as well as teachers. Now, here I was, parading down those same halls with only a small piece of cloth covering my nakedness.

My steps echoed on the wood floor of the old gymnasium. I stopped for a moment to gaze at Jacob in the team photo hanging near the entrance to the locker room. He looked so very handsome in his uniform.

"What do you want from me?" I whispered.

Jacob just kept smiling back at me, unchanging, but the gym now seemed eerily silent, as if it, too, was waiting for a response. A chill went up my spine. I shook my head. I didn't want to think about Jacob anymore.

The old boys' locker room was as eerily silent as the gym. The locker room and showers at VHS were filled with boisterous boys after last-period gym—talking, yelling, cracking jokes and swapping insults. I imagined the old locker room and showers here had been much the same once. I didn't suppose teenagers were that different way back when. I'd bet my balls that guys were just as interested in sex then as now. I kind of doubted they were able to have sex as often as we did now, but that was only a guess. I knew guys like me had to stay completely hidden; at least, that's the impression I got. That must've sucked—or not, if you get what I mean.

I pulled off my towel and hung it on a hook no doubt used by countless guys before me. I wished I could see back into the past and get a good look at the guys who had once used this locker room. I don't so much mean checking them out in the showers, if that's what you're thinking. I just wanted to get an idea of what they looked like and how they acted. Were they like the boys I knew, or were they somehow different?

I pulled out a metal basket from one of the lockers. The baskets had once been used by athletes and gym-class inmates just like the lockers at VHS, but now I kept my soap and shampoo in one of them. Another basket held washcloths, and a couple of others each held a towel. I carried my supplies into the shower area and adjusted the water so it was just warm, but not quite hot.

The water refreshed me as it cascaded down my naked body. I worked shampoo into my hair and then began to wash my face, chest, and the rest of my body. I enjoyed the warm soapy feeling immensely. I think I could have just stood there all day.

As I continued to soap up, I shivered. I added a bit more hot water to the mix. The water flowing over me immediately felt warmer, but the sensation was fleeting. I adjusted the water to make it even hotter with the same result. I felt almost as if I was taking a hot shower outside in the winter. Steam billowed from the cascading water and I began to breathe faster. I didn't want to turn around. I knew what I'd see if I did. I forced myself to turn. I froze. Jacob stood there gazing at me.

I'd begun to hope that Jacob would leave me alone, but I knew in my heart he'd be back. I didn't understand what he wanted from me. I'd given him back his coin only to find it around my neck again soon after. Was there some weird connection between Jacob and the necklace? Was he forever doomed to reach out for it but never possess it more than temporarily? Was I doomed to be haunted by him forever? I was scared enough by the simple fact that Jacob was a ghost. The fact that he'd forced Boothe to bring that coin to me is what truly terrified me. Boothe wasn't an easy one to force into anything.

Why me? What did Jacob want?

This was the first time I'd seen Jacob outside my bedroom. I didn't like it. It was bad enough he appeared to me at night in my room, but now here he was while I was taking a shower. It wasn't even properly dark out.

Jacob stepped closer. The cold seemed less intense this time, but perhaps it was only the warmth of the shower. There were no windows in the shower area to frost over as there were in my room, but there was no sign the cold was bitter enough to freeze the water droplets on the floors and walls. Still, the steam coming off the hot water was intense enough that it partly obscured Jacob. It was as if we were standing in a fog bank.

I wasn't wearing the coin. I'd left it upstairs in my room when I'd stripped for my shower. Jacob reached out to me the same as always, however, just as if I was wearing it. I felt the same rising fear I did every time he approached. Jacob had not tried to harm me yet, but I couldn't shake the fear.

My heart raced as Jacob closed in on me. Had he gotten so close to me before? He kept coming. I fought to keep myself from backing away. I stood there in the shower, shuddering from the chill of Jacob's presence and from fear. My breath came faster even as I tried to calm myself.

Jacob closed in on me. I stood my ground, but I was beginning to tremble violently. A scream threatened to rise up out of my throat, but I swallowed it. Jacob gazed directly into my eyes. His eyes were green and his hair black! I'd never been able to make out such details before. I realized with a start that his face was far less bluish-purple than before, too. He didn't look natural, but his appearance wasn't quite so ghoulish. Was it a trick of the light?

I cried out as Jacob reached out and touched me. He touched me! The fingertips of his right hand grazed my chest. His fingers felt chilly but not quite cold. I backed against the wall. Jacob stared directly into my eyes as he ran his hand over my chest. I wanted to bolt, but I could do nothing but keep staring into those eyes.

Then, he was gone. I didn't even blink. He was simply gone.

The water was now far too hot. I adjusted the temperature and just stood there in the warm spray. My breath slowly returned to normal, and my heart slowed. I looked down. My penis stood straight out from my body. I was rock-hard. That, as much as anything, disturbed me.

I turned off the shower and walked into the locker room to grab my towel. My arousal didn't diminish. I dried off, hung up my washcloth to dry, and put my soap and shampoo back into their basket. I walked back to my room, still freaked out by my encounter with Jacob in the showers.

It wasn't until after I'd dressed and was sitting in my chair by the reading lamp that my penis calmed down. I didn't understand why my body had reacted so powerfully to Jacob. He had touched me, but he merely ran his fingers over my chest. Jacob had been handsome in life and looked as if he'd had a good body, too, but he was dead—cold and dead. His face had appeared less purplish-blue this time, but he still looked dead. I had not felt any attraction for him in the showers. I'd felt only fear. So why...I didn't want to think about it.

I called Tim and asked if he could come over. I told him only that Jacob had appeared to me again and I was scared. He said he was on his way and hung up.

I walked downstairs and waited for Tim in the entrance hallway. The quiet in the old school disturbed me. I kept expecting to see Jacob come toward me. I jumped when, some minutes later, Tim knocked on the glass of the front doors.

As soon as Tim was inside I pulled him to me and hugged him. He wrapped his strong arms around me and held me tight.

"Dane, you're shaking."

When did I start trembling again, or had I never stopped?

"It was...so much scarier this time," I said.

Tim kept holding me. He kissed my forehead. I felt better, but an edge of fear wouldn't let me go.

"Let's walk to the gym. I want to look at his picture again," I said.

Tim held my hand as we walked down the hallways toward the old gym. We crossed the basketball court, and I shined my flashlight on the photo of Jacob Brubaker that hung on the wall near the stage.

"He has black hair and green eyes," I said.

"You could see that when he appeared to you?"

"Yes."

It had to be so. The old photo was in black and white.

Tim and I walked into the boys' locker room and on into the showers. The floor was still wet, but there was no sign of Jacob. I didn't expect him to be there, but I felt compelled to look.

Tim and I walked to the cafeteria. I needed something hot to drink. My hands were so unsteady I couldn't fill the kettle with water. Tim took over and made us mugs of hot tea. I didn't know what was wrong with me.

"Was it *that* scary?" Tim asked. "I know it must be frightening. I'd be scared for sure, but you've never been like this before, or is it always like this and I just didn't realize it was this bad because I didn't see you so soon after?"

"I don't know why I'm so scared. The first time was terrifying. The next a little less so. This time...this time was worse than the first. It wasn't that different from before, only..."

"What?"

"Let's wait until we get up to my room to talk about it. I feel exposed here."

I could tell by the look in Tim's eyes that he was worried about me. I felt guilty for making him worry. Jacob didn't try to hurt me. There was no real reason why I should be so afraid...other than the fact he was a ghost and he'd touched me!

Tim carried our steaming mugs up to my room because I was too shaky to keep from spilling mine everywhere. Once there, we sat close together and sipped our tea. I should have thought to offer Tim coffee. He loved coffee.

"So, what was different this time?" Tim asked.

"It was less cold, I think. There was more color to him. He came closer than ever, but I was able to make out the color of his hair and eyes this time. That's not the big thing, though. He touched me."

"He touched you?"

"Yeah. I was showering. He reached out and touched my chest with his fingertips, then he ran his fingers over my chest."

"For how long?"

"A few moments, I guess, but it might have been longer. I don't know. He was staring straight into my eyes while he did it. I couldn't look away."

"You tried to look away and couldn't?"

"I…I don't know. I don't think I tried. I just couldn't stop looking."

"What did it feel like?"

"Chilly, not cold, just cool, but it wasn't the touch of the living."

I was silent for a few moments.

"Anything else?" Tim asked.

"I…I didn't realize it until after he was gone, but…"

"What?"

"I got hard."

"You got a hard-on?"

"Yeah. I didn't even know it until I looked down, but…I was hard. It didn't go away for about five minutes or so. I don't understand it. I wasn't turned on by him touching me. I was scared, just scared."

Tim was silent.

"Are we okay, Tim?" I asked.

"Yeah," he said. "It's okay. I wouldn't go telling Brandon or Jon you got a hard-on for a dead boy, but it's okay."

"I'm sorry."

"You don't have to be sorry, Dane. Come on. We both get hard looking at other guys sometimes. It's no big deal."

"I guess, but...this wasn't like those times. I wasn't attracted to him. I didn't even feel it happening."

"I'd say your mind was on other things."

"Yeah, but it still freaks me out I got hard for a dead boy."

"Is that why you're so scared?"

"I don't know. I don't really know why I'm so scared. Maybe because he touched me. Maybe because he didn't come to me in my bedroom this time. I don't know. I just...I thought I could deal with this, but now I'm not so sure. I just feel messed up."

"I think I'd feel pretty messed up if a dead boy came in while I was showering and touched me," Tim said. "That's not exactly the kind of thing that happens every day."

"Tim, do you think I might be crazy? No one has ever seen this ghost but me. Maybe I just think I see him."

"Dane, most people believe in ghosts. If that many people believe, then lots of people must have seen them. Besides, someone else has seen the ghost: Boothe. Why would he risk getting arrested and go to the trouble of coming here to get rid of Jacob if Jacob wasn't real?"

"Yeah, that's true. Boothe is only interested in Boothe. I wonder if Jacob came after Boothe the way he did me just a few minutes ago."

"Surely even a dead boy has better taste than that," Tim said.

"Well, I'm not sure why Jacob touched me. Maybe it was sexual, and maybe it wasn't. Maybe he kept coming after Boothe and touching him. Maybe he did something worse. What if Jacob touches me every time he comes? I don't know if I'll be able to sleep knowing I could wake up and find him groping me. It's creepy. What if it doesn't stop there?"

Tim had no answer for that. He just hugged me. I wished he could hug me forever.

Tim put our mugs of tea to the side, leaned in, and kissed me. He held me close and kissed me until I forgot about Jacob. We would have done more, but my parents might have walked in, and that would've been as scary as any ghost.

I don't know how long we kissed. It was never long enough. Some minutes later Tim and I pulled apart. He smoothed back my hair. I yawned.

"Why don't you get some rest," Tim said. "Get into bed, and I'll stay here with you until you fall asleep."

"I love you," I said.

"I love you, too."

I undressed and climbed into bed. Tim tucked me in and sat beside me holding my hand. His presence was comforting. I thought about how lucky I was to have such a wonderful boyfriend. Soon, I fell asleep.

Shawn

"You are such a girl," Tim said.

"What?"

"That's like the eighth shirt you've tried on and the fourth pair of pants. Pick something already. It's only a date."

"*Only a date?*" I could hear my voice going up an octave.

"Okay. Okay. I'm sorry. I know you've been stalking Tristan since he first set foot in Verona, and I know you're totally obsessed with him..."

"Funny."

"Yeah, but not so far from the truth. Is it?"

I had no answer for that.

"Seriously, Shawn. Tristan has seen you in everything you wear to school. Just pick out something already."

"Are these jeans okay?" I asked, although why I was asking my little brother for fashion advice I did not know.

"They're perfect. They're just a little tight so they show off your hot ass."

"Tim!"

"Well, you do have a hot ass. Don't freak out. It's just an observation."

I wasn't entirely sure about that, but I didn't want to think about it. Besides, Tim had Dane now.

I stood there bare-chested, staring into my closet. Tristan had seen me in everything I'd worn to school... I reached out and pulled out a white tank top and slipped it on. It was just a little tight. I pulled out a light-weight, pale-green flannel shirt and pulled it on.

"How's this?" I asked, turning around.

"Perfect, as long as you don't button up the shirt."

"Give me a little credit, will you?"

Tim stood back and checked me out.

"Yeah, perfect. You're all set. Now, you'll have time to do something with that hair."

"My hair? What's wrong with my hair? Tim? Tim?"

My little brother walked off, laughing. I hurried after him.

"Tim, what's wrong with my hair?"

"I was just messing with you. Will you relax already? This isn't the first time you've gone out with Tristan, after all."

"Yes, but this is our first *real* date. We went strictly as friends on our other date, so it wasn't really a date. This is totally different!"

"You're acting like a lovesick girl."

"Casey would smack you silly if she heard your girl comments."

"Yeah, but what she doesn't know won't hurt me."

I rolled my eyes.

"So, I seriously look okay?"

"You look fine, Shawn. Besides, don't you think Tristan is interested in more than the way you look? He's about the least-shallow person I know."

"Yeah, you're right. I'm just nervous. I don't want to screw this up."

"Shawn, he already knows you. He knows what a doofus you are sometimes."

"Thanks a lot."

"What I'm saying is you don't have to impress him. He already likes you. Just relax, have a good time, and try not to dive across the table and rip his clothes off."

"Thanks, Tim."

"Yeah, yeah, now leave me alone. I have to get ready, too."

"Have a date with Dane?"

"No. He's coming over the second you're out of the apartment so we can fuck."

"Tim!"

"I'm kidding, just kidding...probably."

I decided not to pursue the matter further. I hoped Tim was displaying his quirky sense of humor, but I also knew he was probably getting it on with Dane at every opportunity. I would have if I was him.

Tristan and I would not be getting it on at every opportunity. We wouldn't be getting it on at all. The most I could hope for was a closed-mouth kiss, and maybe we'd go no further tonight than holding hands. The thing was, that was okay. I'd rather hold hands with Tristan than go all the way with Blake.

I walked into the bathroom and shaved again. I put on some cologne. I was nervous but also ecstatically happy. This was it! This was the beginning. I'd waited so long to date Tristan, and tonight was the night.

I checked myself out in the mirror. I did look good. I'd never be on the cover of a magazine, but so what? Tim was right, anyway. Tristan was not shallow. My looks were secondary. I grinned. I like that Tristan liked me for me and not just the way I looked. It made me feel very good about myself. Blake made me feel good about myself in a physical way. He was obviously turned on by my body. Tristan made me feel even better because he liked all of me, or at least most of me. No one was perfect after all.

It was still a little early, but I told Tim "goodbye" and headed out. I was picking Tristan up at his house, and we were walking together to The Park's Edge. We'd gone there together on Valentine's Day. I wish we could have gone as a couple then, but going as friends was way better than nothing. Besides, that "date" meant a lot to me. In my heart, we weren't just friends even then.

I didn't want to show up early and appear too eager, although Tristan knew all too well how badly I wanted to date him. I was just this side of pathetic, at best. No one had ever had such an effect on me before.

Spring was slowly making its presence known. The grass was greener, daffodils and tulips were beginning to appear, and other flowers were just beginning to push up out of the earth. It would be a while before daisies, peonies, and all the other flowers I couldn't name were blooming, but just the hint of their presence lightened my heart.

Most guys didn't seem to notice flowers. Did I because I was gay, or was that just me? Either way, I guess it didn't matter. I counted myself lucky that I did notice them. There was so much to enjoy in life if you only looked, and I'm not just talking about flowers. Yeah, I know that's easy for me to say now. Tristan and I are going on our first date! It was just as true when I thought Tristan was dating Nate London and back when Tim and I were still living with Dad and Tom. Maybe even more so then, because I needed whatever happiness I could find in life. Maybe life had a way of compensating those who didn't have it so good.

I hoped I didn't act like a total doofus tonight. As Tim had pointed out, Tristan was well acquainted with my less-than-suave characteristics, but I wanted him to see the strong, confident, romantic Shawn tonight. I needed him to understand that I was more than the Shawn who acted goofy at school, more than the Shawn who had a three-way with Blake and Marc.

Just relax. Be yourself. He likes you.

I took a deep breath. Yeah, that's what I was going to do. I was just going to relax, be myself, and have a good time. I was not going to turn my long-anticipated date with Tristan into a problem.

I smiled as I headed for Tristan's house. This was it.

I walked up the steps and knocked. Tristan opened the door moments later. He was dressed in black jeans and a black, long-sleeved dress shirt which was unbuttoned to reveal a deep-purple, tight-fitting shirt underneath. He looked so handsome, sophisticated, and sexy.

"I am starving," Tristan said.

"Me, too." The funny thing is I didn't realize it until just then.

I couldn't help but gaze at Tristan now and then and smile. I noticed he grinned back at me. After a few blocks, I burst out laughing, and it didn't take Tristan long to join me.

"So much for appearing suave," I said.

"You are suave. You're also intelligent, charming, sexy, funny, courageous, and a few other things. All of them together add up to you."

"Intelligent?"

"Yes."

"I don't know about that. I even went to the library to pick out a book to read so I could talk to you more intelligently, but...I don't know. I couldn't find anything that interested me. I didn't even know what most of the books were about. I don't feel very intelligent."

"Oh, but you are, Shawn. There are all kinds of intelligence. I love books, but there are brilliant people who never read a book in their lives. I would like to introduce you to books, but only because I think you'd really enjoy them."

"Maybe you can help me pick out something."

"Let me think about it. I'll try to come up with something I think you'll enjoy. I love reading. I'd like to share that with you."

I smiled a big dopey smile just then, and I didn't care if I looked like a fool. Tristan liked me! That's all that mattered.

We walked on in companionable silence. The fact that we didn't have to say anything to enjoy each other's company made me feel all the closer to Tristan. It wasn't like that with Blake. We had incredible sex, but when the sex was over, there was nothing left. I did get a similar feeling when I was with Marc, but it wasn't the same. I wanted to get naked with Tristan in the worst way, but I just wanted to be with him.

Tristan and I entered The Park's Edge and were ushered to a booth along the wall. The booth was completely enclosed on three sides and seemed almost like a separate little room. It was comfortable and cozy—in other words, perfect.

"So how is Tim?"

"Horny," I said. "You have to ask?"

Tristan laughed.

"Let me rephrase that, how are things between you and Tim?"

"Great. Now that he can have Dane in his room with the door closed, there's much less tension between us. I can't believe Dane's mom agreed to that, but it's made my life so much easier."

"I'm surprised she's willing to allow it, too, but it is logical. Tim and Dane will have sex one way or another. There's nothing anyone could do to stop it, short of keeping them both locked up."

"True. The important thing is I don't have to be the bad guy now, at least not in this area. I rarely have to get onto Tim about anything else. Thank God."

"I'm sure it's rough."

"Yeah, he is a great brother. I just don't tell him that too often. His ego is big enough."

"I envy you having a brother. Taylor was a lot like a brother to me, but now…"

I reached across the table and gave Tristan's hand a squeeze.

"So, what looks good," Tristan said.

"What doesn't?"

Our waiter arrived, took our drink orders, and departed.

"So, what are you thinking about ordering?" Tristan asked.

"I'm thinking the grilled salmon with fettuccine—rich tomato-basil cream with grilled fresh salmon, pine nuts, olives, onion, Romano cheese, chives, garlic, and basil."

"That does sound good, but I'm leaning toward the Caesar's salad with grilled chicken breast," Tristan said. "Crisp romaine, freshly grated parmesan and croutons tossed with our classic Caesar dressing."

"I'd wonder if just a salad is enough, but I've seen the salads here," I said.

"I planned ahead and didn't eat lunch so I'd have a shot at finishing it."

"I'm sure I'll be taking part of my supper home."

"School is going to be over in a month, can you believe it?" Tristan asked.

"I can't wait. I like school, but juggling school and work gets to be a little much. I plan on putting in more hours this summer, but I'll still have more free time than now."

"I'm going to miss everyone."

"You'll still see everyone this summer. We all hang out."

"True, but it won't be the same as seeing everyone daily."

"I hope you and I can spend a lot of time together," I said.

"Me, too, but I'll also need time to myself."

"Absolutely. I need alone time, too, and it's hard to get when Tim is around so much. Don't worry. I know I've been your stalker, but I'm not the clingy type. I want to do my own thing, too."

"I wouldn't say you've been stalking me. Close, but not quite."

Tristan grinned, and my heart soared. Yeah, yeah, I know. How sappy, right? I don't care!

"I'm a solitary creature," Tristan said. "At least I have been. I want to change that somewhat. Sometimes, I think I spend too much time with my art or with my nose poked in a book. I feel as if I'm drawing life and reading about it instead of living it. In Tulsa a lot of people thought I was aloof and even a little snobbish, but the truth is I was just pursuing my own interests. Don't get me wrong, I enjoy the company of others. As much as I love school, lunch with the gang is the highlight of my day. The Brandon & Jon Show alone is a blast. It's just that I'm so interested in reading great novels, drawing, and painting that I largely live in my own head. Like I said, though, I want to change that. I guess you could say I want to be more balanced."

"Does that mean you're imbalanced now?"

Tristan threw the paper wrapper of his straw at me.

"Hey, has Dane seen his ghost again?"

"Did my mention of the word imbalanced make you think of Dane?" I asked.

"No. I quite firmly believe in ghosts, especially here recently."

"The latest, at least I think it's the latest, is the shower incident."

"Shower incident?"

"Yeah, Dane told Tim that the ghost appeared to him while he was showering at home. What's more, it touched him."

"Touched him?"

"Yeah, it felt his chest."

"That would be unnerving."

"Dane is pretty spooked."

"I would be, too, but I'd also be fascinated. A ghost actually touched him."

"It was nearly a grope. I don't know how I'd feel about that."

"Yeah. Dead boys have never been my type."

"You're most discerning," I said.

"I'd love to get a look at Dane's ghost."

"I'm not sure I'd want a look. It's interesting, but stuff like that freaks me out. Hey, what did you mean when you said you firmly believe in ghosts, *especially here recently?*"

"Well, I told you about my cousin appearing to me the night he died."

"Yeah?"

"I saw him again, two nights ago."

"What happened?"

"He came into my room and looked at me. He was only there a few moments, but I know it was really Taylor. I'd been reading, and I felt someone looking at me. When I looked up, there he was. He was there just to check on me and make sure I was okay. He never spoke, but I know that's why he was there."

"Were you scared?"

"No. I was startled, the way you are when someone surprises you. It's not fear, just momentary shock."

"I think Dane is telling the truth," I said. "I don't think he's crazy, either, although Tim says Dane is beginning to wonder. He's the only one who has seen the ghost."

"I think it's far more likely he's being haunted than going insane. I don't think ghost sightings are nearly as rare as most believe."

Our food arrived. My pasta was delicious, and Tristan's salad was enormous. Neither was a surprise. We sat and ate and talked and laughed. I was finally having the date with Tristan I'd dreamed about for so long. I hoped this was the beginning of a long and serious relationship, but I wasn't going to get ahead of myself. I planned to enjoy what I had, and if our feelings for each other deepened, so much the better.

An hour later, Tristan and I sipped our drinks while the waiter boxed up my fettuccine. I don't think I ate a third of it. Tristan ate most of his Caesar salad but not all.

When we stepped outside, darkness had fallen. I drew close to Tristan, and he took my hand. The marquee lights of the Paramount lit the sidewalk with flashing light as we passed underneath. I couldn't wait until Tristan and I could watch a movie there together, sitting close, my arm around his shoulder, perhaps sharing a kiss. That's not quite true. As eager as I was for that event, I could wait. I was content to walk by Tristan's side, holding hands, as we left the lights of the old theatre behind. Tristan even leaned his head against my shoulder for a while as we walked and talked. I don't think I could possibly have been any happier.

I walked Tristan home under the moonlight. We paused before his door. I didn't want to move too fast, but…I leaned in and kissed him. Tristan kissed me back.

"I had a wonderful time tonight," he said.

"Does that mean we can go out again?"

"Of course," said Tristan.

I gave him a hug.

"Good night," I said.

"Sweet dreams."

Tristan turned and went inside. I walked down the steps. Sweet dreams. There was little doubt of that.

I walked home in the moonlight, humming to myself. I felt as if I was inside a movie, a musical to be precise. I was only a step away from dancing and singing my way down the sidewalk. I laughed out loud at the thought, then looked around to see if anyone noticed my bizarre outburst. I was quite alone, but I truly didn't care if I made a fool of myself or not. I hadn't been this happy...ever.

I felt like running, but I wanted to savor this moment. My date with Tristan was magnificent! Yes, I'd said and done a few less-than-intelligent things, but Tristan didn't care. Tim was right. Tristan liked me, imperfections included.

I walked on, thinking my thoughts of Tristan, noticing how the moonlight gave everything a silvery-bluish glow. I loved the night. It was mysterious and romantic, quiet and peaceful. I wanted to take Tristan on a moonlit picnic. We could eat and talk and lie back and watch the stars. There was so much I wanted to do with Tristan. I was glad I'd met him now. I just knew that one lifetime with him wouldn't be enough. What if we hadn't met until we were thirty or forty? I supposed the "what ifs" didn't matter. There were too many of them to consider anyway.

Once home, I ran up the stairs, entered the apartment, and gave Tim a big hug.

"Whoa! If you were any happier you'd turn into a Disney character. I take it your date went well?"

"It was wonderful! Tristan was wonderful! The whole night was..."

"Let me guess, wonderful?"

"Yes!"

I hugged Tim again.

"You are *so* lucky Brandon and Jon aren't here to see this. You'd never hear the end of it."

"I wouldn't care."

"If I didn't know better, I'd say you were drunk."

"I'm drunk on love!"

"Oh, my God. I cannot believe you just said that. You are such a dork."

"Yes! I am!"

I laughed. Tim laughed, too, and I have no doubt he was laughing at me, but I didn't care.

"I was just getting ready to have some coffee. I'll make you some tea," Tim said. "Sit down, lover boy."

I sat at the table while Tim put a kettle on in the kitchen.

"Where's Dane? I thought he'd be over tonight."

"We had a quick fuck, and then he went home."

I raised my eyebrow.

"Actually, he had tons of homework, so he was busy tonight. I've been writing a paper while you've been out having fun."

"Sounds fair."

"Shut up, or I'll tell Brandon and Jon what a dork you are."

"Oh, like they don't already know."

"Yeah, I guess it is common knowledge."

I stuck out my tongue.

Soon, we were sitting across the table from each other, Tim with his coffee and me with my tea.

"So, did you get any?" Tim asked.

"Tim! My goal with Tristan isn't to get some. I just want to be with him."

"Come on. I know you're in love with him, but isn't the ultimate goal in any romantic relationship to get naked?"

"It's a goal, a part of the relationship, but it's not the ultimate goal."

"So you didn't get any."

"It was our first date, Tim. I want more than just sex with Tristan. If I just wanted sex, I'd call up Blake."

"Or Marc." Tim grinned.

"Or Marc. I want Tristan, yeah. I want him so bad I can't stand it. I want his companionship and his love even more than that. If we start out with sex, that's most likely all it will ever be. If we take it slow, we'll have time to become intimate friends, then lovers."

"Is that you or Tristan talking?"

"Both. I wanted to start dating him the moment he walked into Ofarim's that night, but even then I wanted more than just to get into his pants. I probably would have screwed things up by moving too fast. Sometimes, I think with my dick. That doesn't change my intentions, though. I want sex, but I want everything else, too."

"Yep. You're in love."

"Don't you want more than just sex with Dane? Don't you have more? I know you're both horny little bastards, but isn't there more between you than just sex?"

"First of all, neither of us is little, thank you very much. Second of all, there is more than just sex between us. Sex is a big part of our relationship, but I get what you're saying. I love Dane. He's my best friend as well as my boyfriend. What I'm saying, though, is that getting to sex, getting to that level of physical intimacy, is the goal of any romantic relationship. You see what I mean?"

"Maybe we're talking about the same thing, just with different emphasis. The goal is to become intimate, but it's the non-physical parts of that intimacy that are truly the goal. Sex is biology. Intimacy is emotion. I've been physically intimate with Blake and Marc. I haven't been with Tristan, but I feel closer to Tristan. I have feelings for Marc, but not nearly as strong as I have for Tristan. Blake…well, I like Blake, but there's nothing there but sex. If sex was the ultimate goal, then a hookup would suffice. Sex is intimate, but it's got to be combined with emotion to really mean something. Without those feelings it's just nature and lust."

"Okay, I guess we are talking about the same thing. You're just so love-struck you're thinking like a poet."

"Me? A poet?"

"I didn't say you were a poet; I said you're thinking like one. You're so in love with Tristan that you'd be spouting Shakespeare if you knew any."

"Well, you're thinking like a horny, teenaged boy."

"Which is exactly what I am!"

Tim laughed, and so did I.

"I'm glad you're happy, Shawn; you deserve to be happy. I don't often say it, but I appreciate everything you do for me. I don't know where I'd be if it wasn't for you. Maybe I'd be at home still getting beat on. Maybe I'd be living on the streets. I don't know, but...I know you've sacrificed a lot. I'm going to get a part-time job this summer to help out. I'm going to start pulling my weight a little more. You've been letting me just be a kid, but I'm not really a kid anymore."

"I just want us to have a chance, Tim. I want us to be happy. You've made sacrifices, too, and you've helped me out in ways you don't even realize. I don't know if I could have done this all on my own. You're a really good brother."

"Damn, why wasn't I taping this?"

"As if I would have said that if you were recording it. I mean it, though, Tim. I'm lucky to have such a good brother."

"Me, too." Tim paused. "Do you think Tom will ever change, Shawn? He wasn't always... I don't understand how he could have gone so bad."

"I don't know, Tim. Part of me wishes he could be here with us, but I'm afraid that's just a fantasy. I don't know why he is like he is. If he was here, it would probably be much the same as before. Even if he wasn't in prison, I wouldn't want him here, not after everything he did, not after the way he treated us both."

"I wasn't exactly kind to you back then."

"You were afraid, Tim. No one can blame you for that. I don't. I understand. You were never as bad as Tom, not even close."

"He really would have killed Brendan, wouldn't he?" Tim asked.

"Yeah, I think so."

"Are you afraid of what will happen when he gets out?"

"Yeah, but I don't worry about it. Tom probably does blame me for getting caught, but he would have gotten caught even if I hadn't slowed him down and helped Brendan get away. Taking a gun to school... How could he not have gotten caught?"

"You saved Brendan's life and maybe the lives of others."

"Maybe. Maybe not. It's all over now, anyway. I wish things could be different, but wishing won't make it happen. How did we get on this topic anyway? I want to talk about Tristan!"

Tim rolled his eyes.

"So talk, but I get to talk about Dane!"

"Deal, but no sexual details."

"Are you sure?" Tim grinned.

We sat there talking, long into the night. It was one of those times I'd probably remember forever. I certainly hoped so.

Dane

I awakened wearing Jacob's coin. I didn't even notice it until I looked in the bathroom mirror. I didn't remember putting it on the night before. I didn't wear it all that often anymore, but sometimes I felt compelled to do so. I didn't want to wear it, and yet…I did. I usually took it off to sleep, but there it was, resting against my chest. I just stood there and gazed at my reflection: me wearing the coin against my bare chest. For a few moments I felt as if I was someone else.

I'd slept well. I drifted off with Tim at my side and hadn't awakened until my alarm sounded. I had no idea when Tim left.

I wrapped a towel around my waist and headed for the showers as I did every morning. This time I did so with trepidation. What if Jacob was in there waiting for me? What if he appeared and touched me again? Before, I only had to worry about him coming into my room at night. Now, he could appear anywhere at anytime. Or could he? Weren't ghosts bound to certain locations? I knew so little about ghosts.

I couldn't help but look around as I entered the showers and turned on the water. I kept my eyes open during my shower, except when I had to close them to keep from getting soap in my eyes. I scanned the shower room. I knew I was being paranoid, but being haunted by a dead boy has that effect on a person.

I finished my shower without incident, got ready for school, had breakfast, and headed out.

Tim made no mention of Jacob at school, and I didn't either. I just didn't want to talk about him. There was no way I was going to tell the guys about getting hard when Jacob was with me, but even mentioning he'd come to me while I was showering would give Brandon and Jon too much ammunition. I loved it when they joked around, and I didn't mind being the butt of their jokes at times, but I didn't think the whole Jacob situation was funny. I didn't want to be reminded about him, either. He'd been on my mind too much since my disturbing encounter.

I spotted Tim and Shawn talking together between classes. Shawn was just a bit taller, but they were so similar in appearance even strangers had to know they were brothers. I wondered what the odds were of brothers being gay? As far as I knew, their older brother wasn't, but still, that left two out of three. I wondered sometimes if Tim had fooled around with Shawn. Two gay boys living in the same room sounded like a recipe for sex to me. I know incest was supposed to be bad, but I wasn't quite sure if I agreed. Hetero incest could lead to mentally retarded kids, but that couldn't happen with homo incest. I was an only child, so I didn't know if I would have been attracted to my own brother or not. If I had a brother, the thought of sex with him might have been a total turnoff, even if he was attractive. I was hot for a couple of cousins, but they weren't my brothers. An image of Tim and Shawn doing it entered my mind. I banished it, not because it disturbed me, but because I didn't need any help getting turned on.

One thing was for sure, Tim and Shawn were both hot! Maybe the stereotype about all the hottest guys being gay was true. It sure was in my experience; Tim, Shawn, Ethan, and Brendan were all major hunks. Tristan wasn't a stud like the others, but he was extremely handsome and sexy. Nathan and Casper weren't stud muffins either, but they were cute and sexy. I wasn't hard on the eyes, either, if I do say so myself.

Thinking about all the hot gay boys I knew was a mistake. It sexually aroused me to the point of desperate need. Tim and I hadn't messed around last night. I was too frightened and freaked out to think much about sex. Besides, I didn't want Tim to think that I wanted him because Jacob had turned me on. That would have been messed up.

I left school that afternoon with a ton of homework, but that was okay with me because I was still feeling skittish. I knew it was stupid, but feelings don't have to make sense. Tim called around eight. Talking to him made me feel safer. His sexy voice calmed and comforted me. We made plans to try to get together the next night because we were both needing it bad! I was tempted to forget my homework and race over to Tim's place, but if I let my grades slip because I was spending too much time with Tim, there would be trouble. Besides, I took a certain amount of masochistic pleasure in sexually denying myself. Tomorrow evening was going to be hot!

I went to bed about ten. My bed was comfy, but I lay there with my ears strained. I don't know why. I'd never heard Jacob approach in our previous encounters. He didn't appear rattling chains like the ghost of the same name from *A Christmas Carol*. He was just suddenly there. That was worse in a way, and yet the whole clinking chains thing would have freaked me out. My Jacob was way hotter than the one in the Dickens story, if you could get past the whole being-dead thing.

I lay there, thinking about my sexy boyfriend and the things we'd be doing the next evening. I got so worked up I needed to relieve the pressure, but I didn't allow myself. Maybe my worked-up state would cause me to dream about Tim. I hoped so. Now, that would be an intense dream!

I drifted off to sleep, but I don't remember if I dreamed about Tim or not. I awakened with a shiver some time later. I have no idea how much time had passed. It could have been minutes or hours. A gasp escaped from my lips, and my butt hit the floor about two seconds later as I tried to flee. I'd awakened to find Jacob caressing my bare chest. I stood up, putting the bed between us. I grabbed up the sheet to cover my nakedness. I didn't like Jacob seeing my stuff, especially after he'd been caressing me in my sleep. Who knew what he'd done before I'd awakened?

Jacob closed in on me, stepping right through my bed. I backed away, but it was no good. There was no stopping him. In moments my back was against the wall. I shivered from the chill air. It might have been my imagination, but the air felt less chill than before. Still, there was an unpleasant nip in the air.

My breath came hard and fast, and I fought back a scream. Maybe I should've screamed, but I didn't want to explain to my parents why I was screaming. Besides, I didn't think it would do much good. What could anyone do against a ghost?

Jacob grasped my chin and made me look him in the eyes. I struggled against him, but he was strong for a dead boy. I had a momentary fear he was a vampire and not a ghost at all, but I reminded myself that this was reality.

Jacob didn't look purplish-blue anymore. He didn't look alive, but he wasn't zombie-scary dead looking, either. He took his hand away from my chin, and I kept looking at him. I couldn't stop gazing at him, but I wasn't sure if it was because I physically couldn't look away or just didn't want to. Jacob was extremely handsome now that he wasn't all purple. He was better looking than he was in that old team photo in the gym. If he was alive and I wasn't dating Tim, I could have gone for him. Those were two huge points, however. I was dating Tim, and Jacob was dead!

My body didn't share my opinion. It reacted to Jacob again. Jacob pulled the sheet away, revealing my naked body. He ran both hands over my bare chest. I became increasingly aroused. This was sick! I was turned on by a dead boy!

"I'm going to make you mine," Jacob whispered, and then he disappeared.

Shit!

I ran for my bed, jumped in, and pulled the covers up over my head. He'd spoken to me! He'd never done that before! His words disturbed me. What did he mean he was going to make me his? That wasn't possible, and it was wrong on *so* many levels.

I feared Jacob would come back during the night. He'd never appeared twice in one night before, but I felt as if anything could happen now. I tried to sleep, but I couldn't. I kept waiting to feel Jacob pulling back the covers or groping me through the sheets. I eventually did fall asleep, but I wasn't well-rested when I awakened the next morning.

***

I pulled Tim to the side the moment I spotted him the next morning.

"Jacob came back last night," I said. "He spoke to me!"

Tim's eyes widened.

"What did he say?"

"That's the truly scary part. He said, 'I'm going to make you mine.' I'm really scared now, Tim."

"I'll come stay with you tonight."

"Yeah, like my parents would go for that! If they'd caught you sleeping with me the other night, it would not have been pretty."

"Maybe if you explain."

"You want me to tell my parents a dead boy is after me? They'd probably send me off to a shrink."

"They might understand."

"No, they'll think I'm having emotional problems because of everything that happened with Boothe."

"You could show them the coin."

"They wouldn't believe me."

"It's not as if you lie to them a lot, Dane."

"I know, but they're not going to believe I'm being haunted. If I show them that coin, they'll just think I'm delusional. They'll think I found the coin somewhere and have built up the whole ghost thing in my mind. I can almost hear them telling me they believe that I believe I'm being haunted. That will be minutes before they have me taken away."

"Dane, your parents would never have you taken away."

"You know what I mean. They'll try to help me by sending me to a shrink, and I'll be bombarded with questions by someone who is sure I've been hallucinating. Think about it, Tim. I wouldn't even be sure I wasn't nuts if it wasn't for that coin."

"I'm not sure how to help you, but I'll do anything I can," Tim said.

"I know." I smiled. "Just having you in my life helps more than I can express."

Tim hugged me.

"We'd better get to class," I said. "I don't think being haunted by a dead football player will fly as an excuse for being tardy."

"At least it would be original," Tim said.

Tim could always make me smile.

I really wanted to kill Boothe. It was bad enough when he stuck me with a ghost that showed up to scare the crap out of me, but now the ghost *wanted* me. Had Boothe known that would happen? I'm sure he didn't care if it did. Boothe only cared about one person: Boothe.

I didn't exactly know what "I'm going to make you mine" meant, but it couldn't be good. There was a time when I wished a jock would want to make me his, but this is not what I had in mind! For one thing, I had definitely meant a jock who was alive! This was just too messed up.

My past had really come back to bite me in the ass. If I hadn't run away, come to Verona, and been forced by circumstance to work for Boothe, I would never have met him. If I hadn't met him, he couldn't have stuck me with a ghost, and I'd be able to sleep or take a shower without worrying some dead dude was going to molest me. Of course, then I would never have met Shawn, which means I would never have met Tim. I wouldn't be living in Verona with my parents, either. We would still have moved from Marmont probably, but chances are we'd be somewhere else. As much as Jacob freaked me out, Tim was worth it. I'd suffer anything to be with him.

Despite the fact I'd eaten an extra-large breakfast, I was starved by the time lunch rolled around. I took everything I could get when I went through the line: fish sticks, coleslaw, French fries, green beans, and orange Jell-O.

"Dane has finally lost his mind," Brandon said as I sat down.

"Huh?" I asked.

"You got the fish sticks? Are you crazy?"

"They're good," I said.

"There's no accounting for taste," Brandon said. "Well, look who he's dating."

"Hey!" Tim said.

"I was just seeing if you were paying attention, although Dane could do better. He could date a soccer player."

"That sounds like an offer. Finally getting around to kicking for the other team, huh, Brandon?" Jon said.

"That's bat for the other team, dumb ass," Brandon said.

"I didn't want to mix sports. We were talking soccer."

"I wasn't talking about me," Brandon said.

"Sure you weren't. Admit it, you're hot for Dane."

"No offense, Dane, but if I was going to get it on with a guy, which I'm not, you would not be my first choice."

"He'd pick me," Marc said.

"Don't flatter yourself," Brandon said.

"Come on, Brandon. I've seen you check me out in the showers. You can't keep your eyes off my hot ass," Marc said.

"Oh, this is getting good," Casey said.

"You wish," Brandon said to Marc. "You should talk, Mr. Roving Eyes."

"Like you wouldn't look around if you were in the girls' showers," said Marc.

"Don't go there," Jon said. "He'll start drooling."

"Actually, Marc would be a good match for Dane," Brandon said.

"Excuse me," Tim said. "Dane's boyfriend is sitting right here."

"Jacob's here?" Brandon asked, looking around as if he expected him to walk up.

The mention of Jacob made me uncomfortable, but I tried not to show it.

"I think Dane and Tim make a great couple," Marc said.

"Thank you," Tim said.

"So, why don't you have a boyfriend, Marc?" Jon asked. "I thought you and Shawn were going to be an item there for a while."

Shawn looked slightly uncomfortable for a moment, but then he took Tristan's hand and squeezed it. They smiled at each other.

"Tie myself down with just one guy? Are you insane?" Marc asked.

"I like the way you think," Brandon said.

"You'd better not let Jennifer hear you say that," Jon warned.

"I don't see you and Jennifer together much," Nathan said.

"Yeah, you're always hanging out with Jon instead," Brendan pointed out.

"She has her life, and I have mine. We see each other plenty, and when we do…mmm."

"Spare us the heterosexual details," Marc said.

"Yeah, gross," Casper said and grinned.

"I should give you the details just to make you all squirm."

"How would hearing about Jennifer rejecting you make them squirm?" Jon asked.

"Good one, Jon," Casper said.

"Listen, Deerfield, just because you'll die a virgin doesn't mean I will. I've already taken care of that."

"Masturbation doesn't count, Hanson," Jon said.

Brandon and Jon were a welcome distraction. I was still edgy, although I felt a good deal better at school than I did at home. Tim's presence was comforting. He made me feel as if I could endure anything—even Jacob.

"Hey, can you come over for supper tonight?" Tim asked as we walked toward our lockers after lunch. "Tristan is coming over, and Shawn thought it would be cool if you could come, too. It can be a double date."

"Yeah, I'd like that. I don't really want to spend the evening at home. I'm afraid you-know-who will drop in. I'm sure Mom and Dad will let me come."

"Great, I'll tell Shawn you'll be there. He said supper will be at six. It might be a bit later, but you can come over any time. The sooner the better! Shawn doesn't have to work, so he'll be around, but hopefully we can find some alone time. See you later, stud puppy."

Tim kissed me on the cheek and disappeared. Stud puppy. He'd never called me that before. I liked it.

It might not seem like a big thing, but I was really looking forward to supper at Tim's place. I loved spending time with friends and, of course, my boyfriend. Shawn meant a lot to me, and I really liked Tristan, too. I was sexually revved up, but I was looking forward to time with Tim, whether or not we had sex. I loved that boy!

I hurried home and hit the books so I could finish up before going over to Tim's. Keeping busy kept my mind off Jacob, too. I went outside and picked a bouquet of daisies a little before six and then headed over to Tim's. It was a nice evening for a walk—warm, but nowhere near hot. I wore a pair of khaki shorts and a red polo shirt. It was my idea of dressing up for dinner.

Tim greeted me at the door with a hug and a kiss. I gave him the flowers, and he put them in a vase and set them on the table. Tristan was setting the table, while Shawn moved back and forth between a simmering skillet, a large steaming pan, and the oven.

"Supper won't be ready for a while, come on," Tim said.

Tim pulled me to his room, closed the door, and then immediately pulled me to him and kissed me. We worked in some quick kisses at school, despite the no PDA rule. They were mere pecks, however. Now, Tim kissed me deeply, sliding his tongue into my mouth. My hand immediately went into his shorts. We knew we probably didn't have long, so we didn't get naked. We just stood right there, making out, groping each other. Soon, our shorts were around our ankles and our hands were busy. We kept making out and groping until we thought we'd better be getting back.

Shawn was still busy in the kitchen when we returned. Tristan was on the couch talking to him. Tim and I plopped down by him.

"You're going to make someone a good housewife someday, Shawn," Tim said.

"Shhh, don't taunt him. I'm trying to get him trained," Tristan said. "It's hard to domesticate him."

Shawn merely shot them both a look of pretend annoyance.

"So, you still haven't gotten tired of my brother yet," Tim said.

"Not even close," Tristan said.

"You know he's actually been talking about reading a book that hasn't been assigned," Tim said. "I never thought I'd live to see that."

"We're teaching each other a few things," Shawn said. "I'm going to teach Tristan how to play football."

"Really?" I asked.

"Is that so unbelievable?" Tristan asked.

"Well, yeah. I mean, you just don't seem…I don't mean it in a bad way, but you don't seem very athletic."

"Oh, he's athletic—very athletic," Shawn said, wiggling his eyebrows.

"I meant outside of your bedroom," I said.

"Don't go there, Dane," Shawn warned.

I wondered if they'd done it yet.

"I'm not into organized sports, but I like stuff like bicycling or playing soccer with a few of the guys. I just don't like getting too serious about it. I'm not a jock. I don't have the natural athletic talent of Shawn."

Shawn paused a moment to flex his muscles.

"Don't encourage him or we'll have to change his name to Narcissus," Tim said.

"Big word for you Tim," Shawn said. Tim stuck out his tongue.

"I like Shawn's cockiness," Tristan said.

"Yeah, I'm sure you like his cock…iness," Tim said. Tristan smacked him. I laughed.

"Um, who is Narcissus?" I asked, feeling a bit stupid.

"Narcissus was a beautiful youth who fell in love with his own reflection," Tim said. "He pined away gazing at himself, and the narcissus, the flower, sprang up where he died. It's from Greek mythology."

"Oh!"

"How are you doing, Dane?" Tristan asked.

"I'm...okay mostly."

"Just mostly?"

"Yeah, I've been having some...freaky experiences lately."

"Such as?"

"Well, you know about Jacob. He's been showing up more frequently, and he's beginning to scare me. Listen guys, this can't leave this room, okay?"

"Sure," everyone said.

"Jacob actually touched me—twice—and last time he spoke to me."

"I told Shawn about the shower incident," Tim said. "I hope that was okay."

"And he told me, but it went no further," Tristan added.

"That's okay. I don't mind you guys knowing. I just don't want everyone to know."

"This is fascinating," Tristan said.

"You sure you don't think I'm nuts?"

"No. You seem perfectly sane to me."

"And you really believe me?"

"You don't have a reputation for lying, so why wouldn't I believe you?"

"You don't seem surprised that I saw a ghost. Even the first time I told everyone, you didn't seem shocked at all."

"I wasn't. Lots of people have seen ghosts."

"Have you?"

"Yes."

"When?"

"Not too long after my cousin died."

"You saw Taylor?" Tim asked.

"Yes, and I've seen him a couple of times since."

"So, what happened?" Tim asked.

"The first time I saw him was just after I found out he'd died. I was taking it *really* hard and feeling very guilty. I kept wondering if there was something I could have said or done to have kept him from killing himself."

"A lot of us were feeling the same thing," Shawn said. "Brandon just about lost his mind."

"Taylor came to me that night. It was maybe ten. I wasn't in bed yet, and I was just sitting and staring into space. I felt him enter the room. He looked kind of misty white. I wasn't afraid, because I knew it was Taylor. He didn't speak to me, but he gazed at me, and without words, he told me that everything was going to be okay and that I had nothing to feel guilty about. I even heard his voice in my head. One thing that really struck me later is when he said, 'Mark and I will always be together now.' I didn't learn until a few days later that his boyfriend killed himself, too. That's what made me certain I hadn't just imagined the whole thing. That and the fact that it felt so real. It wasn't like a dream at all. It was reality."

"Did it feel cold when he appeared?"

"No," Tristan said. "If it was colder, it wasn't enough to notice."

"It was icy the first time Jacob appeared, but it's been less cold each time. Last time, it was merely chilly."

"I wonder why the change," Tristan said.

"Me, too. I also wonder why it wasn't cold when Taylor came to you."

"I'm afraid I don't know much about ghosts," Tristan said. "I've seen Taylor since then. He came to check on me when my dad died and again right before Mom and I moved to Verona. He appeared to me recently, too. I know he's watching over me. It makes me feel very secure."

"Jacob definitely isn't watching over me," I said. "He scares me. The last two times he touched me. His fingers felt chilly and, well, dead, yet they felt like fingers."

"I think I would have crapped my pants," Shawn said, pouring the contents of the big pan into a colander in the sink.

"That's not the worst of it. The last time, he also spoke to me. He told me he was going to make me his. It freaked me out, and I'm still pretty scared."

"Shit," Shawn said.

I said nothing about Jacob's touch sexually arousing me. There were some things I wasn't going to share even with the closest of friends.

"I'm afraid he'll come back again soon. It was freaky when he haunted me before, but I just don't know how long I can handle him touching me and talking to me. I don't know how to stop him, either."

No one had an answer to that.

"Sorry for bringing everyone down," I said.

"You haven't brought us down," Tristan said. "We just don't know how to help you. If there is anything we can do, let us know."

"I didn't expect any solutions. I just wanted to talk about it with someone. I've told Tim, of course, but I just couldn't mention it at school."

Tim took my hand and held it.

"Okay, supper is just about ready. Everyone, take a seat," Shawn said.

Tristan, Tim, and I sat down at the table Shawn had received as a birthday present from the Selbys. The scent of oregano wafted through the air as Shawn placed a huge bowl of spaghetti in the center of the table. He also put out cooked apples and garlic bread. My mouth watered just looking at it. We all helped ourselves.

"This looks incredible," I said.

"It's called cooking on a budget," Shawn said.

"It's called delicious," Tristan said. "This sauce is incredible. My mom is going to want the recipe when I tell her about it."

"I just doctored up some sauce out of a jar," Shawn said. "I added a little barbeque sauce, some onions, green peppers, and some extra oregano. Apples were on sale at the grocery, so I thought I'd try cooking some."

"I love it," Tristan said.

Everyone did. It was mostly silent for the next several minutes. Everyone was far too busy eating to talk.

I watched Shawn and Tristan as they sat across from each other. It had taken Shawn a long time, but he'd reeled in the boy of his dreams. I knew that look in Tristan's eyes. If he didn't already love Shawn, he was at least falling for him. I was glad Shawn had managed to get Tristan. There for quite a while, I thought he was going to pine away for him. Tristan was beautiful, but it almost seemed their roles were reversed. It would've made more sense to me if the intellectual guy was obsessed with the jock. It was so much easier for Tim and me. We fell for each other on the spot.

Shawn made us hot tea and coffee after the supper things had been put away. He also brought out chocolate-chip cookies he'd baked. I had no clue that Shawn had such a domestic side. I'd never pictured him cooking and baking before. My mental image of him was as a jock: tough, strong, athletic, and virile. I was quickly beginning to realize he was more than that. I wondered if he'd been so all along or if Tristan was bringing out previously hidden qualities. It was kind of cool that he could kick ass on the football field and bake, too, especially when his cookies were so incredible!

"Why don't we play Rook?" Tristan asked after we'd been talking and munching cookies for a while.

"Because we don't know what you're talking about?" Tim asked.

"It's a card game. My parents liked to play it when they visited Taylor's parents. Taylor was really good at it, too. I brought a deck of cards, if you guys think you want to learn. It's not difficult."

"Well, if it's tougher than Old Maid, I doubt Shawn can keep up," Tim said. "He still hasn't quite mastered Candy Land."

"Don't make me kick your butt in front of your boyfriend," Shawn said.

Tim merely grinned in response.

"Here, I'll show you," Tristan said, spreading the deck face up. "There are four colors of cards: green, black, red, and yellow."

"The yellow looks like orange to me," I said.

"Me, too," Tristan said. "I don't think true yellow would be very easy to read on the white background. Anyway, each color has cards numbered from five to fourteen. There is also one Rook card. It's the one that says 'ROOK', and it has a picture of a big crow on it holding a hand of cards in one of its feet.

"Okay, let me deal a round to show you how to play. I'll deal the cards face up just to demonstrate. When you're dealing, you hand out all the cards. Five cards, however, are placed to the side. Those cards are known as the widow. I don't know why they are called that. The game starts with bidding, but we'll get to that in a minute. I just want to show you how to play first.

"The game is played by partners. Shawn and I will be partners, and Tim and Dane are the other team. I dealt the cards, so you get to play a card first, Dane. The idea is to take the trick by playing the highest card."

"Okay, I don't know what I'm doing, but I have a fourteen, so I'll play it," I said.

I put my green fourteen in the center of the table.

"Okay, Dane played a green card, so everyone else has to play green as well, unless you don't have any green cards. Then, you can play any color you want."

Shawn played a five, Tim a twelve, and Tristan played a ten.

"Okay, Dane won that trick because the fourteen is the highest card, but I want to explain a few things before he picks the cards up. Some of the cards are worth points. Fives are worth five points, tens are worth ten points, and fourteens are worth ten points. The Rook is worth twenty. The goal of the game is to get as many points as you can and keep the other team from getting points. In this hand, Dane won twenty-five points. I didn't want Dane to get my ten, but as you can see, that's the only green card I have, so I had to play it. Okay, Dane, since you won that hand, you get to lead again. Pick up the cards and place them in a pile near you, face down."

"Um, I'll play my green thirteen, then."

Shawn played a six. Tim sat thinking, since he was out of green cards. He placed a red ten on the table. I put down a black eight.

"Okay, Dane won that hand, too. Tim made a smart move. Since he was out of green, he could play any color, and he gave his partner a ten. As you can see, I've got a black ten in my hand, but I don't want Dane to get it, so I played a different card.

"Now, here's where it gets a little unpredictable. During every game, one color is the trump. Let's say red is trumps. Any red card will take any card of any other color. For example, a red five will take a black, yellow, or green fourteen. The Rook still beats everything because it's always a trump card, no matter what color is trumps. Okay, Dane, it's still your lead. Play another card. Stick with green, because I want to show you something."

I played a green eleven, Shawn a seven, Tim played a red five, and Tristan played a red eleven.

"Now, I won this hand because I played the highest trump card." Tristan said. "Tim and I could play trumps because we don't have any green cards. You see how it gets a little unpredictable? You may have the highest card in a color, but someone else may trump in.

"Okay, now let me explain bidding. I told you about the point cards. There are 120 points total in the deck. At the beginning of the game, each player bids how many points he thinks he and his partner can take. Whoever bids the highest, gets to play first and gets to name the color of trumps."

"So, if I have a lot of black cards and I bid the highest, I can name black trumps?" Tim said.

"Exactly, which is why you want to be the high bidder if you can. The catch is that if you don't make your bid, that bid is taken away from your score. For example, let's say I win the bid at eighty-five, but Shawn and I only manage to get seventy-five points.

Since we didn't make my bid, eighty-five points are deducted from our score."

"So you don't get the seventy-five points you made?" I asked.

"No. If we made eighty-five points or more, then we'd get those points. The other team gets whatever points it makes, because it doesn't have to match a bid."

"What about the widow?" I asked.

"Okay, whoever gets the bid each game, also gets to pick up the widow. If any cards in the widow are better than those in your hand, you can trade them."

I picked up the widow which I'd dealt face down and turned it over.

"As you can see, the Rook card is in the widow. That happens sometimes."

"So, if I had the top bid, I could take out the Rook and those two black cards in the widow and play them?" Tim asked.

"Exactly. You could take out whatever cards you wanted and replace them with your worst cards."

"Cool."

"So, the advantages of winning the bid is getting to name trumps and getting to look through the widow. Of course, sometimes the widow doesn't have any good cards at all. You never know in advance. Everyone, throw in your cards. I'll deal again. This time, don't let anyone see your cards, and we'll bid."

Everyone but Tristan made a lot of mistakes the first few hands. I forgot about trumps and played a black fourteen only to have Shawn trump it with a yellow six. His victory was short-lived, however, because Tim played a yellow eleven, and Tristan couldn't play a higher trump because he still had black. The game was kind of like a battle. A lot of laughing, taunting, and teasing went on. I was glad Tristan was teaching us how to play. I thought I might even get good at it eventually.

The game lasted until one team reached 500 points. Shawn and Tristan won the first game. The final score was 520 to -110. Yeah, that's right, Tim and I had negative 110 points. We didn't make our bid a few times and had our bid deducted from our total, which Tristan said was called "getting set."

Tim and I actually beat Shawn and Tristan the next game, and we rubbed their noses it in. We played three games, which took about two hours. It was a blast!

"We have to play that again sometime," I said at the end of the evening.

"You're just saying that because you won the last game," Tristan said.

"No, I'm saying that because I intend to win the *next* game."

Tim walked me home in the moonlight. We held hands, and he kissed me as we stood on the doorstep. I walked inside, perfectly content. I didn't even think about Jacob as I fell asleep in my comfy bed.

Shawn

"Shawn. Shawn! Would you answer the question please?"

"Uh, Churchill?"

Laughter erupted around me in my first-period U.S. History class.

"A noble effort, Shawn, but incorrect," Mr. Pennington said.

I could feel myself turn slightly red.

"Can anyone else tell me about Truman's involvement with the war effort during the final months of F.D.R.'s administration?"

"F.D.R. kept him out of the loop even though Truman was the Vice President, so his involvement was minimal," said Jennifer, Brandon's girlfriend.

"That's correct. Truman was rather frustrated by the situation. Here was the man who would be leading the country if President Roosevelt died or was incapacitated, yet F.D.R. kept him largely out of the loop, as Jennifer put it. Shawn, can you tell us why this was a particularly bad policy?"

I knew Mr. Pennington would be getting back to me, so I'd been paying attention.

"Because Roosevelt was in very poor health, and he knew it. It was very likely that he would die before the end of the war, and he did."

"That's right..."

I began to drift off again, although I kept paying as much attention as I could manage because I knew Mr. Pennington might fire another question in my direction. I usually paid attention in my classes, especially history. Some of this World War II stuff was kind of boring, but I was interested in the whole F.D.R./Churchill thing.

The rest of the class passed without incident, as did the next, but then Brandon stopped by my locker after second period.

"Great job in U.S. History," Brandon said then laughed.

"Does Jennifer tell you everything?"

"Only the most important stuff. Let me guess, you were off in lala land thinking about your dream boy."

"Um...yeah," I said.

"I knew it! You homos are so pathetic!"

"So why do you hang around us?"

"You have great entertainment value. It's the same reason I hang out with Jon."

"I'll tell him you said that."

Brandon only grinned and went on his way.

Word had spread about Tristan and me. In VHS, if you were spotted holding hands with someone, a lot of assumptions follow. When you're a guy holding the hand of another guy, that's especially juicy news. VHS either has more than its share of homos or more of us are out, but either way, Tristan and I were a topic of the rumor mill. It would have been a bigger deal if I was the first football player to openly date a boy, but Brendan and Casper had already been there and done that.

A few guys gave me some shit, but it was just rude comments and name-calling. I didn't let on, but even those hurt. When someone calls you a cocksucking faggot, it doesn't exactly raise your self-esteem. It's more the way it's said and the belligerence behind the words than the words themselves that hurt. After all, it's true. Not only do I suck cock, I love sucking cock, and I'm good at it! I am a faggot, although I much prefer the term gay or even homo. Calling a guy like me faggot is like calling a black guy nigger. It's a putdown. I don't like being called a cocksucker, either. I mean, I wouldn't call a hetero guy a pussy-eater, even though that's probably an accurate description of most heteros. So yeah, the names and slurs hurt, but I don't let on. I just glare back, flip the asshole off if a teacher isn't around, or even give the jerk a shove.

I'm well aware that the situation could be much worse. When I think of the shit that was done to Mark and Taylor—like when those guys beat Mark up so bad he had to be put in the hospital. Then, there were the things Dane had told me about his old school.

My past wasn't exactly a fairytale, no pun intended, but I was damn lucky to be living in Verona.

***

Tristan walked into Café Moffatt and took a seat in a booth. He looked so very handsome in his jeans and a black, long-sleeved pullover. I walked over as soon as I'd finished topping off the ice water for my tables.

"Hey, I don't get off for another fifteen minutes."

"Yeah, I know. I hear this place has hot busboys. I thought I'd check them out."

"Watch it," I said. Tristan smiled.

"Hey, can you get me a cup of hot tea?"

"What do I look like, a waiter? Oh, yeah…"

"You are such a goof."

I fetched Tristan's tea and made my rounds to make sure all my customers were happy. A large part of my pay came from tips, after all. Besides, I did want to do a good job. Being a waiter isn't exactly prestigious, but being a crappy waiter is worse.

At the end of my shift, Tristan and I headed out the door.

"I don't know if I'm ready for this," I said.

"Shawn, we're going to the library, not into battle."

"Libraries make me feel stupid. There's so much knowledge there, so much I don't know."

"Shawn, no one knows everything in all those books. You aren't stupid. When are you going to realize that?"

"I'm kind of stupid."

"Shawn, quit putting yourself down. I mean it. The only thing stupid about you is that you have yourself convinced you're stupid. We talked about this before. Everyone has their own type of knowledge."

"I'm sorry."

"Don't be sorry, but quit putting yourself down."

I knew Tristan was a little pissed at me, but I guessed that was just because he liked me. I knew I had self-esteem issues in the intelligence department, but knowing and doing something about them were two different things. How could I just start thinking I was intelligent when I thought of myself as kind of dim for so long? I guess it was something I'd just have to keep working on.

We entered the dreaded library. I hushed my fears that I wouldn't be able to understand whatever book we picked out for me to read. An even bigger worry was that I just couldn't get into it. I'd tried picking out something before, and I couldn't even come up with something that halfway interested me.

"So what interests you—other than football?" Tristan asked in a quiet voice.

"There are books on things besides football? Why?"

Tristan raised an eyebrow.

"Okay, okay, um...I kind of like history now. I used to think it was boring, but Mr. Pennington makes it kind of cool."

"Hmm," said Tristan.

We browsed around for several minutes without saying much. None of the titles caught my eye. A lot of them made no sense to me.

"Alexander the Great," Tristan said after a while.

"What about him?"

"I think you might like reading about Alexander the Great."

"Maybe."

"He's extremely interesting and not just because he conquered most of the known world in his time. If he lived now and was our age, I'm sure he'd be a football player."

"Is that a dig?"

"No. Alexander was big into competition and doing things that had never been done before. The more impossible the task, the more he was obsessed to complete it. He actually came to believe he was a god. He was also gay."

"I've heard he was gay, but is that true?"

"At the very least he was bi and more than likely gay. He had a lover named Hephaestion and other male lovers as well. He nearly went insane when Hephaestion died."

"Okay, he does sound interesting."

In a couple of minutes, Tristan had located the section that included Alexander biographies. I was surprised there were so many!

"Here," he said, handing me one at last. "I've heard this one is the best. It's not been out long, either, so it will include the latest discoveries."

"Latest discoveries? Didn't Alexander die 2,000 years ago?"

"Yes, but new archaeological information is always being discovered about Alexander."

I just nodded. I had no idea.

I read the back cover of the book.

"I think I would like to read this," I said to Tristan. What's more, I meant it.

"I told you we would find something. You are in great danger now, however."

"What do you mean?"

"You think you're going to read just that book, but by the time you're finished you'll want another one. You'll get interested in the Ptolemies of Egypt or Greek History, and you'll pick up a book on that, which will get you interested in something else and so on."

"Oh, so it's like you've tricked me into taking a bite of a magic apple or something. Thanks a lot."

Tristan grinned. "And you thought I was a nice guy."

Tristan picked up a couple of books before we left: a biography of William Shakespeare and *The Trees* by Conrad Richter.

"I've heard of Conrad Richter before," I said. "Where?"

"You've probably read *The Light in the Forest*.   It's assigned reading in a lot of schools."

"Yeah, I remember now. I kind of liked it."

"I think you really like books and are just afraid to admit it. You're a closet reader," Tristan said.

"I was only experimenting, and I might have been drunk. I'm not a reader, I swear," I said as if I was a straight boy trying to explain away a sexual encounter with a bud. Tristan just shook his head.

We checked out our books. Yes, believe it or not, I do have a library card, although previously I'd only used it to check out books I needed for school and magazines about football or fitness.

"That was a lot easier than I expected," I said as we walked down the front steps.

"Did you expect to have your fingerprints taken at the front desk?"

"No, I mean, finding a book I actually want to read."

"I knew you'd find something. You're a lot deeper than you think."

"Well, I hope so!"

Tristan laughed again. That's something I liked about him. He laughed easily and often. He was quiet at times, but he was upbeat.

"Let's go to my place and grab something to eat," Tristan said. "I'm going to need something, since you talked me into attending boot camp."

"A little three-on-three football is not boot camp."

"It sounds exhausting," said Tristan.

"No, it sounds fun. You'll want to play again before we're finished. Besides, that was the deal. You introduce me to reading for fun, and I introduce you to football."

"I'm just teasing you, Shawn, but I am a little apprehensive."

"Why?"

"I'm not an athlete like you. That stuff comes so easily to you that you don't even think about it. Taylor was like that with soccer. I used to watch him play when we visited. He was so graceful on the field. He was like a wildcat: strong, sleek, and lethal. He was powerful and beautiful."

"It sounds like you were in love with him."

"I guess I was in a way, but it's more accurate to say I loved him. We were like brothers."

Tristan got quiet. I'd learned that meant he was sad, upset, or hurting inside.

"I'm sorry."

"No. It's okay. Sometimes I just forget Taylor is gone, you know? It's as if he's still out there, playing soccer. Then I remember, and I feel the loss all over again. It will pass soon. I know he's safe now, so everything is okay. I'm just feeling a little sorry for myself."

Tristan had a unique way of looking at grief, yet maybe he was right. If those who died did go onto a better place, then grief really was just those left behind feeling sorry for themselves because they missed who was gone. I guess that wasn't a bad thing, either, but it was a new take on grief.

Tristan brightened up almost immediately. It was as if a dark cloud had passed over and was now gone. I hugged him close, and then we walked on.

"So who is playing with us?" Tristan asked. "I forgot to ask before."

"Brendan, Casper, Marc, and Nate."

"You invited Nate?"

"Yeah, I'm trying to patch things up with him. I was a dick when I thought you two had something going."

"I think you had him confused. He had no idea why you were hostile. Maybe I should tell him."

"Don't you dare!"

"Ohh, I love having leverage."

"You're just a little-bit wicked, you know that?"

"Just a little bit."

"Well, I'm trying to make up for being a jerk. I invited Marc, too, because I want you guys to get to know each other better."

We walked on to Tristan's house. He led me into the kitchen. His mom was sitting at the kitchen table, sipping coffee and reading *Country Living*.

"How was the library?" she asked.

"It was full of books, Mom," Tristan said, giving her a hug.

"How are you, Shawn?"

"I couldn't be better."

I think I turned ever so slightly pink. I was just sure Tristan's mom could tell I was in love with her son by the tone of my voice. She smiled.

"Want me to fix you boys something?"

"No, we'll just make sandwiches. We're heading over to the park to play flag football in a while," Tristan said.

"Football?"

"Don't act so surprised, Mom."

"I've just never heard you mention football before."

"Shawn and I are introducing each other to new things. He's reading a book. I'm playing football."

"You make such a cute couple."

"Mom!"

"Well, you do."

I knew Tristan was out to his mom, but I almost couldn't believe she was talking about Tristan and me as a couple.

"I think you're good for each other, and Shawn is very handsome."

"Uh, Mom, he's sitting right there."

336

I laughed, even though I was a little embarrassed, too.

"You'll have to excuse me, Shawn. I'm just happy Tristan is dating such a nice boy."

"I'm happy I'm dating Tristan. He's wonderful." The tone of my voice said how much I loved him.

If Brandon and Jon had been there, they would've been playing fake violins and giving me a rough time, but I was safely hidden from their gaze.

Tristan and I made bologna-salad sandwiches and sat down at the kitchen table with his mom. Tristan poured us both iced tea.

"Do you have any college plans yet, Shawn?" Tristan's mom asked.

"College is kind of up in the air at this point. I plan to go, but I don't know when. I don't see how I can go before Tim graduates from high school. Then he's going to need help with school expenses, so I may have to wait until after he graduates from college. I have decided that I am going to school even if I don't graduate until I'm thirty."

"Tristan has told me how you're taking care of your brother. What you're doing for him is very admirable."

"Well, I'm doing it for us. I get a lot out of it, too. I don't know if I could handle being truly on my own."

"Well, I'm very impressed. I think Tristan has made a very good choice."

I smiled.

We finished up and headed out to the park.

"I hope Mom didn't embarrass you too much," Tristan said.

"Just a little. I'm glad she approves of me."

"Why wouldn't she?"

"Well, beyond the obvious reason that I'm a guy, I'm just...surprised."

"Mom has no problem with my sexual orientation. I'm sure she'd like grandchildren—most moms do, I think—but I probably will have a kid. You shouldn't be surprised she approves. In case you haven't noticed, you have a lot going for you."

I smiled again. I smiled a lot when I was around Tristan.

"I've never thought much about having kids," I said. "I think I'd like that, but not too soon!"

"I'm talking about the future. After college, certainly. I don't have to tell you what a responsibility that will be. For all practical purposes, Tim is your son."

"Yeah, no kidding. I feel like his dad sometimes, although mostly I feel like his brother. I'm just glad he's sixteen and not six. If we adopt someday, let's stick with an older kid."

"Are you proposing to me, Shawn Myer?"

I turned a little red—yet again.

"Let's just say I hope we'll be together for a long time."

"I hope so, too."

Those four words filled me with such happiness I thought I might float right off the sidewalk. I felt as if I had proposed and Tristan had said "yes."

We walked on to the park in silence. We didn't need words. We didn't need anything. This...this was happiness.

Brendan and Casper awaited us by the volleyball courts. Brendan held a football in one hand, idling tossing it into the air and catching it. I was a talented football player, but Brendan...he was a football god. I seriously wouldn't be surprised if he ended up in the NFL.

The weather was on the chilly side. Casper was wearing a blue-plaid flannel shirt over his t-shirt, and Brendan was wearing a red IU sweatshirt. Tristan had his long-sleeved pullover. I was the only one dumb enough to wear only a t-shirt. My arms were chilly, but I figured I'd warm up when we began to play. At least, I was wearing jeans like everyone else.

Marc showed up soon, smiling and cheerful. He had dressed for the cool weather too—sweat pants and a forest-green, long-sleeved shirt that set off his blond hair. Nate arrived three minutes later. He gave Tristan a smile and nod and said "hey" to everyone.

I didn't feel quite so stupid after Nate arrived. He was wearing a muscle shirt that completely left his arms bare. He had nicely muscled arms. I experienced a momentary flash of jealousy, but then I reminded myself there was nothing going on between Tristan and Nate beyond friendship. I made it a point to be nice to Nate.

"So, how do we play?" Tristan asked. "Is this like flag football in gym?"

"Pretty much," Brendan said. "When the other team has possession, just try to grab the flag of whoever has the ball. When your team has the ball, try to keep the other team from doing the same. The quarterback will call the plays, but there's only so much you can do with so few players."

"I can handle that," Tristan said.

I began to feel a little uneasy. Tristan wasn't the athletic type. What if he got hurt? No one was going to hurt anyone else on purpose, but accidents happened. What if Nate plowed into Tristan and broke his glasses? What if Brendan fell on Tristan?

I can't believe it. I sound like someone's mother.

What was I worrying about? This was flag football. Tristan wasn't a jock, but that didn't mean he was a weakling. He was a lot bigger than Casper, and I wasn't worried about Casper.

You're not in love with Casper, either.

I smiled. Was this what love did? It wasn't a bad price to pay. I was being ridiculous, anyway. Tristan was not made of glass. If he did get hurt, which wasn't likely, he'd deal with it like any other guy, and then he'd be okay.

"Okay, how about teams?" Brendan asked.

"I think Brendan and Casper should be on one team and Shawn and Tristan on the other. We shouldn't split up boyfriends," Marc said.

"But what about you and me?" Nate asked in a tone that suggested they were a couple, too.

"Oh, you just wish you could land a boyfriend as hot as me," Marc said.

I wondered about Nate's sexual orientation. Not long ago, I thought he had something going with Tristan, but I was completely wrong about that. Nate seemed entirely comfortable around gay guys, but that didn't mean he was gay. In fact, it might mean he was hetero. The guys who were the least comfortable around out gay guys were usually closeted gays or questioning guys who hadn't figured things out yet. I guess it didn't matter.

"Which team would you like?" Nate asked.

"I think I should be with Brendan and Casper. You and Brendan are the big guys. That will balance it out."

No one had a problem with that, so we set up the boundaries and goal lines and prepared to play.

Brendan called the shots for the other team, no surprise there. I deferred to Nate. To be honest, I was a better player, but I wanted to receive some passes.

We won possession on the coin toss. Our plan was for me to break into the clear if possible, then Nate would pass to me. If I couldn't get into the clear, he'd make a dash for it. Tristan's job was to keep Casper and Marc busy.

Brendan plowed into me and knocked me on my ass. We were taking it easy since it was flag football, but contact was allowed, at least for blocking. While I was on my butt, Tristan darted past the other team and toward the goal line. Nate passed to him, and I made it to my feet just in time to see Tristan catch the ball and race across the line with Marc hot on his heels. My mouth dropped open. Here I thought I was the jock in our relationship.

Tristan grinned. Brendan and Nate just gaped at him, as if they couldn't believe he'd pulled it off.

"I think you guys have a secret weapon. You should go out for football this fall, Tristan."

"I don't think so. I have a feeling football practice would kill me. Besides, that was beginner's luck. I have an incredible store of clumsiness I haven't begun to tap yet."

No one scored for the next fifteen minutes or so. Brendan and Nate couldn't seem to get past each other. There were tons of incomplete passes. Casper and Marc were a menace. They might not be football players, but they were fast. I thought I might repeat Tristan's performance when I broke into the clear and caught the ball, but Casper nabbed my flag about two seconds later. I didn't even see him coming.

Brendan intercepted the next pass, and this time he did get past Nate, as well as Tristan and me. He tied up the score.

Nate faked a pass to Tristan on our next play and then tried to maneuver his way down the field. Casper and Marc were all over him, and Brendan was coming in for the kill. Nate made a short pass to me, and I tore off toward the goal line. This time, I could hear Casper coming up behind me and closing fast. I sprinted and scored!

We played for another half hour, but I was the last to score, which meant our team won!

After the game, we all headed across the street to Ofarim's for something hot to drink. All that running around had warmed me up, but my arms were chilled, and the warmth of the restaurant was welcome.

We all squeezed into one booth. I was wedged between Tristan and Marc. My boyfriend and my almost-boyfriend were getting along wonderfully. I guess that shouldn't have surprised me, but I was relieved nonetheless.

I'd joked around with Nate during the game and had dropped all pretense of hostility toward him. He seemed to have forgiven me for being an ass before.

Scotty approached our table with menus, but we all ordered hot chocolate, except for Nate, who ordered coffee. Scotty was a sophomore at VHS. I worked with him in Ofarim's occasionally, but he was mostly there when I wasn't. He had a good sense of humor, so I enjoyed those times we were waiting tables together.

"You're sure you don't want to go out for football this fall?" Nate asked Tristan as we waited on our drinks.

"No, thanks. I'll leave football to Shawn."

"Yeah, it might be embarrassing for Shawn if you end up being a better player," Brendan said mischievously. "You definitely outdid him today."

"Hey! I scored a goal, too, if you remember. I believe that's how our team kicked your butt."

"Yeah, but that catch was beautiful. If you want to give up that whole studious persona and become a jock, I think you can handle it, Tristan."

"Yeah, right! If the practices didn't kill me, I'm sure the first game would. No, thank you. I did have fun playing today, though. We should do this again. I'm glad Shawn talked me into it. I wasn't exactly eager."

"Not eager to play football?" Nate asked. "And I thought you were smart."

"If Shawn and I hadn't cut a deal, I wouldn't have played today."

"What deal?" Brendan asked. "Was it something sexual?"

"You're getting as bad as Brandon and Jon," Marc said.

"No, it wasn't sexual. I agreed to give football a try if Shawn would read a book."

I suddenly felt somewhat embarrassed, although I'm not sure why.

"So what are you reading, Shawn?" Marc asked. "*War & Peace* or *The Little Engine That Could?*"

"Something in between, smart ass, a biography of Alexander the Great."

"I've read three books on him," Brendan said. "He's fascinating."

Brendan read about Alexander the Great?

"Yeah, he was a homo like you. It figures you'd be into him," Nate said.

Casper pelted Nate with a wadded-up napkin.

"Chill. I'm just kidding. I did a World Civ report on him. I think I might be Alexander reincarnated."

"You wish," said Brendan.

Maybe I was going to have to adjust my ideas about jocks. I never really thought of Brendan and Nate having interests beyond sports. Brendan had read three books on Alexander? That couldn't have all been for school. Maybe I was the only dumb jock. I definitely wanted to give this reading thing a try.

Our drinks arrived. I think I enjoyed holding the warm mug as much as I did drinking the hot chocolate. Our conversation turned from Alexander back to football, then to soccer, and then to chocolate-chip cookies, for some reason. It's kind of weird how conversations move from one topic to another like that. One minute you're talking about a book report and the next you're on funerals, not that we talked about funerals as we sat there, but you know what I mean. Weird.

Dane

I was in the VHS restroom near the library when it happened. No, I'm not talking about something like *that*. Tim and I could use his place now, and restroom sex had never been our thing. Gross! I mean something scary. I'd just rinsed the soap off my hands when I raised my head and cried out. I could see Jacob's reflection in the mirror! My ghost had followed me to school, and he was standing right behind me! I turned quickly, but he was gone.

"I know it's big, Dane, but it's not that scary," Jon said as he zipped up his pants and walked to the sinks.

"Huh?"

"Hello? Dane? Are you in there?"

"Um, yeah."

"There's no point in teasing you if you aren't going to react," Jon said.

"Oh, I'm sorry. What did you say?"

"Forget it," Jon said. "Are you okay?"

"I…um…I guess so."

"Do you often scream in the boys' restroom for no reason?"

"I just…thought I saw something in the mirror. It freaked me out."

"O-k-a-y," Jon said as if I was a mental patient. "Are the leprechauns after you again?"

"Funny."

I walked back out into the hallway. I had not imagined it. I'd seen Jacob standing behind me wearing his VHS letterman's jacket. He looked more real than ever. I could almost have mistaken him for just another student, except his face was still slightly discolored, and he looked a bit out of place and time. His clothes were just a little off. His jacket, for instance. It was similar yet not the same as those worn by the jocks at VHS nowadays.

Jacob had left me in peace last night. After Tim walked me home, I'd crawled into bed and didn't awaken until it was time to get up for school. I hoped that meant he'd leave me be, but no such luck. Maybe I had imagined him after all, but no, my imagination wasn't that good. I hadn't even been thinking about Jacob before he appeared. My mind had been on other things this morning, like the spaghetti and the Rook game of the night before. I'd been in a great mood all morning and then: bam!

Was I going to start seeing Jacob everywhere? What if he started haunting me in my classes? What if he accosted me on my way home from school? How could I escape from a ghost?

Damn that Boothe! He had royally screwed me over, yet this wasn't Boothe's fault. He was a selfish jerk and had no problem dumping his troubles on someone else, but Jacob had forced him to pass that coin onto me. Even if I didn't know it for a fact, it would've made sense. Boothe didn't like me, but he wouldn't have gone to the trouble of tracking me down if he could have saddled just anyone with that coin. He wouldn't have put himself in unnecessary danger, either. Boothe was far from blameless, but Jacob was the driving force.

I calmed myself. There was no reason to blow things out of proportion. The situation was bad, but I'd been in worse spots. I feared Jacob. I was uneasy because I never knew when he was going to pop up, but he'd never tried to harm me, and there was no reason to fear he'd become dangerous. It was a scary situation, but a dead Jacob wasn't nearly as dangerous as a living Boothe.

The rest of the day passed pleasantly enough. Brandon and Jon teased me about eating not only my lunch but half of Tim's. I had been hungrier lately, but maybe that was because of the frequent sexual activity with Tim. We burned up a lot of calories! Tim said I wore him out as much as football practice did.

I walked home after school, dumped my backpack in my room, and then walked down to the cafeteria. I found a note on the refrigerator door. Mom and Dad had driven up to South Bend to check out some antique mall and then to have supper. Mine was in the refrigerator. All I had to do was heat it up.

I wasn't hungry enough for supper yet, so I grabbed a couple of chocolate-chip cookies and walked to the gym. I went to the large football-team photo near the stage and stared at Jacob

Brubaker. I wondered who he'd been and what his life was like. Tim and I had planned to do some more research on him, but other pursuits had demanded our time. It had been easy enough to discover he was killed by being hit by a car, but other details were harder to find. I had gone to the library again a couple of times to see what I could uncover, but all I'd dug up was references to his participation in sports and a few school clubs. Jacob was a star athlete. He'd earned a letterman's jacket. He was the top contender to become the quarterback in the 1949-50 school year, but his death had brought everything to an abrupt end.

"Handsome, wasn't I?"

I jumped and cried out. I turned quickly. Jacob was standing not two feet away. He looked almost alive. His face was only slightly blue-tinged. The air perhaps felt cooler, but if so, the difference was so little I couldn't be sure. This time, there had been no warning that Jacob was coming. My mind raced back to that morning in the restroom. There had been no advance warning then, either—no intense cold, no frost forming on glass. I'd been too shaken up to think about it then.

Jacob stepped closer, and I backed up against the wall.

"You're not wearing my coin," Jacob said. "I want you to wear it."

"I, uh…"

I trembled. Jacob was speaking to me. He'd only done so once before now, and then only those few words that so disturbed me: "I'm going to make you mine."

"You don't have to be afraid of me," Jacob said. "I understand why you were afraid before. I know I wasn't looking my best. I'm coming back now, though, thanks to you. I won't hurt you, Dane. I'm grateful."

"I…I don't understand."

"You will."

Jacob closed in on me. I darted away from him, into the boys' locker room. I'm not sure what I thought I was doing. There was no escaping a ghost. Jacob walked through the door and smiled at me.

"Don't be afraid."

"It was Boothe's idea to rob your grave! I was just working for him! I was desperate. I'm sorry!"

"It's okay, Dane. Without Boothe and you, I wouldn't have been able to come back. I'm not angry about you disturbing my grave. In fact, I'm grateful. It's just a shame that Boothe took the coin and not you. It would have made things so much easier. It's you I've wanted since that night."

There it was. I had been the target all along. I already knew it, yet hearing it stated out loud chilled me to the bone.

"I want to show you my appreciation, Dane. I know about your fantasy. I heard you talk about it in this very room."

Jacob came closer. I backed into the lockers. I wanted to run, but there was no escape. Wherever I went, he'd find me.

Jacob was only inches from me now.

"Please. Whatever you're going to do, please don't!"

"But it's what you want, Dane. I know it, and you know it, too."

Jacob gripped my upper arms. He was strong—as strong as a living boy with his build. Jacob leaned in. I turned my head. He grasped my chin in one hand and made me look at him. He pressed his lips against mine and kissed me. I tried to pull away, but he kissed me harder, forcing my lips to part. He slipped his tongue into my mouth. His lips and tongue were warm. He felt—alive. Jacob kissed me deeply, then leaned back, smiling.

"You can't tell me you didn't like that."

"But, you're dead!"

"I'm not dead. I was never truly dead. I was just…waiting."

I shook my head.

"No. No, you're dead! This isn't right! It's…"

"Do I look dead to you?"

I gazed at Jacob. I couldn't even detect the slight purple tinge anymore.

348

"No."

"Did I feel dead when I kissed you?"

I shook my head. I'd panicked when he began to kiss me and then again when he forced his tongue into my mouth. The thought of his cold, wet, likely rotting tongue nearly made me retch, but then it hadn't been like that at all.

"You're not alive," I said.

"Close enough," Jacob said.

"Not for me."

I swallowed hard, ready for him to become angry.

"You'll change your mind about that soon enough."

Jacob moved to kiss me again.

"No. Please!"

"You know you like it."

"I have a boyfriend!"

"I'll make you forget all about him," Jacob said.

Before I could protest that I'd never forget about Tim, Jacob kissed me again. He pressed his body into mine and kissed me deeply. My own body began to react. I tried to break away. Doing this was wrong on so many levels. Jacob wouldn't let me go. He held me in place and kissed me as if he was trying to devour me.

"I know your fantasy," he whispered into my ear right before he gently chewed on my earlobe. A wave of pleasure coursed through my body. I fought it. I couldn't allow myself to feel this.

Jacob's hands were all over my body.

"No. Stop. Please stop," I pleaded.

Jacob shut me up by forcing his tongue into my mouth. Jacob's body pinned me against the lockers as he held my head in place with his left hand. His right hand wandered and groped. He gripped the front of my jeans. I fought him, but he was too strong for me. I tried to bring my knee up to nail him in the nuts, wondering if I could even hurt a ghost (or whatever he was) that way, but my legs were firmly pinned. I could barely move.

Jacob kept kissing me. He kept groping me through my jeans. I was aroused despite myself. Before long, I began to moan into Jacob's mouth. My own body betrayed me. I was so turned on I couldn't stand it. Jacob groped me, then rubbed his crotch into mine. I could feel the hardness in his pants. He rubbed against me harder and harder while his tongue invaded my mouth. I moaned into Jacob's mouth as I lost control. My orgasm surged through my entire body. I'd never felt anything so intense in my life. If Jacob hadn't had me pinned to the wall, I would have slid down it. That's just what I did when he released me. He stood over me, smiling.

I looked up. Jacob looked powerful and beautiful. He looked full of life. He smiled at me again, and then he disappeared. I just sat there on the floor, panting.

I was exhausted. I was almost too weak to pull myself up and sit on the bench. I remained there a few moments. My stomach rumbled. I was ravenously hungry. I walked out of the locker room and made my way to the cafeteria.

I warmed up the lasagna Mom had left for me and wolfed it down. Then, I made myself a salami and Colby Jack cheese sandwich and devoured it. Two more sandwiches followed as did most of a bag of sour cream & onion potato chips. My mind kept going back to what had just happened in the old locker room. I didn't want to remember. I felt so guilty. I should have been stronger. I should have had more control. Jacob should not have been able to get me off. I had a boyfriend! I loved him! Despite what Jacob said, he was dead! I'd seen him lying in his casket with my very own eyes. He'd been hit by a car decades ago, and he'd lain in his grave ever since—until Boothe disturbed him. I loathed Boothe. If I ever got my hands on him…but no, that was stupid. Boothe was far too much for me to handle. It was best to hope he never returned to Verona again. I doubted he would. He'd done what he'd set out to do: saddle me with a dead boy!

I wanted to clean up, but I was afraid Jacob might molest me if I tried to take a shower. Instead, I climbed the stairs to my room, grabbed a clean pair of boxers, and headed for the boys' restroom. I cleaned myself up and changed underwear. I stood there staring at myself in the mirror when I was finished, feeling more guilty by the second. I'd cheated on Tim, and I didn't like the way I felt about myself.

I didn't know what I was going to do. Should I tell Tim or keep it from him? I didn't want to hurt Tim, but not telling him felt like messing around behind his back. I didn't want to tell him what I'd done, but I knew the guilt would probably eat me alive if I didn't. There were disadvantages to being the new me. The old me would have reveled in the intrigue instead of feeling guilty. Despite my predicament, I liked the new me a whole lot better.

I walked to Tim's place. I wasn't sure if he'd be home or not, but I didn't want to call. I couldn't talk about this on the phone. When he opened the door, he gave me a grin. I felt worse than ever about what had happened.

On the way over, I'd promised myself I'd come right out and say what I had to say. If I let myself stall even a little, I might spend hours with Tim and never have the balls to tell him what had happened. I'd tell him and take the consequences.

"Tim, I…I've got to tell you something," I said even before the door was closed behind us.

"Shoot," he said.

"I cheated on you."

That did it. My eyes watered, and a sob escaped my throat. My pain was increased exponentially by the look on Tim's face. He looked as if I'd just slapped him.

"No," he said, shaking his head. "You wouldn't do that."

"I did," I said. "I'm sorry."

I was sniveling like a pathetic loser.

"Who?" Tim asked, his lower lip beginning to tremble. "Marc? Blake?"

I shook my head.

"Jacob."

"Jacob? Dane, Jacob is a ghost. He isn't real. Well, he's real, but you cannot have cheated on me with a ghost. It isn't possible."

"I did."

"What did you do, Dane?"

I told Tim exactly what happened.

"You jerk. Don't scare me like that. Don't come telling me you cheated on me when you didn't. It's not cheating if you aren't a willing participant. Dane, Jacob raped you. You're not responsible for what happened."

"He didn't rape me. He didn't...you know."

"Just because there was no penetration doesn't mean it wasn't rape. You tried to stop him. You tried to get away. You couldn't. He forced you. That's rape in my book."

"But, I...I came."

"So? Listen, if someone pinned me to the wall and kept groping my stuff I'd come sooner or later, too. That's not cheating, Dane. That is your body's natural reaction."

"So you're not mad?"

"What I am is worried. Dane, I had no idea Jacob could or would do something like that."

"I didn't, either."

"Forget all this cheating talk, Dane. That's crazy. You did not cheat on me. I'd kick Jacob's ass if I knew how to find him."

"Well, short of digging him up, I don't think you can. I'm not even sure he's in his grave anymore. He was solid this time. If I didn't know he was a ghost, I would've thought he was a real, live guy. He's been getting more and more lifelike. This afternoon he was almost the same as living. I don't know what he is anymore."

"We've got to find some way to protect you against him."

"I'd love that, but how do you protect yourself against someone who can walk through walls? He felt completely solid to me, but he still walked straight through the door."

"Maybe you should wear a cross or something."

"He's a ghost, Tim, not a vampire."

Tim pulled me to him and held me close. Despite the Jacob situation, I felt safe with Tim. I wished I could be with Tim all the time, but that wasn't going to happen. My parents wouldn't allow it. If I could explain to them why I needed Tim to be with me, they might have allowed it, but I couldn't explain. How do you tell your parents you're being molested by a ghost without them sending you off to the nut house? It can't be done.

Shawn was out, so we made good use of the time. I needed to be with Tim then. There were all the usual attractions of his naked body against mine, but being with him made me feel safe and secure. When we were finished, Tim held me as we lay on his bed. We both fell asleep. I didn't awaken until Tim nudged me. I could hear Shawn moving about the loft. Tim and I dressed and walked into the living room.

"I'm not going to ask what you guys were doing," Shawn said.

"Actually, we were sleeping," Tim said.

"Yeah, and I bet I know what wore you out."

We grinned but didn't say anything.

"I'm going to walk Dane home. I'll be back in a bit," Tim said.

"I may be in bed when you get back. I'm exhausted."

Shawn yawned. He looked worn out.

Tim walked me home in the moonlight. It was romantic and wonderful.

"I'm glad we're okay," I said.

"We're more than okay. We're perfect."

I stopped for a moment, pulled Tim to me, and kissed him on the lips.

"I don't deserve you."

"Sure you do," Tim said. "I just hope I deserve you."

"You do."

We kissed again and walked on. When I'd walked to Tim's place I'd feared things might be over between us. I guess that was pretty stupid of me. I guess I just panicked. Now things were better than ever. It would take more than a ghost to come between Tim and me.

353

***

"I am so hungry," I said as Tim and I walked out the front doors of VHS.

Tim arched an eyebrow.

"I meant for food, but that, too."

Tim grinned.

"Let's go get something," he said. "Ofarim's? We can annoy Shawn."

We walked the few blocks to Ofarim's. The bell jingled as we opened the door. Shawn looked up from the counter and smiled. We slipped into a booth. Shawn carried milkshakes over to a couple sitting on the other side of the restaurant and then came to us.

"Do you need menus or do you know what you want?"

"I'll have a triple cheeseburger, fries, a corndog, a Coke, and a large chocolate shake."

Shawn's eyes widened slightly at my large order but said nothing.

"I think I'll have a hot dog, fries, and a Coke," Tim said.

"It'll be ready in a few."

Shawn brought our Cokes right out. I immediately sucked half of mine down. I loved the bubbly sweetness of it.

"I wish it would warm up already," I said. "Why does it take so long for spring to really get going?"

"You're just impatient. Besides, it's pretty warm out now. Think of how cold it was two months ago!"

"Yeah, I'm impatient. I'm like that sign I saw once. It said something like, 'May God grant me patience, and I want it right now!'"

Tim laughed.

Our orders were up sooner than expected. The scent of my burger, corn dog, and fries was heavenly. I stuffed my mouth full of fries almost as soon as they were on the table. Tim took a bite of his hot dog and sighed.

"What?" I tried to ask with my mouth full. I think it came out as, "Wmmff?"

"I feel guilty," Tim said. "Here we are stuffing our faces, and Shawn is stuck waiting tables. He works so hard, and I feel like I don't do anything."

"I seem to remember you offered to get a part-time job, but Shawn didn't want you to do it."

"Yeah, he was afraid my grades would suffer, and he said he wanted me to remain a kid while I could."

"So, there you are. You help out around the apartment, right?"

"Yeah. Shawn and I share the cleaning. I think I'm going to start doing most of it, though. It's only fair. He's working to support both of us. He shouldn't have to come home and clean after school and work."

"Problem solved then. Take on more of the housework. I'll even help you."

"I really lucked out getting a big brother like Shawn. Tom's a loser, but Shawn is so cool. Sometimes, I wonder about what my life would be like without Shawn."

"Don't worry about that. You do have Shawn. He's a hero in my book, not only for saving my life but for everything he does for you and for the way he stepped aside when he noticed how you and I felt about each other."

"Are you ever sorry you didn't just stick with Shawn?" Tim asked.

"No. I love your brother, but I don't think we could have ever been boyfriends. There was too much of a past between us for us to feel romantic about each other, you know? Shawn and I would probably have never been more than friends with benefits.

We're still friends, so all I'm missing out on is the benefits, and I have all the benefits I can handle with you."

Tim laughed.

"You know we'd better not let Shawn hear us talk about him like this. He'll expect us to carve a statue of him or something," I said.

"Yeah, his ego is big enough. He's been walking on air since he landed Tristan. I never thought he'd go for a guy like Tristan. They're such an odd couple. Tristan is extremely good-looking, but he's an artist and such a bookworm. Shawn is a typical jock. Maybe opposites do attract."

"Look at us. You're a jock, and I'm definitely not. My idea of playing football is tossing a ball back and forth. You get out on the field and knock guys on their ass."

"And get knocked on my ass," Tim added.

"Yeah, seeing one of those big linebackers coming for me would scare the crap out of me."

"I just think it's fun."

"See, we're different in a lot of ways, but don't you think that makes things interesting? I like those differences. I don't want to date myself."

"Yeah, I see what you mean. I guess it's the same with Shawn and Tristan."

I tore into my cheeseburger.

"Are you eating for two, Dane?" Tim asked.

"No, but if you want to try to get me pregnant, I'm up for it."

"I'll take you up on that," Tim said.

Tim began eating his hot dog in a suggestive manner. He looked as if he was practicing giving head. I laughed. I was becoming aroused, too, until he took a big bite.

"Oww," I said.

"I only bite hot dogs," Tim said.

Tim finished his hot dog and fries long before I finished my meal. We sat and talked and joked around. Tim was a boyfriend and a best friend combined.

I was finishing off my milkshake when my breath caught in my throat. There, only a few paces away, was Jacob.

"He's here," I said.

"I know Shawn's here. He took our order, remember?" Tim teased.

"Not Shawn. Him," I said, pointing.

Tim turned around for a look then turned back to me.

"Who? Where?"

"Right by the jukebox."

Tim took another look.

"There is no one by the jukebox."

"He's standing right there!"

"Dane, calm down. Who's standing there?"

"Can't you see him?"

"See who?"

It was obvious that only I could see Jacob.

"Jacob," I said.

"The ghost?"

"Yes! Why can't you see him?"

"I don't know anything about ghosts," Tim said.

"You probably think I'm nuts, don't you?"

"I think no such thing."

I smiled.

"Thanks, Tim."

"Does he look...dead?"

"No. He looks alive. If you could see him, you'd think he was just another guy."

Jacob looked so sexy leaning up against the jukebox. He grinned at me, and some '50s song began playing. I didn't know the title, but some guy was singing, "oh, my darling, my love," or something like that. It was freaky.

"How did he do that?"

"Do what?" Tim asked, gazing at the jukebox, straining to see.

"The music."

"What music?"

"Can't you hear it?"

"No."

"I think I'm going crazy, Tim."

I was on the verge of tears. I wanted to scream.

"You're okay," Tim said, gazing at me with a worried expression.

I was on the verge of panic, but I also felt drawn to Jacob. What was I thinking? The last time I'd encountered Jacob, he'd backed me up against the lockers and molested me. Tim had gone so far as to call it rape. I wanted nothing to do with Jacob. Even if he wasn't dead—a major turnoff, by the way—he was dangerous.

Jacob stepped closer.

"Shit, he's coming this way."

Tim stood and faced in the general direction of Jacob. I stood up, too. Jacob looked me up and down and smiled.

"Hot," he said.

"Leave me alone."

"That's not what you want. I know what you really want."

"Where is he?" Tim asked. "Tell me so I can stay between you."

"Three feet to your right, about four feet in front of you."

Tim moved, trying to block Jacob.

"Not bad," Jacob said, looking my boyfriend up and down. "I might want some of that."

"Leave him alone!" I said.

"Are you talking to me?" Tim asked.

"No, to Jacob."

"Don't worry. You're the one I want. I'm going to make you mine," Jacob said.

I shook my head. Jacob looked at Tim again.

"I'm much hotter than your boyfriend. I can make you feel things he can't."

"Just leave me alone. I'm not interested in you."

"Where is he?" Tim asked.

"He's...never mind."

"Liar. You know you want me. The sooner you admit it, the easier this will be for all of us."

What I hated most was that a part of me did want him, and I didn't understand why. Jacob faded before my eyes.

"He's gone," I said.

"Are you okay?" Tim asked.

"I think so."

It was a lie, and little did I know it would be the first of many. I wasn't okay. I wasn't okay at all.

Shawn

Whoa. So Alexander the Great did have a thing for guys. He was, at the very least, bisexual and most likely gay. Alexander and Hephaestion were friends since boyhood and were way more than friends. The historian who wrote the biography I was reading came right out and said they were lovers. Alexander nearly went insane when Hephaestion died. I thought of Mark and Taylor for a moment. Mark had gone insane when Taylor killed himself. He was so overcome with grief he totally lost it. That must have been what it was like for Alexander, only he didn't kill himself. Alexander had at least one other lover, a Persian boy named Bagoas. Man, that would be a big scandal if it happened now, but it wasn't a big thing back then. The Greeks even believed that man/boy relationships were more important that man/woman relationships. Wouldn't the religious fundamentalists go nuts if they were suddenly transported back to Ancient Greece? I smiled to think about it.

I put my book away. Break time was over. I liked working at Ofarim's, but it was restful to lose myself in a book for a few minutes. Yeah, this is me, Shawn, talking. I know I sound more like Tristan, but he was right about books, at least about this particular book. Before, I'd always spent my breaks taking a short walk in the park or thumbing through a football magazine. Reading just a few pages of a good book allowed my mind to go to a whole different place. Not only that, I could bring that place with me when I returned to work.

At first, I really didn't know if I'd get into the whole reading thing. I was interested in the book Tristan helped me pick out, but being interested in it and actually reading it were two different things. I was relieved I was into it. I didn't want to have to disappoint Tristan by telling him I wasn't, and I couldn't lie to him. Well, I could, but I didn't want to, and he'd find me out, anyway. If he began talking about Alexander, it would become obvious fast if I hadn't read the book. There were no worries there. I liked it well enough. I actually looked forward to reading it. Why hadn't any of my English teachers assigned something cool to read instead of the boring stuff they handed out?

I cleaned tables and took orders while thinking about Alexander and Hephaestion. It was cool that the most powerful guy in the ancient world was gay. I wondered what Brandon and Jon would have to say about that? I grinned, but I didn't think I'd bring it up. If I started talking Ancient Greece, they'd want to know why. Then, I'd have to tell them I was reading a book, and they would let me have it. It was best not to give those guys ammunition.

Business picked up, and I was kept hopping most of the rest of the night. I liked it that way. Not only did I get more tips, time passed a good deal faster. Right before closing, the bells on the door jingled and Blake walked in. He was wearing his letterman's jacket over a white tank top. My eyes involuntarily fell to his crotch. His tight jeans left little to the imagination. I quickly took my eyes off his package, but it was too late. Blake gave me a knowing smirk.

"What's up?" he asked.

"I'm getting ready to close up. It's been a busy night."

"Maybe you should stay a little late."

There was no mistaking Blake's suggestive tone.

"I have a boyfriend, Blake."

"He doesn't have to know."

"I couldn't do that to him."

"But you want it."

"No. I don't."

"Don't lie to me. I bet you're getting hard right now, aren't you?"

I didn't answer. I was getting hard. I couldn't help it. Memories of getting it on with Blake filled my mind before I could prevent them.

"That's what I thought. You do want it. You want me to shove you over the counter and make you moan my name."

"No. I mean, yes, maybe I do want it, but I don't want it. I love Tristan."

"I bet he can't make you feel the way I do. Has he ever held you down and pounded you?"

"We've, uh, never had sex."

"Are you fucking kidding me? Not even a blowjob?"

"No."

"Fuck, you must be going nuts. You need it worse than I do."

"I'm not having sex with you, Blake."

"What your boyfriend doesn't know won't hurt him, Shawn. He doesn't have to know."

"I'll know."

"So?"

"Blake, if I wasn't dating Tristan, I'd be ripping your shirt off right now, but I am dating him. I love him."

"You aren't even getting any from him!"

"There's more to it than sex, Blake."

"Oh, come on! With guys it's always about sex. If you aren't getting any, it's time to move on."

"No."

"Then, at least take care of your needs while you've got the chance. Keep dating him if you want. Date him and have sex with me."

"No."

Blake looked disgusted. He shook his head.

"You'll come around. I know how bad you want this," he said, groping his bulge. "I'll see you later, Shawn. Call me when you change your mind."

Blake left without another word.

I locked the door behind him and flipped the sign to "Closed." I finished cleaning up, trying to force Blake from my mind. I focused on each small task as if the world would blow up if

I didn't do it properly. It was one of those times when I wished I could just shut off my mind and stop thinking.

I turned off the lights, let myself out, and locked the front door. I don't even remember the trip home. I just remember walking up the stairs and opening the door to find Tim studying at the kitchen table.

"Have a good night, bro?" Tim asked.

I looked at him and almost cried.

"Shawn, what's wrong?"

"Blake came to Ofarim's right before I closed up."

"And?"

"I feel so guilty," I said. I had to fight the tears back, which was especially hard for me because I almost never cried.

"Shawn, you didn't!"

My lower lip trembled, and I bit it.

"You had sex with Blake?"

"No."

"No? Then why do you feel guilty?"

"Blake came on to me. I wanted him soooo bad."

"But you didn't have sex with him. Did you touch him?"

"No."

"Did you let him touch you?"

"No."

"I don't get it, then."

"I love Tristan!"

"Well, duh, but what did you do that's so bad? Why do you feel guilty? Just tell me exactly what happened."

"Blake came in. He wanted to do what we'd done before after closing."

"Which is?"

"None of your business. He wanted to have sex. That's as much detail as you're getting."

"Okay, so then what?"

"I was behind the counter. Blake couldn't see, but I…"

"Was hard and throbbing?"

"Thank you for trying to turn this into pornography."

"Yeah, yeah, but I'm right, aren't I?"

"Yes. I was so…worked up it was all I could do to keep myself from jumping on him and ripping off his shirt. Blake could even tell how bad I wanted him."

"Blake is an aggressive guy. I bet he pushed you."

"He tried to talk me into it."

"But nothing happened?"

"No."

"I feel like smacking you upside the head. You had me worried. I thought you'd gone and fucked up everything by cheating on Tristan, but you didn't do anything."

"I just told you what happened! I *wanted* to do it with Blake. I wanted him so bad I thought I was going to have an accident in my pants."

Tim actually looked as though he was going to laugh for a moment, probably over the accident-in-my-pants part.

"Let me spell it out for you, Shawn. Cheating is having sex with someone other than Tristan. Not cheating is not having sex with someone other than Tristan. You didn't have sex with Blake. You didn't touch him. You didn't let him touch you. There was no physical contact. I fail to see the problem."

"But I *wanted* him."

"Let me say this slowly: Big—Fucking—Deal! So you wanted him, that's nothing! Listen, I love Dane, but sometimes I see a hot guy and I get so hard I'm afraid my zipper is going to burst from the strain. Sometimes I feel like jumping on a guy and ripping his clothes off. That's just nature. It's a natural physical reaction. I'm sure Dane gets hot for other guys, too. In fact, I know he does.

Before you started dating Tristan, we even discussed…well, never mind."

"What?"

"Trust me, you don't want to know."

"Just tell me."

"Okay, you asked for it. Dane and I talked about having a three-way with you. We figured we could seduce you into it."

"Tim, that is way too much information."

"I told you that you didn't want it hear it, but you insisted! The point is I get hot for other guys, and so does Dane. That doesn't mean we don't love each other. I'd never cheat on Dane, and I know he wouldn't cheat on me."

"Maybe I am making too big of a deal out of this."

"Duh! Listen, I know you love Tristan, but you didn't do anything wrong. In fact, you just passed a test. Blake was right there. He wanted it. You wanted it. But, you didn't do it. You could have cheated on Tristan, and he never would have known. No one would have known except for Blake and you. You shouldn't feel guilty. You should feel proud of yourself."

"I think saying I should feel proud of myself is going way too far."

"Either way, you did nothing wrong. That's the point I'm trying to make, and if you don't get it soon, I am going to beat it in."

"Do you think I should tell, Tristan?"

"No."

"But I want to be honest with him."

"There's honesty, and there's too much information. He already knows you get turned on by other guys. He gets turned on by other guys. He has to; it's as simple as that. He knows you had sex with Blake before you started dating him. Therefore, he knows you find Blake attractive. I'm sure he doesn't want to hear about it."

"Are you sure?"

366

"Yes. I know Dane gets hot for other guys, but I don't want to hear about it. Seriously, Shawn, get a grip. This whole, I-did-something-wrong thing is in your head. Hell, even I know that no matter how bad you want Blake, the only way he's going to get you is if he ties you up and forces you."

"Now I feel like an idiot."

"Go with that feeling. You are an idiot, but I love you anyway."

"Thanks, Tim."

"For calling you an idiot? Anytime!"

"No, for talking me through this and pointing out I'm an idiot."

"Well, you're usually pretty smart, but don't ask me to repeat it, because I won't."

I laughed.

"Okay, unless you have another imaginary crisis, I need to get back to my homework."

"No, that's it for now. Thanks."

"Then get the hell out of here."

"Night, Tim."

"Night, dumb ass."

I was worn out, physically and emotionally. I showered to get rid of the smell of cooking grease and then brushed my teeth. I still felt a little bit guilty, especially since I was still horny as hell, but Tim was right. I had worked myself up over basically nothing. If I'd groped Blake or even allowed him to grope me, I would have done something wrong, but neither had happened. Wanting it and doing it were two different things. No one was locked up for wanting to rob a bank or wanting to vandalize a house. As long as I didn't do anything sexual with Blake, it didn't matter whether I wanted him or not.

I climbed into bed. I needed to stroke really badly, but I didn't. I was afraid I might picture Blake if I did. I masturbated a lot since Tristan and I weren't doing it, but I always thought of him when I was getting myself off. I didn't want to risk cheating on Tristan even in my own mind. I loved him so much!

I awakened the next morning surprised I didn't have a wet dream during the night. I'd gone to sleep fearing I'd dream about doing it with Blake, and then I'd feel all guilty again. Tim would no doubt have told me dreaming about Blake wasn't cheating, either, but I still would have been afraid there was some psychological reason for me dreaming about him. So, I was more than happy I hadn't had a wet dream even though it meant I was on the verge of having a case of blue balls, which is no fun at all.

I took care of business in the shower, thinking about what I'd like to do with Tristan someday. I wanted Tristan badly, but I was content to wait. Well, I wasn't entirely content, but when you're in love with someone, it's easier to wait. Just making out with him and doing a little groping was sexy as hell. This might sound crazy, but it was almost better than sex. Besides, I figured we'd take the next step soon. We wouldn't go all the way yet, but I had a feeling I'd get to see Tristan completely naked. The thought of doing oral with him drove me out of my mind with lust. That's what got me off in the shower. I just hoped Tim didn't hear me moan.

I was really curious about what Tristan looked like naked. I'd felt enough to know he had a firm body, and he was at least average in size. Believe it or not, I hadn't even seen him shirtless yet. I was dying to do so. Something about a guy's chest really got me going. I knew Tristan wasn't built like Brendan or Blake or even me, but he didn't have to be muscular to be hot. I thought slim and defined guys were totally sexy. Marc had some muscle, but I'd describe him as more slim and defined than muscular, and he was sexy as fuck.

I wondered why being around Marc didn't trigger the same intense sexual arousal I'd experienced the night before with Blake. Maybe because Marc hadn't come onto me since I started dating Tristan. Maybe it was because there was more than just sex between us. I thought of him as a friend. Blake and I weren't friends. We weren't enemies, but we'd never done anything together except have sex. We got each other off and went our separate ways. Now that I thought of it, that was probably the difference. Marc was a friend. Blake was just a fuck.

I greeted Tristan at his locker after I'd gathered up the books I needed from my own. He smiled at me, and I fell for him all over again. I gave him a hug and kissed him on the cheek. I was so thankful I hadn't done anything with Blake the night before. I never wanted to do anything to screw up what I had with Tristan. I walked him to class, gave him a quick peck after making sure no teachers were watching, and went on my way.

"Sicko," Devon said as he passed me.

"Jealous?" I asked.

Devon's expression contorted to one of disgust. I laughed and went on my way.

The whole thing with Blake seemed like less of a big deal in the morning light. My little brother was right. I guess I was just paranoid that something was going to screw up my relationship with Tristan. I didn't know what I'd do if we didn't work out.

I was glad Blake didn't go to VHS. Blake was used to getting what he wanted, and I had little doubt he'd try to get into my pants again. If we went to the same school, he might become a real problem. I wasn't looking forward to dealing with his advances, but at least he had to drive about fifteen miles to try to seduce me.

Nothing of note happened until lunchtime. The cafeteria always offers some kind of excitement, even if it was just Brandon and Jon going at each other. Dane provided the entertainment for the day, but it kind of freaked me out. We were all talking and laughing when Dane shouted.

"Leave him alone!"

Dane was staring into space near Tim. He'd yelled loud enough to attract the attention of the nearest tables, but everyone went back to gossiping when there was nothing to see. Those of us sitting near Dane, however, were treated to a ringside seat for weird.

"He's not interested in you. He can't even see you," Dane said.

He was glaring at the same spot, at absolutely nothing.

I looked toward Brandon and Jon, waiting for one of them to make a smartass remark, but they were just staring at Dane. They were probably thinking what I was thinking. Dane was seeing his ghost again.

"Is he here?" Tim asked quietly.

"He's standing right beside you, and he's leering at you. I don't like it."

Jon made a face at Brandon that clearly indicated he thought Dane had lost his mind. I didn't know what to think. I kind of believed in ghosts, but why could only Dane see this one? My doubts were increased by the fact we were at school. I knew Dane had supposedly seen him here before, and he sure acted as if he was seeing something now, but there was nothing to see. I could believe a ghost might hang out in the spooky old school where Dane lived, but in this one? Unlikely, at best. Maybe Dane really was losing it, or maybe it was just a big joke.

I looked over at my brother. He looked worried and frightened. No, this wasn't a joke. Dane wouldn't do that to Tim. Perhaps Tim was in on it, but I didn't think he was that good of an actor.

"Stop it! Just stop it!" Dane said.

Dane was clearly upset. I doubted he was a good enough actor to fake what was going on. He looked worried and frightened, too, and he was on the verge of tears. No one at the table was talking. Brendan, Ethan, and Nathan looked worried for Dane. Marc, Casper, and Nate looked embarrassed for him. Casey looked as if she didn't know what to think, and Brandon and Jon looked as though they thought Dane was nuts. Tristan gazed at Dane evenly as if he was trying to read Dane's mind.

"If you touch him, I'll hate you forever," Dane said.

Now, he was clearly angry. No, there was no way he was faking this.

"He's gone," Dane said in the next moment.

Tim reached across the table, grasped Dane's hand, and gave him a reassuring smile. At least it was meant to be reassuring. Tim was scared.

"Sooo, nice weather out, isn't it?" Nate said after an uncomfortable silence.

For some reason, that got Brandon and Jon to giggling. I could tell they were trying to hold it in, but it wasn't working. Dane didn't seem to notice. He just shoveled mashed potatoes and green beans into his mouth as if he hadn't eaten for days. He only took his eyes away from his tray to look at Tim now and then. It was the most bizarre lunch our table had seen in quite some time.

I was worried about Dane. He was either haunted by the ghost of a dead football player, or he was losing his mind. Neither was good. I was glad the guys hadn't made fun of him. They were probably worried about him, too. I had the additional worry of Tim. My little brother loved Dane. What if something bad happened to Dane? What if he went insane? How would Tim deal with that? How could I help him deal with that? I decided not to think about it too much. I just hoped everything would be okay.

Dane

It was time to rid myself of Jacob. My recent encounters with him right in VHS were the final straw. I didn't like Jacob's growing interest in Tim. He'd said he wasn't interested in him, but he sure acted interested! What if he started molesting my boyfriend, or worse, what if he did something to Tim to get him out of the way? I couldn't let him hurt Tim. I wouldn't!

I didn't know if my plan would work, but I had to try something. Boothe had been plenty desperate to pawn off Jacob's coin on me. Jacob had started haunting me soon after the coin came into my possession. There was a good chance the coin was the key. I was determined to destroy it.

I didn't figure merely smashing the coin into an unrecognizable hunk of silver would be enough. I had to melt it. I couldn't accomplish that on a kitchen range, so I hunted out Dad's old Coleman stove and his sinker-making supplies. Long ago, Dad had been big into fishing. I have vague memories of him making sinkers out of lead. I remembered I was allowed nowhere near the stove while he was melting lead and pouring the molten metal into molds. Silver wasn't lead, but it was a soft metal, and I figured Dad's old stove would do the trick.

I set up shop in a corner of the old basement. I had some trouble lighting the stove, but soon I had it going. I placed the iron dipper on the blue jets of flame, and soon the old remnants of lead began to run down the inner sides.

I looked around as I pulled out the coin and dropped it chain and all into the white hot dipper. I half feared Jacob would try to stop me, but there was no sign of the ghost who haunted me. He was too late now. The coin was lying in the thin layer of molten lead, and soon it too would begin to melt. I watched and waited, but nothing happened. The coin refused to melt. Minutes passed and still nothing. It seemed I'd underestimated the temperature needed to melt silver. It obviously had a much higher melting point than lead. Disappointed, I turned off the stove and carefully dumped the coin onto the floor.

Once everything had cooled, I put away the stove and the supplies and picked up the coin. Lead now adhered to it in places, but otherwise it was unchanged.

I wasn't ready to give up yet. I went in search of Dad's tin snips. When I located them, I cut the coin into several small pieces. I walked outside and scattered the pieces in distant parts of the yard. I returned to my room wondering if cutting the coin into little bits was enough. Now, I had only to wait and see if the link to Jacob was broken. Perhaps I'd sent him back to his grave. I crossed my fingers and hoped for the best.

Night came, and I crawled into bed. Still no sign of the ghost. I lay there with my eyes open for the longest time, hoping and fearing—hoping I'd rid myself of Jacob, at last; fearing the solution had been too easy and that I wasn't rid of him at all. I think waiting this night was worse than any of the others. If Jacob didn't appear, it likely meant I was rid of him forever. If he did…my troubles were far from over.

The minutes passed, and still I was alone. My eyes grew heavy, and I drifted off to sleep. Sometime in the night, I began to dream. I could feel myself smile even in my dream. Tim was lying on top of me, his naked body pressed against mine. He was kissing me and holding me tight. I felt so safe and comfortable—so loved.

I grew quickly aroused. I'd had wet dreams about Tim before. They were almost as good as actual sex. I'd often wished I could dream about Tim at will, but I contented myself with his infrequent dream visits. A small moan escaped my lips and then another.

I opened my eyes. Jacob muffled my scream by locking his lips onto mine and shooting his tongue into my mouth. I struggled, but Jacob held me down. He kissed me and pressed his naked body into mine.

It was then that I felt cold metal pressed between our bare chests, metal the shape and size of a half dollar. Jacob pulled back and gazed into my eyes.

"You didn't really think you could rid yourself of me that easily, did you? You didn't really think Boothe hadn't already tried that?"

My face grew sullen.

"Stop fighting it, Dane. We were meant to be together. I've waited for you all these years."

"You only want me because Boothe was smart enough to escape."

"Boothe? Why would anyone want him? No, Boothe was only a means to an end. I didn't come to him as I come to you. I didn't bring him pleasure. I tormented him until he did what I wanted. I knew he wouldn't hesitate to pass the coin onto you. It's you I've wanted all along."

"The coin is the key, isn't it?"

"Still trying to think of ways to rid yourself of me? Why are you so determined to push away what you most need?"

"I don't need you!"

"Someday you'll be amazed you even thought of trying to get rid of me. You won't know how you lived without me."

"Liar."

"You'll come around. Until then, I'm going to bring you more pleasure than you've dreamed possible."

Jacob began to grope me.

"No!"

Jacob clamped his mouth on mine again. He kept me pinned with the weight of his body while he molested me with a free hand. I felt violated and used. I experienced exquisite pleasure and then guilt over the pleasure. When the pleasure was so intense it was nearly painful, Jacob forced me onto my stomach. I struggled, but only half-heartedly. My mind was a mass of confusion.

I knew what he was going to do to me. At the last moment, I tried to cry out, but he shoved my face into the pillow. Blinding pain exploded into my mind, and I bit down on the pillow hard. With the pain came a wave of pleasure. The pain and pleasure mixed until the two were one. Jacob took me by force, but then I gave myself up to him. I'd never experienced such perfect bliss before. The pleasure was too great to push away.

After minutes or hours, I don't know which, such exquisite pleasure erupted in my mind and body that I blacked out. When I awakened I was alone. I would have thought the experience was a dream, but I could still feel the aftereffects in my body and the coin that hung around my neck. I collapsed onto the sheets and fell immediately into a deep sleep.

I momentarily thought I'd been dreaming when I awakened the next morning, but the soreness inside me and the coin hanging around my neck told me what I'd experienced was no dream. The mere memory of it aroused me.

I climbed out of bed and walked to the mirror. The coin lay against my bare chest. There was no sign I'd cut it to bits. It looked exactly the same as always. I began to pull the chain over my head, but I let the coin fall back onto my chest. I gazed at myself in the mirror. I wasn't sure I knew the boy who was looking back at me.

I arrived at school a bit early. Tim met me at my locker and gave me a peck on the lips.

"So, any sign of Jacob last night?" he asked.

"No. No, I didn't see him."

"That's good. I was worried he'd try to get at you after what happened yesterday."

"No, everything is fine. I slept like a baby last night."

"Great."

Tim walked me to class, all smiles. I smiled back at him, but it was only a fake smile plastered to my lips. I wasn't sure why I'd just lied to my boyfriend. I told myself it was so he wouldn't worry, but that wasn't the whole truth or even most of it. I didn't want him to know what had happened in my bed last night. I didn't want him to know that a part of me enjoyed it.

At lunch, I paid little attention to my friends. I was vaguely aware of Brandon and Jon going at each other, but I was too busy trying to satisfy my gnawing hunger to pay attention. When I finished my lunch, I was still hungry. I went back for another.

"Two lunches?" Jon asked.

"Dude, why don't you weigh three hundred pounds?" Brandon asked.

"I just get really hungry sometimes," I said distractedly.

"Sometimes?" Brandon asked. "You've been eating more than Jon and me combined for days."

"Have I?"

"Uh, yeah. It's hard not to notice."

"Well, I don't feel any fatter."

"He's not," Tim said, grinning.

"Please, no homo-sex stories," Jon said. "I'm still eating."

"Come on, you know you love homo-sex stories," Ethan said.

"You wish."

"Once upon a time..." Ethan said and then laughed. He didn't continue.

The rest of the day was uneventful except for a brief moment between my last two classes when I thought I saw Jacob walking down the hallway. It was more than a glimpse, but I didn't get a truly good look, so I didn't know if I'd actually seen him or not.

Tim walked me home after school, but something was off between us. Something was off with me. I didn't feel quite like myself. Still, I enjoyed walking beside my handsome boyfriend. Tim made me feel safe.

We kissed at the door, and then Tim headed home. I walked up to my room, dumped my backpack, and pondered doing my homework. Instead, I undressed, wrapped a towel around my waist, and walked down to the showers in the boys' locker room.

I took my time shampooing my hair and soaping up. I looked up at every odd noise—more mysterious sounds of the old school, I realized. I lingered in the showers for nearly an hour, then shut off the water and dried myself. I walked out into the gym and peered at the old team photo. There was Jacob gazing out at me as if he could actually see me.

I walked back up to my room, dressed in some comfy sweats and a t-shirt and sat down to do my homework. My room was too quiet. I felt as if I was surrounded by nothingness.

I finished my assignments. I watched TV. I played video games. Time crawled by. At ten, I undressed and crawled into bed. I lay there watching the reflections of headlights play out on the ceiling. My fingers wandered up over my bare skin and grasped Jacob's coin. I immediately grew aroused.

"Miss me?"

I turned my head. Jacob stood at the windows, the moonlight making him little more than a shadow. I slid out of bed and walked to him. I put my arms around him and hugged him close. I kissed him on the lips. I was immediately filled with a sense of contentment.

Jacob kissed me deeply. There wasn't the slightest trace of coldness in him now. He didn't possess the warmth of life, yet I could almost swear he felt ever-so-slightly warm. I crushed my naked body against him, the wool of his letterman's jacket was slightly scratchy on my skin.

Jacob ran his hands down my back and onto my butt. He gripped me as he worked his tongue ever more deeply into my mouth. I panted with desire when he gently pushed me away.

Jacob slowly undressed, first taking off his jacket, then his button-down shirt. The sight of his bare chest filled me with desire. I'd always been attracted to guys with muscular chests, and Jacob had a beautifully muscled torso.

Jacob seductively unzipped his pants and slid them down over his hips. He pushed his boxers down and beckoned to me. I stepped toward him, and he gently but firmly pushed me to my knees. I leaned in. Jacob ran his fingers through my hair, grasped the sides of my head, and moved my head back and forth. I lost myself. Giving Jacob pleasure was my pleasure.

Time had no meaning. Jacob was outside of time, and so was I when I was with him. When Jacob pushed me away, I wasn't sure if minutes or hours had passed. I'd been lost in a dreamlike state of perfect delight.

Jacob pulled me to my feet and kissed me again. I never wanted him to stop. He led me to my bed. He pushed my face down and climbed on top of me. I moaned as white hot pain exploded in my mind. This time, the pain was pleasure. I wanted it. I yearned for it. I needed it. Jacob wasn't gentle. It was as if he could read my mind and know exactly what I wanted. Yet I knew he wasn't so much concerned with my pleasure as his. Even that was as I wanted it.

Jacob shoved my face into the pillow as I cried out with joy. I couldn't hold it in. I'd never felt anything like the sensations I experienced when I was with Jacob. All my sexual experiences before seemed bland compared to what I experienced now. I believed Jacob had not come to Boothe as he had to me. Boothe would not and could not have given up such pleasure.

Jacob went at me harder and harder until the pleasure was nearly too much to bear. I screamed into my pillow with delight as both Jacob and I finished at the same time. Jacob rolled me over onto my back, leaned down, and kissed me.

"I told you I'd make you mine," he said and grinned.

He turned to walk away, but I grabbed his hand.

"When will you return?" I asked.

"Tomorrow."

With that he was gone, dissolving as if he'd never been there at all.

I lay on my back. I was completely, utterly satisfied. I closed my eyes and fell into a contented sleep.

***

The days that followed blurred together. I was vaguely aware of attending school, eating lunch with my friends, and occasionally kissing...Tim. What I remembered the most, other than my nights with Jacob, was food. Corn dogs, hot dogs, green beans, applesauce, donuts, cereal, hamburgers, and more. I loved to eat. By all rights I should have weighed a ton, but my intense physical activity with Jacob burned. calories at an insane rate. I'd never experienced such intense, passionate sex. With Jacob, sex was a contact sport. Our sessions together left me winded and drenched with sweat.

I looked forward to Jacob's nightly visits with eager anticipation. Had he failed to show up, I don't know what I would've done, but he was there each and every night, and each night was better than the last. Jacob was my addiction. He'd been right all along. I was his. I only wondered why I'd struggled against him. If it was possible to die from pleasure, I was in mortal danger, but I would have given my life for one night of such bliss. Anyone would have done so.

Sometimes, I felt guilty, as though I was cheating on Tim. It wasn't really cheating, though. Jacob was a ghost. He wasn't a real boy. At least, that's what I told myself. I knew it wasn't entirely true, but it's not as if I'd stopped seeing Tim. I still cared about him. It's just that…he didn't seem to matter as much anymore.

I began to see Jacob more frequently—on the street, in the hallways at school, and in the school parking lot. The sightings were no longer fleeting. Jacob seemed fascinated with life in Verona and particularly at VHS. Jacob had changed. When he was with me he seemed almost real—so close, in fact, that the difference no longer mattered. I believed, however, that it was my own perception of Jacob that had changed. The more time I spent with him, the more perfectly I could perceive him. Perhaps I possessed some natural psychic ability that was becoming honed with experience. Regardless, Jacob was quite real to me, and I couldn't bear the thought of losing him.

I first became aware of a new turn of events between second and third period when I overheard two girls talking about the dreamy new boy with black hair and green eyes. I paused for a moment but then dismissed my thought as ridiculous. Just before lunch, however, I spotted Jacob not far from my own locker. It wasn't the Jacob sighting that was significant, however. Two girls were speaking to him! I immediately felt faint. Jacob looked up and grinned at me.

I just stared at him for a moment. He beckoned me closer. I walked toward him.

"I don't know many people yet," Jacob was saying. "I do know Dane. He lives near me. Right, Dane?"

"Uh, yeah."

"You don't look so good, buddy."

"I, um…I just feel…I guess I just need to eat something."

Jacob went on talking to the girls. My mind reeled. I was accustomed to seeing Jacob myself, but never before had others been able to see him. There was a time when I thought I was losing my mind because I was the only one who could see Jacob. I didn't know then if he was real or if he was all in my head. I'd known for some time he was real, but up until now he was invisible to everyone but me. I guess my ability to perceive Jacob hadn't improved. He'd actually become visible, but *how?*

I peered at Jacob. He was dressed as I'd seen him before. The only thing missing was his letterman's jacket. He was dressed in a plaid, button-down shirt and tan pants. He looked slightly out of place, but perhaps I only thought so because I knew he was dressed in clothing from the late 1940s. The girls he spoke to obviously didn't notice his odd attire, but then perhaps they were too busy checking out Jacob's well-muscled body. Jealousy burned in my chest. Jacob looked up at me. He bid the girls goodbye, walked over to me, and whispered in my ear, "Don't worry, you're the one I want." His words immediately set me at ease.

Jacob moved on before I had the chance to speak to him. My mind was filled with questions. How was it that others could see him now? What was he doing here? Had he somehow managed to enroll, and if so, how did he pull it off? Was he actually attending classes, or was he just appearing here and there in the hallways? How was any of this even possible? How could he explain not having parents, or a home, or records? I shook my head. Questions were inundating me faster than I could think them.

My astonishment only increased when Tim and I walked down to the cafeteria for lunch. I was so ravenously hungry as I approached the lunch line I took no note of my surroundings, but when I came out of the line with my tray and headed toward my usual table I stopped dead in my tracks.

"What's wrong?" Tim asked.

"Nothing. I'm just…distracted."

"You're distracted all the time now," Tim said irritability.

It was true. My thoughts were more on Jacob than anyone or anything else. Tim often had to repeat what he said to me. I hadn't been spending much time with him, and when I did, it was almost as if he wasn't there. Everything had changed.

We walked on toward the table. Tim and I sat in our usual spots. Casper smiled at us.

"This is Jacob. He's new. I asked him to join us," Casper said.

"We, uh, met briefly in the hall," I said.

"Yeah, you're Dave, right. No, that's not it," Jacob said, pretending confusion.

"Dane."

I tried not to stare. How had he done this? My mind was reeling.

"Yeah, that's right. Dane."

"I'm Tim."

Tim and Jacob shook hands. Tim gave no indication he had just shaken hands with a ghost. My mind continued to race as it had since I'd spotted Jacob talking to the girls in the hallway. How was this possible? Was I dreaming?

Not staring at Jacob required a continual struggle. No one had a clue they were having lunch with a dead boy, except for me. Was he still a dead boy? He looked plenty alive, and he was sure alive in my bedroom. When I was with him, I didn't even think about him being dead. I don't think I could have stomached sex with him if I did. I never thought about it when I was with him, at least not in those terms. I thought about how real he seemed but not the fact that he wasn't truly alive.

I was pulled away from my thoughts by Shawn's voice.

"You've got to come out for football this fall. We desperately need some talented guys. If you were the quarterback at your old school, you must be good."

Huh? I pulled myself out of my own thoughts. What had I missed?

"I'll think about it. I want to get settled in first," Jacob said.

"Moving can be disorienting," Tristan said. "I just moved here a few months ago. It took me forever just to unpack."

"Yeah, I have a lot of things to learn. Verona is really…different. It's a new experience for me."

"Oh, it's very different," Jon said.

"Yeah, for one thing we have the largest collection of gay boys in Indiana," Brandon said. "You're sitting with most of them."

Jacob smiled.

"You don't seem bothered by that," Marc said. His voice sounded hopeful. I didn't like it.

"I'm not." Jacob grinned. Was he flirting with Marc? I burned with jealousy.

"Uh-oh. I think we've got another one on our hands," Brandon said to Jon. "We might have guessed, since Casper brought him to the table. I think he's got some kind of gaydar thing going."

"He can't be worse than the rest of them," Jon said.

"Can't I?" Jacob asked. The mysterious tone in his voice was evident.

"Oh, you sound like fun," Marc said.

I wanted to slap Marc. Could he be any more obvious? He was practically drooling over Jacob. I had half a mind to jerk him to the side after lunch and tell him to knock it off, but I couldn't do that, could I? I couldn't tell him to back off because Jacob was mine. I was supposed to be dating Tim, after all. I glanced at Tim for a moment and felt a momentary pang of guilt. Tim just didn't seem as important to me anymore. He was still the same Tim, but Jacob was…so much more.

"You want this?" Jacob asked me, pushing his tray forward. "I'm just not hungry today."

I looked down. I'd finished my own lunch without even realizing it. Jacob had moved his food around so that it looked as if he'd eaten some of it, but I couldn't remember him taking a single bite. Did he eat?

"Um, yeah, thanks. I'm really hungry today."

"Today?" Brandon asked.

"Blow me, Brandon."

"Go for it, Brandon!" said Jon. "You know how you love cock."

Brandon flipped him off, but what I noticed most was the smirk Jacob gave me. A chill ran up my spine. I glanced at Tim and then looked back at Jacob. There was something about the smile on his lips that made me uneasy. Warning sirens went off in my head. I needed to talk to Tim. I needed to let him know what was going on, but how could I? I definitely couldn't tell him *everything*, but what if Jacob tried to hurt him? No, I was being paranoid. Jacob had only pretended interest in Tim so he could get me. He had what he wanted now, so Tim was in no danger. If that was so, why did I feel uneasy?

Perhaps because a ghost is hanging out with your friends, and they don't have a clue.

I was in the Twilight Zone. Jacob joked and laughed with the guys as Tim and I carried our trays away from the table. I gave one backwards glance to see Marc gazing dreamily at Jacob. I wanted to punch him in the face. Jacob was mine!

"Are you okay?" Tim asked.

"Huh? Yeah."

"You seem angry."

We dumped our trays.

"Whatever."

"Dane, have I done something to make you mad?" Tim asked as we walked toward our lockers.

"No."

"You act as though…kind of as if you don't like me," Tim said.

I looked at him. The pained expression on his face was clear to read. My old feelings for him rose briefly to the surface, but how could I explain? Doing so would only hurt him. I technically wasn't doing anything wrong. Jacob was a ghost. Whatever I did with him didn't count.

"I like you. You're my boyfriend."

"You haven't seemed much like a boyfriend lately."

"I've just been busy, Tim."

"You still seem mad."

"I'm not mad! Okay?"

"You'd be a little more convincing if you didn't shout when you said it," Tim said.

"I'm sorry. I'm just…well, I am angry, but not at you."

"Who, then?"

"It's no big deal. I'll get over it."

"You know, I'm here if you need me, Dane."

I turned and looked at Tim.

"Yeah, I know and thanks."

I hugged Tim. We parted to go to our lockers, and I promptly forgot about him. I had to find out what was going on with Jacob. I had to figure out the Marc situation, too. If he thought he was going for Jacob, he was sorely mistaken. I'd make him very sorry if he tried anything.

I kept my eye out for Jacob after school. I didn't spot him until I was outside, and sure enough, Marc was talking to him! I eyed Marc angrily as I approached.

"Dane," Jacob said.

"Hey, Dane," Marc said in a cheerful voice, as if he wasn't trying to steal my boyfriend. I paused for a moment, realizing what I'd just thought. It didn't matter. Marc needed to keep his hands off Jacob!

"Marc, I need to get going," Jacob said. "Dane promised to help me catch up in a few of my classes. I'll see you tomorrow, though, okay?"

"Oh. Yeah, okay. You can count on it."

Could Marc be any more obvious? What a slut.

"Later, guys," Marc said.

I waited until Marc was out of hearing range and then turned to Jacob.

"Why are you being so friendly with him? You saw how he was looking at you!"

"That's your first question?" Jacob asked. "You don't want to know what I'm doing here and why others can see me?"

"Well, yeah, but I don't like the way Marc flirted with you!"

"Dane, relax. I told you before, you're mine. I don't need anyone else. I don't want anyone else. You belong to me. I have no physical interest in Marc."

"Well, he's sure interested in you! He'd drop to his knees for you in an instant if you snapped your fingers."

"Perhaps, but I won't snap my fingers, Dane."

I smiled. *Take that, Marc.*

"So, what is going on? I didn't think anyone except me could see you."

"They couldn't—until recently. Thanks to you, Dane, I'm getting stronger."

"Thanks to me?"

"You've heard of the power of love. You're bringing me back, Dane."

"Is that even possible?"

"I'm standing here, aren't I?"

"Yes."

"Well, there it is. I was never really dead, Dane. Close, but not dead. You're bringing me back."

"I don't understand. The newspaper said you were hit by a car. You were walking along the road, and a car accidentally struck you and killed you."

"It wasn't an accident."

"Not an accident?"

"No. My boyfriend ran me down on purpose."

"Your boyfriend?"

"Not much of a boyfriend, huh?" Jacob asked as we walked further away from the school.

"No. Why did he run you down?"

"He couldn't deal with what he was. He wanted to break things off. It was partly my fault. I threatened to expose him if he broke up with me. I would never have really done that. I was just trying to keep him with me. I loved him, but he was a coward. He lived in fear of being found out. He didn't have the courage to stay with me, so I tried to make him. I thought he'd be able to deal with the situation if he gave it a little time. I made a mistake, obviously, but a well-intentioned mistake. He needed me, and I needed him. Back then, well it wasn't like now. I thought I'd never find someone. I knew how hard it would be to find another if I let him get away. I know how hard life would be for him, too. I pushed him too far, and he tried to kill me."

Jacob's voice seemed sad.

"He ran you down and you didn't die? I don't understand. I saw you in your grave. You were...decomposing."

"That was just my body, Dane. What I am now...this is a new me. I'm almost fully alive again, thanks to you."

"Almost? Does that mean you can become completely alive?"

"Yes. Would you like that?"

"Yes!"

"How much?"

"More than anything!"

"You'll help me, then?"

"Of course! I'll do anything!"

Jacob smiled.

"That's what I've been waiting to hear. Soon, very soon, we can be together forever."

Jacob hugged me, and we walked on.

"How did you manage to enroll in school?" I asked. "How about records and all that?"

"I didn't enroll."

"You just...showed up?"

"Of course. Where's the fun of attending classes?"

I laughed.

"But when you're really alive again...what will you do? How will you..."

"Let me worry about all that," Jacob said.

I nodded. I felt really tired. I noticed the Jacob looked over his shoulder now and then. He'd been doing so since we left school.

"What do you keep looking at?" I asked.

"Not what, who. Tim is following us."

"Shit. Jacob, listen. I need to talk to Tim soon. I haven't been fair to him. I guess I've been cheating on him. I haven't thought of it as cheating because you're not...well it was as if you're not...real. That's not really true, though, and once you're alive again...well, I've got to tell him."

"Why? Are you saying you prefer him over me? Has Tim *ever* made you feel the way I do? Even once?" Jacob asked angrily.

"No, that's not what I'm saying! No one has ever made me feel the way you do. It will still be like that when you're truly alive, won't it? When I'm with you, it seems almost magical. We won't lose that, will we?"

Jacob grinned.

"You like that, don't you?"

"How can you ask? I'd almost sell my soul for that! Anyone would! If I died while being with you, I'd die happy."

"It will always be the same, Dane. I'm concerned about Tim, though."

"I'll break up with him. I'll do it right now if you want. I'll do anything you want. I've got to be honest with him about this. Well, not completely honest. He doesn't need to know that you're a ghost. Soon, you won't be, anyway. I just mean that I can't see you behind his back. I know that's what I've been doing. I told myself it wasn't really cheating when I bothered to think about it at all, but it is, and I can't go on hurting him. Tim has been good to me."

"You're so kind and innocent," Jacob said, running his finger along my jawline.

"I don't know about that, but I have to talk to Tim. I have to tell him that you and I are going to be together. The sooner I do it, the better off we'll all be."

"Yes, but don't tell him just yet. Let me handle Tim for now."

"Handle him?"

"He may be angry because you're walking with me. I want to make sure he doesn't hurt you."

"Tim would never hurt me."

"Very well. I'm sure you know best."

"I'll go talk with him right now," I said.

"No. You look tired. You need to rest. Get some sleep, have something to eat, and I'll come to you later. Soon, with your help, I'll be alive once again."

I grinned.

"I can't wait," I said.

Jacob walked me to my doorstep. I didn't let him kiss me, for I feared Tim might still be following us. I'd been far too careless and uncaring recently. I'd thought only of my own pleasure. It was as if the old Dane was coming back. I was going to set that right as soon as possible. I'd tell Tim the truth, that I loved him, but I wanted to be with Jacob. Perhaps, we could even still be friends.

I smiled at Jacob and walked inside. I was hungry again but too tired to eat. I was practically asleep on my feet. I definitely needed a nap.

Shawn

I smiled across the table at Tristan. We were sharing a late supper of Chicken Scallopini at The Park's Edge. I'd never tried it before, but Tristan convinced me to, and I was glad. It was made with chicken breast, onion, roma tomatoes, bacon, mushrooms, white wine, butter, oregano, and spinach fettuccine.

"You're smiling again," Tristan said.

"What can I say? I like being with you."

"I like being with you, too."

"Are you sorry you made me wait?" I asked. "Are you sorry we didn't start dating sooner?"

"No. I had to be sure of you first. I had to make sure I wasn't falling for the wrong guy again."

"Falling for me? You were falling for me when I first asked you out? You never told me that!"

"I needed time, and you didn't need any encouragement."

I laughed.

"That's true. I hope I wasn't too pushy. I tried to take it slow like you wanted."

"You were a little pushy, but in a good way. I could tell you were making a real effort to keep things casual, and that told me you were truly interested in me and not just in having sex with me."

I was on the verge of saying, "I'd do anything to be with you," but that sounded way too melodramatic and like something out of a bad romance novel. Instead, I smiled again.

"So, what do you think now?" I asked.

"I think I'm safe. Well, as safe as anyone can be. You're not like that boy back in Tulsa."

"I told you I wasn't."

"I know, but I had to make sure. That's why I wanted to be friends first. I needed to be sure."

"And now you are?"

"We wouldn't be sitting here if I wasn't."

'You're worth the wait."

Tristan smiled.

"We are so lucky Brandon and Jon can't hear all this," he said.

"I don't know. They'd probably just say something like 'too easy' and let it go."

"Brandon and Jon really are incredible. There aren't that many hetero guys who would sit at the homo table. You know they have to take crap because of it."

"Yeah, and some people probably think they're gay, too."

"Exactly. That's why I admire them so much. It takes courage to be out, but they put themselves on the line when they don't have to. It's important to be out, so people can see what we're really like instead of letting their imaginations run wild. I think guys like Brandon and Jon are doing something even more important. They openly accept us, even though they aren't like us."

"We'd better not let them hear us talking about them like this or there will be no living with them at all."

Tristan grinned.

"I feel almost guilty being this happy," I said.

"Why?"

"Tim and Dane are having some problems. Tim hides it from everyone else, but he told me he thinks Dane is losing interest in him. It will tear him apart if they don't work out. He's already upset."

"Well, you know, Shawn, they probably won't work out. Dane is Tim's first boyfriend. Tim is Dane's first real boyfriend, too, isn't he?"

"Yeah."

"It's very unlikely they'll stay together. There are so many changes coming up in their lives: graduation, college..."

"Don't say that."

"Why?"

"Because those same changes are coming up in our lives, and I don't want to think about them."

"You don't have to think about them, but things will change. There's no guarantee you and I will go to the same university. There are no guarantees in life, period."

"Are you saying you don't think we have a future?"

That thought upset me more than I can express.

"No. I'm not saying that. We may stick together through all the changes in our lives. Shawn, I love you. I've liked you since the day we met, and somewhere along the way I began to love you. I want us to make it. I want us to always be together. What's important is right now. This time will never come again. Even if we grow old together, now will always be the most important time. I don't want to mess up the present by worrying about the future. We can plan for it, certainly, but I don't want to ruin the present by thinking about all the bad things that can happen. We could both walk out of here and be killed crossing the street. A million other things could happen, and some of them will. Knowing that should make us appreciate what we have, right here, right now. I don't want to let it take away from what we've got."

I smiled.

"I wish I was as smart as you about such things. You're right. I know. I just get worried when I think about certain things. I guess I'm just afraid of losing you."

"You are in no danger of that now, so just be happy."

"I'll do my best. I've been doing a pretty good job, even with worrying. I like what you said about this time never coming again. If we are both killed when we step out that door, it's okay really, because we've had this. I'd rather us not be killed, of course, but you know what I mean."

"Yeah, I know," said Tristan, with yet another grin.

My own grin faded. Tristan reached across the table and grasped my hand.

"Tim will be okay, Shawn."

"I just don't like seeing him in pain, and I know the situation may get much worse. If Tim and Dane break up..."

"You'll be there to help Tim through it—and Dane, too, no doubt."

"I feel a little more like a parent every day."

"Is that a bad thing?"

"No, but it hurts. I know Tim is in pain now, and I know that pain may get much worse. It's as if...I feel the pain for him."

"You sound like a parent, at least like mine. I remember my dad telling me he wished he could be sick for me. I think I can understand what he meant."

"I do understand."

"Things may work out yet between Tim and Dane. Like I said, it's unlikely they'll be together forever, but that doesn't mean they won't have the rest of their high-school years together. When they move on, the situation may be much less painful for Tim than you imagine."

"I guess we're getting back into the don't-worry-about-all-the-bad-things-that-*could*-happen discussion."

"Exactly. Besides, even if you knew things were going to end badly between Tim and Dane, thinking and worrying about it in advance only increases your pain. It won't help them."

"I guess you're right. I just have a bad feeling about their relationship. Tim says Dane has become distant."

"He's become distant with everyone," Tristan said.

"Yes, he's...well, I don't like to say it, but he seems more like the old Dane."

"He was a pretty nasty piece of work at one time, wasn't he?" Tristan said. It wasn't a question. I'd told him about my first encounters with Dane.

"Dane didn't care about anyone but himself when he first came to Verona. I know his life was hard then, but all he cared about was getting what he wanted. I don't sense the same belligerence in him I did then, but he doesn't seem to care about any of us now. He doesn't even seem to care that much about Tim. For a while there, Dane had eyes only for Tim, but now…"

"Dane seems rather interested in Jacob, doesn't he?" Tristan said.

"Yeah. I don't know what to make of that. It's as if…it's as if Dane is kind of intimidated by Jacob, maybe even a little afraid of him, but…the way he looks at him…it's no wonder Tim is upset. That look in Dane's eyes…"

"Pure lust," Tristan said.

"Exactly. Poor Tim."

I looked up. Tristan was gazing at me with compassion.

"I'm sorry. I'm ruining our evening by obsessing over Tim."

"It just shows how much you care about him, which is one of the things I like about you. Besides, our evening isn't ruined. I do think you need to get your mind on other things. You know you'll be there when Tim needs you. Other than that, there's not much you can do."

"You're right. Maybe you can help me get my mind off Tim later by making out with me on the couch."

"Oh, the sacrifices I make for you," Tristan said, grinning.

I let out a long breath and forced myself to relax. The Park's Edge was beautiful, the pasta was delicious, and Tristan…he was my dream boy. I had problems, but didn't everyone always have problems?

"I'm very happy *right now*," I said.

"Now is the time that matters most."

Tristan and I ate and talked and laughed. When we finished, we paid the check and departed. We walked in moonlight and starlight holding hands. I wished I could save moments like this to experience again and again. Neither of us spoke a single word, but our clasped hands and the feelings we shared expressed more than could ever be put into words.

Tim wasn't home. Tristan and I kicked off our shoes and sat on the couch. I pulled Tristan close and pressed my lips to his.

Our mouths parted and our tongues entwined. I focused entirely on Tristan: kissing him, holding him close, feeling his heart beat against my chest. I pulled his shirt free and slid my hands up his bare chest. His skin was so smooth, his body so firm. I wanted to rip his shirt away, but I controlled myself and kissed him ever more passionately.

Tristan's hands weren't idle. The feel of his hands sliding over my pecs and abs was so sensual. I had yet to be naked with Tristan, yet the feelings he inspired within me were more intense than anything I'd ever experienced with Blake. My heart pounded; my breath came heavy and fast. I ran my hand over Tristan's flat stomach and lower still. We kissed each other with fevered passion. I wanted us to rip each other's clothes off and take each other right there on the couch, but at the same time, I wanted to keep going just as we were. I couldn't imagine anything more pleasurable or intense.

Just when I was worked up to the point that pleasure nearly became pain, I heard Tim's footsteps on the stairs. Seconds later, he entered. Tristan and I reluctantly stopped kissing and groping each other but remained sitting close.

"Am I interrupting something?" Tim asked with a smirk.

"Yes, but we'll forgive you...this time," I said.

I didn't ask about Dane. Tim knew I was there if he needed or wanted to talk. For that matter, Tristan was there for him, too. I wanted to give Tim his space.

Tim did look a little down. I looked at Tristan.

"Hey, why don't we play cards or Monopoly or something?" Tristan suggested, no doubt to draw my brother in and help pull him out of his mood.

"Not Monopoly," Tim said. "You two will gang up on me."

"Us?" I said with feigned innocence.

"Yes, I know you too well."

"Okay, cards then," I said. "Hmm, how about Bullshit?"

"Yeah!" Tim said.

"Is that a card game?" Tristan asked.

"You haven't heard of Bullshit?" Tim asked.

"Not as a card game."

"It's pretty simple," said Tim. "The first player lays all the matching cards he has face down on a pile, starting with twos, and he tells how many he's putting down. If no one says 'bullshit', the next player lays down his threes on the pile. If no one says "bullshit", the next player players his fours and so on."

"And if someone says 'bullshit'?" Tristan asked.

"Then the player turns the cards he put down face up to prove he really played what he said. If he was bullshitting, he has to pick up the entire pile of cards. The object is to get rid of all your cards, and sometimes you have to bullshit about what you're putting down, hence the name of the game."

"What if someone calls 'bullshit' and the other player really did put down all the cards he said he did?"

"Then that player has to pick up the entire pile."

Tristan laughed.

"Sounds like fun."

"Yeah, but I think we need popcorn," Tim said. "I'll make some before we start."

While Tim was busy making popcorn, I poured sodas over ice. I was sorry my make-out session with Tristan had to end, but cards did sound like fun. There was more to life than sex, and a game of cards would help Tim get his mind off Dane.

We stayed up late playing Bullshit and eating popcorn. Tristan had an amazing ability to bullshit. He'd make a killer poker player, I'm sure. I never could tell when he was bluffing. I thought I had him a couple of times, but I ended up with a fist full of cards. Tim was worse. He had to pick up the entire pile six times when he read Tristan wrong. Tristan won all the games except one, and that one went to Tim. That made me the biggest loser, but I didn't care. I had a blast! I wondered what the game would have been like if Brandon and Jon had been there.

I walked Tristan home after our game. It was a little chilly out but not bad at all. Spring had a firm hold now—finally. Tristan and I walked close together. I put my arm around his shoulder. I loved the closeness with Tristan, the intimacy. I was in desperate need of sex, but even that painful need was tinged with pleasure. Maybe I was some kind of masochist. I don't know. More likely, I was just enjoying what the present had to offer.

Tristan and I kissed on his doorstep. Our lingering kiss flamed the fires of my passion. I had to fight to keep myself from giving Tristan a grope. I feared his mom might be watching through the curtains. It was an irrational fear, but I was more than content to feel his warm body pressed against mine as we kissed.

Tristan went inside, and I walked back home. I wished once more I could save this moment to experience over and over again.

***

Dane was extra weird during lunch. I seriously thought he was going to jump on Jacob and hump him. Tim was visibly upset and actually got up and left the table. I thought about going after him, but I figured he needed his space. Dane either didn't notice or didn't care when Tim left. I'm not sure he knew any of the rest of us were there. For all he knew, he was sitting alone with Jacob.

Jacob, for his part, spared Dane a rare lustful glance but seemed more interested in joking around with Brandon and Jon and getting all buddy-buddy with everyone else. I have to admit he possessed a good deal of charisma. He could even have charmed me if his presence wasn't so upsetting to my brother. While Dane was insensitive and borderline cruel in this actions, Jacob had done nothing wrong. He didn't overly encourage Dane. I didn't even know if he was aware Dane and Tim were a couple.

The longer I sat there, the angrier I became. Dane sat there completely unconcerned that my brother, his boyfriend, was likely off somewhere crying. Well, Tim probably wasn't crying. He was like me; he didn't cry easily. Still, he was hurting because his boyfriend was drooling over another boy and acting as though he didn't give a damn about him. Dane was reverting to his old ways.

I'd had enough. I stood up. I began to reach across the table to grab Dane, but Tristan's hand closed over my forearm. He shook his head. I let him lead me away. Neither of us said a word as we dumped our trays and made our way out of the cafeteria. I was too angry to speak. I knew I had to get myself under control or I'd be shouting, and the last thing I wanted to do was shout at my boyfriend.

"Just take a few deep breaths," Tristan said. His voice was soothing and calm. I did as he said. "You looked ready to kill Dane back there."

"I was going to jerk him out of his seat and have a talk with him, but you're probably right. I think I would have ended up pounding him."

"Casey was trying to warn you off, but you weren't paying attention."

"She was?"

"Yes."

"I can't believe Dane! Did you see how he was looking at Jacob—and with Tim sitting right there? When Tim left, Dane didn't even look up. He didn't even care!"

"I know."

"Maybe I should have gone after Tim."

"No. You did the right thing. He'll need you later, but I think he needs to be alone now."

"How can Dane treat him like that? They were so happy. How can Dane fuck everything up just because he's hot for this new boy?"

"I don't know, Shawn. It doesn't make any sense to me, either."

"It's like the old Dane is back. I really thought he'd changed. I don't know. Maybe he's just playing us all for fools."

"You really think that?"

"No, but I think he is reverting to his old ways. I don't understand, though. I know he loves Tim…loved him anyway.

How could that change so fast? How could it just go away? Poor Tim."

"I don't have any answers for you."

"I'm gonna kick his ass."

"Shawn, that won't help Tim. It will only get you into trouble."

"I still want to beat the crap out of Dane."

"Let's look for another solution."

"It's hard to maintain my fury with your calming influence," I said.

"That's the idea."

Tristan leaned in and kissed me. I kissed him back—hard. We pulled apart when someone cleared his throat.

"Mr. Hahn, hey," I said.

"Hi, Shawn. Hello, Tristan."

Mr. Hahn smiled at us and walked on.

"He could totally have busted us for P.D.A." I said.

"You jocks can get away with anything," Tristan said, teasing me.

"I don't think that extends to kissing another boy in school."

I laughed. I was still pissed at Dane, but I felt a good deal better. Kicking his ass would have been a mistake. Part of me still wanted to do it, but Tristan was right, it wouldn't help Tim.

I tried to keep myself from worrying about my brother during my afternoon classes. I only saw Tim once—right before school let out. I didn't say anything meaningful to him, but I gave him a hug. Brandon saw us hugging but didn't make any smart comments about incest or anything like that. I could tell by his expression he was worried about Tim, too.

I was distracted as I took orders and bused tables in Ofarim's that evening. I usually enjoyed working, but for the first time I wished I was home instead. I wanted to be there in case Tim needed me. Then again, he'd made no effort to talk to me after school. If he wanted to talk to me, he easily could have then. I had to quit worrying about everything! How did Tristan do it? He was more compassionate than I was, yet he had the ability to keep things from getting to him. He acted when it was time to act and didn't obsess over "what ifs." I had a lot to learn from him.

Tim was sitting at the table, quietly doing his homework when I came in from work.

"Are you okay?" I asked.

Tim didn't speak. He just shook his head.

"If you need to talk, I'm here, okay?"

Tim nodded. I felt as though I should do or say more, but he obviously wasn't in the mood to communicate. He knew I was there if he needed me. That's what was important at the moment.

I made myself a cup of tea, then sat down across from Tim and started in on homework I was too tired to do. Just sitting felt good. My feet were tired, and getting my shoes off was a pleasure.

Tim all but ignored me, but I think he liked that I was there. We quietly worked without speaking. When the words began to blur I closed my books, kissed Tim on the forehead, and bid him goodnight.

I brushed my teeth, then went to my bedroom, stripped, and climbed into bed. One advantage of being so very tired was that crawling into bed felt so very good. I lay there naked, with my hands behind my head, staring up at the ceiling. I was too tired to think of anything just then. I lay there, feeling my muscles relax. The sheets were soft and the mattress comfy. I slipped into complete contentedness.

As tired as I was, I didn't immediately fall asleep. I lay there in drowsy pleasure. Maybe in my next life I could be a cat and just lie around sleeping all day.

Sometime later—I don't know how much later—Tim quietly entered my room. He was wearing only his boxers, and his hair was tousled.

"Can't sleep?" I asked, drowsily.

He shook his head.

"Shawn, can I sleep with you tonight? Please? I don't want to be alone. I just need to feel someone beside me."

In answer, I held open the covers. Tim snuggled in beside me. I wrapped my arms around him and held him close. He didn't speak, but I could hear him softly crying. I just kept holding him as we both drifted off to sleep.

***

I woke up alone the next morning. Tim had slept with me most of the night. I had awakened a few times to feel his warm body beside me. I must admit it was kind of nice to have someone in bed with me. Someday, Tristan and I would share a bed, and I could snuggle up against him every night.

I climbed out of bed and grabbed a pair of boxers from my dresser drawer and walked towards the bathroom. Tim and I were rather casual about the way we dressed—or didn't—in the apartment. I slept naked and saw no reason to slip on clothes just to take them off again when I reached the bathroom. Tim and I were accustomed to being around naked guys in the locker room and showers at school, so it was no big deal. Well, I did like the scenery at school, but you know what I mean. I hadn't thought about it last night, but Tim had worn boxers to bed. Maybe it was his way of telling me he didn't have an ulterior motive. There was a time, not so long ago, when my little brother had expressed a sexual interest in me. That had disturbed me a bit. While I found incest kind of arousing in the abstract, it was a different matter when it involved me and my brother. Tim was a hot boy, but he was my brother, and I just couldn't think of him sexually. Well, not much anyway. I think incest is one of those things that is hot as a fantasy, but not as a reality. Anyway, once Dane entered the picture, Tim hadn't shown the same sexual interest in me, which was a relief. I kind of wonder if his interest in me stemmed solely from the fact that Tim was just a horny little bastard. I guess it didn't matter. Whether Tim wanted sex with me or not, it was not going to happen.

I heard the water running as I approached the bathroom. I entered. Tim was rinsing off, so I just waited my turn. He spotted me as he finished, so he just left the water running. He nodded to me as he stepped away from the shower and reached for a towel.

I stepped under the warm spray of water. I loved our shower. It didn't offer privacy, but Tim and I didn't need any. I loved the feel of the tiles under my feet. I loved the openness of the shower. The shower head was a large one, too, and I could stand directly under it. It was like standing in my own private rain shower.

"How are you doing?" I asked Tim as I worked lilac shampoo into my hair.

"Better, but…"

I wanted to tell him everything would be okay, but I didn't know if it was so.

"Thanks for letting me sleep with you last night," Tim said.

"No problem; it was kind of nice."

Tim finished drying off and left. I rinsed out the shampoo and put in lavender conditioner. I soaped up my body and luxuriated in the hot water flowing over me. I thought of the shower as a spa. I loved the hot water and the scent and feel of the shampoo, hair conditioner, and soap. I wondered if enjoying a shower was a homo thing or if all guys liked it or if it was just me. I guess it didn't really matter. I liked what I liked.

After breakfast, I drove Tim to school. He wasn't happy, but he wasn't as upset as the night before. Tim was strong. He could handle a lot. He already had. I knew he was still hurting, but he was dealing with it. Just before we both got out of the car, I patted his leg.

"I love you, little brother."

"I love you, too, Shawn."

Sometimes, it's important to say things like that. Now was one of those times.

Tim and I walked toward school together. Brendan, Casper, Ethan, and Nathan surrounded us as we neared the doors. They talked and laughed and even made Tim smile.

I spotted Tristan at his locker and cut away from the group.

"Hey," I said, grinning. I grinned a lot when I was around Tristan. I'm sure Brandon and Jon would say I grinned like an idiot, but I don't care.

"Hey." Tristan grinned too. His smile could just about make me melt. "How's Tim?"

"He had a rough night. He seems better this morning, but..."

"Yeah. I wish there was something we could do..."

"I don't know what we can do, since you won't let me beat up Dane."

Tristan gave me a stern look.

"I'm just kidding! I did want to kick his ass yesterday, but I've calmed down, and I know you're right. That's not the way to handle the situation."

"Come on," Tristan said, putting his arm around my shoulder. "Let's go to class."

"Homos," Devon growled when he spotted Tristan with his arm around me.

"Closet case," I retorted.

"What's that supposed to mean?" Devon asked, stopping dead in his tracks.

"You know what it means, Devon."

"I'm not a closet case! I'm not a sick fag...a homo like you."

"Get off it, Devon. No one would be so down on gays unless he was trying to hide something. You'll be a lot better off if you just admit to yourself and everyone else you like guys. Maybe you'll even get some."

Devon began to sputter with anger and exasperation. He reminded me of a tea kettle boiling over. Devon couldn't even get a complete syllable out. Tristan and I walked on. We were twenty feet down the hallway before Devon regained enough control of himself to shout after us.

"Fucking faggots! You guys make me sick!"

Tristan tightened his grip on me, as if afraid I might turn and go after Devon. I didn't even feel anger, though. What I felt was pity for Devon. He was pathetic in a way. I really did think he was a closet case. I'd seen him checking out guys in the locker room and showers after gym class when we were younger. It wasn't the usual guy-comparing-himself-to-another type of checking out, either. I knew lust when I saw it. Devon would be better off if he admitted what he was. There was really no helping someone who wouldn't even admit the truth to himself. Devon was one disturbed boy.

Tim sat with us at lunch. I half expected him not to show, but he was sitting there in his usual spot when I arrived. It was the same scene as the day before. Dane was obsessed with Jacob and all but ignored Tim. Jacob was being all buddy-buddy with the guys and showing Dane just enough interest to keep him on the hook. A mental image of Dane dressed as a dog pawing at Jacob's knees entered my mind. I would have laughed, but the situation wasn't funny.

Tim didn't seem overly upset by Dane's interest in Jacob or in Dane's lack of interest in Tim. He just coolly observed him like a scientist watching a test subject. I didn't know whether to be relieved or frightened. Love gone wrong could lead to violence. I couldn't imagine my little brother stabbing his ex-lover to death, but something about the scene frightened me. Tim was far too calm.

I observed Jacob myself. There was something about him that just seemed a bit off. I couldn't figure out just what that something was, but it was there nonetheless. His clothes were almost odd in a way and yet not quite. He kind of looked as if he was dressed for an episode of that show *Happy Days* that was set in the 1950s, but then again, it wasn't as if he was wearing a black leather jacket with his hair slicked back. Sometimes, Jacob used an odd word or phrase. The other day Jacob said something about Jon always casting an eyeball when a sexy girl was around. He also said he was "cranked" over maybe joining the football team next fall and that he was "frosted" about all the homework he was assigned. I could tell what he meant each time, but who talked like that?

I guess it didn't matter. For the most part, Jacob was just like any other guy at VHS. I didn't particularly like him, but then my perceptions were clouded by the whole situation with Dane. There was no proof Jacob knew there was anything going on between Tim and Dane, so I couldn't even fault him there. It was Dane who was acting like a self-centered jerk.

I was talking to Tristan at the end of the school day when Tim approached us. He looked on edge, as if he'd drunk an entire pot of coffee, which, I might add, he had done before.

"Shawn, I *really* need to talk."

Tristan leaned in and gave me a peck on the lips.

"I'll see you later, Shawn. Have a good evening, Tim."

Tim waited until I'd gathered my books and we'd walked outside before he began. No doubt he didn't want anyone listening in.

"I need to talk to you about Dane," he said.

"Yeah, I know it's rough, Tim. I'm really sorry about…"

"No. Listen. Something is wrong with him. He's acting really bizarre and out of character. This whole thing with Jacob…the way he's drooling over Jacob and ignoring me…"

"That's not out of character for Dane. That's the old Dane. I think he's coming back. The old Dane was a jerk," I said.

"No! It's more than that! It's as if Jacob has some kind of power over him. It's as if Dane is possessed! Something is not right about Jacob. Who is he, anyway? Where did he come from? Is he in any of your classes or anyone else's? I've been asking around. He doesn't share a single class with anyone I know!"

"Tim, I'm really sorry Dane is being such a jerk. I know how much it must hurt you, but you can't lay the blame on Jacob. I don't particularly care for him, but Dane is the one who's the problem. I know you love him and you don't want to believe he could be like this, but…"

"No. Dane does love me! I know he does! It's Jacob!"

"Tim…"

"I have an idea about what's going on."

"Okay, what do you think is going on?"

"I want to check something out before I tell you, just to make sure."

"Check what out?"

"Drive me to Dane's house."

"Tim, I don't know if that's such a good idea. I have work in a few…"

"Please, Shawn."

Tim looked so pathetic I gave in. A few minutes later, I pulled up in front of the old Verona school. We walked to the front and knocked on the door. No one answered. Tim tugged on the door and it opened.

"Tim, what are you doing?"

"Come on," he said.

"Tim!"

My little brother wasn't listening. He went right in. I followed him.

"Tim, we can't just walk into someone's house."

"Mr. and Mrs. Haakonson won't care. I've let myself in lots of times. They almost never hear anyone knocking at the front door."

Tim led me down the short entrance hallway, turned right, and led me down a longer hallway. He turned left at the end and headed for the gym where we'd played dodge ball and basketball with the guys. He pushed open the oak and glass doors that led into the old gym.

"What are we doing here?" I asked.

"You'll see."

He walked toward the far end of the gym to a large football-team photo that hung on the wall between the stage and the boys' locker room. Tim gazed at the photo for a moment and then pointed.

"I knew it! Tell me that isn't the boy who sits with us at lunch. Tell me that's not Jacob."

"So? There's a resemblance. What of it?"

"That's not just a resemblance. He looks *exactly* the same!"

"And?"

"Think about it. Jacob even dresses a little odd. That vintage clothing he wears?"

"He doesn't dress that odd—just a little retro."

"Not retro. Those aren't clothes that look like those worn in the late 1940s. They *are* clothes that were worn in the 1940s."

"What are you saying?"

"I'm saying that Jacob from school is Dane's ghost!"

"That's crazy, Tim."

"Maybe so, but it makes sense. Jacob looks *exactly* like the boy in the photo. He dresses as though he's not quite clued in to what guys wear now. He uses weird phrases that no one uses. Dane even said the ghost's name is Jacob."

I had noticed Jacob's clothing and odd vocabulary. I'd been thinking about both earlier in the day. Still…

"Boothe went to a whole lot of trouble to pawn this ghost off on Dane," Tim said. "Boothe put himself in great danger of getting caught, and from what Dane has told me about him, he wouldn't do that without reason. I believe Dane has been seeing a ghost. I've believed him all along. He wouldn't lie to me. I also believe him about the coin. That means there are supernatural forces at work."

"This is all just crazy, Tim."

"Crazy, but true! Jacob has an unnatural power over Dane."

"Dane just wants his dick," I said. "I'm sorry to say it, but it's true."

"No! It's more than that! Dane loves me! I know he does! I was upset last night because I didn't understand. I was too hurt to think things through. The feelings Dane has for me couldn't go away that quickly. It doesn't make sense! Jacob is controlling

Dane. It's not just lust. He's possessed, I tell you! Jacob is possessing Dane!"

"Tim, I'm really sorry things have gone bad with Dane, but..."

"God dammit, listen to me! Dane is in danger! Jacob was a ghost. Now he's become a real boy. He's not Pinocchio! What about the way Dane eats *all* the time? No one can go on eating and eating like that without gaining weight. If anything, he's losing weight. It's not natural! Jacob is draining Dane's life away somehow! He's killing him!"

Tim grew silent for a moment. I didn't say anything. What could I say? Tim was talking crazy, yet...

"That's it!"

"What's it?" I asked.

"Jacob isn't a real boy—yet. He's sucking the life out of Dane. As Dane gets weaker, Jacob gets stronger. Jacob won't become fully alive until...Dane dies..."

"Tim..."

"We've got to find Dane before it's too late! We've got to stop Jacob!"

"Tim, get hold of yourself! This is all nonsense."

"We've got to find him!"

"Tim! Stop it!"

I grabbed my little brother and shook him. He was becoming frantic.

"No!" he yelled.

Tim slapped my hands away.

"Tim..."

"Shawn, please! I know you think I'm crazy, but please help me! If you love me, help me find Dane! I'm begging you! Please!"

Tim cried his eyes out. The whole idea was insane, but I knew Tim could not rest until we found Dane. At least then maybe we could get to the bottom of things. Jacob? A ghost? No way! At least we could find Dane, talk to him, and prove to Tim that Dane wasn't possessed. The things I did for my little brother...

Tim and I walked back outside and climbed into the car. I drove to Ofarim's first, went in, and talked to Agnes. I explained my predicament. I didn't tell her about Tim's crazy theory, of course, but I explained how he was terribly upset and needed me. Agnes was understanding. I thanked her profusely and walked back out to the car.

"So, any idea where to look?" I asked as I climbed back in the Cutlass.

"Let's just drive around and see if we can spot him."

I pulled out and drove slowly past The Park's Edge, The Paramount, and on. We passed homes, the gas station, the library, the bank, and stores. Soon, we drove by Café Moffatt and our own apartment. We drove on, but there was no sign of Dane.

I didn't say so out loud, but looking for Dane was a complete waste of time. We could more easily have cornered him after school and talked through things then. Tim was in a nervous frenzy, however. While I thought he was worked up over coincidence and imagined danger, he was convinced that Dane's life was at stake. I couldn't just tell him he was being stupid and leave it at that. He'd just go off on his own looking for Dane, and he was acting a little too crazy just now to be set loose on Verona.

I hated missing work. We needed the money, and I didn't like canceling out on such short notice. I could think of a hundred things I'd rather be doing with my time, too. Making out with Tristan immediately sprang to mind.

"Shawn?"

"Yeah?"

"Thanks."

"For what?"

"For humoring me and for helping me. I know you think I'm nuts."

"Can you read minds now?"

"No." Tim smiled briefly, but his smile faded quickly. "I know what I've told you is farfetched, but I also know it's the truth. I can *feel* it, Shawn. Maybe I am crazy, but I have to make sure Dane is okay. I know I'm not crazy, though. I know I'm right. Either way, thanks for being here with me right now. Thanks for helping me."

"I know you're worried. I don't believe Dane is in any danger, Tim. I don't believe Jacob and Dane's ghost are one and the same. I know you do, however. I wouldn't be much of a brother if I didn't help you."

Tim closed his eyes for a moment. He looked as if he was concentrating.

"Drive to the south, out toward the Selby place."

I turned the car, taking us one step further into weird. I was afraid to ask why Tim wanted me to drive south. I didn't want to hear about little voices in his head or whatever was going on in there. What if Tim really was losing it? What if this whole thing with Dane was just too much for him? I was glad I'd taken off work. Tim wasn't himself.

As I drove, I tried to think of a way to soothe Tim's fears. The odds were against us finding Dane. I had half a mind to take Tim home, give him a couple of sleeping pills, and put him to bed. I'd never seen him so agitated before. If only I could talk him out of his crazy...

"There, there he is! Slow down," Tim said.

I could spot two figures way ahead. I couldn't begin to tell who they were.

"Are you sure that's Dane?"

"Yes, it's Dane, and Jacob is with him."

Unless he had the eyes of an eagle, there was no way Tim could be sure who was up ahead. I'd come this far, so I figured I might as well humor him. What was that old saying? In for a penny, in for a pound? I closed the distance a little.

"Don't get closer. I don't want Jacob knowing we're tailing them."

"So, we're just going to follow them?"

"For now."

"Okay."

This was definitely not the best use of my time. Following two distant figures who might or might not be Dane and Jacob was not a thrill. Time somehow slipped by, however, for darkness fell. I looked at the clock on the dashboard.

"What the...?"

"What?" Tim asked.

"What time have you got?"

"Um, 4:30, why?"

That's what the clock on the dashboard read. I checked my own watch. It was the same.

"Why is it dark, Tim?"

Tim looked around as if he had only then become aware that darkness had fallen.

"Eclipse?"

I didn't answer. I just didn't know.

I wanted to turn on the headlights. There was no moonlight. Had I not been driving so very slowly, I couldn't have made my way. As it was, I had to close in more to be able to make out the figures ahead.

"I'm cold, turn on the heater," Tim said.

It was chilly in the car. I turned on the heater.

Headlights appeared to the south, meeting us. They illuminated the figures ahead for a moment. One of them was wearing a letterman's jacket. Even as we looked he took it off and put it on his companion. An old pickup passed by soon. At first I thought it might be Ethan in his uncle's old Ford, but this truck looked even older.

"Is that snow?" I asked.

Tim leaned in toward the windshield and looked up as if he needed to gaze into the sky to see the white flakes that were beginning to fall. There were just a few at first, but then more and more until it was a regular snowfall.

"This is crazy!" I said. "It's not supposed to get nearly cold enough for snow."

I turned on the radio to see if I could pick up a weather forecast.

"This has been the Burns and Allen Show with George Burns and Gracie..."

I turned the dial to hear Tarzan's signature yell come over the speakers. I tried again, and some guy was singing the words "some enchanted evening." I turned the dial further and was assaulted by a country song about ghost riders in the sky. Why was there never a weather report when I needed one? I made another attempt to find what I was seeking.

"...presents Fibber McGee and Molly..."

Some of the words in the radio programs began to register in my mind. Burns and Allen? Fibber McGee and Molly? I'd never heard the programs, but...

"What is this?" I asked. "Old-time-radio night?"

I kept trying to find the weather, but all I could get was old songs I didn't recognize.

"This is too weird," I said.

"See! I told you something bizarre is going on!" Tim said. "Why is it dark at 4:30 p.m.? Why is it snowing when the temperature wasn't supposed to get below, like, sixty? What's with the music and the old radio shows?"

Tim looked up for a moment and his face lit up.

"We're in the past!"

"Tim! Come on! We are not in the past. It's some kind of oldies night on the radio."

"On *all* the stations at once? And what about the darkness? It's night! Our watches say it's early evening, but it's night!"

"Tim..."

The headlights of another car appeared through the snow. Moments later, it passed by. It was a Model A. My stomach sank. Tim looked me in the eyes again.

"We're in the past, I tell you! Jacob is taking Dane back to the night he was killed, and we've been pulled in with him!"

"Tim, that's crazy!"

"Then explain all this! Go on! Explain it!"

"I...can't."

"Oh, my God!" Tim said.

"What?"

"Don't you see what Jacob is doing? Jacob was murdered! He was murdered, and now he's going to make Dane take his place! That's why he put his jacket on Dane! He knows someone is going to run him down, most likely very soon. That's how he's going to do it! When Dane is killed, Jacob will become fully human!"

I didn't know what to think of Tim's line of reasoning, but there was no denying something truly bizarre was going on. Another car appeared in the northbound lane. This one was going faster. It accelerated even as we watched.

"Stop that car! Don't let it hit Dane!" Tim screamed.

Tim slammed his foot down on mine and shoved the accelerator to the floor. The Cutlass fishtailed and roared directly toward Dane and Jacob...

Dane—Slightly Earlier That Same Evening

I grinned when I saw Jacob waiting for me at my locker.

"I thought you'd forgotten about me," I said.

"About you? Never."

Those words were all it took to soothe my worries and ease the hurt I'd felt in my heart.

"It's time, Dane."

"I'm so tired," I said. It was true. I was exhausted, and I think I might have killed for a candy bar.

"I know," Jacob said, pushing my hair back off my forehead. "You still want to help me, don't you?"

"Yes, but I'm worn out…"

"Don't you love me? You said you'd do anything…"

"Yes! Yes, I love you!"

"Then come with me."

I nodded. I put all my books in my locker and followed Jacob out of the front entrance of VHS. I barely had the energy to walk. I didn't know what was wrong with me. I was probably coming down with something. I hated that. I hated to be sick. I swayed.

"I don't feel so good."

"You're just hungry. We'll take care of that."

I leaned on Jacob, and he led me through the streets of Verona. I grinned when he pulled me toward Ofarim's. Scotty came to our table to take our orders. Jacob ordered a triple cheeseburger, large fries, a corn dog, onion rings, a large Coke, a large chocolate shake, and a banana split for me. He ordered only a Coke for himself, which I knew he would only pretend to drink.

Devon entered with Zac while I was eating. His upper lip curled in an angry snarl, but he backed off when Jacob stared him down. I had nothing to fear from Devon with Jacob around. I have a feeling he could have taken on both Devon and Zac.

It took a good long while to finish my feast, but Jacob was patient. He kept talking about his plans: joining the football team, maybe becoming quarterback, buying a car, and more. I didn't know how he planned to join the football team when he wasn't even enrolled in school, but Jacob could probably surmount any obstacle. A boy who could come back from the dead—or almost dead, as he put it—could probably do just about anything.

When we stepped out of Ofarim's it was after four. We began walking again. I was still so very tired, but I felt better. At least I didn't sway when I walked.

"Where are we going?"

"You'll find out soon enough."

We walked down the sidewalk. Jacob began to lead me through the streets of Verona. It was a truly beautiful spring afternoon. I looked at Jacob beside me. He was so very handsome. He was wearing his letterman's jacket again. It was the first time he'd worn it since he'd begun appearing at VHS. I couldn't believe he'd soon be as real as me. Knowing I could help him live again filled me with contentment. Maybe then we could be boyfriends.

We walked beyond the town limits. I grew a little weaker with every step. I was coming down with something. I just knew it. I'd be missing school the next day for sure. Mom would probably drag me to the doctor's office. I was determined to go forward, however. I had to do this. I had to help Jacob. He needed me.

"Is it much further?" I asked.

"No, Dane. It isn't much further now."

I noticed a road sign that said, "Roger's Road," and knew we were close to the Selby Farm where Ethan, Nathan, Casper, and Brendan lived. I knew there was something I should be remembering about the road, but my mind was foggy. We walked on a bit more. I looked around then stopped. I closed my eyes and opened them again.

"But, how?"

It was nighttime, but it couldn't be. Only a few minutes had passed since we left Ofarim's, and it wasn't much after four then.

"What?" Jacob asked.

"It's night!"

"Yes."

"But it shouldn't be night."

"You're confused, Dane. Of course, it's night. Remember? I picked you up at your house a little after nine."

"You did? I thought we just came from Ofarim's."

Jacob laughed.

"No. I took you home because you were tired, then I picked you up just a few minutes ago."

"Oh."

I didn't remember any of that at all. I really was coming down with something.

"When this is over, we have to get you into bed," Jacob teased.

We walked on, my mind reeling. I could have sworn…but it was night. There was no denying the darkness.

An old car passed us going back toward town. I could hear Dinah Shore singing *Baby It's Cold Outside* for a moment as the car passed. My mom loved Dinah Shore, and I'd probably heard that song a hundred times. The song sure fit the weather at the moment. Spring had slipped away. It was chilly—cold, even. Hadn't it been warm earlier? What happened? I began to shiver. I gazed at Jacob beside me. Flakes of snow drifted from above, alighting in his hair. Jacob grinned.

"Not long at all now."

"I didn't know it was supposed to get this cold tonight," I said.

"The weather forecast called it a return to winter," Jacob said.

The snow, which had barely been a few flakes before, came down harder and faster. I felt colder than ever but didn't know if the temperature was dropping fast or if it was just a symptom of whatever illness was taking me over.

"I can't believe it's snowing! The flowers are already blooming, and now it's snowing!"

"Weird, isn't it?" Jacob observed, yet the tone of his voice indicated he didn't think it weird at all.

I felt lightheaded. I began to wonder if I was dreaming. Maybe I was back home in bed, experiencing a feverish dream. I didn't feel feverish. I shivered in the growing cold. I'd worn only a short-sleeve t-shirt.

"Maybe we should go back," I said. "It's too cold."

Another vehicle passed. This time it was an antique truck. My grandfather had driven one like it. I'd seen a picture of it.

"No. Here," Jacob said. He took off his letterman's jacket and helped me into it.

"Better?"

"Much," I said.

I wanted to hug Jacob and tell him how much I loved him. He was so good to me.

The snow came down harder still, and the wind got up. My ears began to ache, and my face began to grow numb.

"This is crazy," I said.

"Not much further," Jacob said. "We'll get this done as fast as possible, and then we can get warm."

"Warm sounds good."

Another car passed going north. This one was a Model A.

"That's three!" I said.

"Three vehicles driving down the road? I know it's a little late, but…"

"Three old vehicles! Very old!"

"I think I heard something about an antique-car show," Jacob said.

He didn't sound convincing. Everything was so…dreamlike. Antique cars, a near-blizzard in spring, my unusual exhaustion—

yeah, I probably was dreaming. If this was a dream, why couldn't I have dreamed something a bit warmer!

I staggered and nearly fell. Jacob grabbed my arm and kept me from falling face first in the gravel at the side of the road.

"I want to help you, Jacob, but I can't keep going."

"Just a little farther," Jacob said. He slipped my right arm over his shoulder and supported most of my weight.

"I feel dizzy. My heart feels as if it's barely beating. I feel...something's wrong, Jacob."

"It's almost time," Jacob said, looking at his watch.

I was so cold, so tired, and so disorientated I hardly cared anymore. We stopped. Jacob wrapped his arms around me. I buried my face in his chest, trying to keep warm.

"It will all be over soon, Dane, and then I'll be alive again. I'll owe it all to you."

I grinned, but Jacob couldn't see, because my face was buried in his chest. He was so warm.

I could hear another car coming, heading north towards town like the others. I couldn't see the car because I was facing Jacob, but I could hear it coming nearer and nearer. Jacob gripped my shoulders tightly and pushed me back just enough so he could look into my eyes.

"I couldn't have done this without you," he said. "I'll never forget you."

He leaned in and kissed me deeply.

The car grew closer. Something about the whole situation suddenly felt very, very wrong. I tried to turn and look, but Jacob held my arms so tightly I cried out in pain. Reflexively, I tried to break his hold. I jerked my head toward the oncoming car as it veered into the southbound lane and accelerated. All I could see were oncoming headlights. I screamed.

The next few seconds whipped by so quickly I was only aware of what happened after it was all over. A second car, gunning its engine, roared down the southbound lane. The driver must have been doing eighty. Jacob screamed, "NO!", even as he shoved me with every ounce of his might into the path of the northbound car. I tumbled to the center line. For a moment I found myself standing between two cars racing toward a head-on collision. I only had time to scream as both cars raced toward me in a crazy game of chicken, with me in the middle. At the last second, the southbound car jerked to the right missing me by inches, then back to the left, fishtailing out of control. Tires squealed, and the northbound car skidded across the lane to miss the other car and jerked onto the shoulder where I'd recently been standing. It passed so close to the other car I expected to hear the screech of metal on metal. There was a loud thud; the northbound car whipped back onto the road and took off. The southbound car skidded to a halt and turned with its headlights shining upon me. I was too exhausted to even try to get out of the road. Doors slammed.

"Dane! Dane are you okay?"

I recognized Tim's voice, but I was too exhausted to answer. I looked up to see him staring down at me with a worried look on his face. Shawn came into view then, too. Together, they pulled me to my feet. I glanced up the road and saw Jacob's still form lying off the shoulder in the snow.

"I need your jacket," Shawn said.

I didn't understand, but I was too tired to argue as he pulled Jacob's letterman's jacket off me and replaced it with his own. Tim led me back toward the Cutlass as Shawn walked toward Jacob's body.

"What's he doing?" I asked after Tim had shoved me into the passenger seat and then climbed in beside me.

I watched through the window as Shawn struggled to put Jacob's jacket on his corpse.

"It has to be this way," Tim said.

I didn't understand. I gazed at Tim. Was I still dreaming?

Shawn glanced around near where Jacob lay and then returned to the car. He slammed the door and looked at me.

"Are you okay?"

"Uh, I'm cold and I don't feel so good..."

"Let's get him back to the loft. He's freezing," Tim said.

Everything was kind of a blur after that until I was in Tim's and Shawn's loft wrapped in a blanket with a mug of hot tea in my hand. I took another bite of a cookie I hadn't realized I was holding until that moment. The early evening light illuminated the windows.

"Dane?" Tim asked.

"Huh?"

"I think he's back," Tim said.

"What do you mean?" I asked.

"You fainted in the car. We brought you back around, but you've been sitting here acting as if you couldn't hear or see us."

"I don't remember anything since the...whatever it was."

"You're going to be okay, Dane," Shawn said.

"What the hell happened?" I asked, feeling more myself by the moment.

"Jacob tried to kill you," Shawn said.

"Why would he do that? We were..." My voice trailed off. I felt horribly guilty, but why hadn't I felt guilty before? What had I done?

"He was killing you so you'd take his place," Tim said.

"Huh?"

"He intended to kill you so you'd switch places," Tim said.

Tim was on the verge of tears. He was clearly shaken by the recent turn of events. I realized how much I loved him. How could I have forgotten that, even for a little while, even for a moment?

"I'm so sorry," I said. I meant for the way I'd treated him. I think he knew it.

"I don't think any of this was your fault," Tim said, but his lower lip trembled.

"I don't know, but I'm so sorry."

"We'll talk about it later, but...I love you."

"I love you, too!" I said.

I hugged Tim. I never wanted to stop hugging him.

"I thought Tim had lost it when he began talking about Jacob possessing you, but I think that's what happened," Shawn said. "He intended for you to replace him. I have no clue how your dying would bring him back to life, but then I don't understand any of this."

"I don't understand," I said. "I know Jacob pushed me into the road, but..."

"Did you notice anything unusual about that car that came at you?" Tim asked.

"Well, it was old..." I looked up. "All the cars I saw when we were walking were old. There was even a Model A! It was almost as though...but Jacob said there was probably an antique-car show somewhere."

"No, there isn't," Shawn said. "What were you about to say before that?"

"Well, it was almost as though we were in the past," I said.

"Exactly," said Tim.

"But that's not..." the word "possible" died on my lips.

"It was bitterly cold and snowing the night Jacob was killed in 1949," Tim said. "Remember the newspaper report?"

"Yeah."

"It's spring. It could snow at this time of year, but the low for tonight was supposed to be 58," Tim said. "What's more, there's nothing about snow or temperatures in the teens on the TV or the radio, AND the snow and cold started less than half a mile from where Jacob tried to kill you. It was only snowing there, nowhere else. It was only cold *there*."

"I don't think..."

"How else can you explain it?" Shawn asked. "I know what you're thinking. I couldn't believe it, either."

"I can't explain any of it!"

"We were in the past," Tim said. "You saw where Jacob was lying after that car hit him. That's where he was found in 1949."

"Is that why you put Jacob's jacket on him?" I asked Shawn.

"Yes, because that's the way he was found. That's why I was checking for our tracks, too, making sure the snow would cover them up."

"Don't you see," Tim said. "It's all exactly as it happened before! But Jacob tried to change the past. He wanted you to die instead of him. That's why he gave you his jacket."

"He gave me his jacket because I was cold. What does the jacket matter, anyway? As soon as my body was found it would be obvious I wasn't Jacob."

"That wouldn't matter. You'd be a John Doe in 1949. Jacob would disappear from that time but be alive here. Jacob put his jacket on you because he knew his death wasn't an accident. He knew that his killer would run down anyone he saw wearing that jacket," Tim said.

"How can you know that?" I asked.

"I don't know it, but it makes sense. Why else would Jacob put the jacket on you? Kindness? I don't think so. Someone wanted Jacob dead. He knew what was going to happen, because it had happened before. He intended for you to take his place."

"I...I just don't know," I said.

"All the pieces fit. If you can come up with a better theory I'm listening, but I'm sure we were in the past," Tim said.

I had no explanation, better or otherwise.

"If we weren't in the past, we'll be hearing about a dead body found on Roger's Road by the morning," Shawn said.

I reached up to my chest with my right hand.

"It's gone! The coin is gone! I was wearing it. I know I was. I haven't taken it off for days."

"It all makes sense," Tim said. "How are you feeling?"

"A whole lot better. I felt as if I was dying, even before Jacob shoved me in front of that car. I was so cold. I swear my heart was barely beating. I was so weak I could hardly move."

"Jacob was sucking the life out of you, like some kind of vampire," Tim said.

I thought for a moment.

"Maybe that's why I was eating so much but not gaining weight."

"He got stronger while you got weaker," Tim said. "Dane, you would have died if that had gone on much longer."

I knew he was right. I had the feeling Shawn and Tim were right about everything. It was all too crazy to believe, but then so was Jacob's coming back from the dead. The world would never be the same to me.

"Guys, can you take me home? My parents will wonder where I am. I don't want to have to explain any of this to them."

"I think that's best," Shawn said. "I think it's best if we don't tell anyone about this. Who would believe it anyway? I barely do, and I was there."

I was soon back in my very own bed. I slept like the dead, if you'll pardon the pun. I awakened strangely refreshed in the morning and felt better than I had in a long time. I even went to school.

There was no mention of a dead body being found that day nor any day after. Shawn, Tim, and I even drove out to the stretch of Roger's Road where it had all happened. We weren't exactly sure where Jacob was killed, but there was no sign of his body anywhere. Tim was right. Somehow, we'd strayed into 1949.

Tim, Shawn, and I kept our secret until many years later. Even if we wanted to talk about what had happened, who would have believed us? I wouldn't have if I hadn't been there.

Jacob troubled me no more. We'd put him back in his grave, and he stayed put this time. I was glad to be rid of him. I didn't even miss the sex. It was like nothing I experienced before or since, but it wasn't natural. Maybe it wasn't even real. I didn't know what

Jacob had done to me, but I saw things much more clearly after he was gone. He'd gained control of me somehow and possessed my thoughts. If Tim and Shawn hadn't stepped in, I would surely have died.

I never saw Jacob again—except a few days later I could've almost sworn he passed me in the hallway at VHS and grinned at me. It was just a glimpse, and when I turned around to look, there was no sign of him. I was sure my mind was playing tricks on me—hopefully.

Tim forgave me. In fact, he said there was nothing to forgive. He laid all the blame on Jacob. I knew Jacob had controlled me. Maybe he'd even largely controlled my thoughts. I wasn't so sure I was blameless, but thinking back, I did almost feel as though it wasn't me. I intended to be on my guard, in any case. I'd never allow myself to slip. I'd never go back to being the old Dane. I loved Tim more than anyone or anything else, and I swore to myself I'd die before I ever hurt him again.

Shawn

Taking orders, making sundaes, and wiping off tables was a welcome normality after the strange events of the evening before. I knew those things had actually happened, but everything all seemed like a dream now. Tim and I haven't spoken about it, and I'd just as soon we didn't. The only indirect mention was made by Dane at lunch when Brandon asked why Jacob wasn't sitting with us. Dane told him he'd heard a rumor that Jacob had moved. The guys thought it weird he'd move again so soon after he'd just arrived in Verona and without so much as a "goodbye." If they only knew the real story...

I had an uneasy feeling all day. Who wouldn't after going through *that*? Dane was mostly back to his old self. I don't mean the old "evil" Dane, but rather the pre-Jacob Dane. Tim and Dane smiled at each other a lot at lunch. Both had that goofy, I'm-so-in-love look, too. Neither Brandon nor Jon gave them a hard time about it. Everyone at the table knew there had been some tension between them. Mostly, everyone seemed pleased Tim and Dane were back to their old selves. I had little doubt Brandon and Jon would start in on them again soon. Then everything would truly be back to normal.

There was a part of me that feared things were not truly over with Jacob. I'd been half afraid he'd be sitting there at our table at lunch as if nothing had happened. I kept expecting him to cross my path in the hallways. There was no sign of him, however. I almost didn't dare to hope it, but he did appear to be truly gone. I sure hoped so—for Dane's sake, Tim's, and even my own.

The bells on the door jingled. I looked up and grinned. There stood Tristan, looking just as handsome as he did the first time I set eyes on him.

I crossed the short distance between us, pulled him to me, and kissed him.

"Let me finish up here, and then we can go to the loft," I said. "I have a few things to tell you about Dane's ghost."

Twenty minute later, Tristan and I were sitting at the table in the loft, sipping cups of hot blackberry tea. I told him everything I could remember about the night before, including my theories. Tristan didn't bat an eye, but then, unlike most, he'd had his own brushes with the supernatural.

"I wonder who killed Jacob and why?" Tristan said.

"According to Tim, Jacob was killed by his boyfriend. Jacob threatened to out him to keep him from breaking up with him. Tim isn't so sure it's the truth."

"It's plausible, at least."

"I guess we'll never know. Did Jacob ever reveal why he was so interested in Dane?"

"No. Maybe because Dane lived in the school where Jacob had once been a jock. Maybe because Jacob preferred him over Boothe. Who knows? Jacob left a lot of unanswered questions behind, but I don't really care as long as he's gone."

"Do you think he is?"

"I don't know. I hope so."

Tristan and I moved to the couch. I pulled him close and pressed my lips against his. We made out and forgot all about Jacob and the weirdness of the past days. I thought about pulling Tristan toward my bedroom, but I knew the time wasn't quite right. It didn't matter. I could wait. I was with the boy I loved, and I had a feeling we'd be together for a good long time. In the end, that's all that mattered.

The End

Information on Mark's upcoming books can be found at markroeder.com. Those wishing to keep in touch with others who enjoy Mark's novels can join his fan club at http://groups.yahoo.com/group/markaroederfans.

Other Books by Mark A. Roeder
Listed in Suggested Reading Order

Outfield Menace

Outfield Menace is the tale of Kurt, a fifteen-year-old baseball player, living in a small, 1950s, Indiana town. During a confrontation with Angel, the resident bad boy of Blackford High School, Kurt attacks Angel, earning the wrath of the most dangerous gang in town. When Angel finally corners Kurt, however, something happens that Kurt wouldn't have imagined in his wildest dreams. As the murder of a local boy is uncovered, suspicion is cast upon Angel, but Kurt has learned there's more to Angel than his bad boy image. Angel has a secret, however, that could get both Kurt and himself killed. *Outfield Menace* is a story of friendship, love, adventure, and perilous danger.

Snow Angel

Angel rescued his boyfriend, Kurt, from a hellish existence, but at the cost of exiling himself from his hometown of Blackford, Indiana. Fifteen-years-old and on the run, Angel must make his way until he can fulfill his promise to return to Kurt. Along the way he faces loneliness, hardships, and a brutal blizzard, but makes new friends and finds acceptance he didn't expect.

Kurt's life is nearly back to normal, but the love of his life is gone. Kurt is determined not to let Angel's sacrifice be in vain, but how can he wait three long years for the return his boyfriend had promised him? What will happen when they are reunited at last? Can they be together, or will Kurt and Angel have to run for their lives?

Snow Angel is a tale of lovers parted, of survival, and a love that cannot be diminished by distance or time.

Ancient Prejudice Breaks To New Mutiny

Mark is a boy who wants what we all want: to love and be loved. His dreams are realized when he meets Taylor, the boy of his dreams. The boys struggle to keep their love hidden from a world that cannot understand, but ultimately, no secret is safe in a small Mid-western town.

Ancient Prejudice is a story of love, friendship, understanding, and an age-old prejudice that still has the power to kill. It is a story for young and old, gay and straight. It reminds us all that everyone should be treated with dignity and respect and that there is nothing greater than the power of love.

The Soccer Field Is Empty

The Soccer Field Is Empty is a revised and much expanded edition of **Ancient Prejudice**. It is more than 50% longer and views events from the point of view of Taylor, as well as Mark. There is so much new in the revised edition that it is being published as a separate novel. **Soccer Field** delves more deeply into the events of Mark and Taylor's lives and reveals previously hidden aspects of Taylor's personality.

Authors note: I suggest readers new to my books start with **Soccer Field** instead of **Ancient Prejudice** as it gives a more complete picture of the lives of Mark and Taylor. For those who wish to read the original version, **Ancient Prejudice** will remain available for at least the time being.

Someone Is Watching

It's hard hiding a secret. It's even harder keeping that secret when someone else knows.

Someone Is Watching is the story of Ethan, a young high school wrestler who must come to terms with being gay. He struggles first with himself, then with an unknown classmate that hounds his every step. While struggling to discover the identity of his tormentor, Ethan must discover his own identity and learn to live his life as his true self. He must choose whether to give up what he wants the most, or face his greatest fear of all.

A Better Place

High school football, a hospital of horrors, a long journey, and an unlikely love await Brendan and Casper as they search for a better place...

Casper is the poorest boy in school. Brendan is the captain of the football team. Casper has nothing. Brendan has it all: looks, money, popularity, but he lacks the deepest desire of his heart. The boys come from different worlds, but have one thing in common that no one would guess.

Casper goes through life as the "invisible boy"; invisible to the boys that pick on him in school, invisible to his abusive father, and invisible most of all to his older brother, who makes his life a living hell. He can't believe his good luck when Brendan, the most popular boy in school, takes an interest in him and becomes his friend. That friendship soon travels in a direction that Casper would never have guessed.

A Better Place is the story of an unlikely pair, who struggle through friendship and betrayal, hardships and heartbreaks, to find the desire of their hearts, to find a better place.

Someone Is Killing The Gay Boys of Verona

Someone is killing the gay boys of Verona, Indiana, and only one gay youth stands in the way. He finds himself pitted against powerful foes, but finds allies in places he did not expect.

A brutal murder. Gay ghosts. A Haunted Victorian-Mansion. A cult of hate. A hundred year old ax murder. All this, and more, await sixteen-year-old Sean as he delves into the supernatural and races to discover the murderer before he strikes again.

Someone is Killing the Gay Boys of Verona is a supernatural murder mystery that goes where no gay novel has set foot before. It is a tale of love, hate, friendship, and revenge.

The Vampires Heart

Ever wonder what it would be like to be fifteen-years-old forever? Ever wonder how it would feel to find out your best friend is not what he seems? Graham Granger is intrigued by the new boy in school. Graham's heart aches for a friend, and maybe a boyfriend, but is Josiah the answer to his dreams? Why is Bry Hartnett, the school hunk, taking an interest in Graham as well? When strange happenings begin to occur at Griswold Jr./Sr. High, Graham's once boring life becomes more exciting than he can handle. Mystery, intrigue, and danger await Graham as he sets out on an adventure he never dreamed possible.

Keeper of Secrets

Sixteen-year-old Avery is in trouble, yet again, but this time he's in over his head. On the run, Avery is faced with hardships and fear. He must become what he's always hated, just to survive. He discovers new reasons to hate, until fate brings him to Graymoor Mansion and he discovers a disturbing connection to the past. Through the eyes of a boy, murdered more than a century before, Avery discovers that all is not as he thought. Avery is soon forced to face the greatest challenge of all; looking into his own heart.

Sean is head over heels in love with his new boyfriend, Nick. There is trouble in paradise, however. Could a boy so beautiful really love plain, ordinary Sean? Sean cannot believe it and desperately tries to transform himself into the ideal young hunk, only to learn that it's what's inside that matters.

Keeper of Secrets is the story of two boys, one a gay youth, the other an adolescent gay basher. Fate and the pages of a hundred year old journal bring them together and their lives are forever changed.

Do You Know That I Love You

The lead singer of the most popular boy band in the world has a secret. A tabloid willing to tell all turns his world upside down.

In **Do You Know That I Love You**, Ralph, a young gay teen living on a farm in Indiana, has an aching crush on a rock star and wants nothing more than to see his idol in concert. Meanwhile, Jordan, the rock star, is lonely and sometimes confused with his success, because all he wants is someone to love him and feels he will never find the love he craves. **Do You Know** is the story of two teenage boys, their lives, desires, loves, and a shared destiny that allows them both to find peace.

Masked Destiny

Masked Destiny is the story of Skye, a high school athlete determined to be the Alpha male. Skye's obsessed with his own body, his Abercrombie & Fitch wardrobe, and keeping those around him in their place. Try as he might, he's not quite able to ignore the world around him, or the plight of gay boys that cross his path. Too frightened of what others might think, Skye fails to intervene when he could have saved a boy with a single word. The resulting tragedy, wise words for a mysterious blond boy, and a unique opportunity combine to push Skye toward his destiny.

Oliver is young, a bit pudgy, and interested in little more than his books and possibly his first kiss. As he slowly gains courage, he seeks out the friendship of Clay, his dream boy, in hopes they will become more than friends. Oliver is sought out in turn by Ken, who warns him Clay is not at all what he seems, but Ken, too, has his secrets. Oliver must choose between them and discovers danger, a link to boys murdered in the recent past, and the answers to secrets he'd never dreamed.

Altered Realities

Marshall only wanted to help his friends, to undo the pain of the past, but a few moments of thoughtless action changed everything. **Altered Realities** is the tale of a changed world. All bets are off. Nothing is as it was and what is to be is transformed too. Mark, Taylor, Ethan, Nathan, Brendan, Casper and nearly the entire cast of the *Gay Youth Chronicles* come together in a tapestry of tales as they all try to deal with the consequences of Marshall's actions. The road to hell is paved with good intentions.

Dead Het Boys

Marshall's experiences with ghosts and the supernatural are legendary, but when a boy a hundred-years dead turns up in his bedroom with the cryptic message "Blackford Manor," Marshall realizes his adventures with the other side have only began. As more specters appear to Marshall, he begins to assemble the pieces of a puzzle that lead him to Graymoor Mansion and a set of crimes more heinous than those of modern day serial killers.

Just over a year ago, Sean's best friend, Marty, was murdered and Sean narrowly escaped the same fate. Now, the evil four, a group of boys who were involved with the death of Marty, have returned. Sean, Skye, and the other gay boys of Verona can do little more than watch and wait for the terror to begin again. Soon, Skye learns of a psychopathic homophobe who is in league with his enemies. Things take a curious turn, however, when one of the evil four is brutally murdered. Suspicion turns to Skye. Has he finally gone too far to protect his friends? Skye isn't the only one with a motive, however. All the gay boys of Verona are suspect. This time around, the shoe is on the other foot.

This Time Around

What happens when a TV evangelist struggles to crush gay rights? Who better to halt his evil plans than the most famous rock star in the world?

This Time Around follows Jordan and Ralph as they become involved in a struggle with Reverend Wellerson, a TV evangelist, over the fate of gay youth centers. Wellerson is willing to stop at nothing to crush gay rights and who better to halt his evil plans than the most famous rock star in the entire world? While battling Wellerson, Jordan seeks to come to terms with his own past and learn more about the father he never knew. The excitement builds when an assassin is hired and death becomes a real possibility for Jordan and those around him. Jordan is forced to face his own fears and doubts and the battle within becomes more dangerous than the battle without. Will Jordan be able to turn from the path of destruction, or is he doomed to follow in the footsteps of his father? This time around, things will be different.

The Summer of My Discontent

The Summer of My Discontent is a tapestry of tales delving into life as a gay teen in a small Midwestern town.

Dane is a sixteen-year-old runaway determined to start a new life of daring, love, and sex—no matter the cost to himself, or others. His actions bring him to the brink of disaster and only those he sought to prey upon can save him. Among Dane's new found "friends" are a young male prostitute and the local grave robber who becomes his despised employer.

The boys of **A Better Place** are back—Ethan, Nathan, Brendan, and Casper are once again dealing with trouble in Verona, Indiana. Drought and circumstance threaten their existence and they struggle together to save themselves from blackmail, financial collapse, and temptation.

Brendan must cope with anonymity after being one of the most popular boys in school. Casper must face his own past—the loss of his father and the fate of his abusive brother, who is locked away in the very hospital of horrors from which Brendan escaped. Letters from his brother force Casper to question his feelings—is Jason truly a monster or can he change?

Dark, foreboding, and sexy—**The Summer of My Discontent** is the tale of gay teens seeking to find themselves, each other, and a better place.

Disastrous Dates & Dream Boys

Disastrous Dates & Dream Boys is the story of teenaged boys who want what we all want, to love and be loved. The boys from *A Better Place* are back. Shawn yearns for a boyfriend, but fears his father's wrath if he discovers the truth. Dane, too, is seeking a soul mate and trying to leave his checkered past behind. He yearns for Billy, but if he approaches him will the result be happiness or disaster? Brendan has created a new life for himself and his boyfriend, Casper, but what happened in his old hometown haunts him and he realizes he must face his father if he is to ever be at peace. Nathan also has issues to resolve with the parents who gave him and his little brother up far too easily. *Disastrous Dates & Dream Boys* is a tale of fathers & sons, lovers & friends, and above all love and understanding.

Just Making Out

Just Making Out is the story of adolescent lovers, a high school boy facing adult responsibilities, and a dead high school football player...all following the dreams of their hearts and just making out...

Dane and Tim are in love. Dane's parents and Tim's older brother do their best to keep them apart, but the teenaged lovers are determined they'll find a way to be together. Just when life gets better for the pair, Dane's old nemesis, Boothe, appears in town with an insane warning about a ghost. The warning turns out not to be so crazy when Jacob, a dead high school football player, haunts Dane. The situation becomes more complex as the ghost slowly becomes more human and expresses an intimate interest in Dane. Tim is at first hurt by the growing relationship between Jacob and Dane, then frightened for his boyfriend's very life. Can he save Dane from the ghost hunk or will he uncover Jacob's dark secret too late?

Shawn has finally gained the attention of his dream boy, but making Tristan his boyfriend is another matter entirely. To complicate matters, Shawn is responsible for his younger brother. Can he make a relationship with Tristan work while he's juggling high school, two-part time jobs, and his new parental responsibilities?

Phantom World

Toby Riester is sixteen, gay, and searching for his first boyfriend. He discovers many potential candidates—Orlando, a cute sixteen year old boy of Latin ancestry who works with Toby at the *Phantom World* amusement park—C.T., a blond, seventeen year old who is obviously gay—and Spike, a well-built sixteen year old from the internet. Each boy has his own seductive qualities and each is more than his seems. One of them, however, is far more dangerous than Toby ever guessed.

Orlando finds himself a girlfriend at **Phantom World**, but that's only the beginning of his story. When he meets his girlfriend's twin brother, Kerry, his world is turned upside down.

Mackenzie Riester is the athletic younger brother of Toby. He has little respect for his queer big brother and joins with his new found friend, Billy, in playing an elaborate practical joke on Toby that becomes more perilous than he ever dreamed.

Phantom World is the story of three very different boys—their triumphs, heartaches, and their search for love and acceptance.

Second Star To The Right

Cedi, an eighteen-year-old British import to the town of Blackford, Indiana, is determined to be a rock star. No one quite knows what to make of the new wild boy in town with his blue hair and overpowering-enthusiasm—not the jocks he torments in revenge, nor his new friends Toby and Orlando. Cedi is certain of his future until his path crosses that of Thad, a tall, dark, older man who tells Cedi he has no talent. Cedi is infuriated, but intrigued. He becomes obsessed with Thad, who wants nothing to do with him. Cedi isn't about to give up, however, and wedges his way into Thad's life. Cedi finds himself caught between his love for Thad and his dream. Just when he has what he thinks he wants, his adventure truly begins...

The Perfect Boy

A specter from the past haunts the halls of Blackford High School, terrorizing anyone who preys on the weak. Rumors say that a Goth/skater boy controls the ghost, but can the rumor be true? A mysterious new boy catches the eye of Toby and his new friend, Daniel Peralta as well. The new boy seems too perfect to be real. Is he or will be become the boy of Toby's or Daniel's dreams?

Cedi is living his fantasy—touring with *Phantom*, the most popular band in the world. Cedi can't quite forget Thad, the older, mysterious novelist he's left behind, but is quickly pulled into a world of concerts, autograph signings, and press conferences. Cedi takes an interest in Ross. Ross has his own demons, however, that may forever prevent him from loving anyone but the man of his dreams.

The Graymoor Mansion B&B

Is turning a haunted mansion into a Bed & Breakfast such a good idea? Sean and his family think so, except for Avery, who believes guests will be scared away by disembodied voices, candles that light themselves, and the ghostly reenactment of the notorious Graymoor Ax Murders.

When the gay boys of Verona went their separate ways, Verona was more at peace than it had been in ages. Skye, the local champion of gay boys, has been gone for five long years, however, and much has changed in his absence. Sean and Nick lived apart during their college years. They've eagerly anticipated their reunion, but what will happen when Ross, the drummer for *Phantom*, comes to stay at Graymoor with the band? Is Nick over his Ross obsession—or is there trouble ahead? Jordan and Ralph have long considered starting a family, but can they surmount the obstacles that stand in their way? The gay boys of Verona, old and new, are together once again.

Shadows of Darkness

Skye, the protector of gay boys and virtual superhero, comes within a hair's-breadth of death when he tackles a new foe. He is saved only by the quick thinking of Devon, his former nemesis, who alone recognizes the nature of Skye's attacker. Marshall, the resident expert on the supernatural, summons help and Skye cannot believe his eyes when the promised help ultimately comes in the form of two young boys. Skye's concept of reality is about to change forever.

Devon is a sixteen-year old boy—again. Now mortal and human, he's back in high school, facing a life both familiar and strange. His former enemies have forgiven him, but can they ever forget? Devon seeks redemption, but his own memories stand in the way. A special boy crosses Devon's path, giving him hope that he may find self-forgiveness and happiness despite his horrific past.

Shadows of Darkness is the latest chapter in the Gay Youth Chronicles and one that takes the tale into a new supernatural direction.

Christmas in Graymoor Mansion

Friends and family gather in stately Graymoor Mansion to celebrate the holiday season, but a blizzard traps them in the massive Victorian home Christmas Eve and all of Christmas Day. To entertain themselves, the guests take turns sharing their Christmas memories and special holiday stories. Join Sean, his family, and friends in their Christmas celebration. There's plenty of food, including wonderful desserts, Christmas cookies, and steaming hot cocoa to go with this set of Christmas tales. This is a collection of previously unpublished Christmas tales to be read year after year.

7845080R0

Made in the USA
Lexington, KY
19 December 2010